MELOWY

Cortney Powell — Writer
Ryan Jampole — Artist
MELOWY created by Danielle Star

PAPERCUTZ™

New York

Meet the Melowies

Cleo

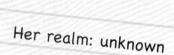

Her realm: unknown

Her personality:
impulsive and loyal

Her passion: writing

Her gift: something mysterious...

Electra

Her realm: Day
Her personality: boisterous
and bubbly
Her passion: fashion
Her gift: the Power of
Light

Maya

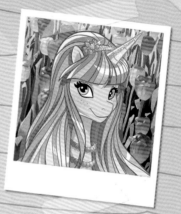

Her realm: Spring

Her personality: shy and sweet

Her passion: cooking

Her gift: the Power of Heat

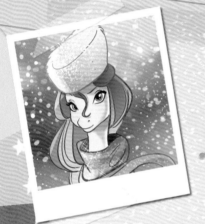

Cora

Her realm: Winter

Her personality: proud and sincere

Her passion: ice-skating

Her gift: the Power of Cold

Selena

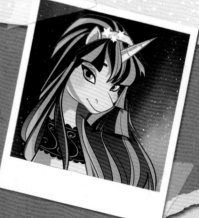

Her realm: Night

Her personality: deep and sensitive

Her passion: music

Her gift: the Power of Darkness

MELOWY

3 in 1

Cover by RYAN JAMPOLE

MELOWY #1 "The Test of Magic"
Editorial Supervision by ALESSANDRA BERELLO and LISA CAPIOTTO (Atlantyca S.p.A.)
Script by CORTNEY POWELL
Art by RYAN JAMPOLE
Color by LAURIE E. SMITH
Lettering by WILSON RAMOS JR.

MELOWY #2 "The Fashion Club of Colors"
Editorial Supervision by ALESSANDRA BERELLO and LISA CAPIOTTO (Atlantyca S.p.A.)
Script by CORTNEY POWELL
Art by RYAN JAMPOLE
Color by LAURIE E. SMITH
Lettering by WILSON RAMOS JR.

MELOWY #3 "Time to Fly"
Editorial Supervision by ALESSANDRA BERELLO and LISA CAPIOTTO (Atlantyca S.p.A.)
Script by CORTNEY POWELL
Art by RYAN JAMPOLE
Color by LAURIE E. SMITH
Lettering by WILSON RAMOS JR.

Editorial Supervision by ALESSANDRA BERELLO and ANITA DENTI (Atlantyca S.p.A.)

Papercutz books may be purchased for business or promotional use.
For information on bulk purchases please contact Macmillan Corporate and Premium Sales Department at (800) 221-7945 x5442

Production—JAYJAY JACKSON
Lettering—WILSON RAMOS JR.
Editorial Assistant—INGRID RIOS
Editor—JEFF WHITMAN
Jim Salicrup
Editor-in-Chief

Special thanks to DAWN GUZZO and KARR ANTUNES

PB ISBN: 978-1-5458-0710-1

Printed in China
May 2021

Distributed by Macmillan
First Printing

THE TEST OF MAGIC

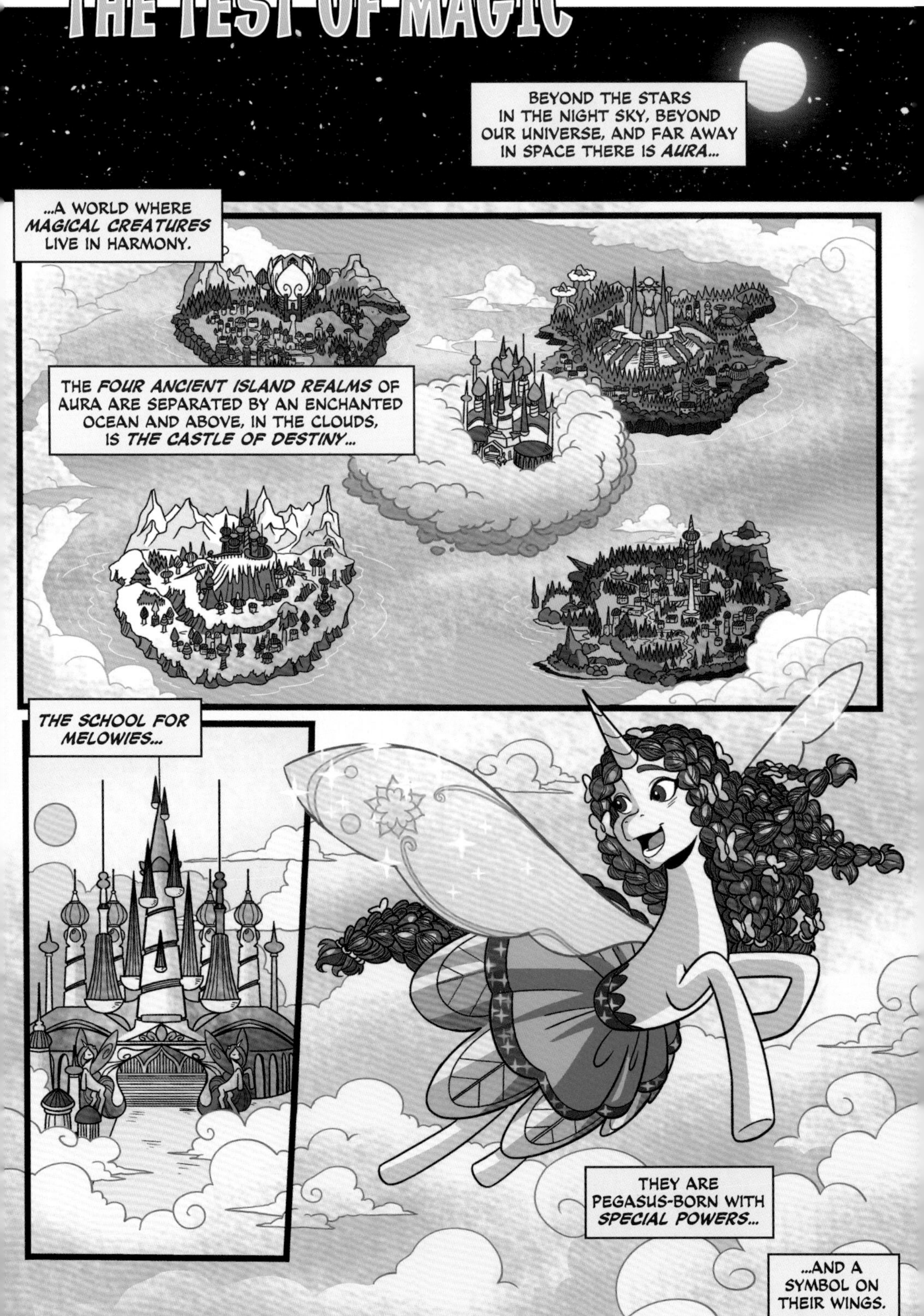

BEYOND THE STARS IN THE NIGHT SKY, BEYOND OUR UNIVERSE, AND FAR AWAY IN SPACE THERE IS *AURA*...
...A WORLD WHERE *MAGICAL CREATURES* LIVE IN HARMONY.
THE *FOUR ANCIENT ISLAND REALMS* OF AURA ARE SEPARATED BY AN ENCHANTED OCEAN AND ABOVE, IN THE CLOUDS, IS *THE CASTLE OF DESTINY*...
THE SCHOOL FOR MELOWIES...
THEY ARE PEGASUS-BORN WITH *SPECIAL POWERS*...
...AND A SYMBOL ON THEIR WINGS.

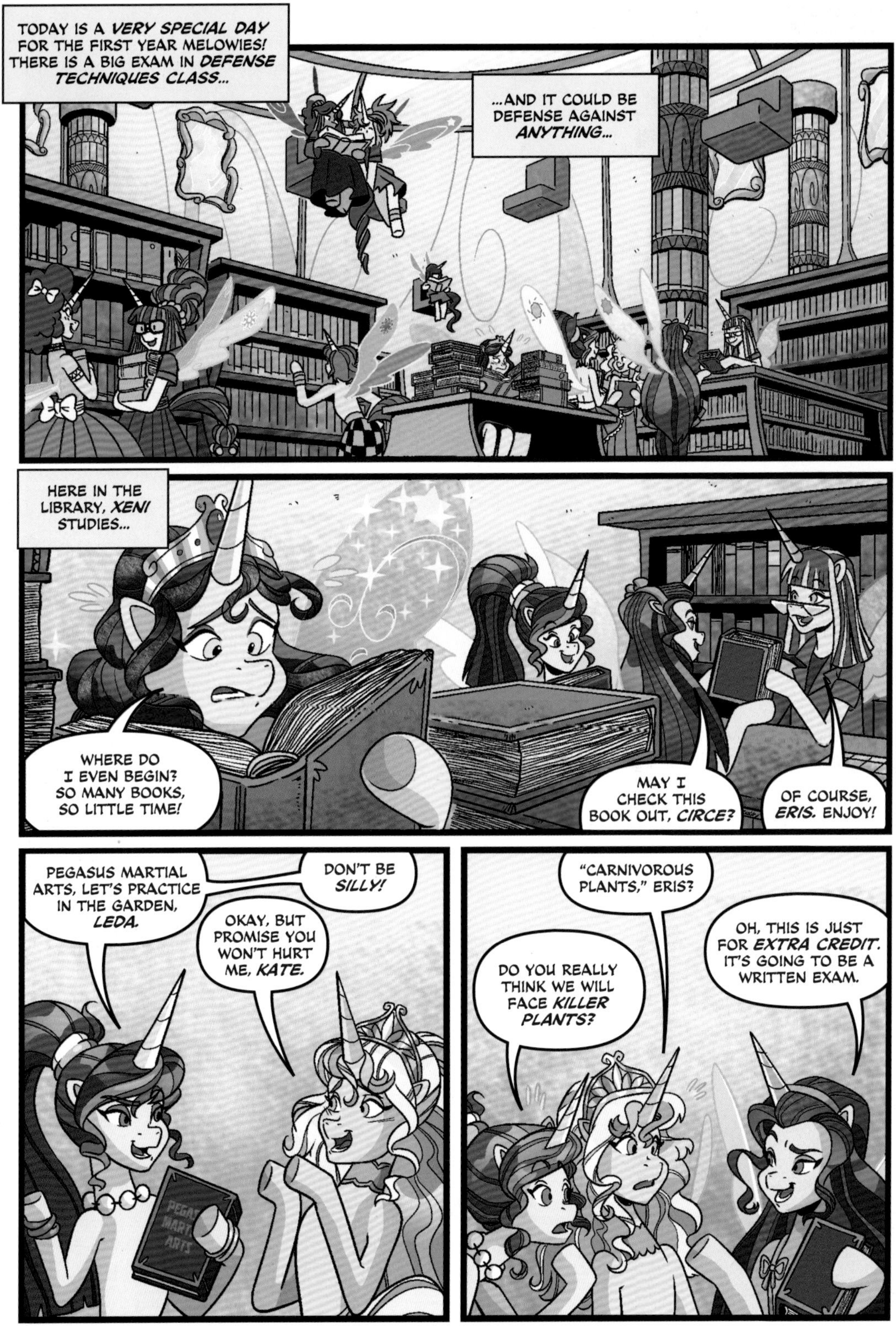
TODAY IS A VERY SPECIAL DAY FOR THE FIRST YEAR MELOWIES! THERE IS A BIG EXAM IN DEFENSE TECHNIQUES CLASS...
...AND IT COULD BE DEFENSE AGAINST ANYTHING...
HERE IN THE LIBRARY, XENI STUDIES...
WHERE DO I EVEN BEGIN? SO MANY BOOKS, SO LITTLE TIME!
MAY I CHECK THIS BOOK OUT, CIRCE?
OF COURSE, ERIS. ENJOY!
PEGASUS MARTIAL ARTS, LET'S PRACTICE IN THE GARDEN, LEDA.
DON'T BE SILLY!
OKAY, BUT PROMISE YOU WON'T HURT ME, KATE.
"CARNIVOROUS PLANTS," ERIS?
DO YOU REALLY THINK WE WILL FACE KILLER PLANTS?
OH, THIS IS JUST FOR EXTRA CREDIT. IT'S GOING TO BE A WRITTEN EXAM.

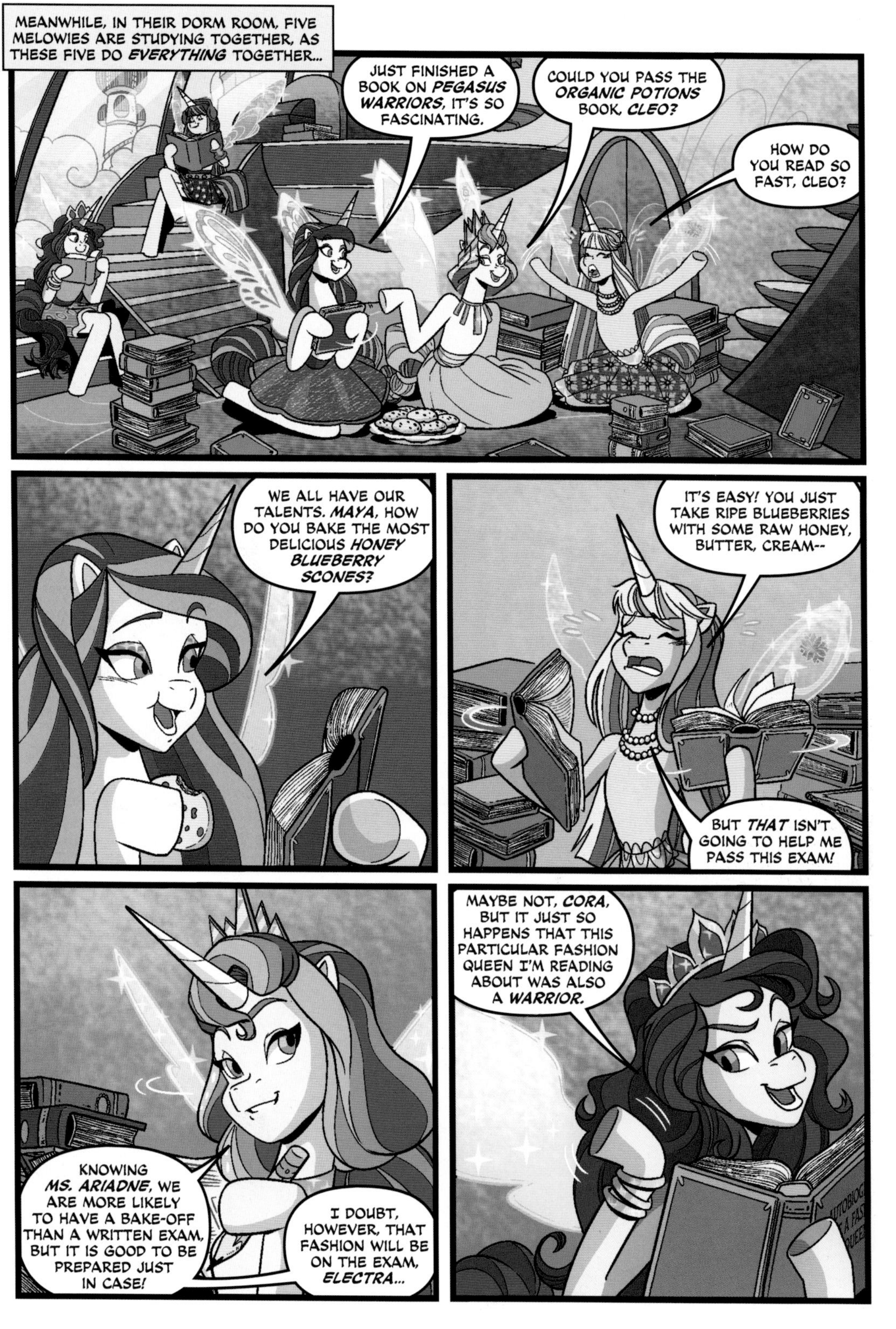
MEANWHILE, IN THEIR DORM ROOM, FIVE MELOWIES ARE STUDYING TOGETHER, AS THESE FIVE DO *EVERYTHING* TOGETHER...
JUST FINISHED A BOOK ON *PEGASUS WARRIORS*, IT'S SO FASCINATING.
COULD YOU PASS THE *ORGANIC POTIONS* BOOK, *CLEO?*
HOW DO YOU READ SO FAST, CLEO?
WE ALL HAVE OUR TALENTS. *MAYA*, HOW DO YOU BAKE THE MOST DELICIOUS *HONEY BLUEBERRY SCONES?*
IT'S EASY! YOU JUST TAKE RIPE BLUEBERRIES WITH SOME RAW HONEY, BUTTER, CREAM--
BUT *THAT* ISN'T GOING TO HELP ME PASS THIS EXAM!
KNOWING *MS. ARIADNE*, WE ARE MORE LIKELY TO HAVE A BAKE-OFF THAN A WRITTEN EXAM, BUT IT IS GOOD TO BE PREPARED JUST IN CASE!
I DOUBT, HOWEVER, THAT FASHION WILL BE ON THE EXAM, *ELECTRA*...
MAYBE NOT, *CORA*, BUT IT JUST SO HAPPENS THAT THIS PARTICULAR FASHION QUEEN I'M READING ABOUT WAS ALSO A *WARRIOR*.

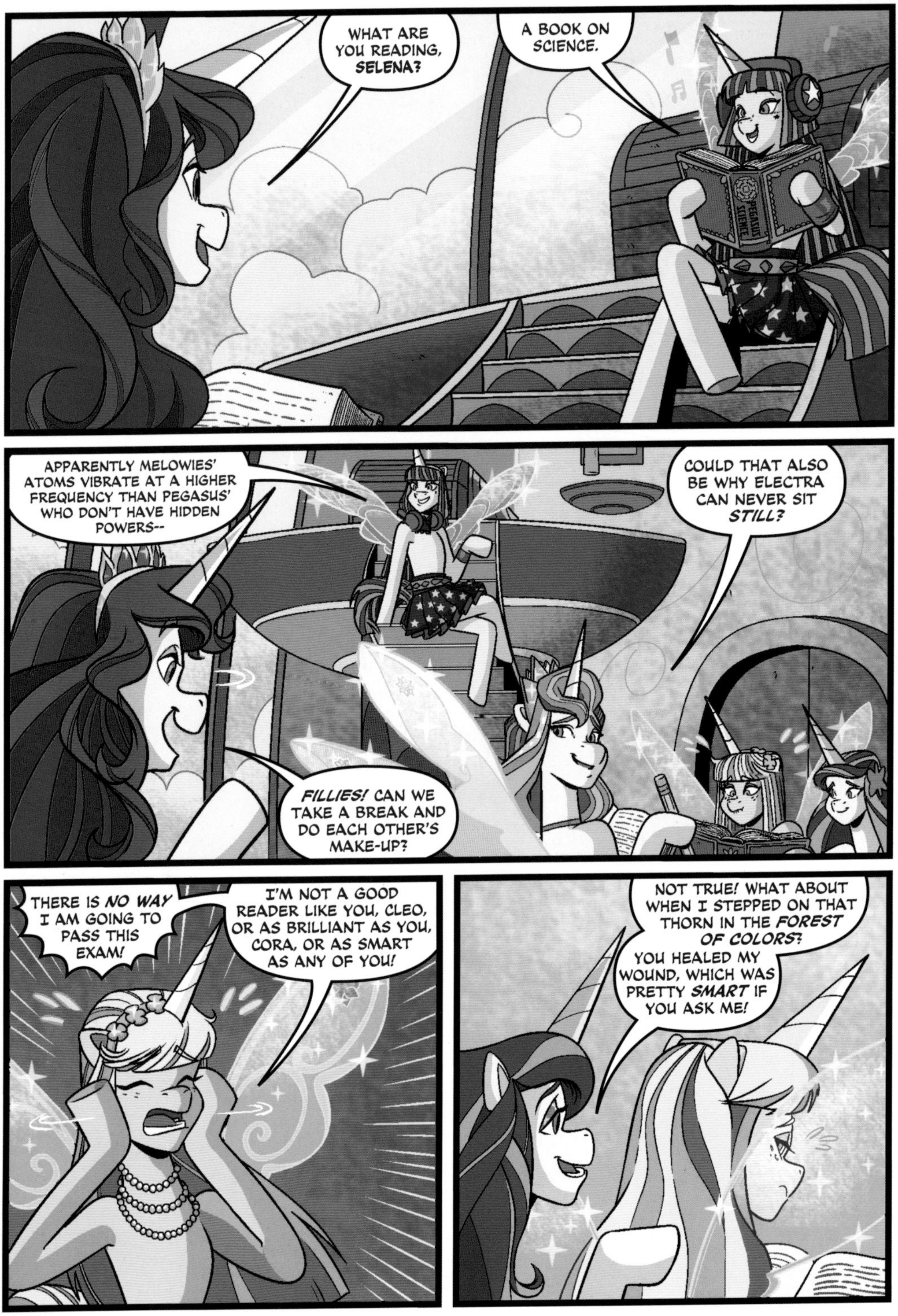
WHAT ARE YOU READING, SELENA?
A BOOK ON SCIENCE.
PEGASUS SCIENCE
APPARENTLY MELOWIES' ATOMS VIBRATE AT A HIGHER FREQUENCY THAN PEGASUS' WHO DON'T HAVE HIDDEN POWERS--
COULD THAT ALSO BE WHY ELECTRA CAN NEVER SIT STILL?
FILLIES! CAN WE TAKE A BREAK AND DO EACH OTHER'S MAKE-UP?
THERE IS NO WAY I AM GOING TO PASS THIS EXAM!
I'M NOT A GOOD READER LIKE YOU, CLEO, OR AS BRILLIANT AS YOU, CORA, OR AS SMART AS ANY OF YOU!
NOT TRUE! WHAT ABOUT WHEN I STEPPED ON THAT THORN IN THE FOREST OF COLORS?
YOU HEALED MY WOUND, WHICH WAS PRETTY SMART IF YOU ASK ME!

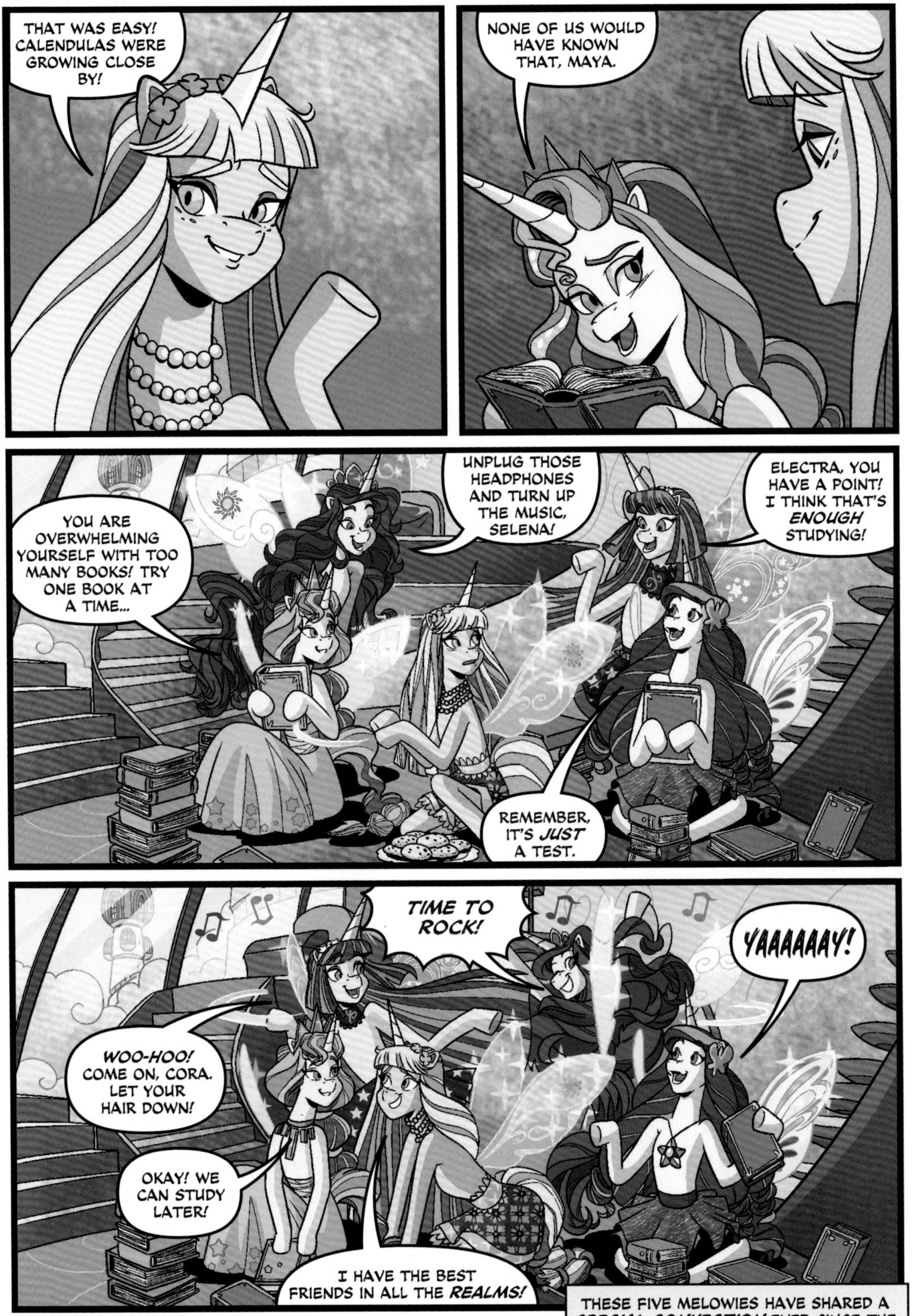
THAT WAS EASY! CALENDULAS WERE GROWING CLOSE BY!
NONE OF US WOULD HAVE KNOWN THAT, MAYA.
YOU ARE OVERWHELMING YOURSELF WITH TOO MANY BOOKS! TRY ONE BOOK AT A TIME...
UNPLUG THOSE HEADPHONES AND TURN UP THE MUSIC, SELENA!
ELECTRA, YOU HAVE A POINT! I THINK THAT'S *ENOUGH* STUDYING!
REMEMBER, IT'S *JUST* A TEST.
TIME TO ROCK!
YAAAAAAY!
WOO-HOO! COME ON, CORA. LET YOUR HAIR DOWN!
OKAY! WE CAN STUDY LATER!
I HAVE THE BEST FRIENDS IN ALL THE *REALMS!*
THESE FIVE MELOWIES HAVE SHARED A *SPECIAL CONNECTION* EVER SINCE THE FIRST DAY OF SCHOOL AT DESTINY...

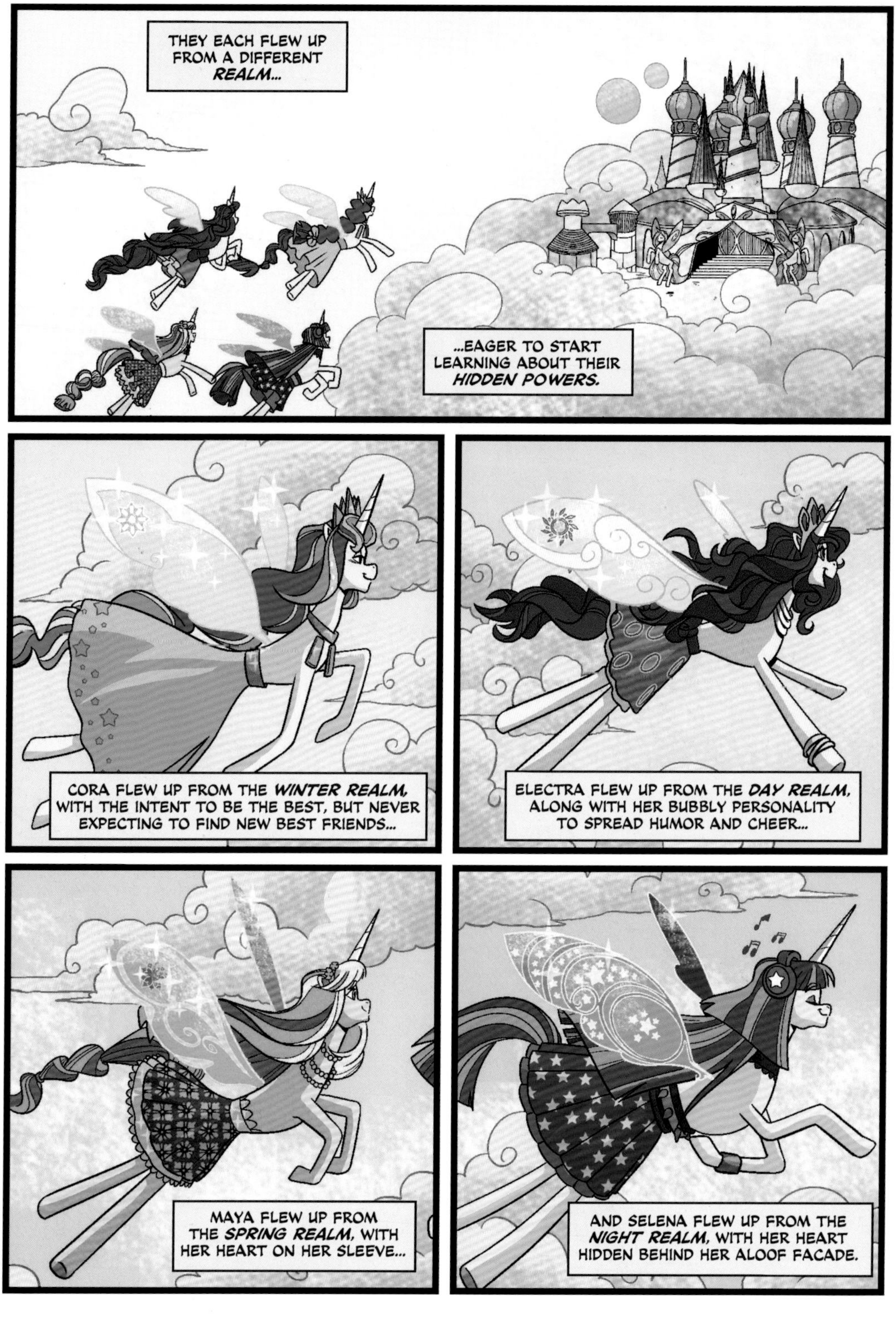
THEY EACH FLEW UP FROM A DIFFERENT *REALM*...
...EAGER TO START LEARNING ABOUT THEIR *HIDDEN POWERS.*
CORA FLEW UP FROM THE *WINTER REALM,* WITH THE INTENT TO BE THE BEST, BUT NEVER EXPECTING TO FIND NEW BEST FRIENDS...
ELECTRA FLEW UP FROM THE *DAY REALM,* ALONG WITH HER BUBBLY PERSONALITY TO SPREAD HUMOR AND CHEER...
MAYA FLEW UP FROM THE *SPRING REALM,* WITH HER HEART ON HER SLEEVE...
AND SELENA FLEW UP FROM THE *NIGHT REALM,* WITH HER HEART HIDDEN BEHIND HER ALOOF FACADE.

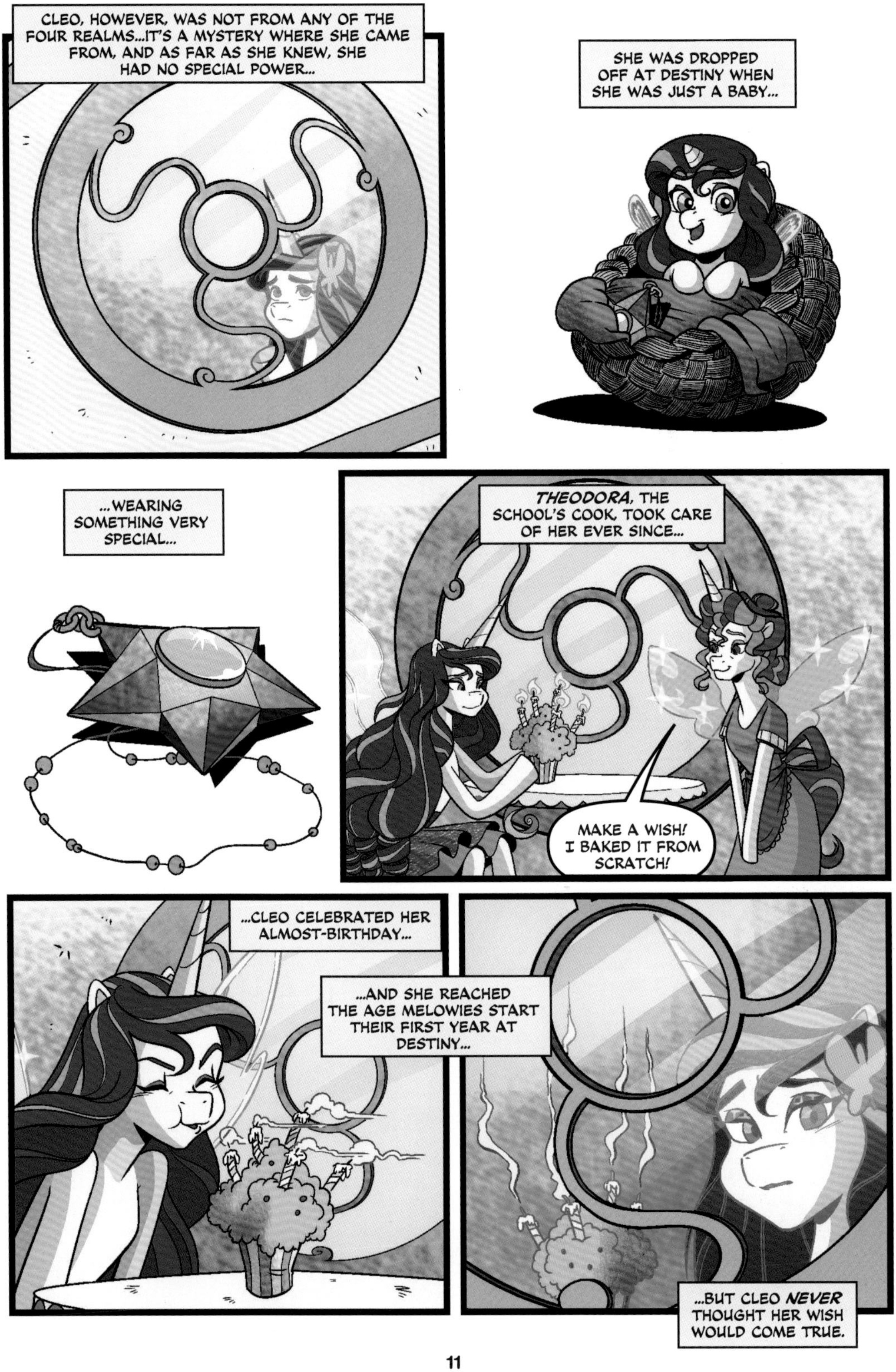

CLEO, HOWEVER, WAS NOT FROM ANY OF THE FOUR REALMS...IT'S A MYSTERY WHERE SHE CAME FROM, AND AS FAR AS SHE KNEW, SHE HAD NO SPECIAL POWER...
SHE WAS DROPPED OFF AT DESTINY WHEN SHE WAS JUST A BABY...
...WEARING SOMETHING VERY SPECIAL...
THEODORA, THE SCHOOL'S COOK, TOOK CARE OF HER EVER SINCE...
MAKE A WISH! I BAKED IT FROM SCRATCH!
...CLEO CELEBRATED HER ALMOST-BIRTHDAY...
...AND SHE REACHED THE AGE MELOWIES START THEIR FIRST YEAR AT DESTINY...
...BUT CLEO *NEVER* THOUGHT HER WISH WOULD COME TRUE.

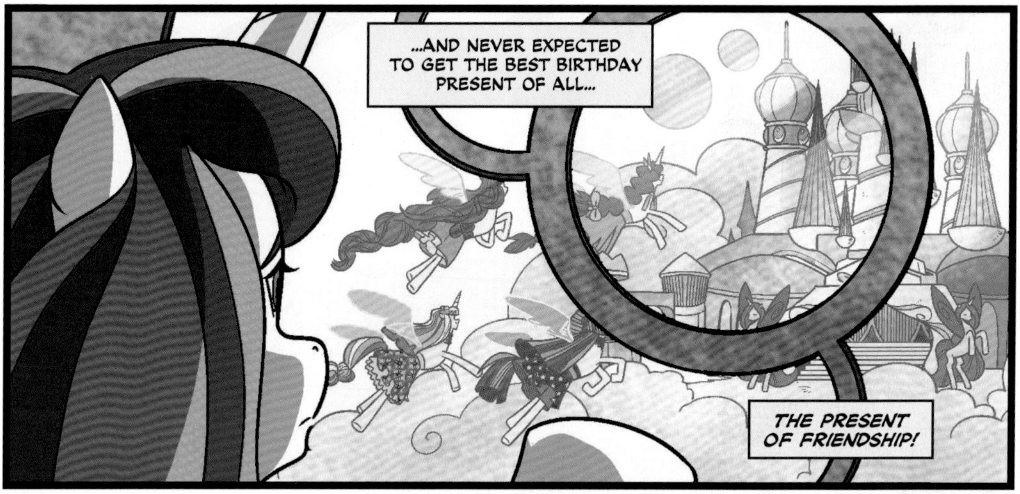
...AND NEVER EXPECTED TO GET THE BEST BIRTHDAY PRESENT OF ALL...
THE PRESENT OF FRIENDSHIP!

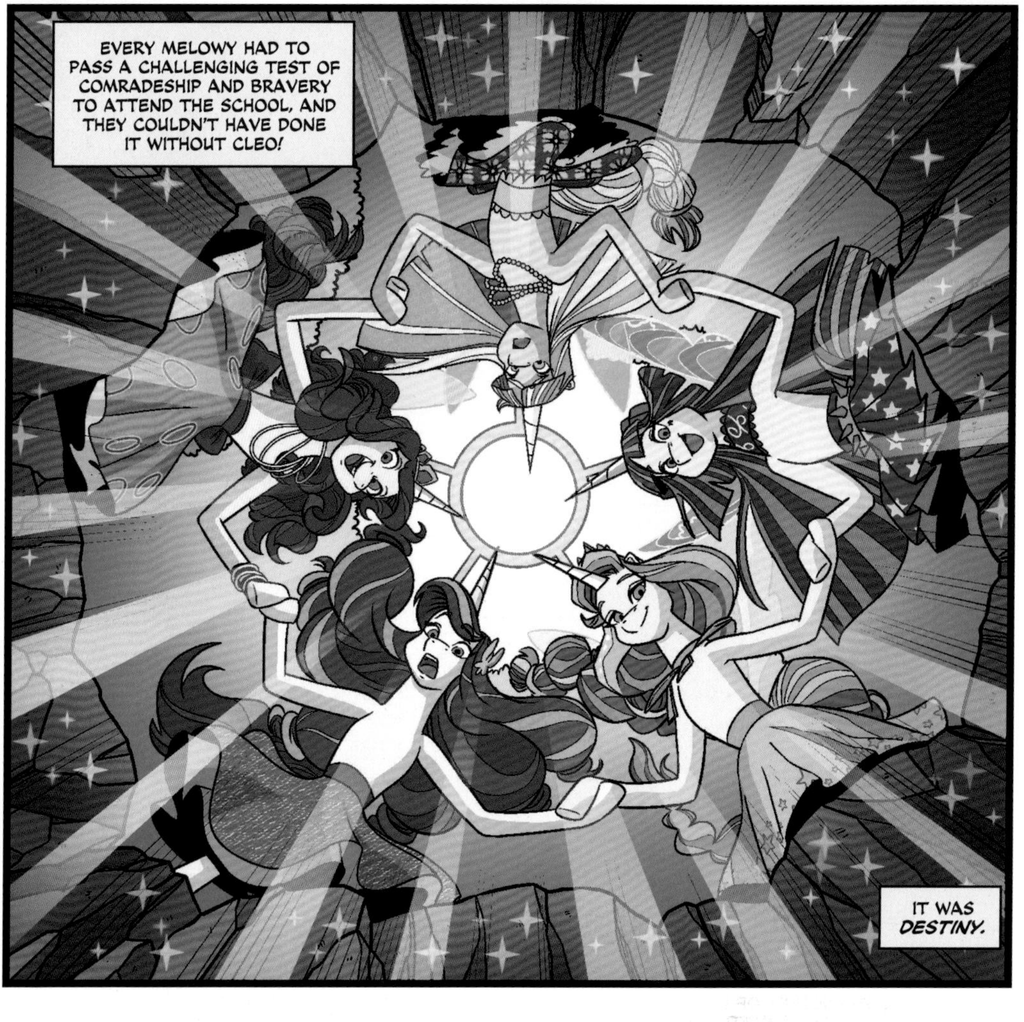
EVERY MELOWY HAD TO PASS A CHALLENGING TEST OF COMRADESHIP AND BRAVERY TO ATTEND THE SCHOOL, AND THEY COULDN'T HAVE DONE IT WITHOUT CLEO!
IT WAS DESTINY.

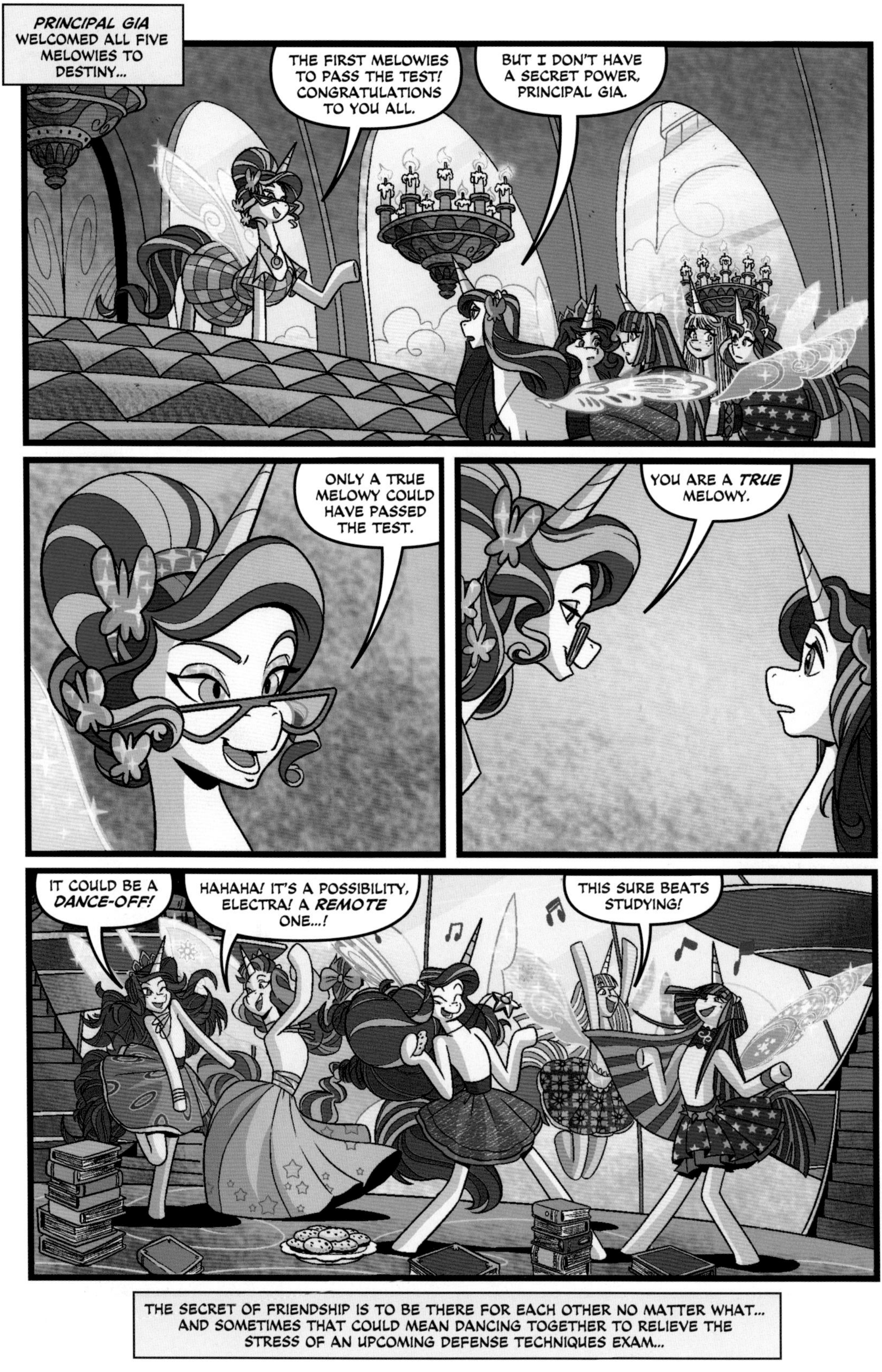
PRINCIPAL GIA WELCOMED ALL FIVE MELOWIES TO DESTINY...
THE FIRST MELOWIES TO PASS THE TEST! CONGRATULATIONS TO YOU ALL.
BUT I DON'T HAVE A SECRET POWER, PRINCIPAL GIA.
ONLY A TRUE MELOWY COULD HAVE PASSED THE TEST.
YOU ARE A TRUE MELOWY.
IT COULD BE A DANCE-OFF!
HAHAHA! IT'S A POSSIBILITY, ELECTRA! A REMOTE ONE...!
THIS SURE BEATS STUDYING!
THE SECRET OF FRIENDSHIP IS TO BE THERE FOR EACH OTHER NO MATTER WHAT... AND SOMETIMES THAT COULD MEAN DANCING TOGETHER TO RELIEVE THE STRESS OF AN UPCOMING DEFENSE TECHNIQUES EXAM...

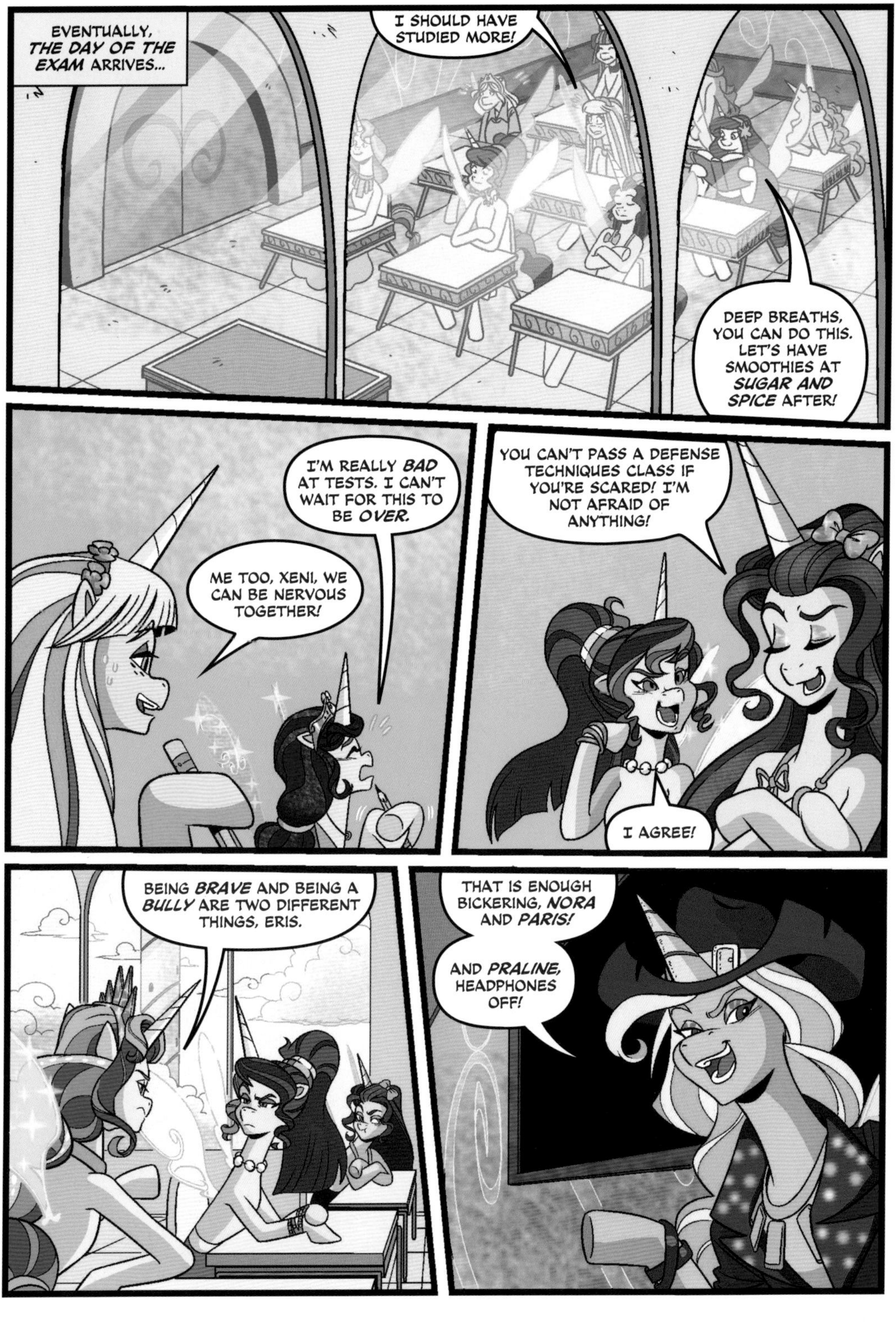
EVENTUALLY, THE DAY OF THE EXAM ARRIVES...
I SHOULD HAVE STUDIED MORE!
DEEP BREATHS, YOU CAN DO THIS. LET'S HAVE SMOOTHIES AT SUGAR AND SPICE AFTER!
I'M REALLY BAD AT TESTS. I CAN'T WAIT FOR THIS TO BE OVER.
ME TOO, XENI, WE CAN BE NERVOUS TOGETHER!
YOU CAN'T PASS A DEFENSE TECHNIQUES CLASS IF YOU'RE SCARED! I'M NOT AFRAID OF ANYTHING!
I AGREE!
BEING BRAVE AND BEING A BULLY ARE TWO DIFFERENT THINGS, ERIS.
THAT IS ENOUGH BICKERING, NORA AND PARIS!
AND PRALINE, HEADPHONES OFF!

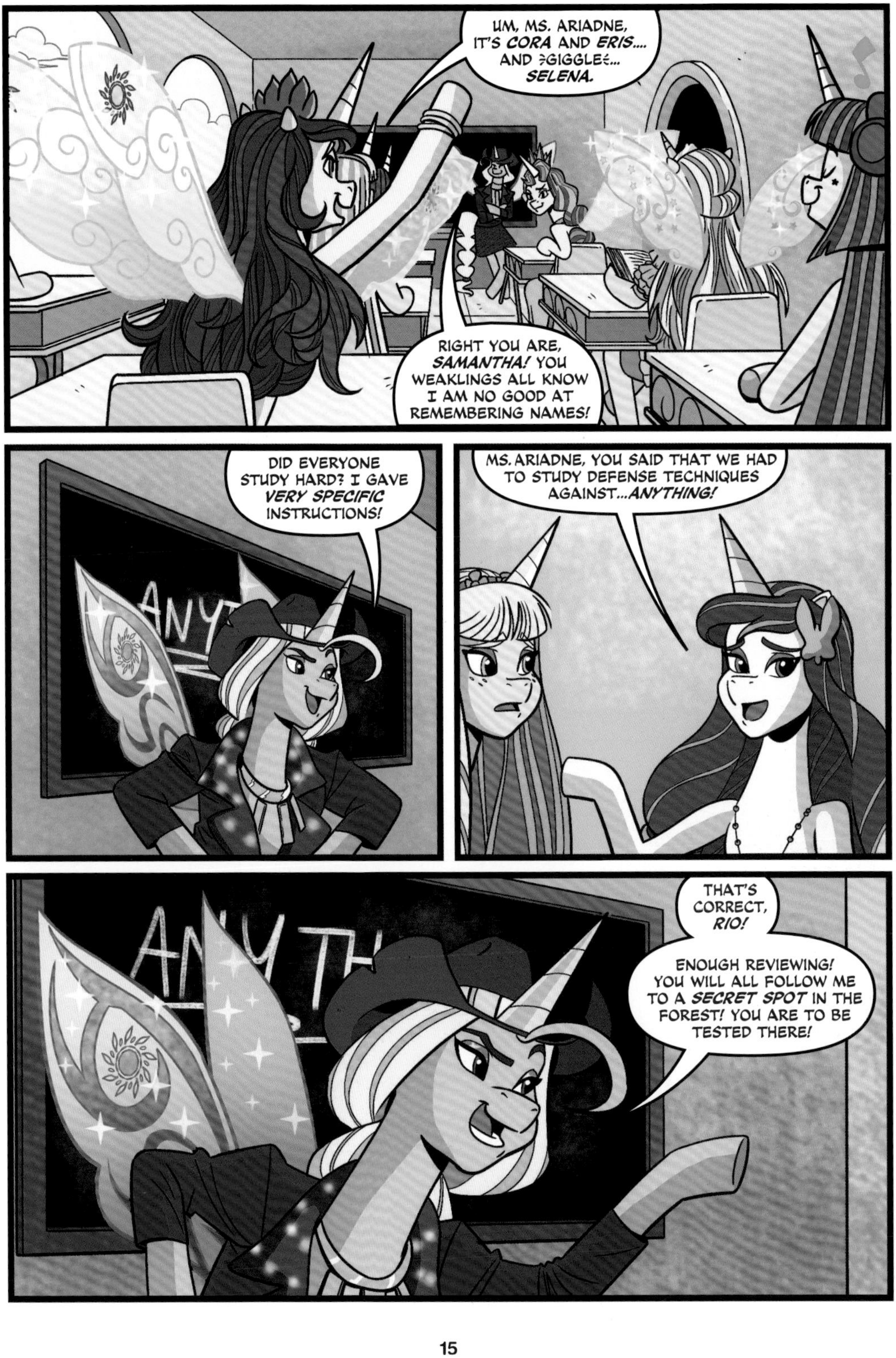
UM, MS. ARIADNE, IT'S CORA AND ERIS.... AND ≥GIGGLE≤... SELENA.
RIGHT YOU ARE, SAMANTHA! YOU WEAKLINGS ALL KNOW I AM NO GOOD AT REMEMBERING NAMES!
DID EVERYONE STUDY HARD? I GAVE VERY SPECIFIC INSTRUCTIONS!
ANY
MS. ARIADNE, YOU SAID THAT WE HAD TO STUDY DEFENSE TECHNIQUES AGAINST...ANYTHING!
ANY TH
THAT'S CORRECT, RIO!
ENOUGH REVIEWING! YOU WILL ALL FOLLOW ME TO A SECRET SPOT IN THE FOREST! YOU ARE TO BE TESTED THERE!

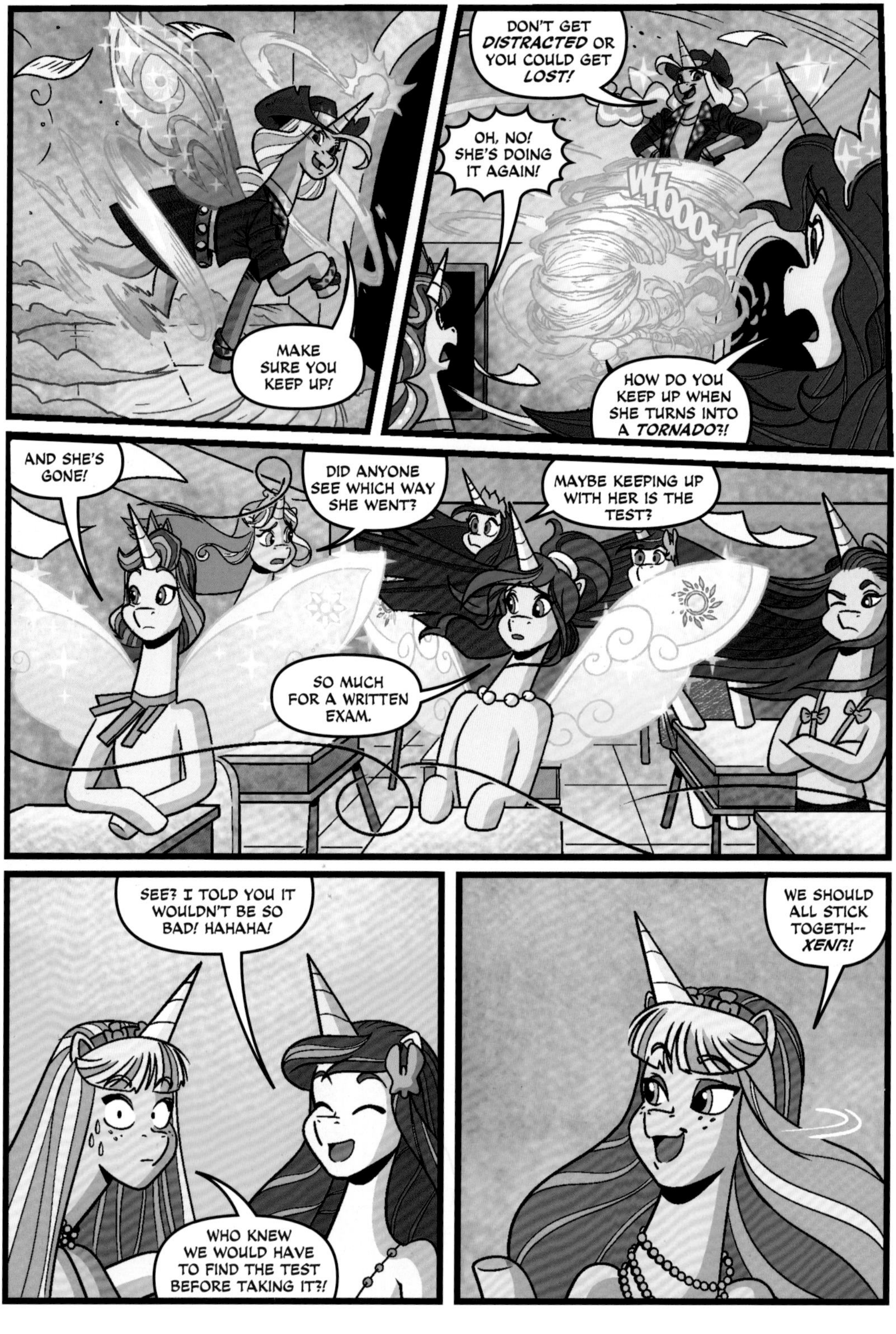
MAKE SURE YOU KEEP UP!
DON'T GET DISTRACTED OR YOU COULD GET LOST!
OH, NO! SHE'S DOING IT AGAIN!
WHOOOSH
HOW DO YOU KEEP UP WHEN SHE TURNS INTO A TORNADO?!
AND SHE'S GONE!
DID ANYONE SEE WHICH WAY SHE WENT?
MAYBE KEEPING UP WITH HER IS THE TEST?
SO MUCH FOR A WRITTEN EXAM.
SEE? I TOLD YOU IT WOULDN'T BE SO BAD! HAHAHA!
WHO KNEW WE WOULD HAVE TO FIND THE TEST BEFORE TAKING IT?!
WE SHOULD ALL STICK TOGETH-- XENI?!

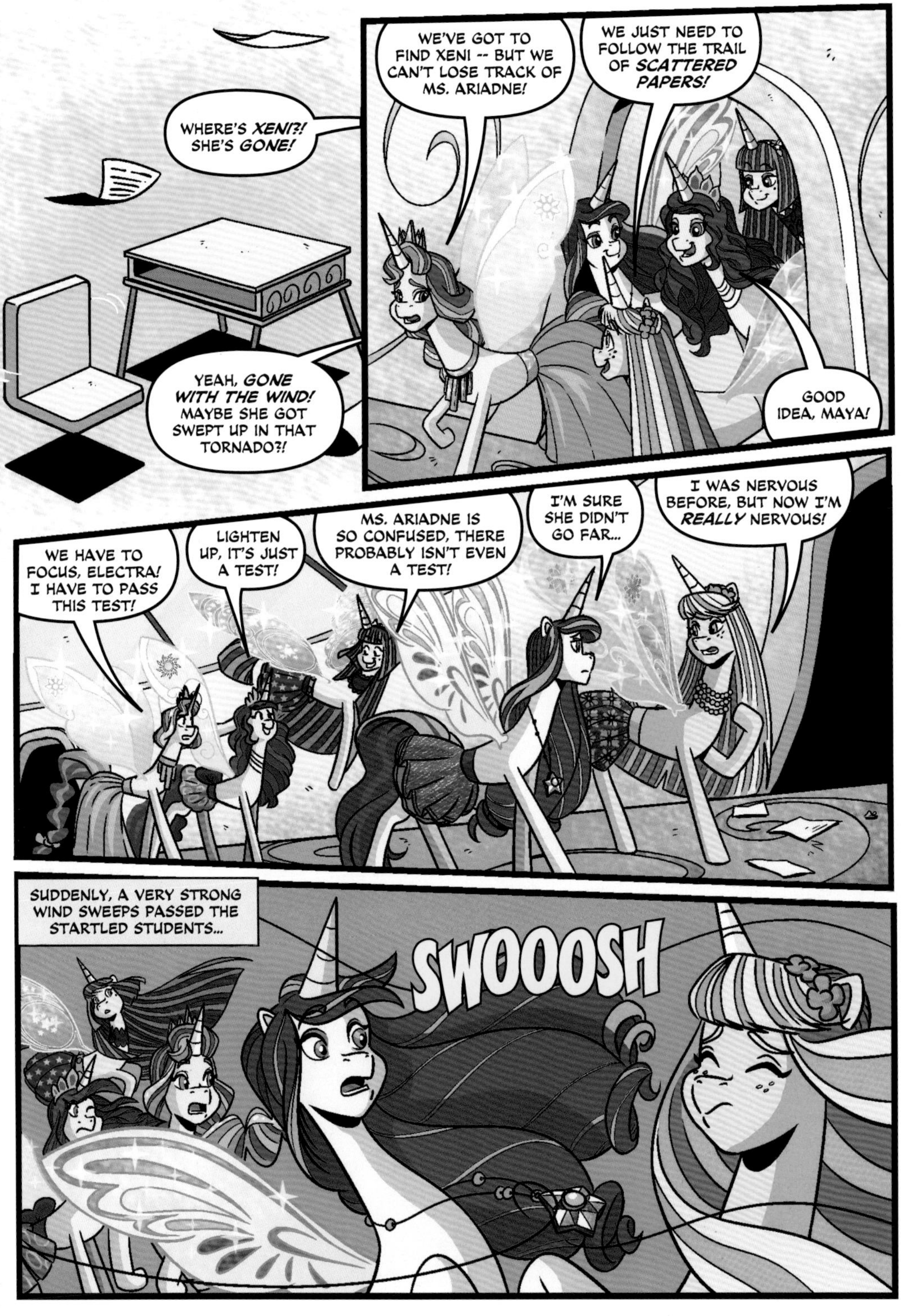
WHERE'S *XENI?!* SHE'S *GONE!*
YEAH, *GONE WITH THE WIND!* MAYBE SHE GOT SWEPT UP IN THAT TORNADO?!
WE'VE GOT TO FIND XENI -- BUT WE CAN'T LOSE TRACK OF MS. ARIADNE!
WE JUST NEED TO FOLLOW THE TRAIL OF *SCATTERED PAPERS!*
GOOD IDEA, MAYA!
WE HAVE TO FOCUS, ELECTRA! I HAVE TO PASS THIS TEST!
LIGHTEN UP, IT'S JUST A TEST!
MS. ARIADNE IS SO CONFUSED, THERE PROBABLY ISN'T EVEN A TEST!
I'M SURE SHE DIDN'T GO FAR...
I WAS NERVOUS BEFORE, BUT NOW I'M *REALLY* NERVOUS!
SUDDENLY, A VERY STRONG WIND SWEEPS PASSED THE STARTLED STUDENTS...
SWOOOSH

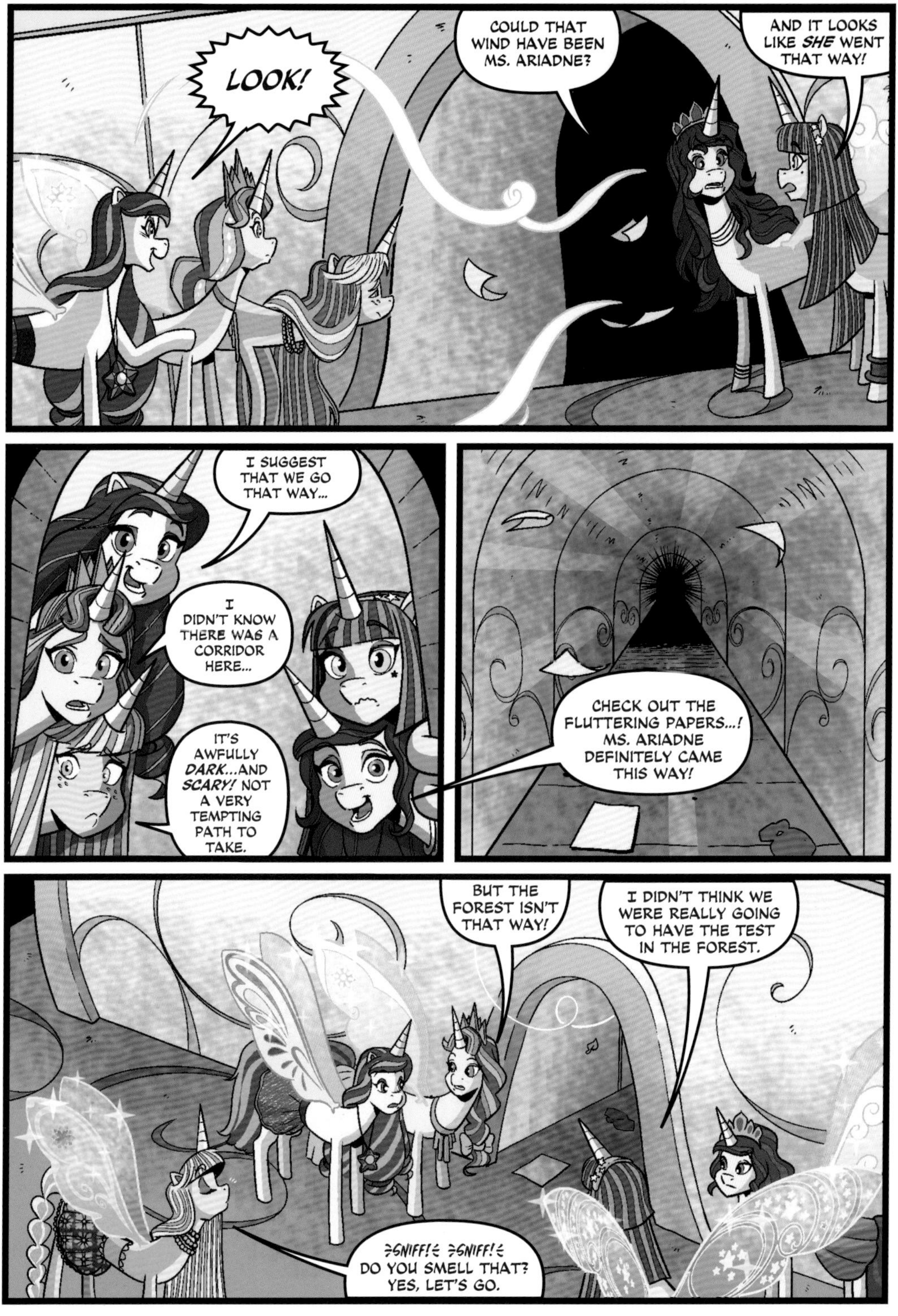
LOOK!
COULD THAT WIND HAVE BEEN MS. ARIADNE?
AND IT LOOKS LIKE *SHE* WENT THAT WAY!
I SUGGEST THAT WE GO THAT WAY...
I DIDN'T KNOW THERE WAS A CORRIDOR HERE...
IT'S AWFULLY *DARK*...AND *SCARY!* NOT A VERY TEMPTING PATH TO TAKE.
CHECK OUT THE FLUTTERING PAPERS...! MS. ARIADNE DEFINITELY CAME THIS WAY!
BUT THE FOREST ISN'T THAT WAY!
I DIDN'T THINK WE WERE REALLY GOING TO HAVE THE TEST IN THE FOREST.
SNIFF! *SNIFF!* DO YOU SMELL THAT? YES, LET'S GO.

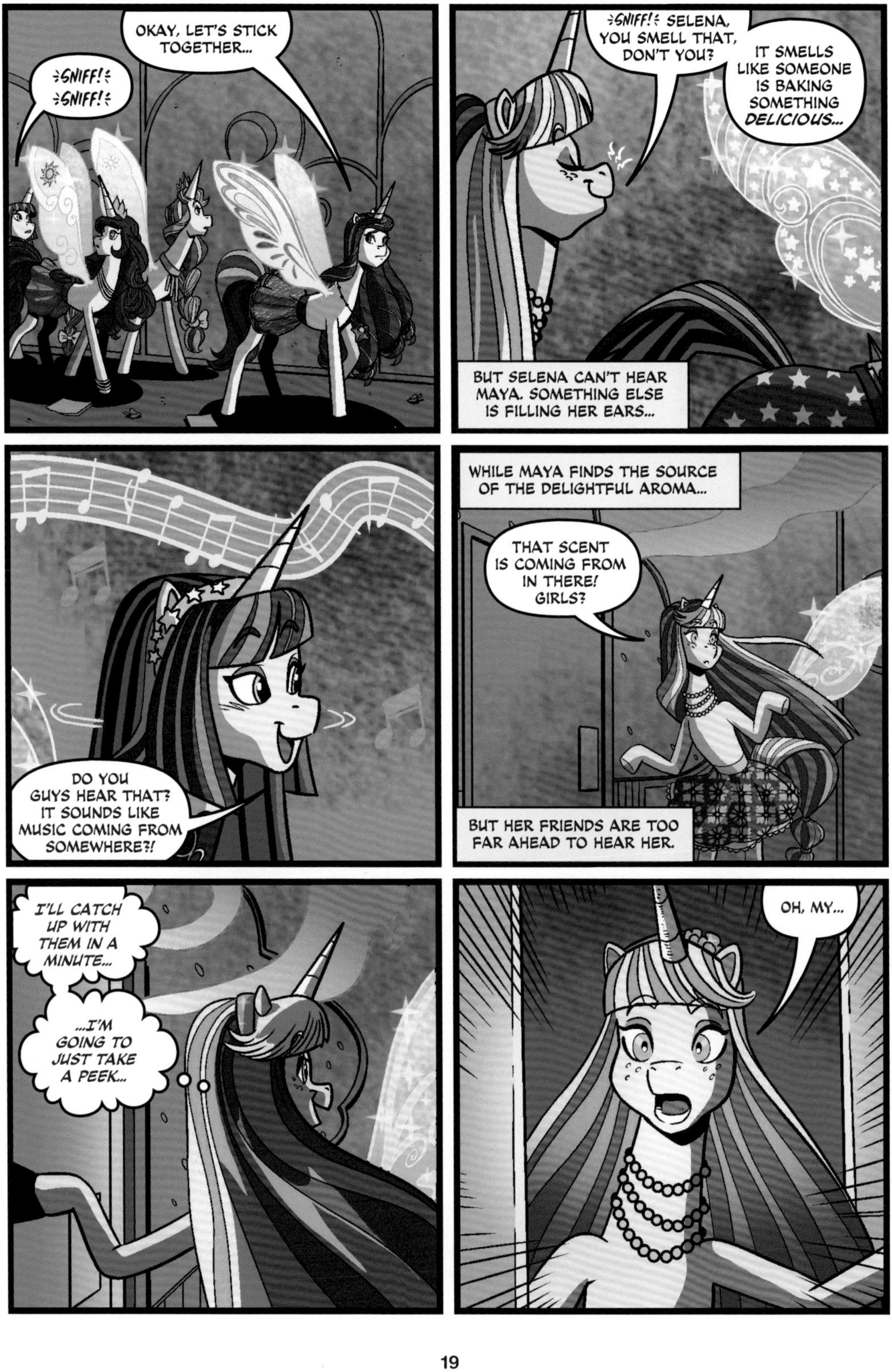
OKAY, LET'S STICK TOGETHER...
SNIFF! SNIFF!
SNIFF! SELENA, YOU SMELL THAT, DON'T YOU?
IT SMELLS LIKE SOMEONE IS BAKING SOMETHING DELICIOUS...
BUT SELENA CAN'T HEAR MAYA. SOMETHING ELSE IS FILLING HER EARS...
DO YOU GUYS HEAR THAT? IT SOUNDS LIKE MUSIC COMING FROM SOMEWHERE?!
WHILE MAYA FINDS THE SOURCE OF THE DELIGHTFUL AROMA...
THAT SCENT IS COMING FROM IN THERE! GIRLS?
BUT HER FRIENDS ARE TOO FAR AHEAD TO HEAR HER.
I'LL CATCH UP WITH THEM IN A MINUTE...
...I'M GOING TO JUST TAKE A PEEK...
OH, MY...

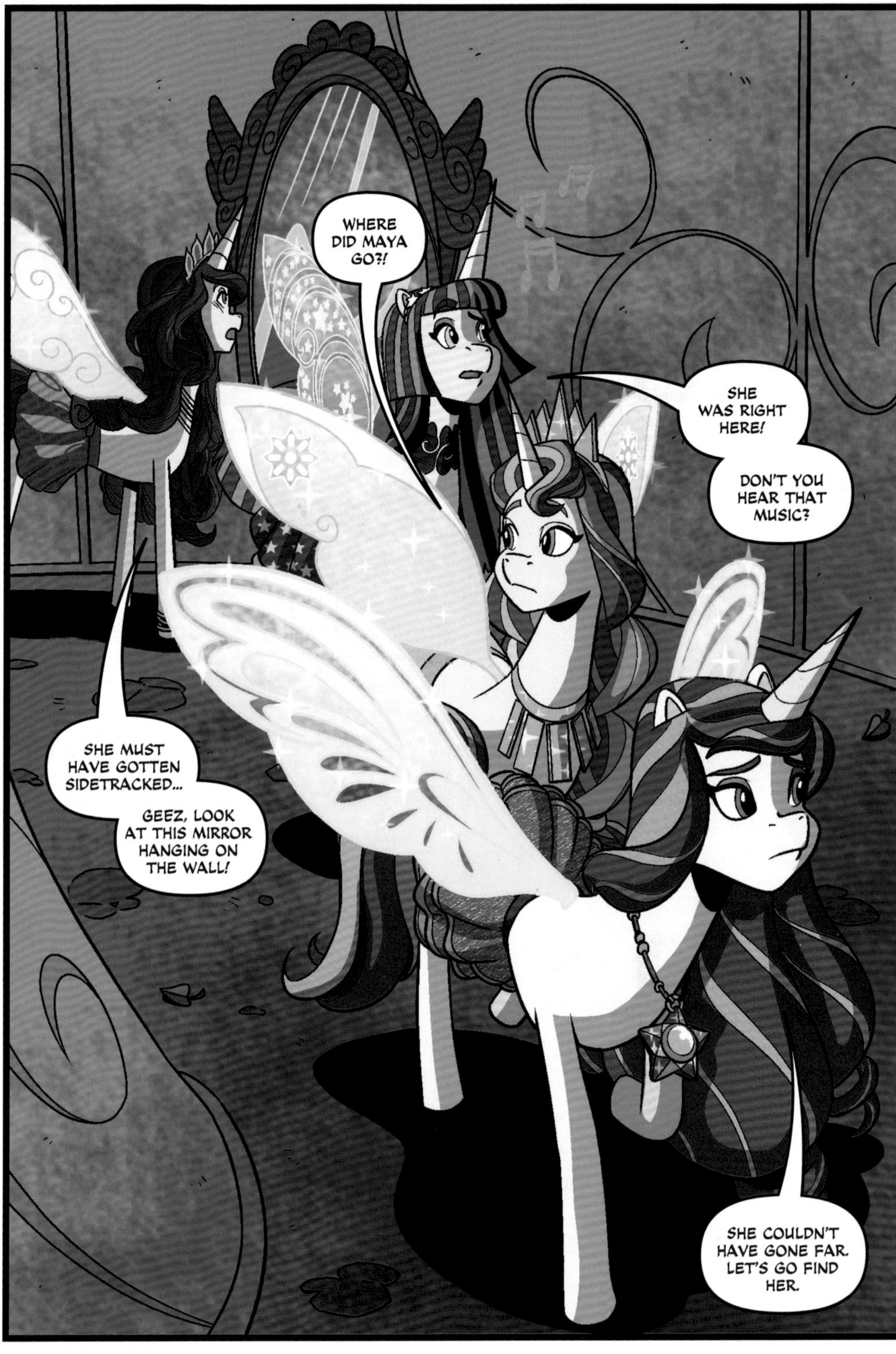
WHERE DID MAYA GO?!
SHE WAS RIGHT HERE!
DON'T YOU HEAR THAT MUSIC?
SHE MUST HAVE GOTTEN SIDETRACKED...
GEEZ, LOOK AT THIS MIRROR HANGING ON THE WALL!
SHE COULDN'T HAVE GONE FAR. LET'S GO FIND HER.

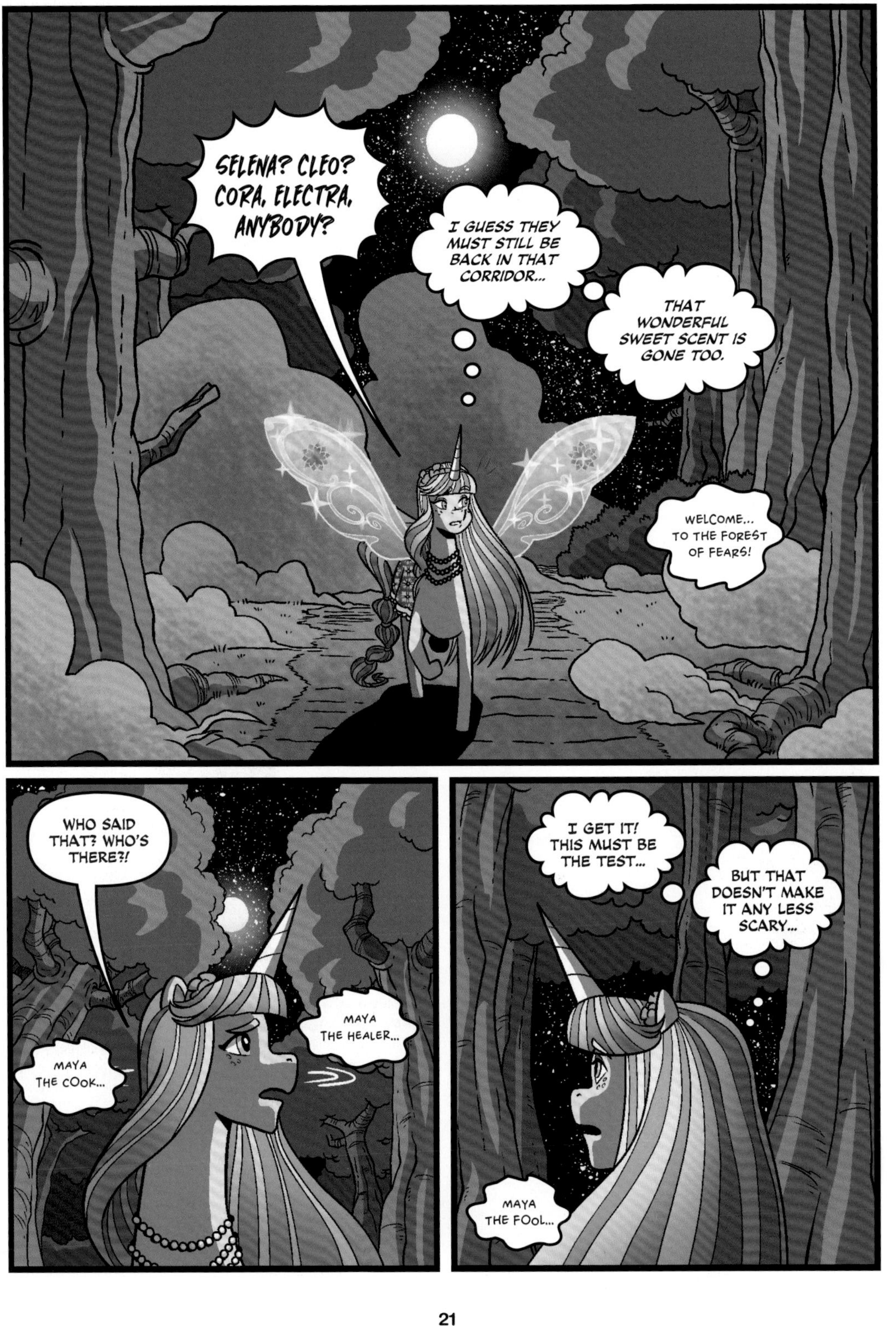
SELENA? CLEO? CORA, ELECTRA, ANYBODY?
I GUESS THEY MUST STILL BE BACK IN THAT CORRIDOR...
THAT WONDERFUL SWEET SCENT IS GONE TOO.
WELCOME... TO THE FOREST OF FEARS!
WHO SAID THAT? WHO'S THERE?!
MAYA THE COOK...
MAYA THE HEALER...
I GET IT! THIS MUST BE THE TEST...
BUT THAT DOESN'T MAKE IT ANY LESS SCARY...
MAYA THE FOOL...

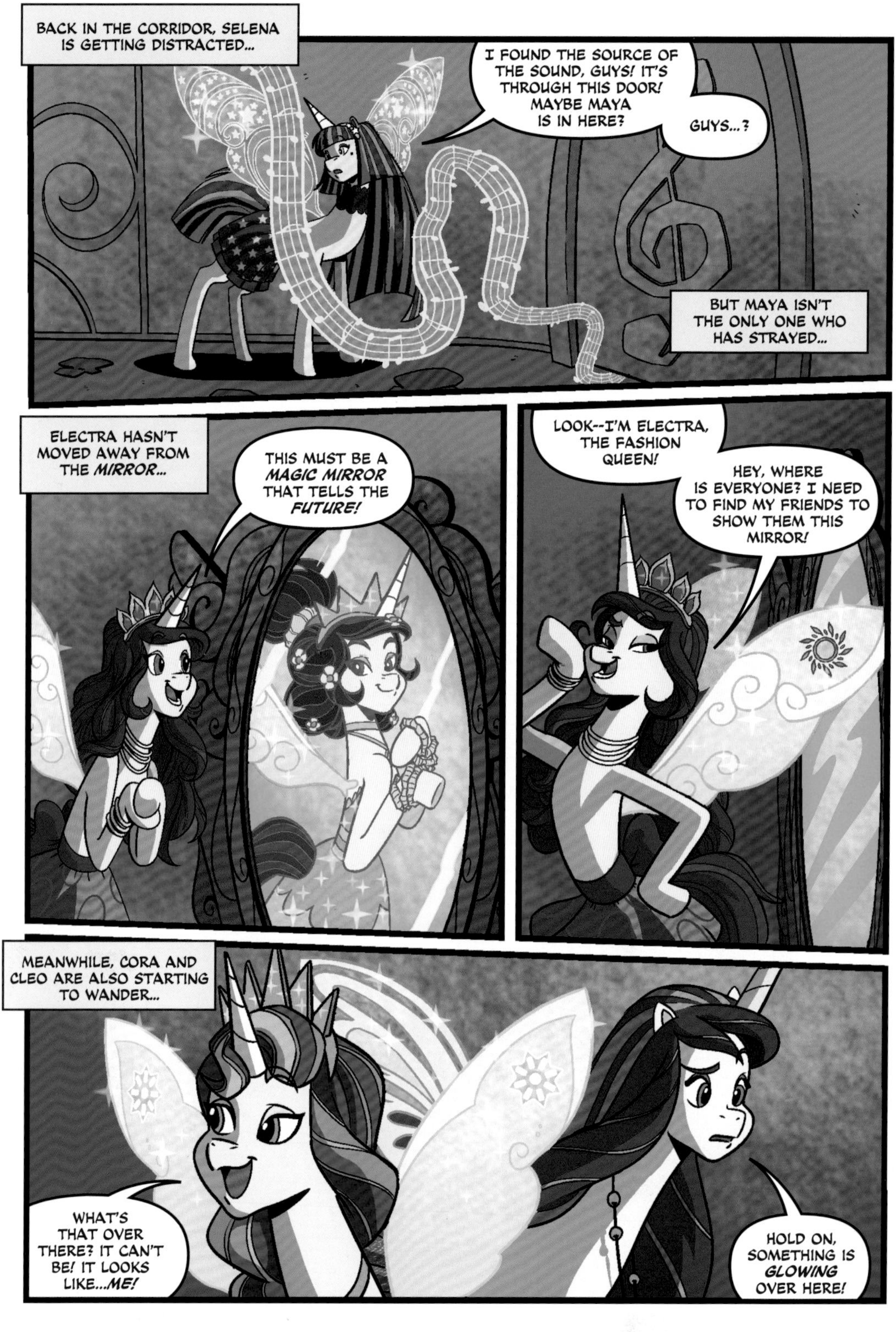

BACK IN THE CORRIDOR, SELENA IS GETTING DISTRACTED...
I FOUND THE SOURCE OF THE SOUND, GUYS! IT'S THROUGH THIS DOOR! MAYBE MAYA IS IN HERE?
GUYS...?
BUT MAYA ISN'T THE ONLY ONE WHO HAS STRAYED...
ELECTRA HASN'T MOVED AWAY FROM THE *MIRROR*...
THIS MUST BE A *MAGIC MIRROR* THAT TELLS THE *FUTURE!*
LOOK--I'M ELECTRA, THE FASHION QUEEN!
HEY, WHERE IS EVERYONE? I NEED TO FIND MY FRIENDS TO SHOW THEM THIS MIRROR!
MEANWHILE, CORA AND CLEO ARE ALSO STARTING TO WANDER...
WHAT'S THAT OVER THERE? IT CAN'T BE! IT LOOKS LIKE...*ME!*
HOLD ON, SOMETHING IS *GLOWING* OVER HERE!

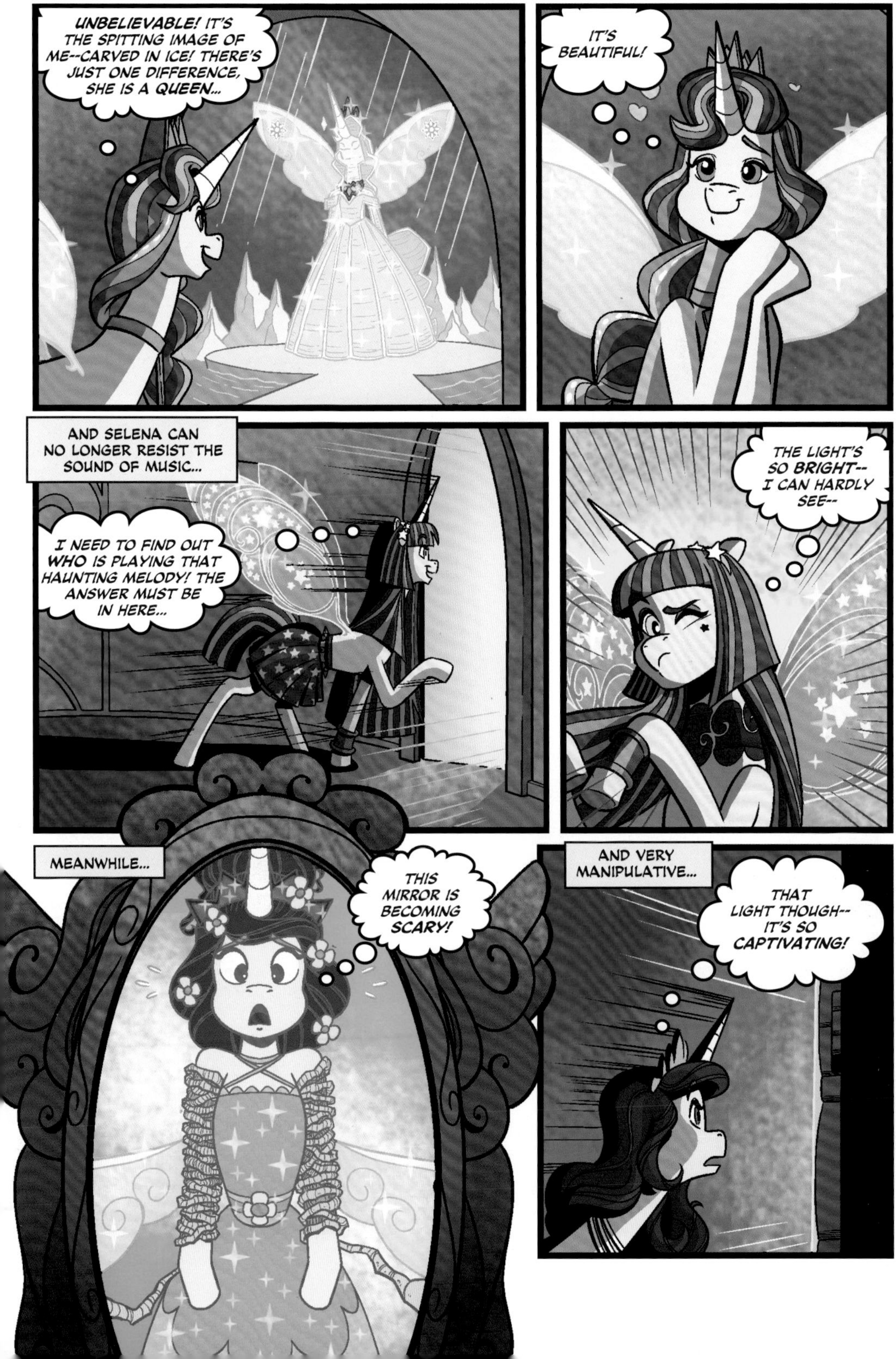
UNBELIEVABLE! IT'S THE SPITTING IMAGE OF ME--CARVED IN ICE! THERE'S JUST ONE DIFFERENCE, SHE IS A QUEEN...
IT'S BEAUTIFUL!
AND SELENA CAN NO LONGER RESIST THE SOUND OF MUSIC...
I NEED TO FIND OUT WHO IS PLAYING THAT HAUNTING MELODY! THE ANSWER MUST BE IN HERE...
THE LIGHT'S SO BRIGHT-- I CAN HARDLY SEE--
MEANWHILE...
THIS MIRROR IS BECOMING SCARY!
AND VERY MANIPULATIVE...
THAT LIGHT THOUGH-- IT'S SO CAPTIVATING!

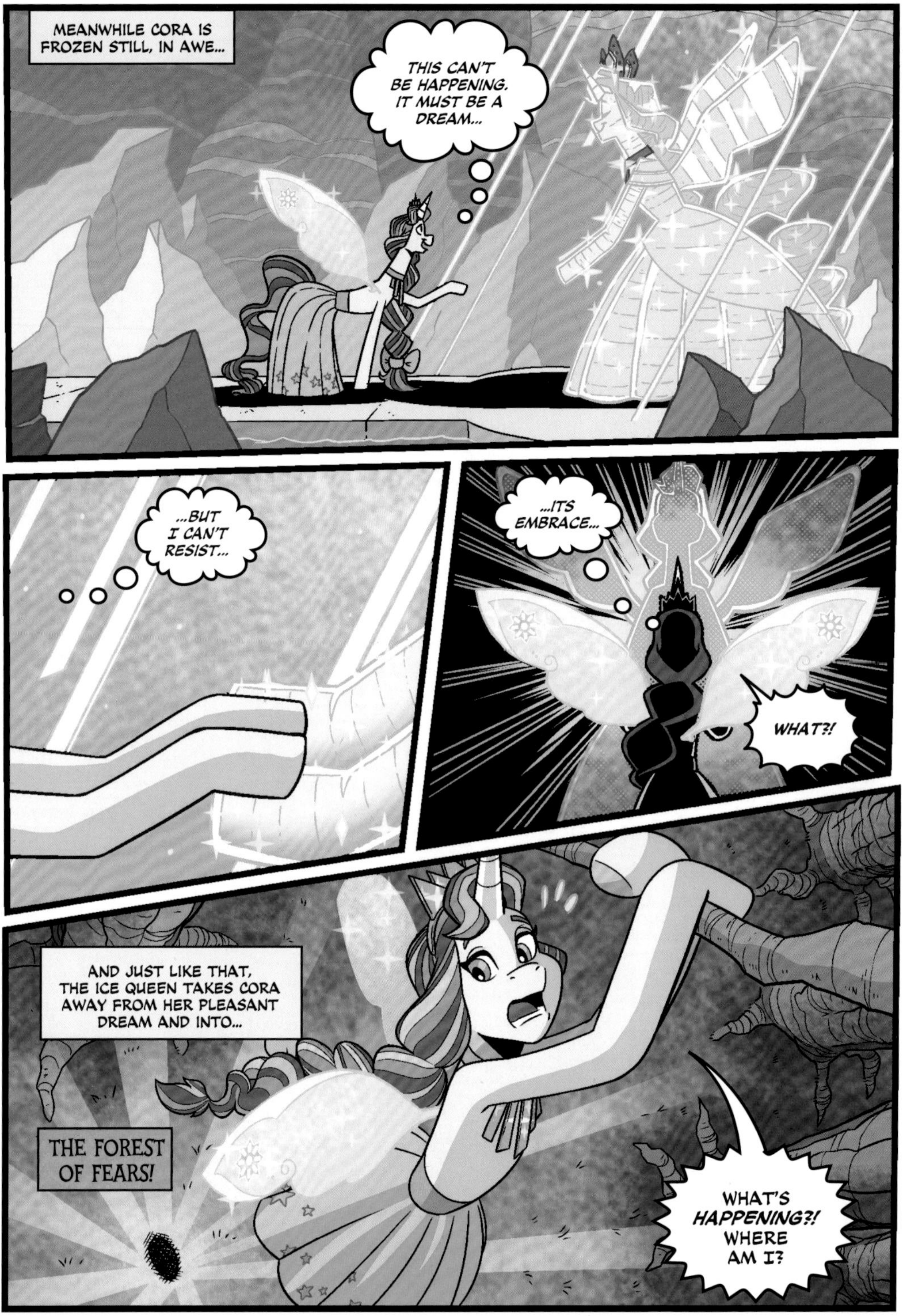
MEANWHILE CORA IS FROZEN STILL, IN AWE...
THIS CAN'T BE HAPPENING. IT MUST BE A DREAM...
...BUT I CAN'T RESIST...
...ITS EMBRACE...
WHAT?!
AND JUST LIKE THAT, THE ICE QUEEN TAKES CORA AWAY FROM HER PLEASANT DREAM AND INTO...
THE FOREST OF FEARS!
WHAT'S HAPPENING?! WHERE AM I?

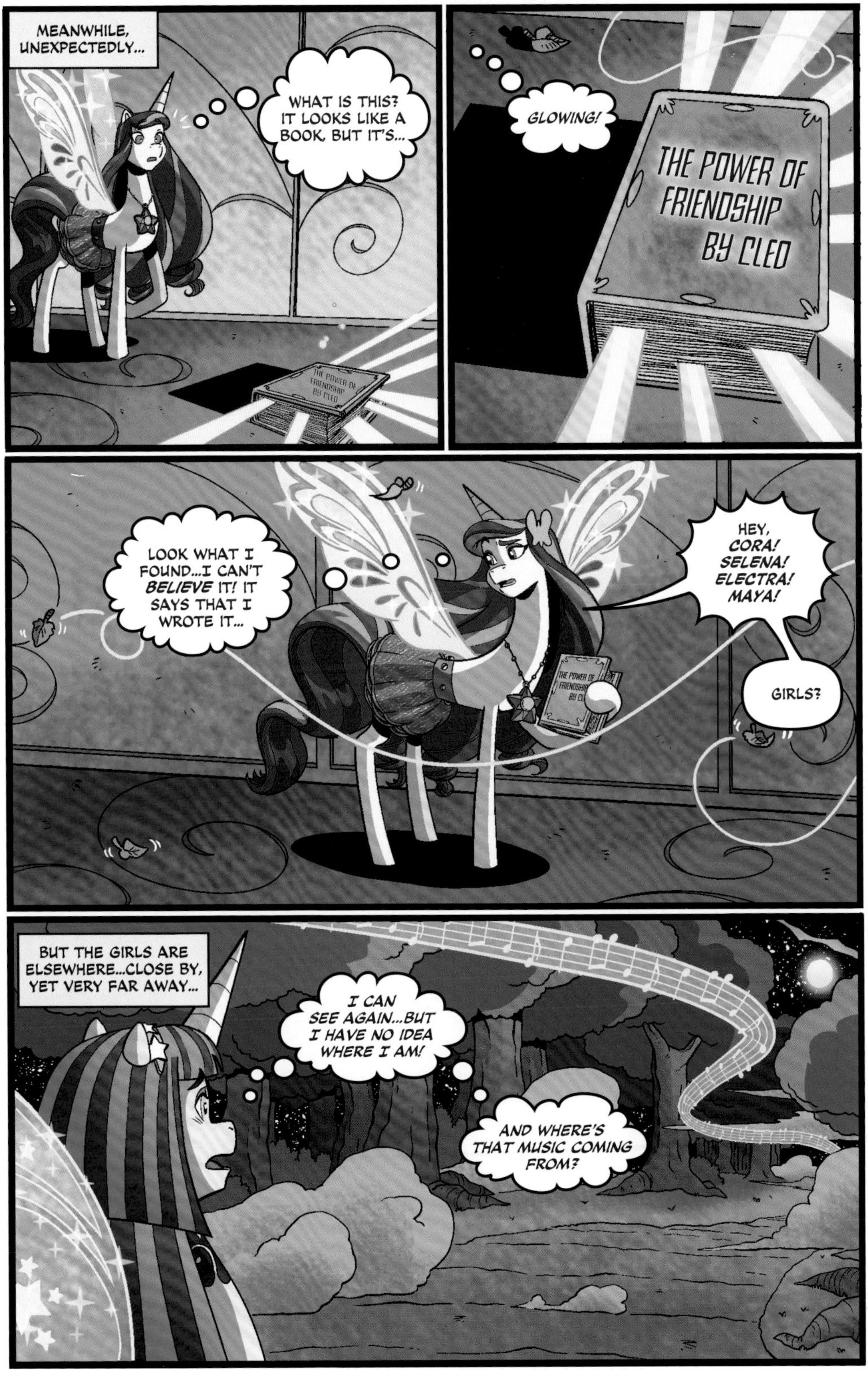
MEANWHILE, UNEXPECTEDLY...
WHAT IS THIS? IT LOOKS LIKE A BOOK, BUT IT'S...
GLOWING!
THE POWER OF FRIENDSHIP BY CLEO
THE POWER OF FRIENDSHIP BY CLEO
LOOK WHAT I FOUND...I CAN'T BELIEVE IT! IT SAYS THAT I WROTE IT...
HEY, CORA! SELENA! ELECTRA! MAYA!
GIRLS?
BUT THE GIRLS ARE ELSEWHERE...CLOSE BY, YET VERY FAR AWAY...
I CAN SEE AGAIN...BUT I HAVE NO IDEA WHERE I AM!
AND WHERE'S THAT MUSIC COMING FROM?

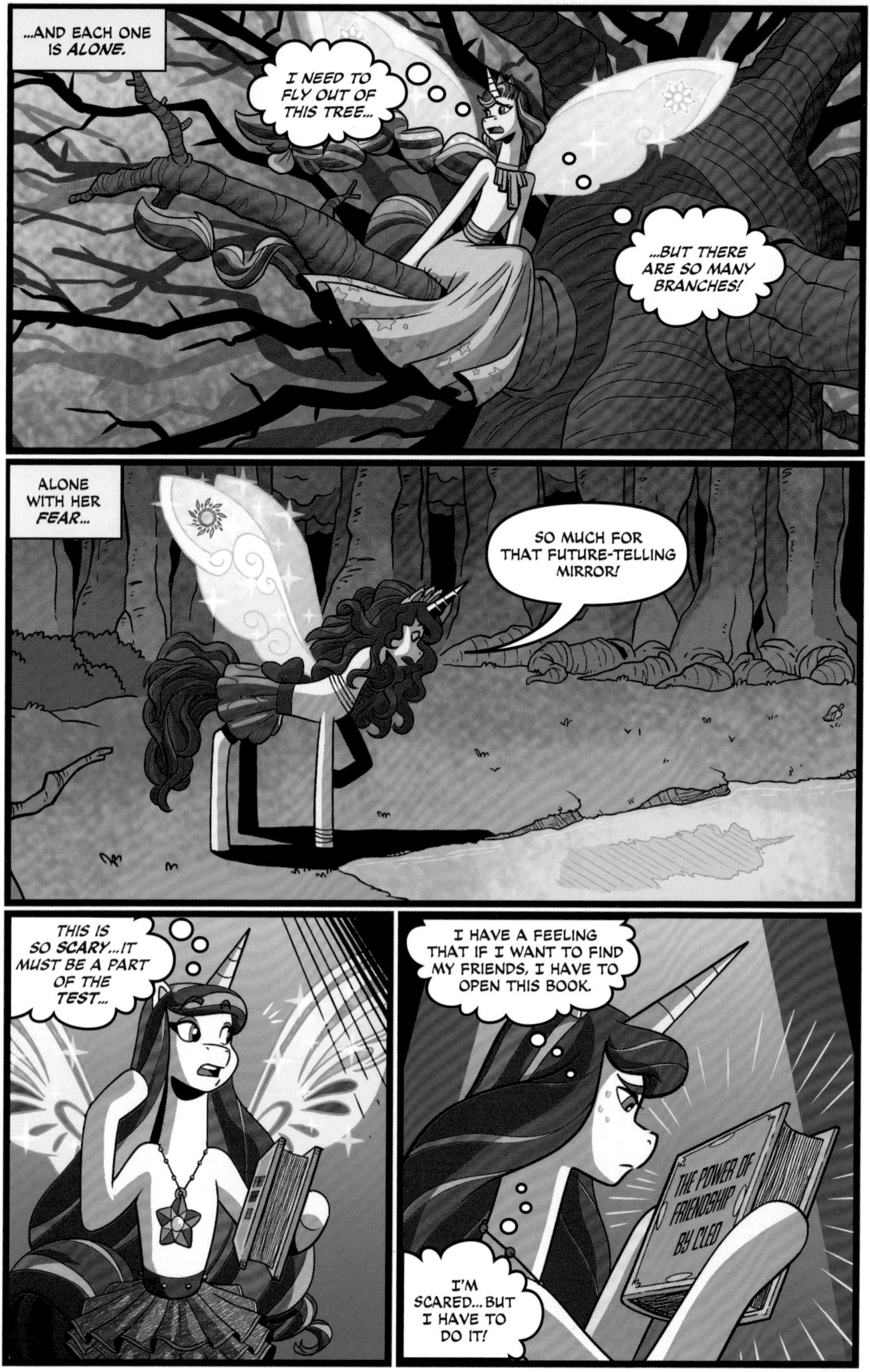
...AND EACH ONE IS ALONE.
I NEED TO FLY OUT OF THIS TREE...
...BUT THERE ARE SO MANY BRANCHES!
ALONE WITH HER FEAR...
SO MUCH FOR THAT FUTURE-TELLING MIRROR!
THIS IS SO SCARY...IT MUST BE A PART OF THE TEST...
I HAVE A FEELING THAT IF I WANT TO FIND MY FRIENDS, I HAVE TO OPEN THIS BOOK.
THE POWER OF FRIENDSHIP BY CLEO
I'M SCARED... BUT I HAVE TO DO IT!

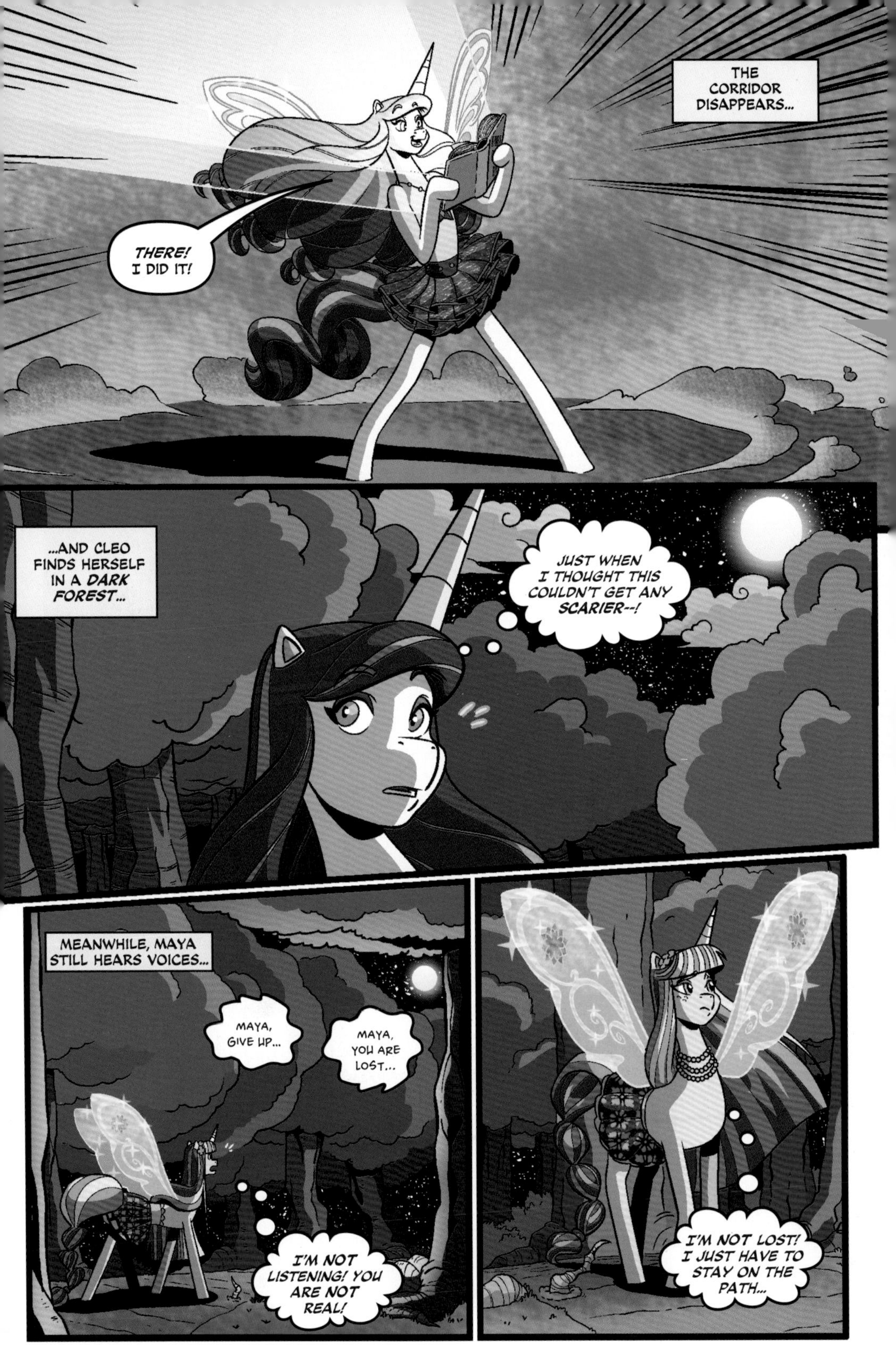
THE CORRIDOR DISAPPEARS...
THERE! I DID IT!
...AND CLEO FINDS HERSELF IN A DARK FOREST...
JUST WHEN I THOUGHT THIS COULDN'T GET ANY SCARIER--!
MEANWHILE, MAYA STILL HEARS VOICES...
MAYA, GIVE UP...
MAYA, YOU ARE LOST...
I'M NOT LISTENING! YOU ARE NOT REAL!
I'M NOT LOST! I JUST HAVE TO STAY ON THE PATH...

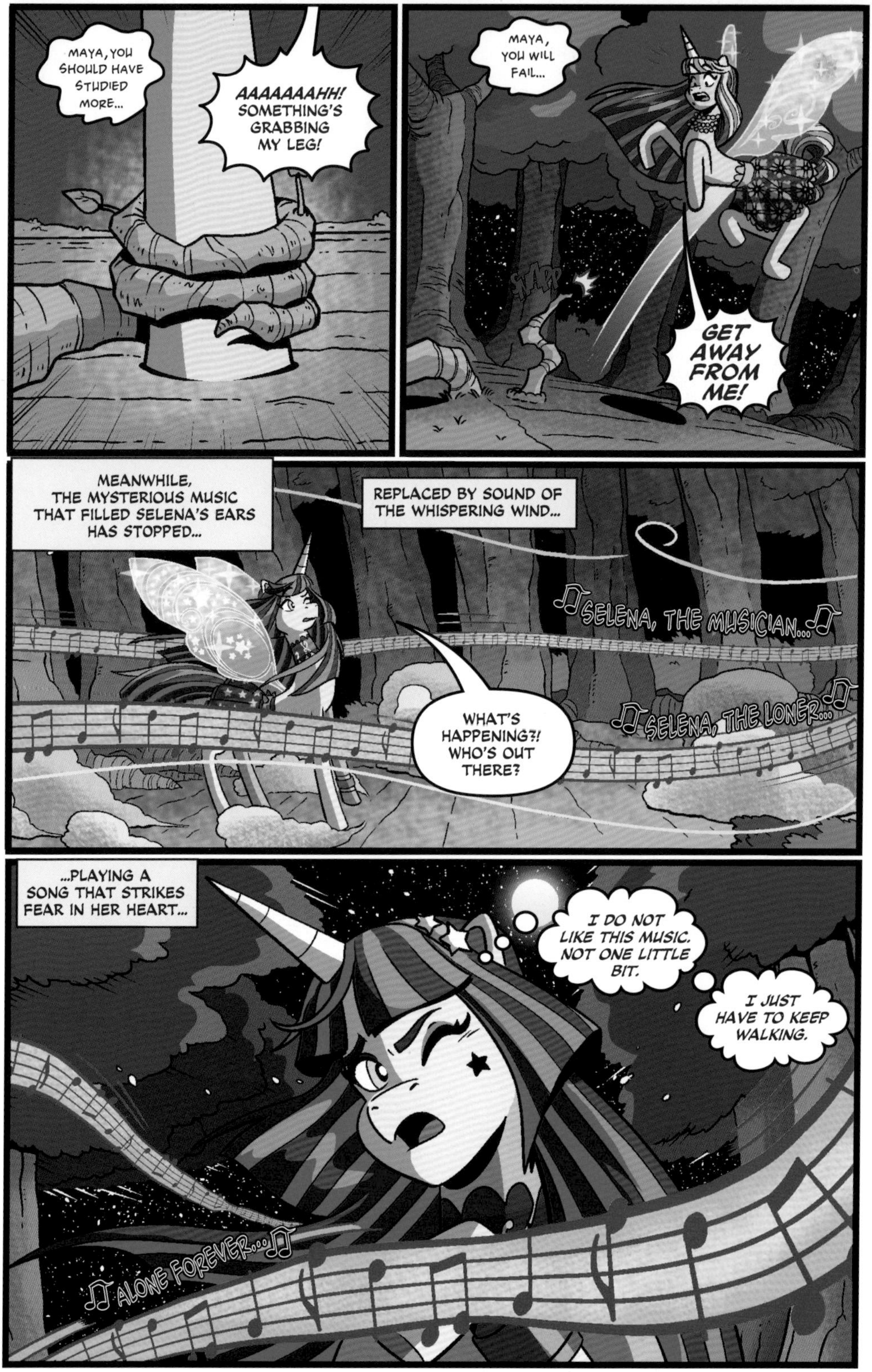
MAYA, YOU SHOULD HAVE STUDIED MORE...
AAAAAAAHH! SOMETHING'S GRABBING MY LEG!
MAYA, YOU WILL FAIL...
GET AWAY FROM ME!
MEANWHILE, THE MYSTERIOUS MUSIC THAT FILLED SELENA'S EARS HAS STOPPED...
REPLACED BY SOUND OF THE WHISPERING WIND...
SELENA, THE MUSICIAN...
SELENA, THE LONER...
WHAT'S HAPPENING?! WHO'S OUT THERE?
...PLAYING A SONG THAT STRIKES FEAR IN HER HEART...
I DO NOT LIKE THIS MUSIC. NOT ONE LITTLE BIT.
I JUST HAVE TO KEEP WALKING.
ALONE FOREVER...

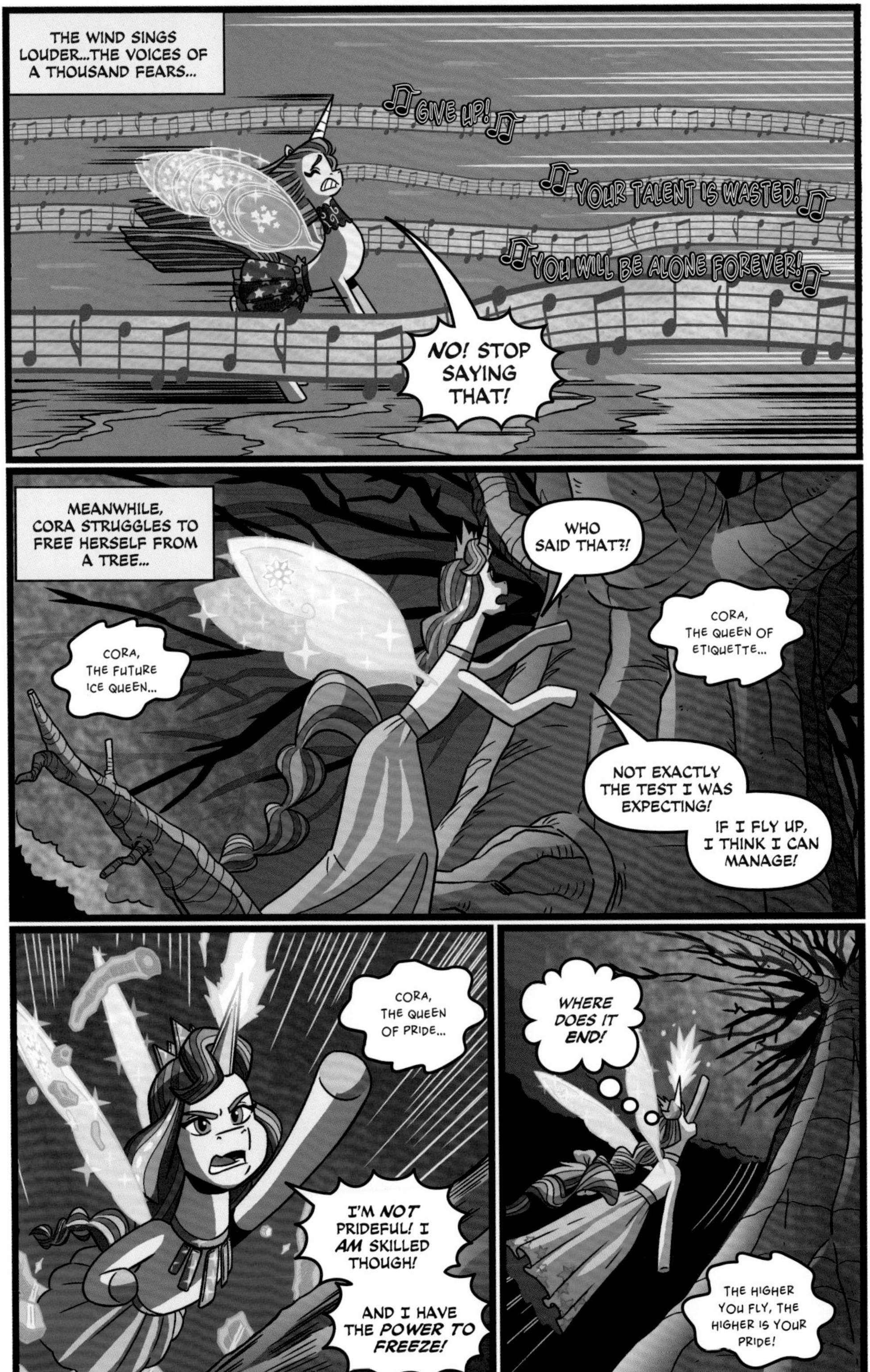
THE WIND SINGS LOUDER...THE VOICES OF A THOUSAND FEARS...
GIVE UP!
YOUR TALENT IS WASTED!
YOU WILL BE ALONE FOREVER!
NO! STOP SAYING THAT!
MEANWHILE, CORA STRUGGLES TO FREE HERSELF FROM A TREE...
WHO SAID THAT?!
CORA, THE FUTURE ICE QUEEN...
CORA, THE QUEEN OF ETIQUETTE...
NOT EXACTLY THE TEST I WAS EXPECTING!
IF I FLY UP, I THINK I CAN MANAGE!
CORA, THE QUEEN OF PRIDE...
I'M NOT PRIDEFUL! I AM SKILLED THOUGH!
AND I HAVE THE POWER TO FREEZE!
WHERE DOES IT END!
THE HIGHER YOU FLY, THE HIGHER IS YOUR PRIDE!

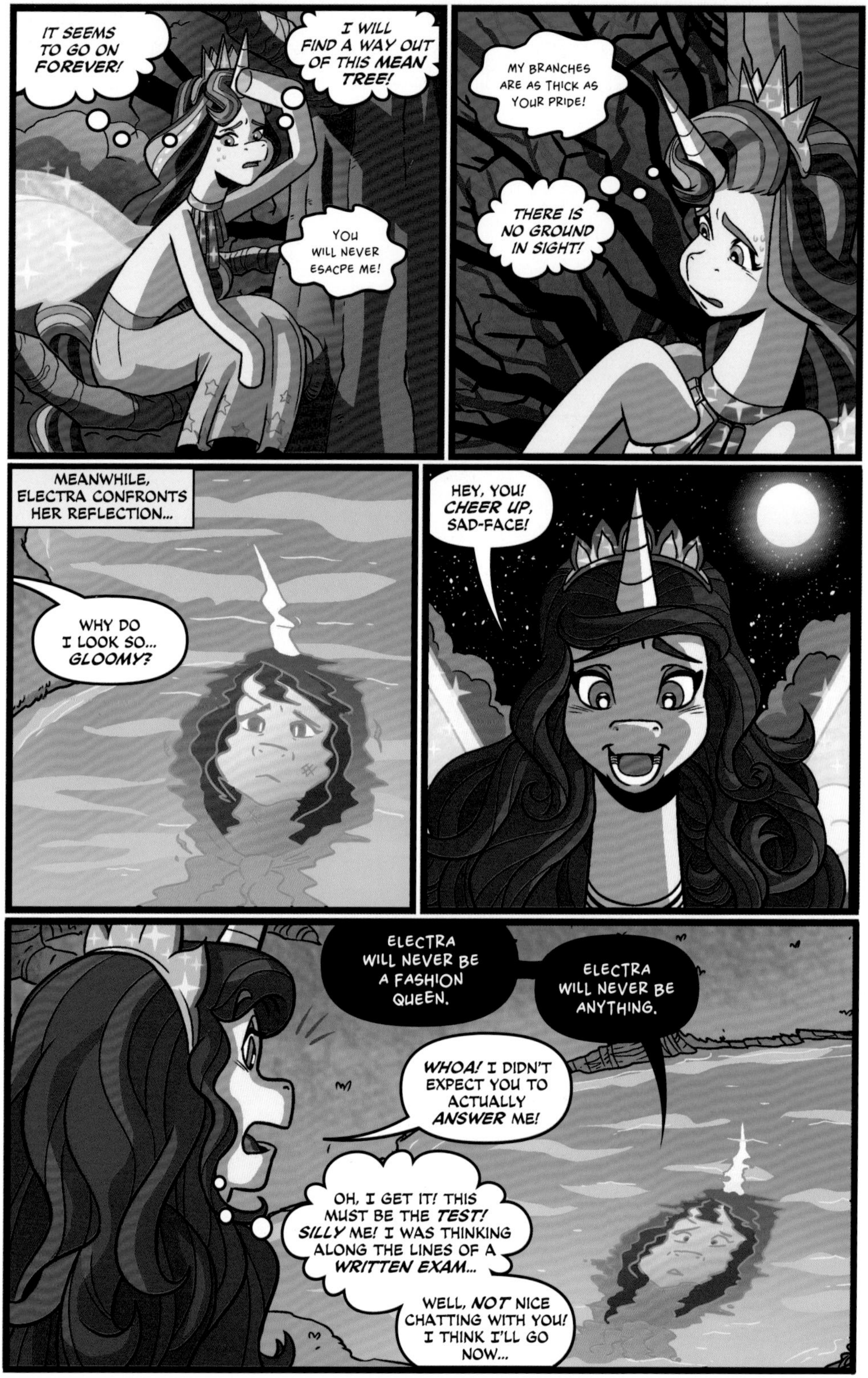
IT SEEMS TO GO ON FOREVER!
I WILL FIND A WAY OUT OF THIS MEAN TREE!
YOU WILL NEVER ESACPE ME!
MY BRANCHES ARE AS THICK AS YOUR PRIDE!
THERE IS NO GROUND IN SIGHT!
MEANWHILE, ELECTRA CONFRONTS HER REFLECTION...
WHY DO I LOOK SO... GLOOMY?
HEY, YOU! CHEER UP, SAD-FACE!
ELECTRA WILL NEVER BE A FASHION QUEEN.
ELECTRA WILL NEVER BE ANYTHING.
WHOA! I DIDN'T EXPECT YOU TO ACTUALLY ANSWER ME!
OH, I GET IT! THIS MUST BE THE TEST! SILLY ME! I WAS THINKING ALONG THE LINES OF A WRITTEN EXAM...
WELL, NOT NICE CHATTING WITH YOU! I THINK I'LL GO NOW...

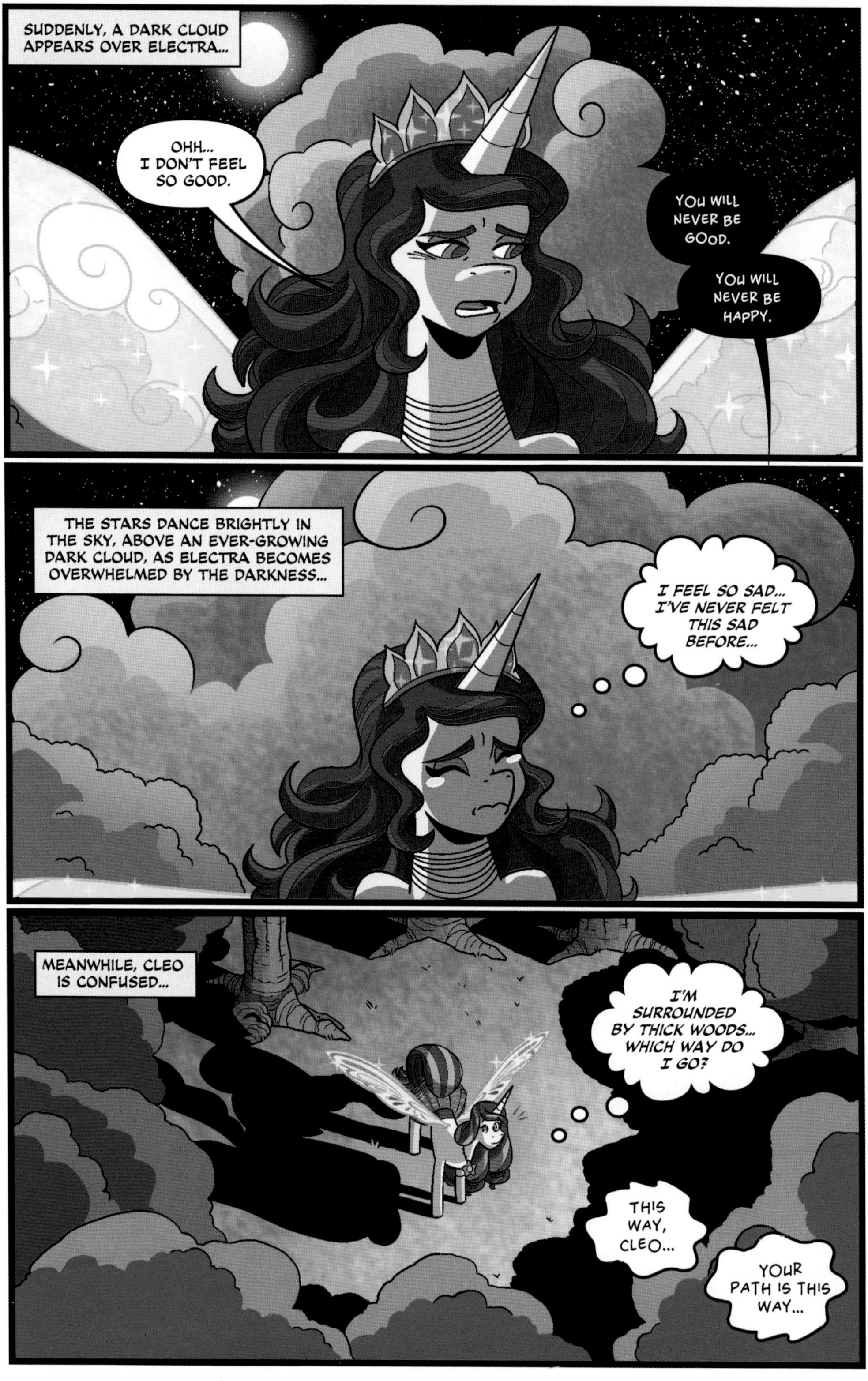
SUDDENLY, A DARK CLOUD APPEARS OVER ELECTRA...
OHH... I DON'T FEEL SO GOOD.
YOU WILL NEVER BE GOOD.
YOU WILL NEVER BE HAPPY.
THE STARS DANCE BRIGHTLY IN THE SKY, ABOVE AN EVER-GROWING DARK CLOUD, AS ELECTRA BECOMES OVERWHELMED BY THE DARKNESS...
I FEEL SO SAD... I'VE NEVER FELT THIS SAD BEFORE...
MEANWHILE, CLEO IS CONFUSED...
I'M SURROUNDED BY THICK WOODS... WHICH WAY DO I GO?
THIS WAY, CLEO...
YOUR PATH IS THIS WAY...

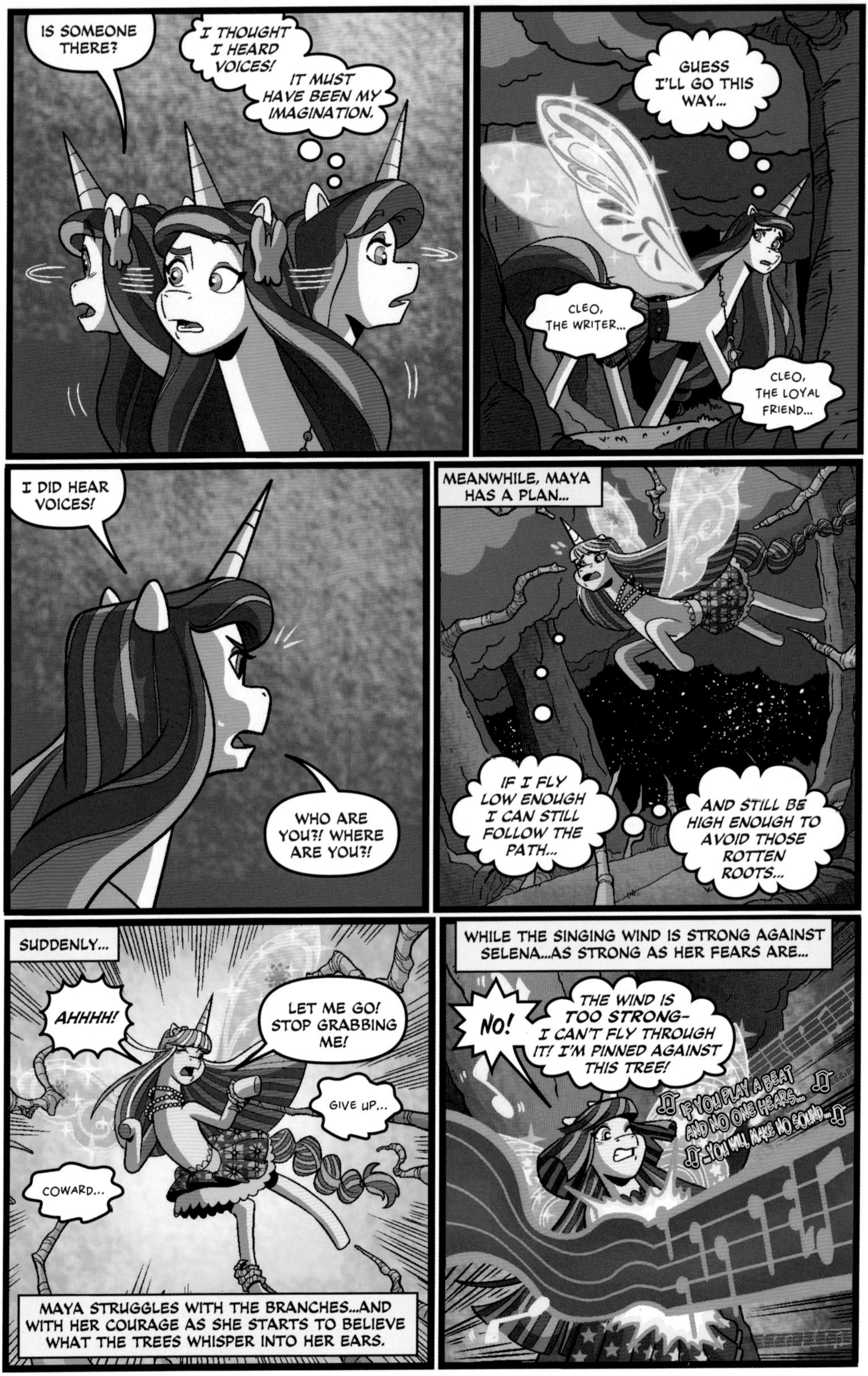
IS SOMEONE THERE?
I THOUGHT I HEARD VOICES!
IT MUST HAVE BEEN MY IMAGINATION.
GUESS I'LL GO THIS WAY...
CLEO, THE WRITER...
CLEO, THE LOYAL FRIEND...
I DID HEAR VOICES!
WHO ARE YOU?! WHERE ARE YOU?!
MEANWHILE, MAYA HAS A PLAN...
IF I FLY LOW ENOUGH I CAN STILL FOLLOW THE PATH...
AND STILL BE HIGH ENOUGH TO AVOID THOSE ROTTEN ROOTS...
SUDDENLY...
AHHHH!
LET ME GO! STOP GRABBING ME!
GIVE UP...
COWARD...
MAYA STRUGGLES WITH THE BRANCHES...AND WITH HER COURAGE AS SHE STARTS TO BELIEVE WHAT THE TREES WHISPER INTO HER EARS.
WHILE THE SINGING WIND IS STRONG AGAINST SELENA...AS STRONG AS HER FEARS ARE...
NO!
THE WIND IS TOO STRONG- I CAN'T FLY THROUGH IT! I'M PINNED AGAINST THIS TREE!
IF YOU PLAY A BEAT AND NO ONE HEARS...
...YOU WILL MAKE NO SOUND...

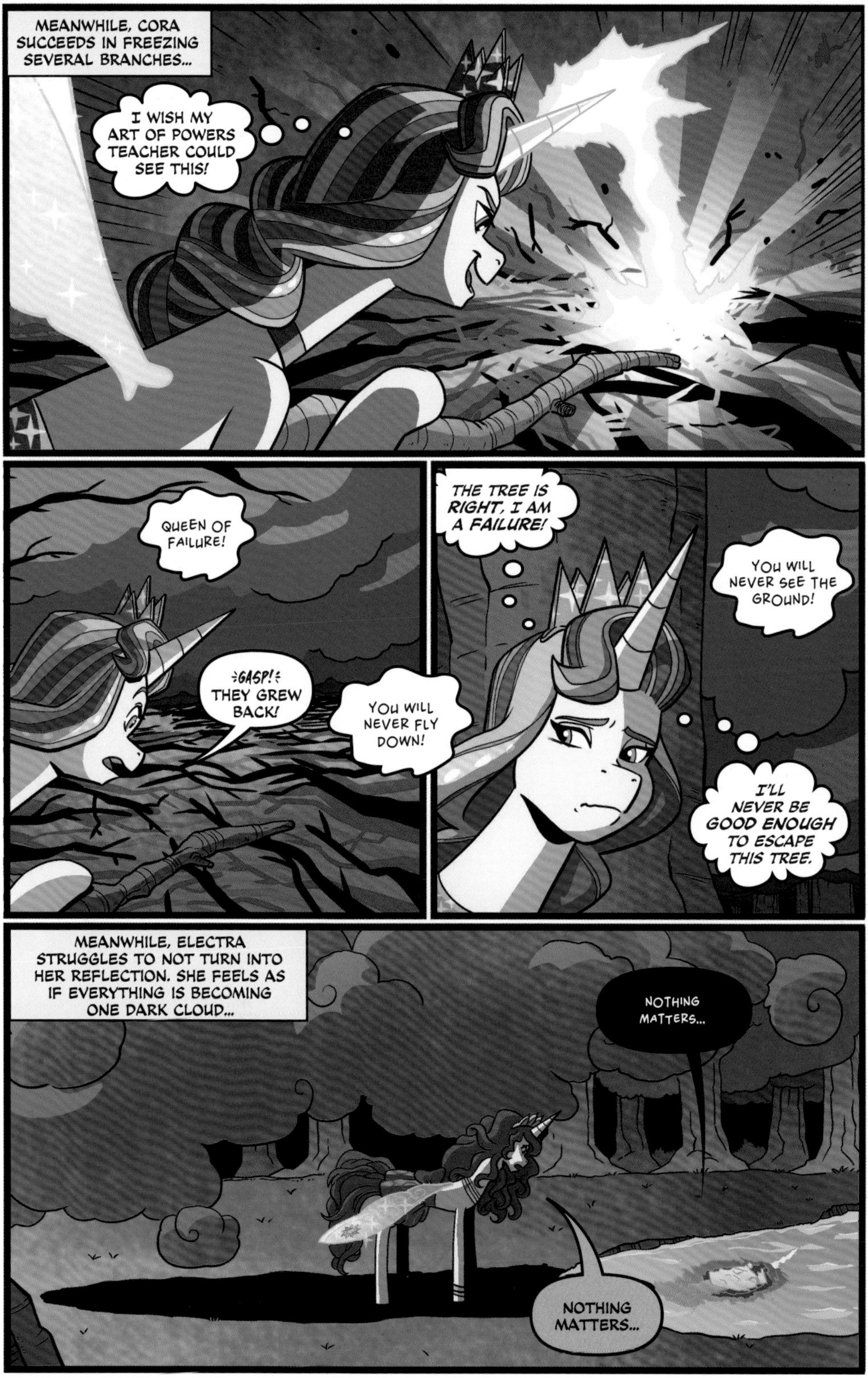
MEANWHILE, CORA SUCCEEDS IN FREEZING SEVERAL BRANCHES...
I WISH MY ART OF POWERS TEACHER COULD SEE THIS!
QUEEN OF FAILURE!
GASP! THEY GREW BACK!
YOU WILL NEVER FLY DOWN!
THE TREE IS RIGHT, I AM A FAILURE!
YOU WILL NEVER SEE THE GROUND!
I'LL NEVER BE GOOD ENOUGH TO ESCAPE THIS TREE.
MEANWHILE, ELECTRA STRUGGLES TO NOT TURN INTO HER REFLECTION. SHE FEELS AS IF EVERYTHING IS BECOMING ONE DARK CLOUD...
NOTHING MATTERS...
NOTHING MATTERS...

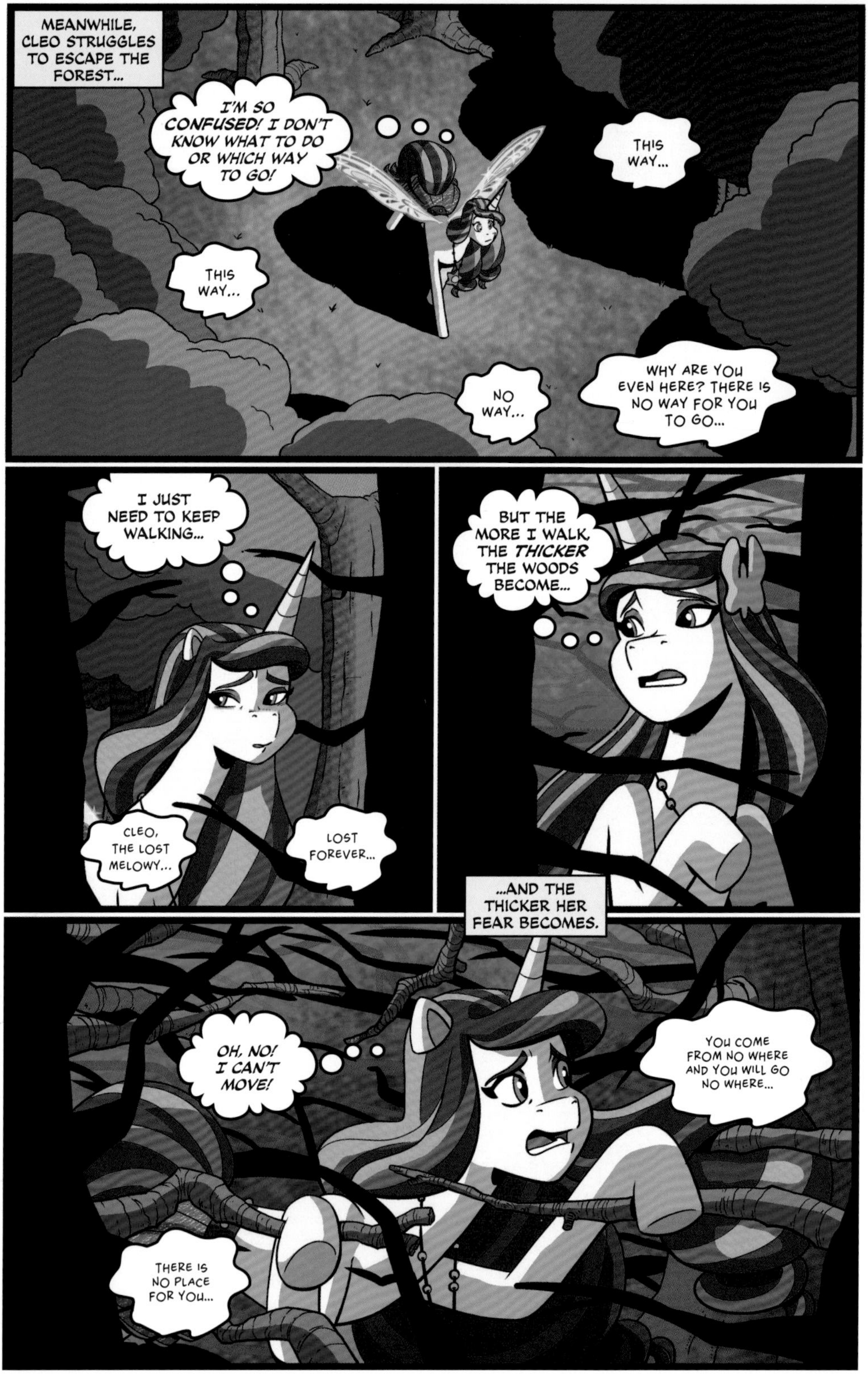
MEANWHILE, CLEO STRUGGLES TO ESCAPE THE FOREST...
I'M SO CONFUSED! I DON'T KNOW WHAT TO DO OR WHICH WAY TO GO!
THIS WAY...
THIS WAY...
NO WAY...
WHY ARE YOU EVEN HERE? THERE IS NO WAY FOR YOU TO GO...
I JUST NEED TO KEEP WALKING...
CLEO, THE LOST MELOWY...
LOST FOREVER...
BUT THE MORE I WALK, THE THICKER THE WOODS BECOME...
...AND THE THICKER HER FEAR BECOMES.
OH, NO! I CAN'T MOVE!
YOU COME FROM NO WHERE AND YOU WILL GO NO WHERE...
THERE IS NO PLACE FOR YOU...

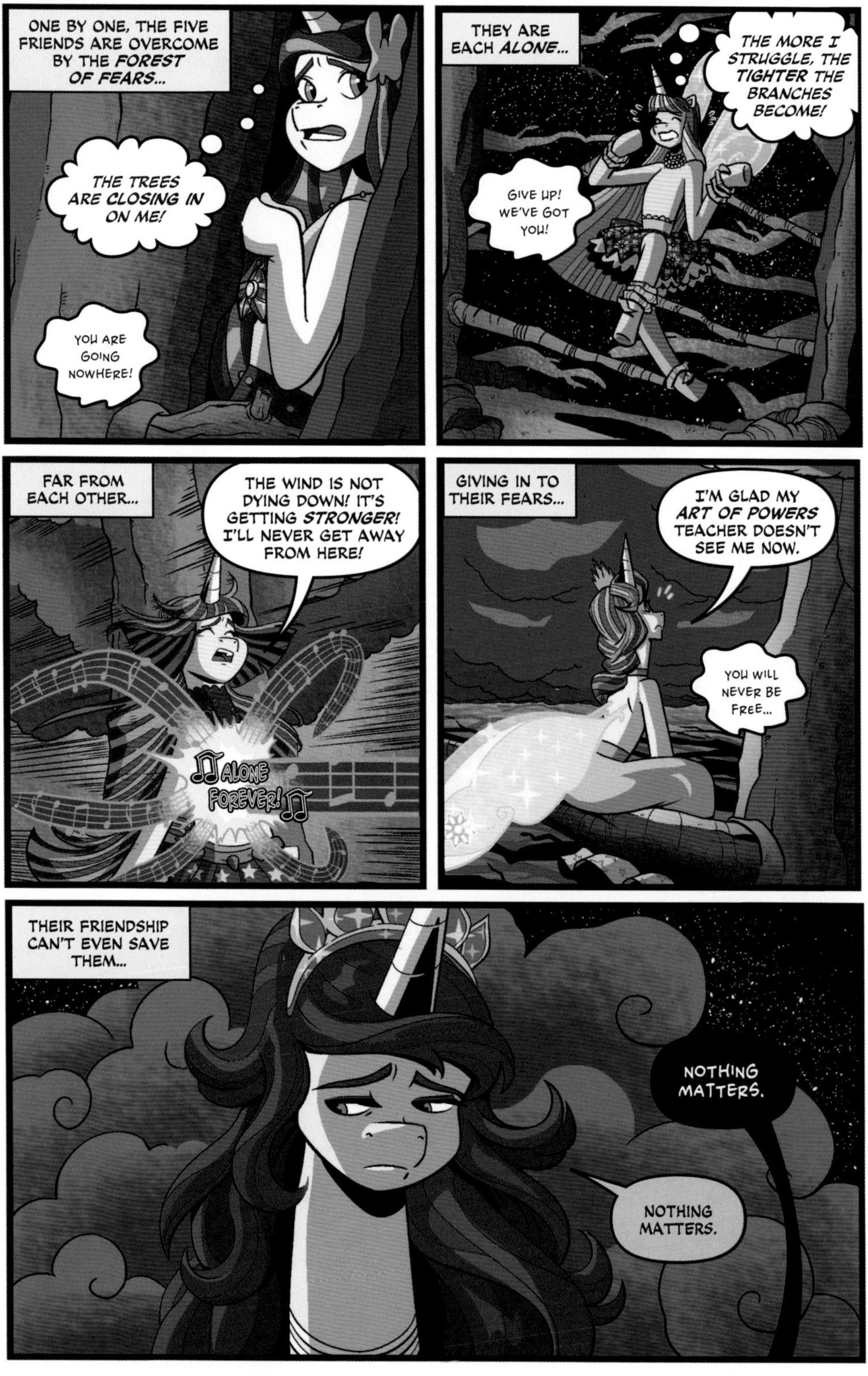
ONE BY ONE, THE FIVE FRIENDS ARE OVERCOME BY THE *FOREST OF FEARS*...
THE TREES ARE CLOSING IN ON ME!
YOU ARE GOING NOWHERE!
THEY ARE EACH *ALONE*...
THE MORE I STRUGGLE, THE TIGHTER THE BRANCHES BECOME!
GIVE UP! WE'VE GOT YOU!
FAR FROM EACH OTHER...
THE WIND IS NOT DYING DOWN! IT'S GETTING *STRONGER!* I'LL NEVER GET AWAY FROM HERE!
ALONE FOREVER!
GIVING IN TO THEIR FEARS...
I'M GLAD MY *ART OF POWERS* TEACHER DOESN'T SEE ME NOW.
YOU WILL NEVER BE FREE...
THEIR FRIENDSHIP CAN'T EVEN SAVE THEM...
NOTHING MATTERS.
NOTHING MATTERS.

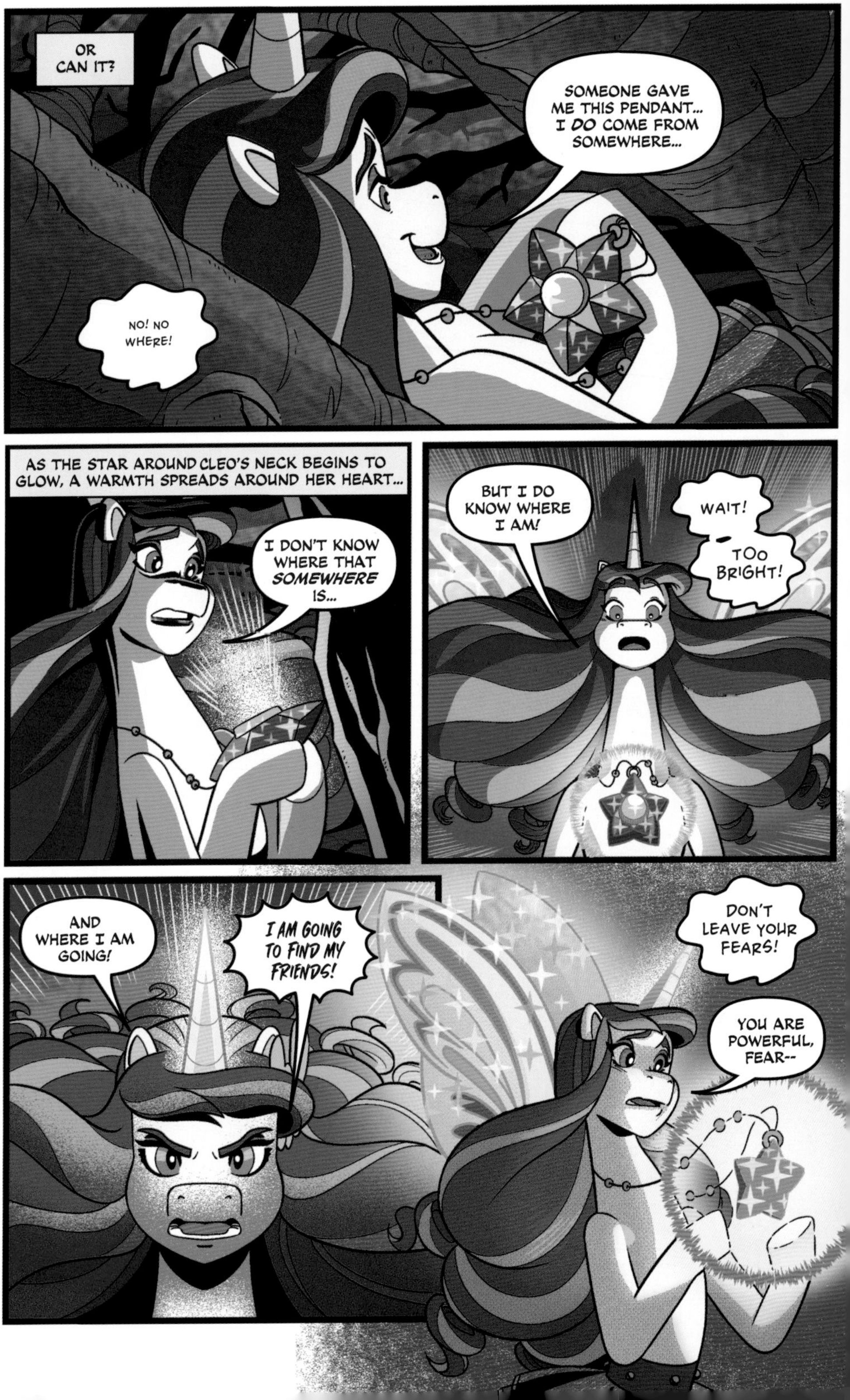
OR CAN IT?
SOMEONE GAVE ME THIS PENDANT... I *DO* COME FROM SOMEWHERE...
NO! NO WHERE!
AS THE STAR AROUND CLEO'S NECK BEGINS TO GLOW, A WARMTH SPREADS AROUND HER HEART...
I DON'T KNOW WHERE THAT *SOMEWHERE* IS...
BUT I DO KNOW WHERE I AM!
WAIT!
TOO BRIGHT!
AND WHERE I AM GOING!
I AM GOING TO FIND MY FRIENDS!
DON'T LEAVE YOUR FEARS!
YOU ARE POWERFUL, FEAR--

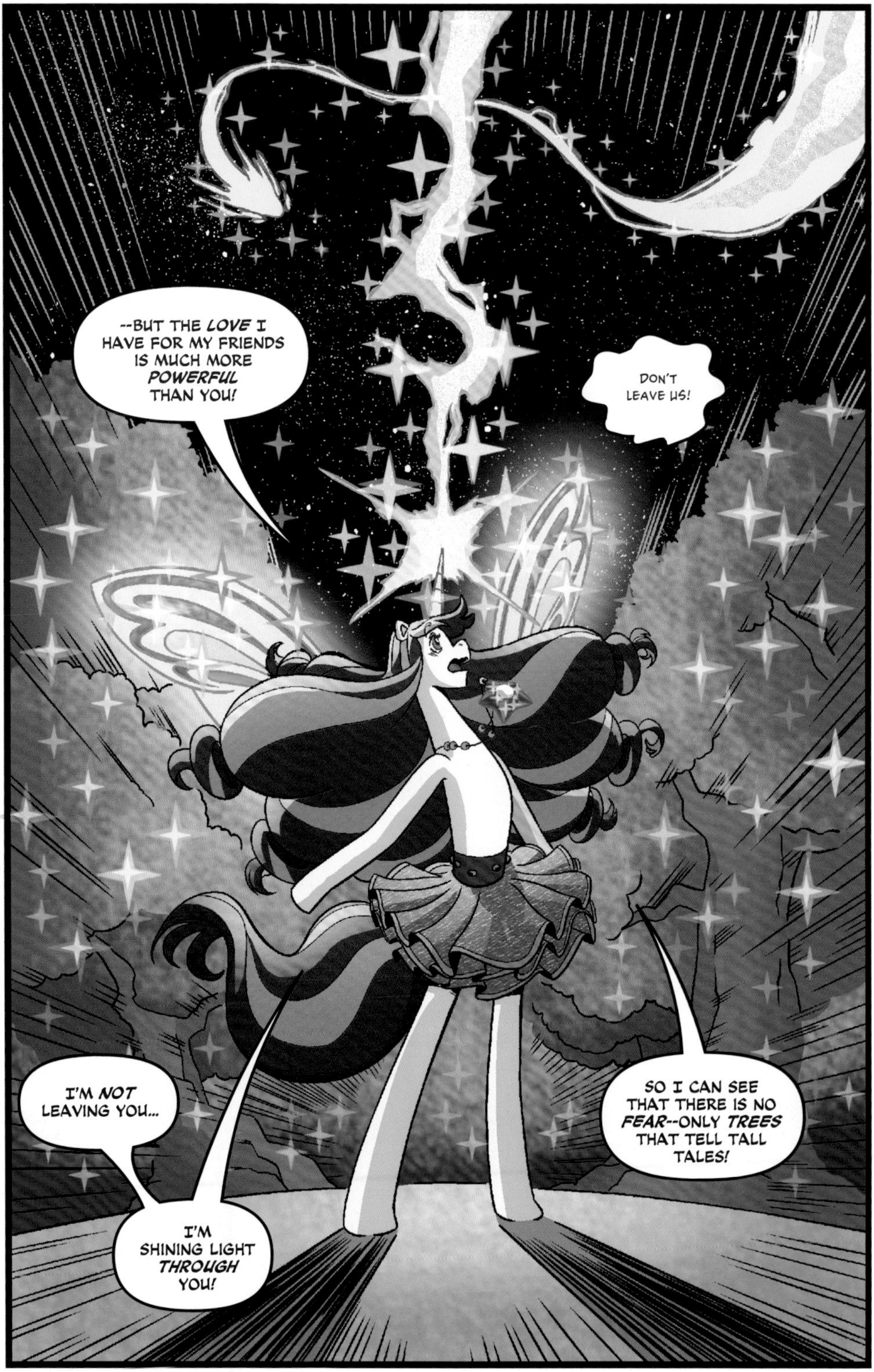
--BUT THE LOVE I HAVE FOR MY FRIENDS IS MUCH MORE POWERFUL THAN YOU!
DON'T LEAVE US!
I'M NOT LEAVING YOU...
I'M SHINING LIGHT THROUGH YOU!
SO I CAN SEE THAT THERE IS NO FEAR--ONLY TREES THAT TELL TALL TALES!

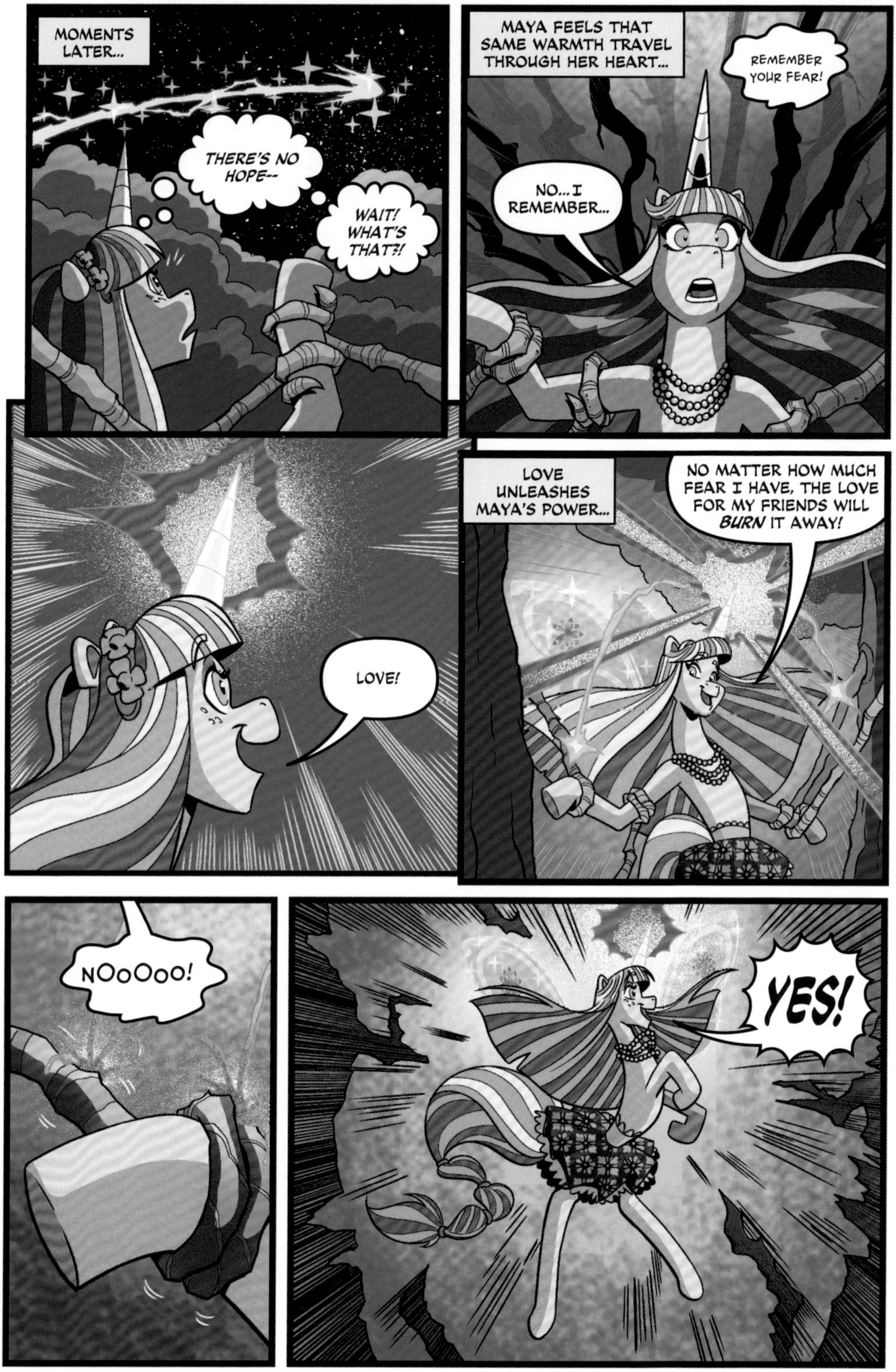
MOMENTS LATER...
THERE'S NO HOPE--
WAIT! WHAT'S THAT?!
MAYA FEELS THAT SAME WARMTH TRAVEL THROUGH HER HEART...
REMEMBER YOUR FEAR!
NO... I REMEMBER...
LOVE!
LOVE UNLEASHES MAYA'S POWER...
NO MATTER HOW MUCH FEAR I HAVE, THE LOVE FOR MY FRIENDS WILL BURN IT AWAY!
NOOOOO!
YES!

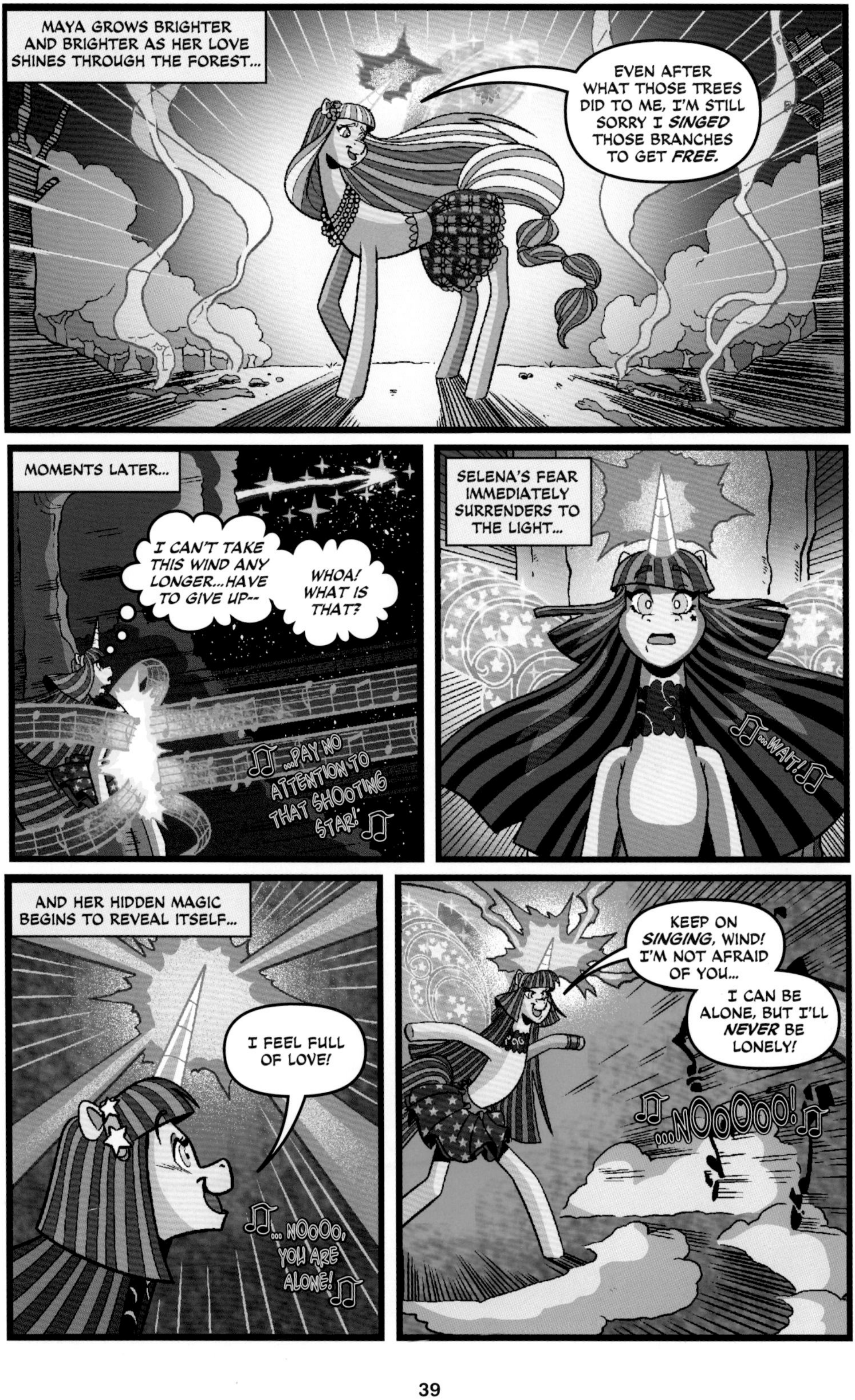
MAYA GROWS BRIGHTER AND BRIGHTER AS HER LOVE SHINES THROUGH THE FOREST...
EVEN AFTER WHAT THOSE TREES DID TO ME, I'M STILL SORRY I SINGED THOSE BRANCHES TO GET FREE.
MOMENTS LATER...
I CAN'T TAKE THIS WIND ANY LONGER...HAVE TO GIVE UP--
WHOA! WHAT IS THAT?
♫ ...PAY NO ATTENTION TO THAT SHOOTING STAR! ♫
SELENA'S FEAR IMMEDIATELY SURRENDERS TO THE LIGHT...
♫ ...WAIT! ♫
AND HER HIDDEN MAGIC BEGINS TO REVEAL ITSELF...
I FEEL FULL OF LOVE!
♫ ... NOOOO, YOU ARE ALONE! ♫
KEEP ON SINGING, WIND! I'M NOT AFRAID OF YOU...
I CAN BE ALONE, BUT I'LL NEVER BE LONELY!
♫ ...NOOOOOO! ♫

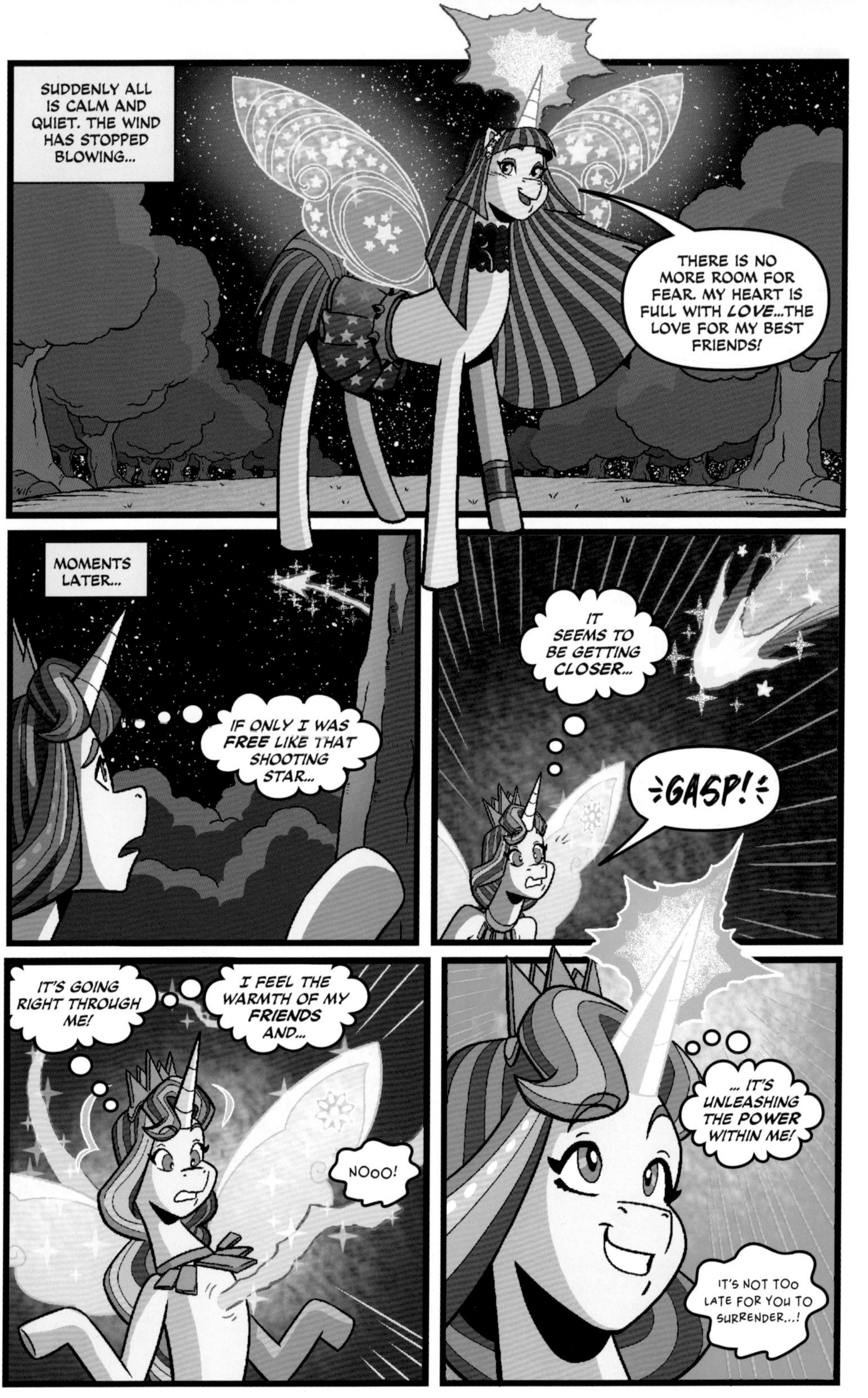
SUDDENLY ALL IS CALM AND QUIET. THE WIND HAS STOPPED BLOWING...
THERE IS NO MORE ROOM FOR FEAR. MY HEART IS FULL WITH LOVE...THE LOVE FOR MY BEST FRIENDS!
MOMENTS LATER...
IF ONLY I WAS FREE LIKE THAT SHOOTING STAR...
IT SEEMS TO BE GETTING CLOSER...
GASP!
IT'S GOING RIGHT THROUGH ME!
I FEEL THE WARMTH OF MY FRIENDS AND...
NOOO!
... IT'S UNLEASHING THE POWER WITHIN ME!
IT'S NOT TOO LATE FOR YOU TO SURRENDER...!

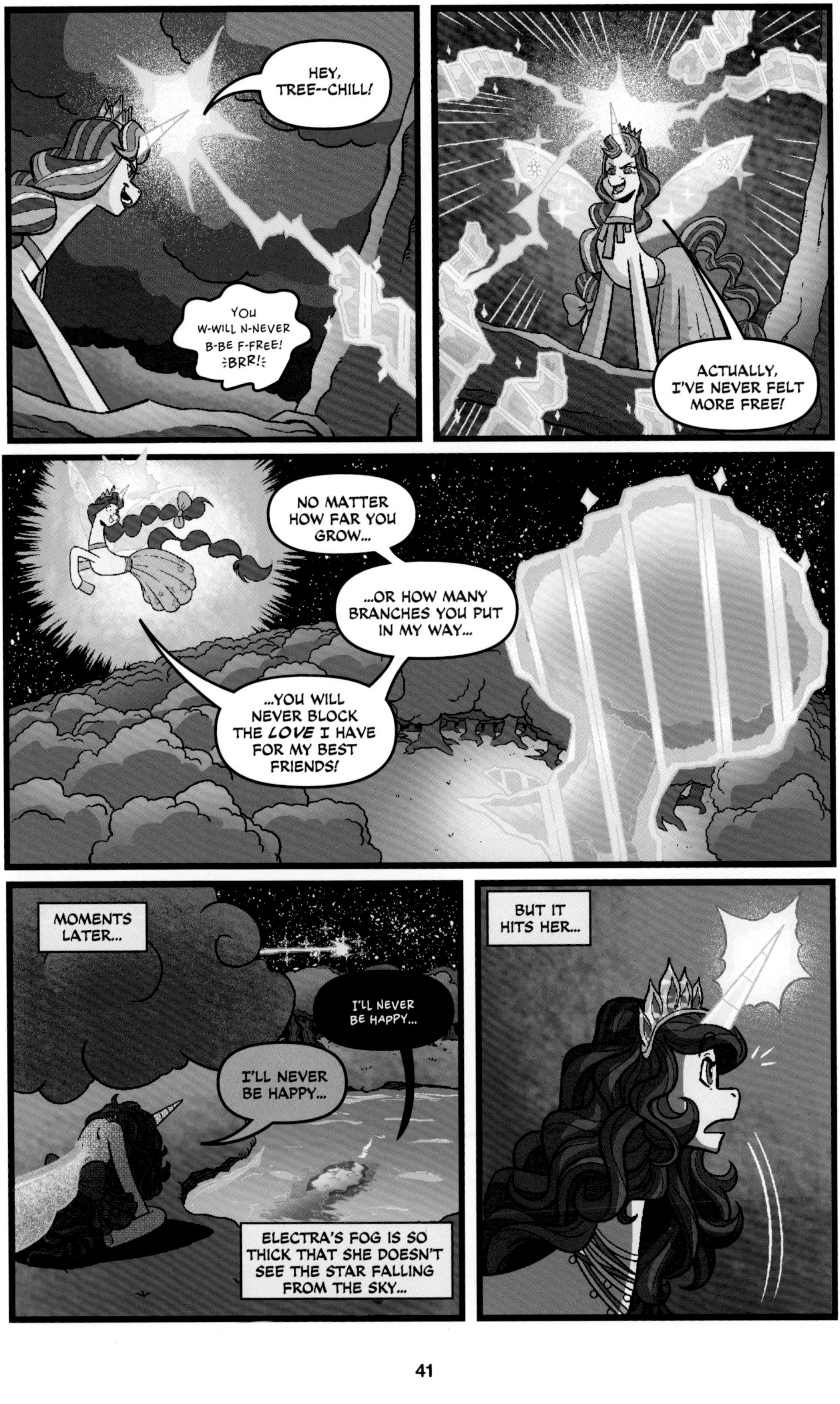
HEY, TREE--CHILL!
YOU W-WILL N-NEVER B-BE F-FREE! BRR!
ACTUALLY, I'VE NEVER FELT MORE FREE!
NO MATTER HOW FAR YOU GROW...
...OR HOW MANY BRANCHES YOU PUT IN MY WAY...
...YOU WILL NEVER BLOCK THE LOVE I HAVE FOR MY BEST FRIENDS!
MOMENTS LATER...
I'LL NEVER BE HAPPY...
I'LL NEVER BE HAPPY...
ELECTRA'S FOG IS SO THICK THAT SHE DOESN'T SEE THE STAR FALLING FROM THE SKY...
BUT IT HITS HER...

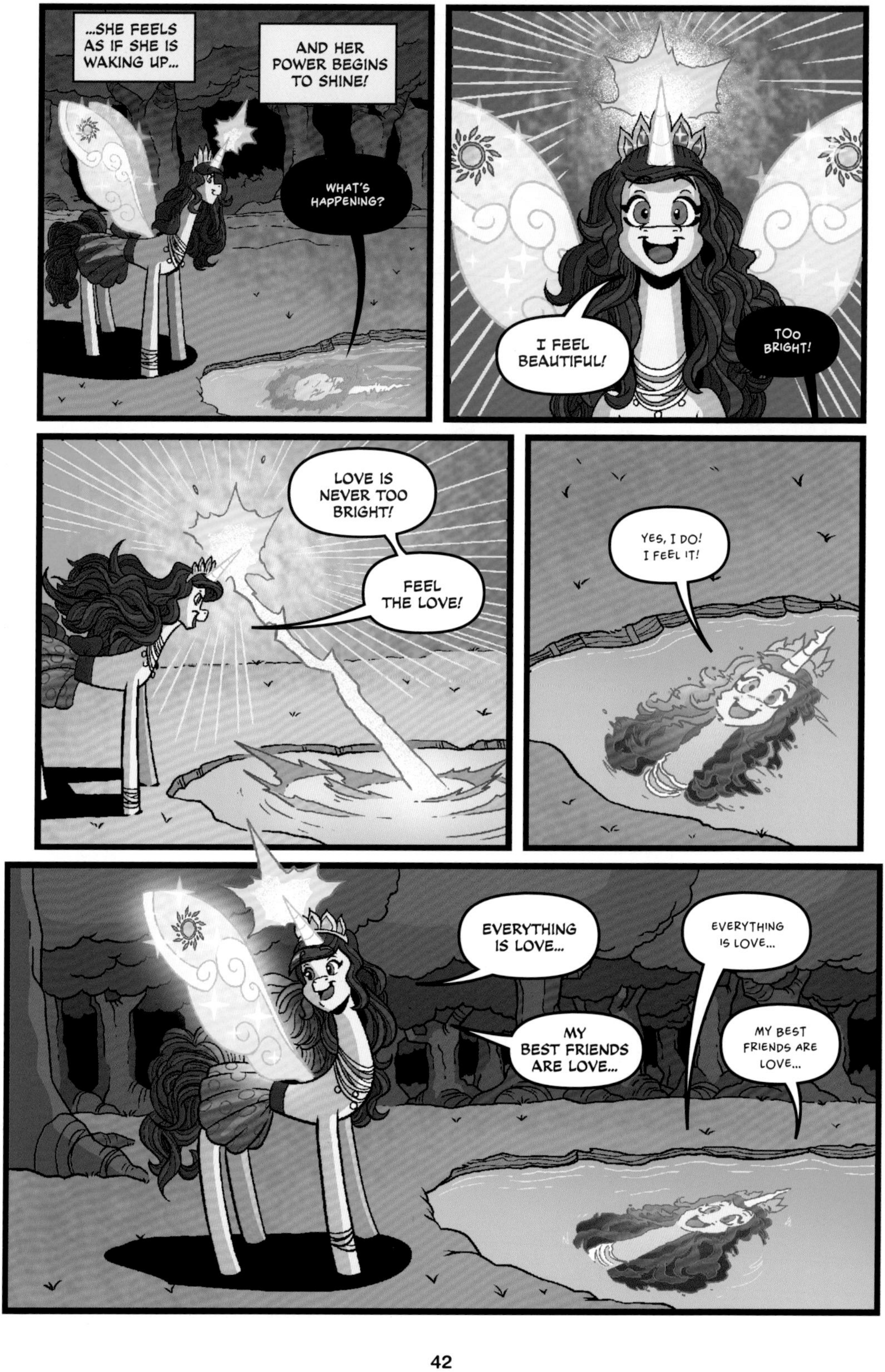
...SHE FEELS AS IF SHE IS WAKING UP...
AND HER POWER BEGINS TO SHINE!
WHAT'S HAPPENING?
I FEEL BEAUTIFUL!
TOO BRIGHT!
LOVE IS NEVER TOO BRIGHT!
FEEL THE LOVE!
YES, I DO! I FEEL IT!
EVERYTHING IS LOVE...
EVERYTHING IS LOVE...
MY BEST FRIENDS ARE LOVE...
MY BEST FRIENDS ARE LOVE...

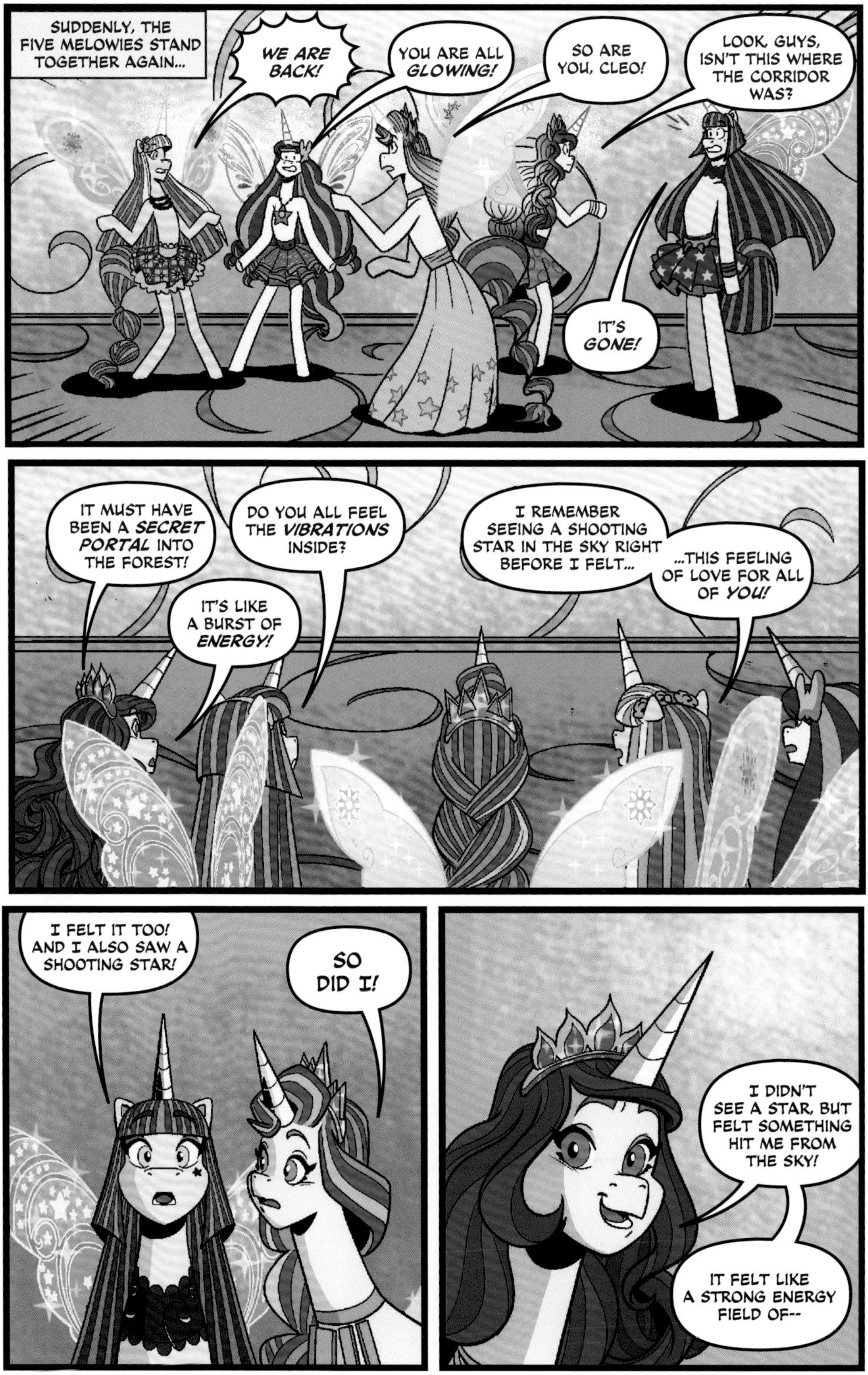
SUDDENLY, THE FIVE MELOWIES STAND TOGETHER AGAIN...
WE ARE BACK!
YOU ARE ALL GLOWING!
SO ARE YOU, CLEO!
LOOK, GUYS, ISN'T THIS WHERE THE CORRIDOR WAS?
IT'S GONE!
IT MUST HAVE BEEN A SECRET PORTAL INTO THE FOREST!
IT'S LIKE A BURST OF ENERGY!
DO YOU ALL FEEL THE VIBRATIONS INSIDE?
I REMEMBER SEEING A SHOOTING STAR IN THE SKY RIGHT BEFORE I FELT...
...THIS FEELING OF LOVE FOR ALL OF YOU!
I FELT IT TOO! AND I ALSO SAW A SHOOTING STAR!
SO DID I!
I DIDN'T SEE A STAR, BUT FELT SOMETHING HIT ME FROM THE SKY!
IT FELT LIKE A STRONG ENERGY FIELD OF--

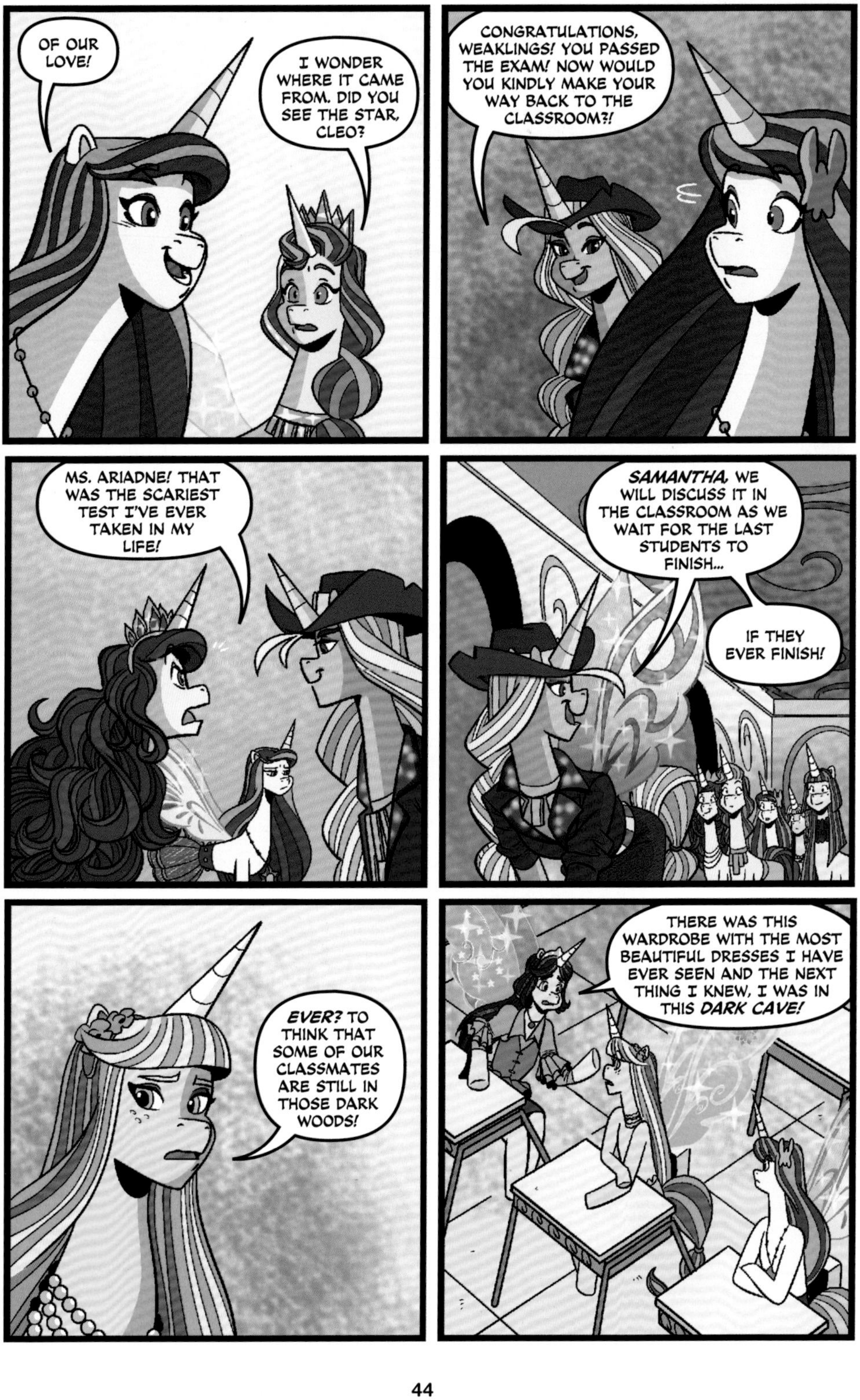
OF OUR LOVE!
I WONDER WHERE IT CAME FROM. DID YOU SEE THE STAR, CLEO?
CONGRATULATIONS, WEAKLINGS! YOU PASSED THE EXAM! NOW WOULD YOU KINDLY MAKE YOUR WAY BACK TO THE CLASSROOM?!
MS. ARIADNE! THAT WAS THE SCARIEST TEST I'VE EVER TAKEN IN MY LIFE!
SAMANTHA, WE WILL DISCUSS IT IN THE CLASSROOM AS WE WAIT FOR THE LAST STUDENTS TO FINISH...
IF THEY EVER FINISH!
EVER? TO THINK THAT SOME OF OUR CLASSMATES ARE STILL IN THOSE DARK WOODS!
THERE WAS THIS WARDROBE WITH THE MOST BEAUTIFUL DRESSES I HAVE EVER SEEN AND THE NEXT THING I KNEW, I WAS IN THIS DARK CAVE!

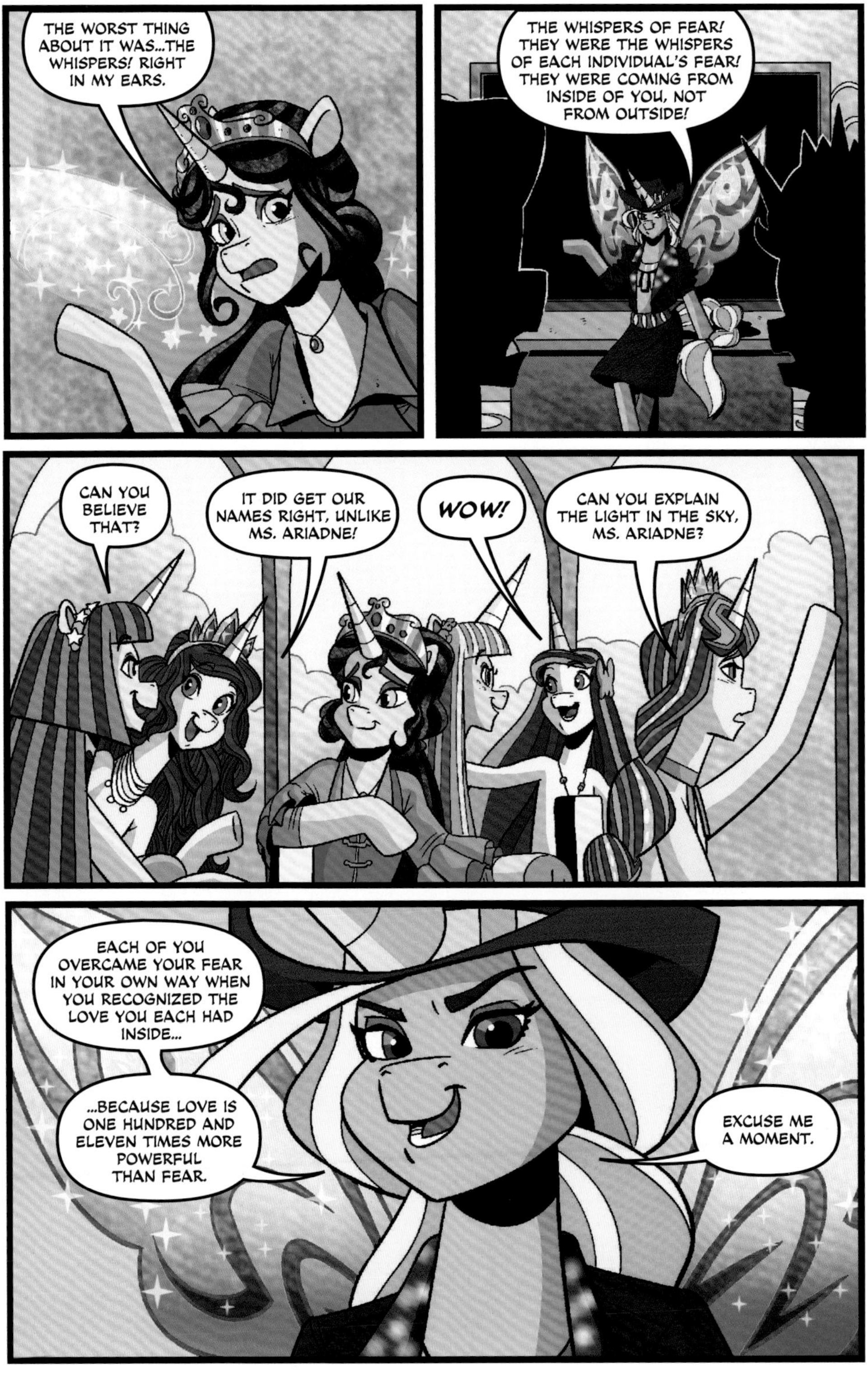
THE WORST THING ABOUT IT WAS...THE WHISPERS! RIGHT IN MY EARS.
THE WHISPERS OF FEAR! THEY WERE THE WHISPERS OF EACH INDIVIDUAL'S FEAR! THEY WERE COMING FROM INSIDE OF YOU, NOT FROM OUTSIDE!
CAN YOU BELIEVE THAT?
IT DID GET OUR NAMES RIGHT, UNLIKE MS. ARIADNE!
WOW!
CAN YOU EXPLAIN THE LIGHT IN THE SKY, MS. ARIADNE?
EACH OF YOU OVERCAME YOUR FEAR IN YOUR OWN WAY WHEN YOU RECOGNIZED THE LOVE YOU EACH HAD INSIDE...
...BECAUSE LOVE IS ONE HUNDRED AND ELEVEN TIMES MORE POWERFUL THAN FEAR.
EXCUSE ME A MOMENT.

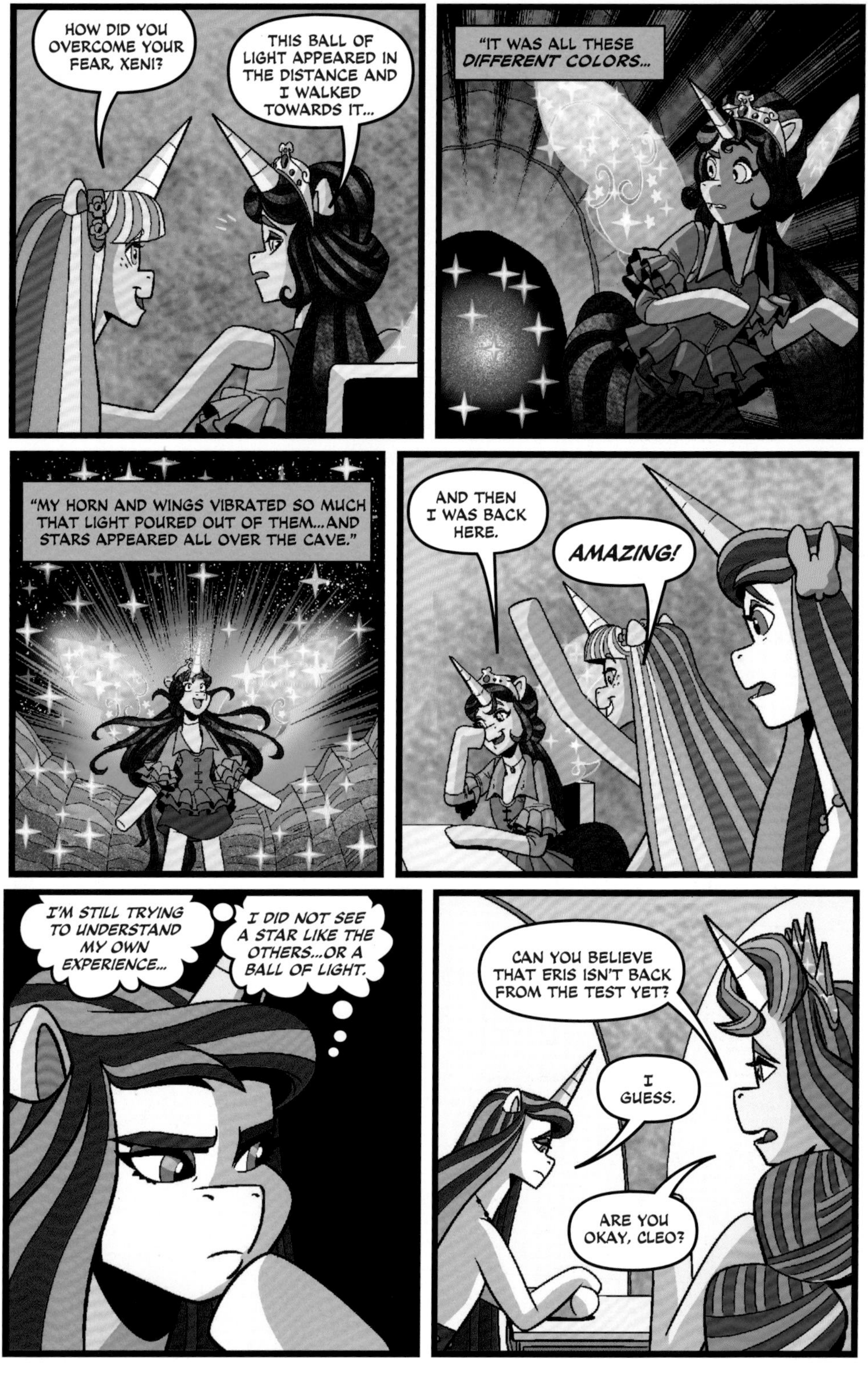
HOW DID YOU OVERCOME YOUR FEAR, XENI?
THIS BALL OF LIGHT APPEARED IN THE DISTANCE AND I WALKED TOWARDS IT...
"IT WAS ALL THESE *DIFFERENT COLORS...*
"MY HORN AND WINGS VIBRATED SO MUCH THAT LIGHT POURED OUT OF THEM...AND STARS APPEARED ALL OVER THE CAVE."
AND THEN I WAS BACK HERE.
AMAZING!
I'M STILL TRYING TO UNDERSTAND MY OWN EXPERIENCE...
I DID NOT SEE A STAR LIKE THE OTHERS...OR A BALL OF LIGHT.
CAN YOU BELIEVE THAT ERIS ISN'T BACK FROM THE TEST YET?
I GUESS.
ARE YOU OKAY, CLEO?

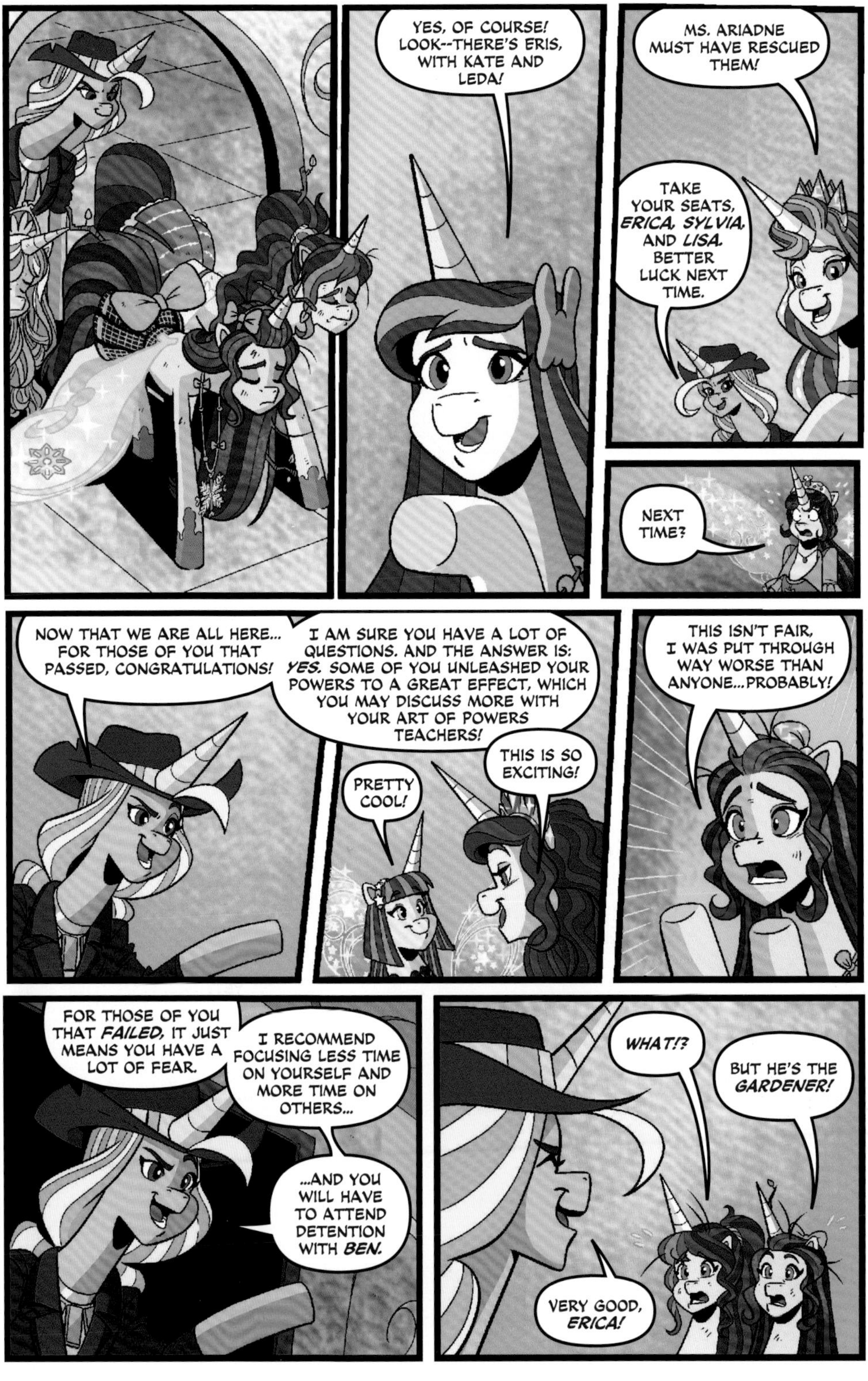
YES, OF COURSE! LOOK--THERE'S ERIS, WITH KATE AND LEDA!
MS. ARIADNE MUST HAVE RESCUED THEM!
TAKE YOUR SEATS, *ERICA, SYLVIA,* AND *LISA.* BETTER LUCK NEXT TIME.
NEXT TIME?
NOW THAT WE ARE ALL HERE... FOR THOSE OF YOU THAT PASSED, CONGRATULATIONS!
I AM SURE YOU HAVE A LOT OF QUESTIONS. AND THE ANSWER IS: *YES.* SOME OF YOU UNLEASHED YOUR POWERS TO A GREAT EFFECT, WHICH YOU MAY DISCUSS MORE WITH YOUR ART OF POWERS TEACHERS!
PRETTY COOL!
THIS IS SO EXCITING!
THIS ISN'T FAIR, I WAS PUT THROUGH WAY WORSE THAN ANYONE...PROBABLY!
FOR THOSE OF YOU THAT *FAILED,* IT JUST MEANS YOU HAVE A LOT OF FEAR.
I RECOMMEND FOCUSING LESS TIME ON YOURSELF AND MORE TIME ON OTHERS...
...AND YOU WILL HAVE TO ATTEND DETENTION WITH *BEN.*
WHAT!?
BUT HE'S THE *GARDENER!*
VERY GOOD, *ERICA!*

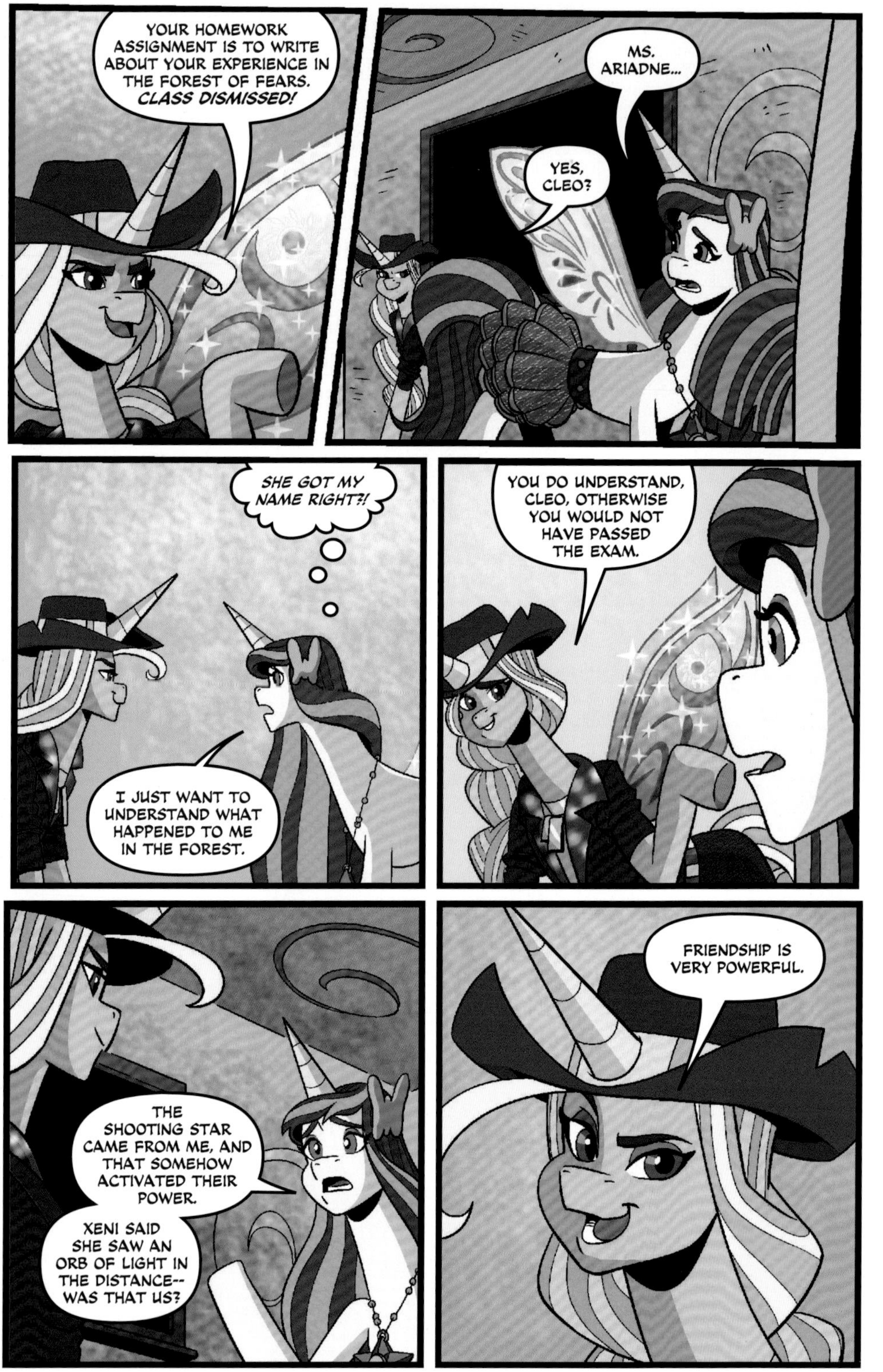
YOUR HOMEWORK ASSIGNMENT IS TO WRITE ABOUT YOUR EXPERIENCE IN THE FOREST OF FEARS. CLASS DISMISSED!
MS. ARIADNE...
YES, CLEO?
SHE GOT MY NAME RIGHT?!
I JUST WANT TO UNDERSTAND WHAT HAPPENED TO ME IN THE FOREST.
YOU DO UNDERSTAND, CLEO, OTHERWISE YOU WOULD NOT HAVE PASSED THE EXAM.
XENI SAID SHE SAW AN ORB OF LIGHT IN THE DISTANCE-- WAS THAT US?
THE SHOOTING STAR CAME FROM ME, AND THAT SOMEHOW ACTIVATED THEIR POWER.
FRIENDSHIP IS VERY POWERFUL.

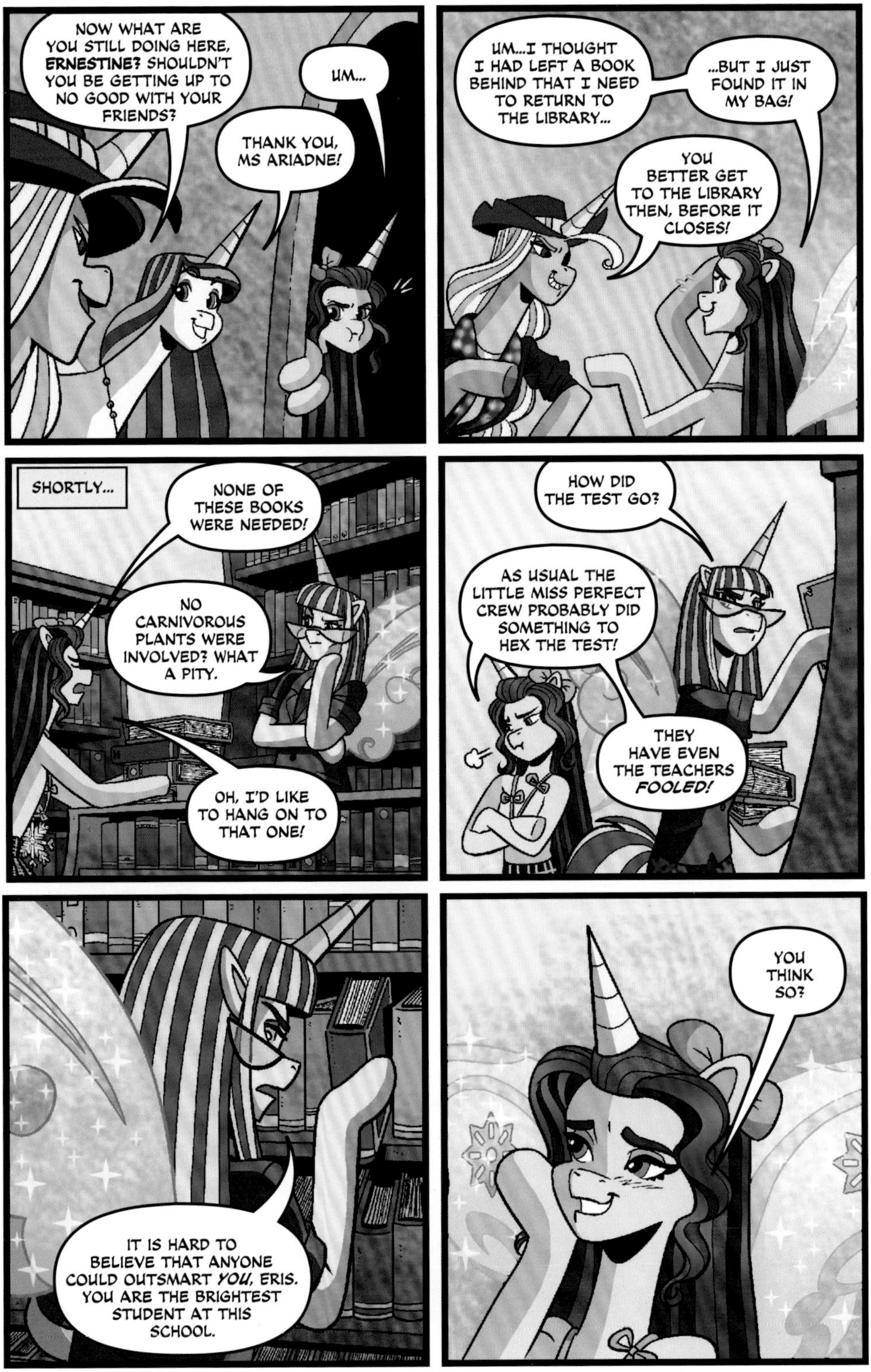
NOW WHAT ARE YOU STILL DOING HERE, ERNESTINE? SHOULDN'T YOU BE GETTING UP TO NO GOOD WITH YOUR FRIENDS?
UM...
THANK YOU, MS ARIADNE!
UM...I THOUGHT I HAD LEFT A BOOK BEHIND THAT I NEED TO RETURN TO THE LIBRARY...
...BUT I JUST FOUND IT IN MY BAG!
YOU BETTER GET TO THE LIBRARY THEN, BEFORE IT CLOSES!
SHORTLY...
NONE OF THESE BOOKS WERE NEEDED!
NO CARNIVOROUS PLANTS WERE INVOLVED? WHAT A PITY.
OH, I'D LIKE TO HANG ON TO THAT ONE!
HOW DID THE TEST GO?
AS USUAL THE LITTLE MISS PERFECT CREW PROBABLY DID SOMETHING TO HEX THE TEST!
THEY HAVE EVEN THE TEACHERS *FOOLED!*
IT IS HARD TO BELIEVE THAT ANYONE COULD OUTSMART *YOU*, ERIS. YOU ARE THE BRIGHTEST STUDENT AT THIS SCHOOL.
YOU THINK SO?

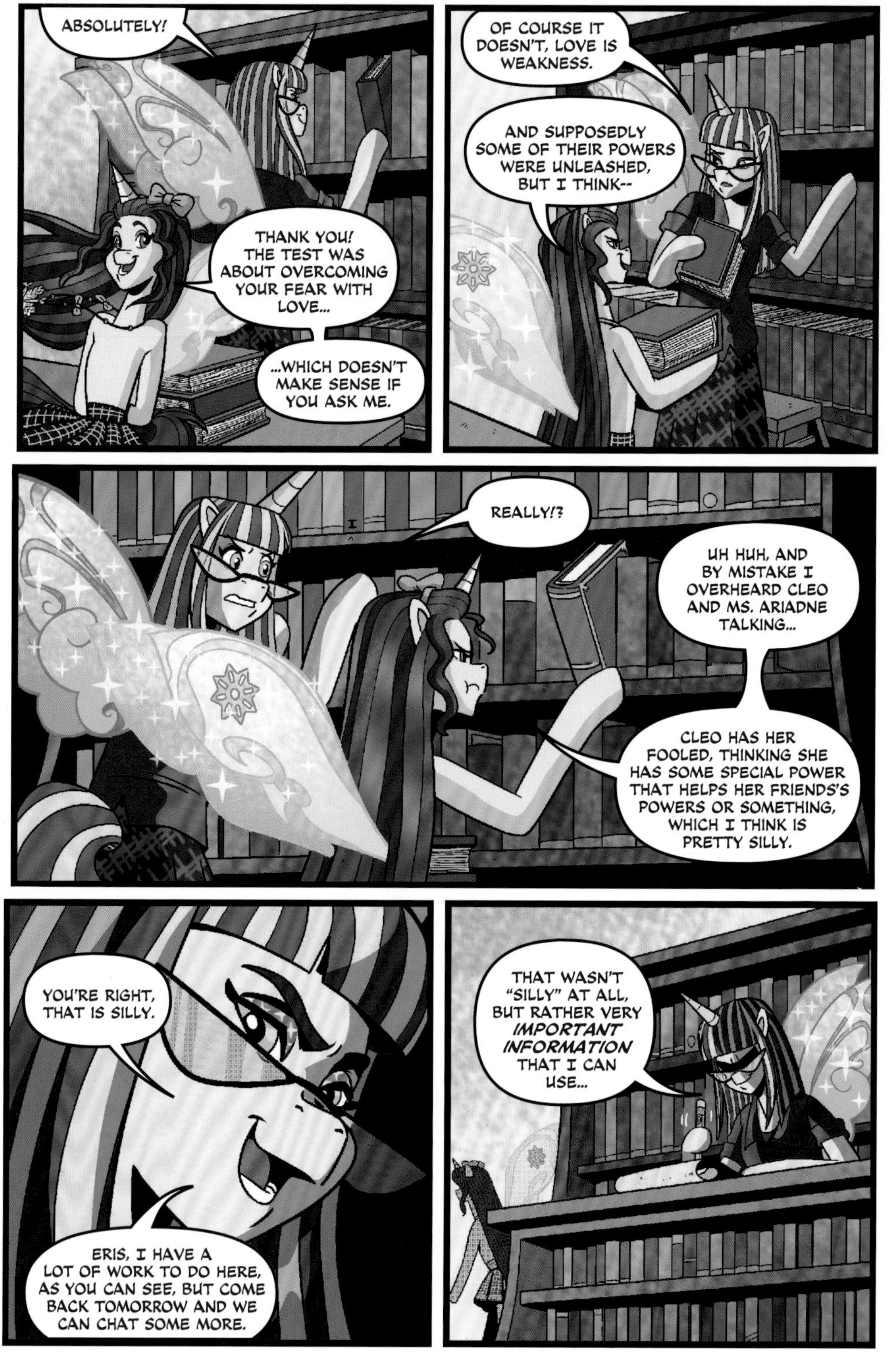
ABSOLUTELY!
THANK YOU! THE TEST WAS ABOUT OVERCOMING YOUR FEAR WITH LOVE...
...WHICH DOESN'T MAKE SENSE IF YOU ASK ME.
OF COURSE IT DOESN'T, LOVE IS WEAKNESS.
AND SUPPOSEDLY SOME OF THEIR POWERS WERE UNLEASHED, BUT I THINK--
REALLY!?
UH HUH, AND BY MISTAKE I OVERHEARD CLEO AND MS. ARIADNE TALKING...
CLEO HAS HER FOOLED, THINKING SHE HAS SOME SPECIAL POWER THAT HELPS HER FRIENDS'S POWERS OR SOMETHING, WHICH I THINK IS PRETTY SILLY.
YOU'RE RIGHT, THAT IS SILLY.
ERIS, I HAVE A LOT OF WORK TO DO HERE, AS YOU CAN SEE, BUT COME BACK TOMORROW AND WE CAN CHAT SOME MORE.
THAT WASN'T "SILLY" AT ALL, BUT RATHER VERY *IMPORTANT INFORMATION* THAT I CAN USE...

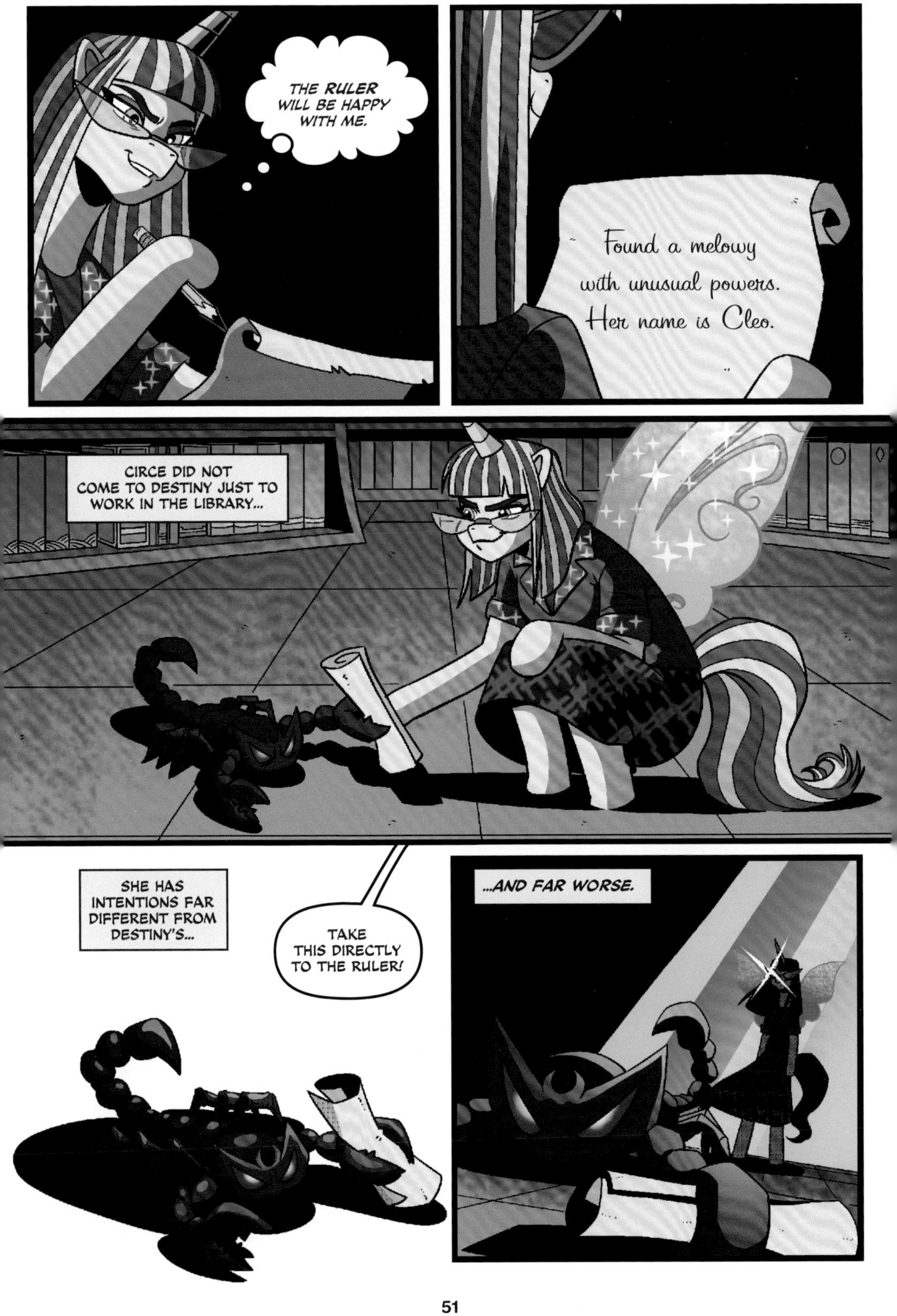
THE RULER WILL BE HAPPY WITH ME.
Found a melowy with unusual powers. Her name is Cleo.
CIRCE DID NOT COME TO DESTINY JUST TO WORK IN THE LIBRARY...
SHE HAS INTENTIONS FAR DIFFERENT FROM DESTINY'S...
TAKE THIS DIRECTLY TO THE RULER!
...AND FAR WORSE.

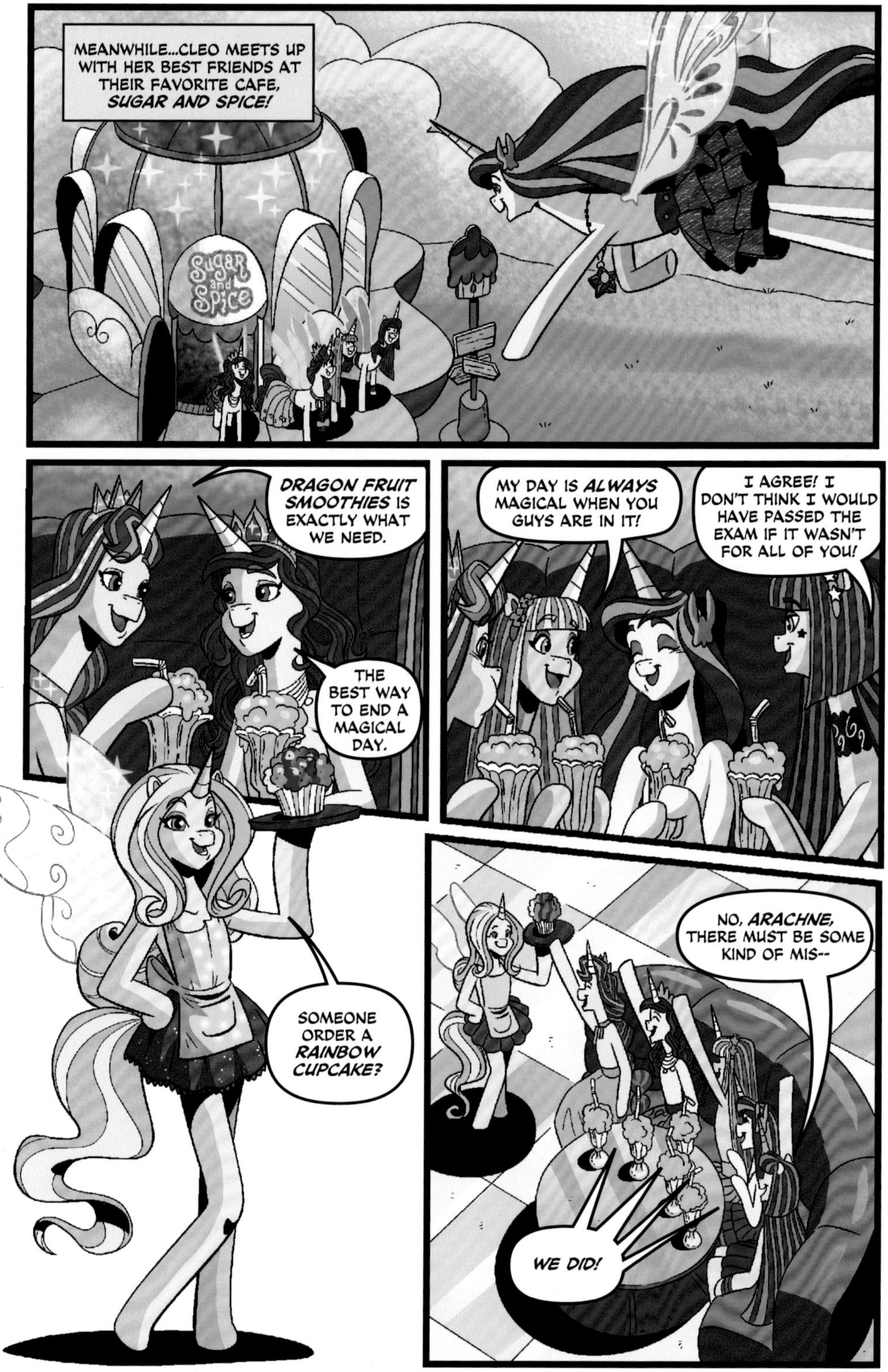

MEANWHILE...CLEO MEETS UP WITH HER BEST FRIENDS AT THEIR FAVORITE CAFE, *SUGAR AND SPICE!*
Sugar and Spice
DRAGON FRUIT SMOOTHIES IS EXACTLY WHAT WE NEED.
THE BEST WAY TO END A MAGICAL DAY.
MY DAY IS *ALWAYS* MAGICAL WHEN YOU GUYS ARE IN IT!
I AGREE! I DON'T THINK I WOULD HAVE PASSED THE EXAM IF IT WASN'T FOR ALL OF YOU!
SOMEONE ORDER A *RAINBOW CUPCAKE?*
WE DID!
NO, *ARACHNE,* THERE MUST BE SOME KIND OF MIS--

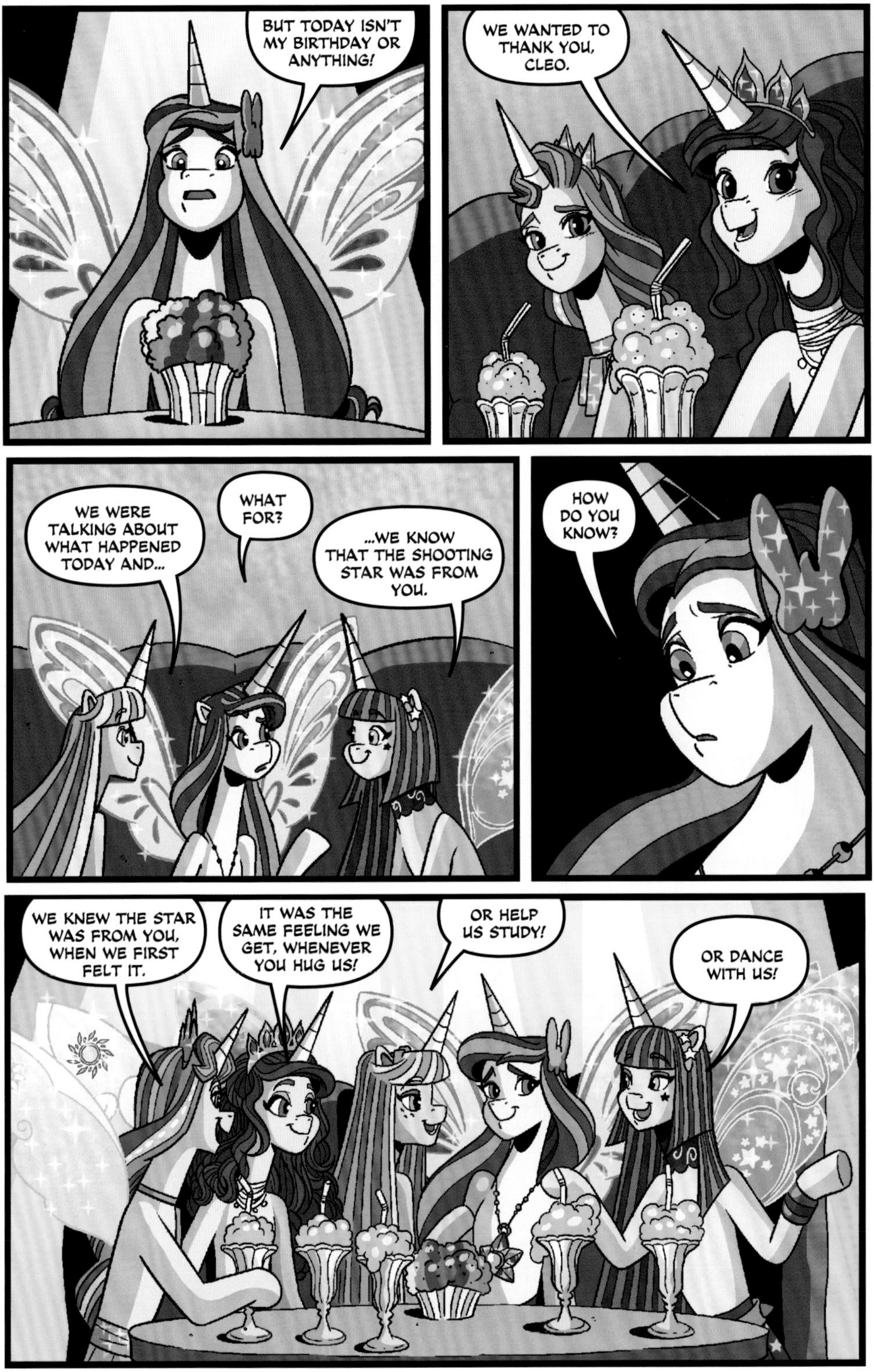
BUT TODAY ISN'T MY BIRTHDAY OR ANYTHING!
WE WANTED TO THANK YOU, CLEO.
WE WERE TALKING ABOUT WHAT HAPPENED TODAY AND...
WHAT FOR?
...WE KNOW THAT THE SHOOTING STAR WAS FROM YOU.
HOW DO YOU KNOW?
WE KNEW THE STAR WAS FROM YOU, WHEN WE FIRST FELT IT.
IT WAS THE SAME FEELING WE GET, WHENEVER YOU HUG US!
OR HELP US STUDY!
OR DANCE WITH US!

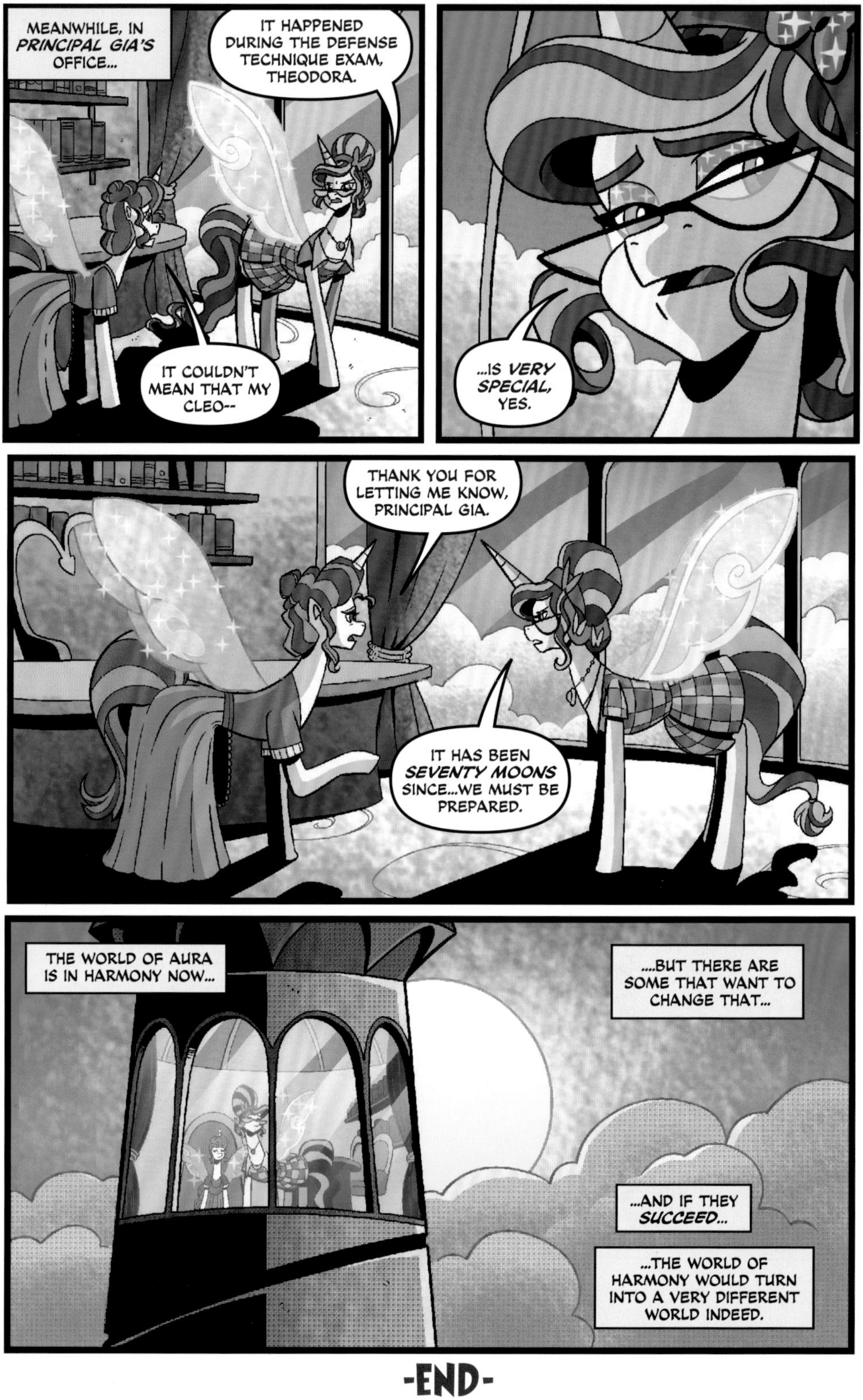
MEANWHILE, IN PRINCIPAL GIA'S OFFICE...
IT HAPPENED DURING THE DEFENSE TECHNIQUE EXAM, THEODORA.
IT COULDN'T MEAN THAT MY CLEO--
...IS VERY SPECIAL, YES.
THANK YOU FOR LETTING ME KNOW, PRINCIPAL GIA.
IT HAS BEEN SEVENTY MOONS SINCE...WE MUST BE PREPARED.
THE WORLD OF AURA IS IN HARMONY NOW...
....BUT THERE ARE SOME THAT WANT TO CHANGE THAT...
...AND IF THEY SUCCEED...
...THE WORLD OF HARMONY WOULD TURN INTO A VERY DIFFERENT WORLD INDEED.

-END-

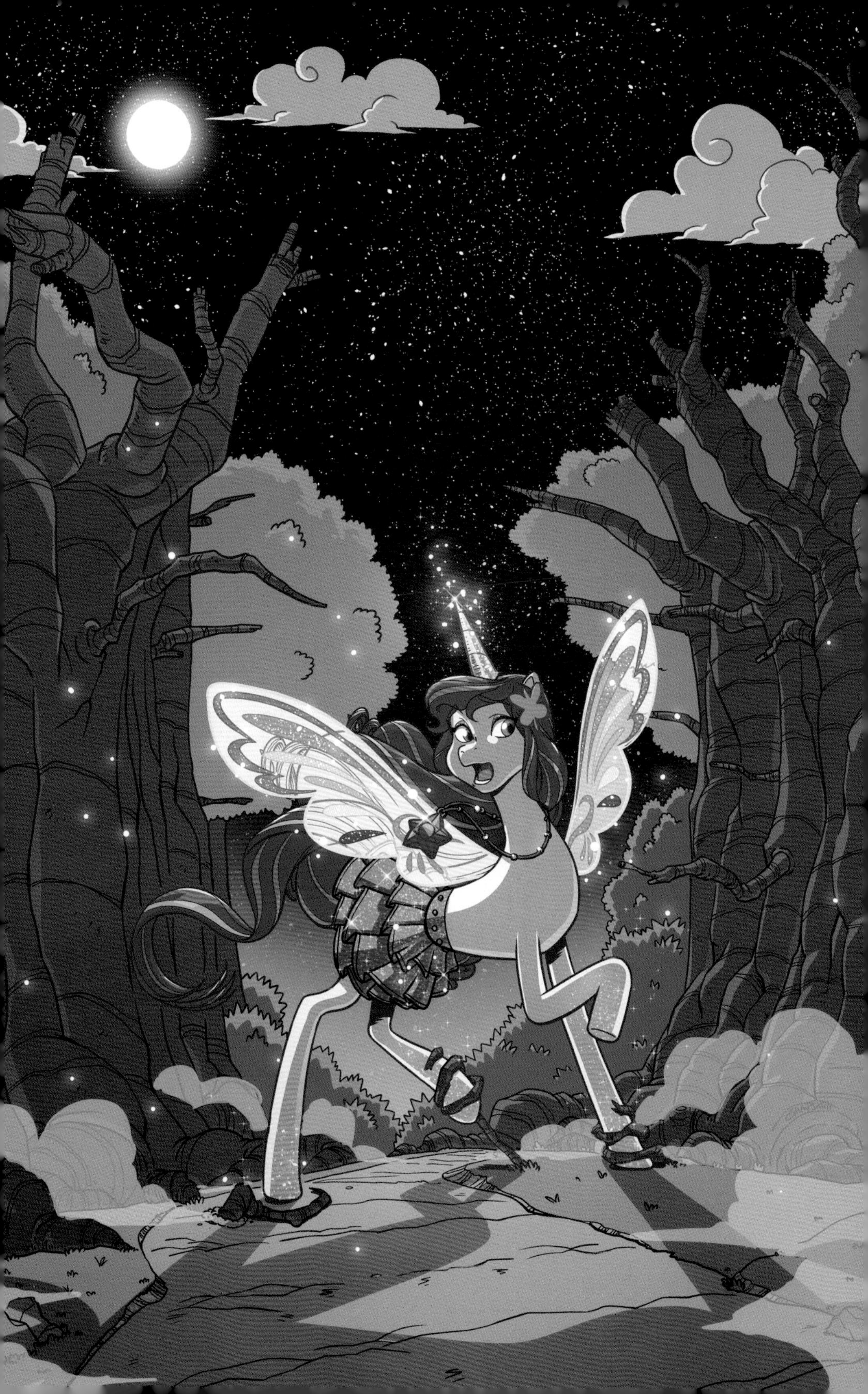

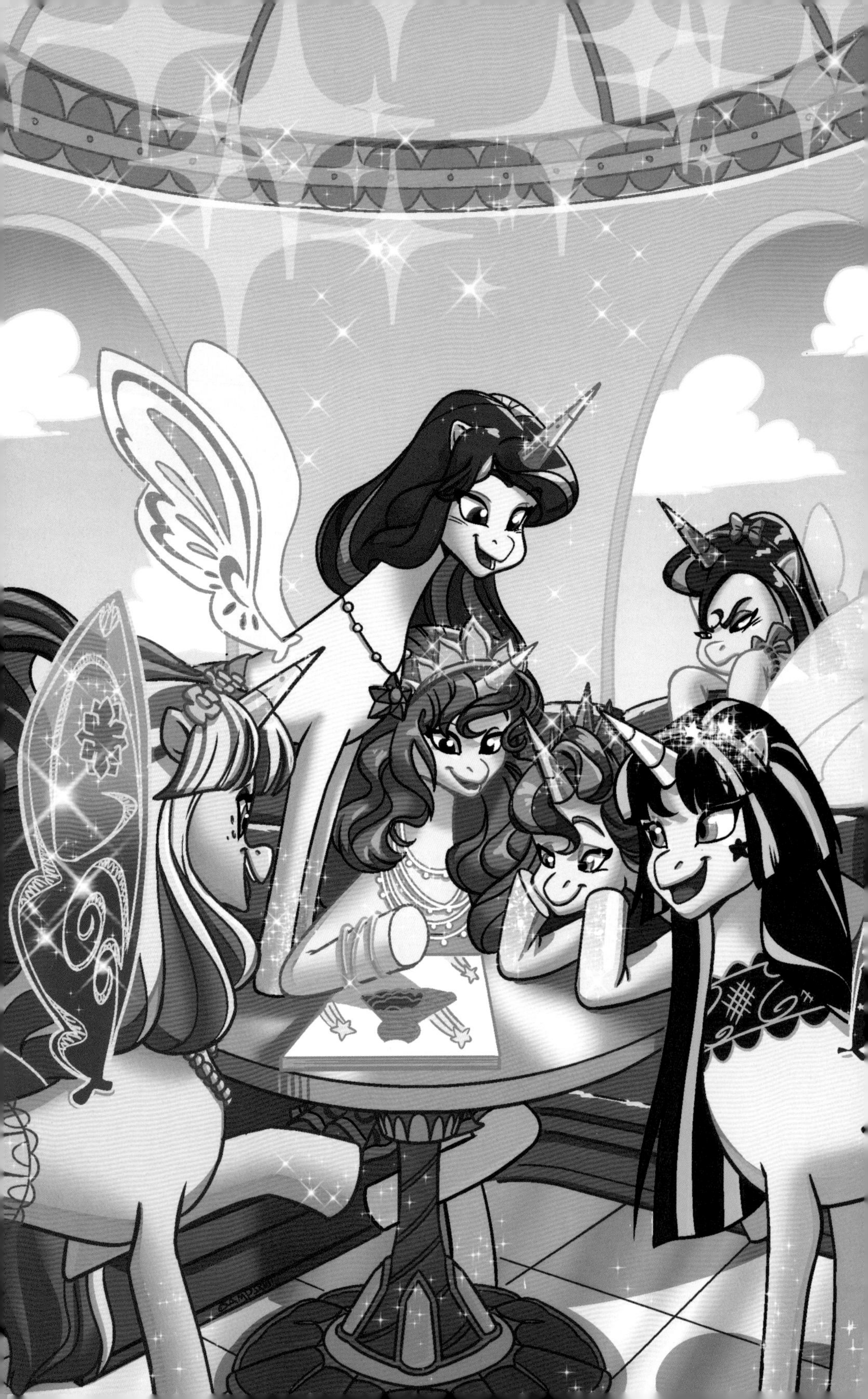

THE FASHION CLUB OF COLORS

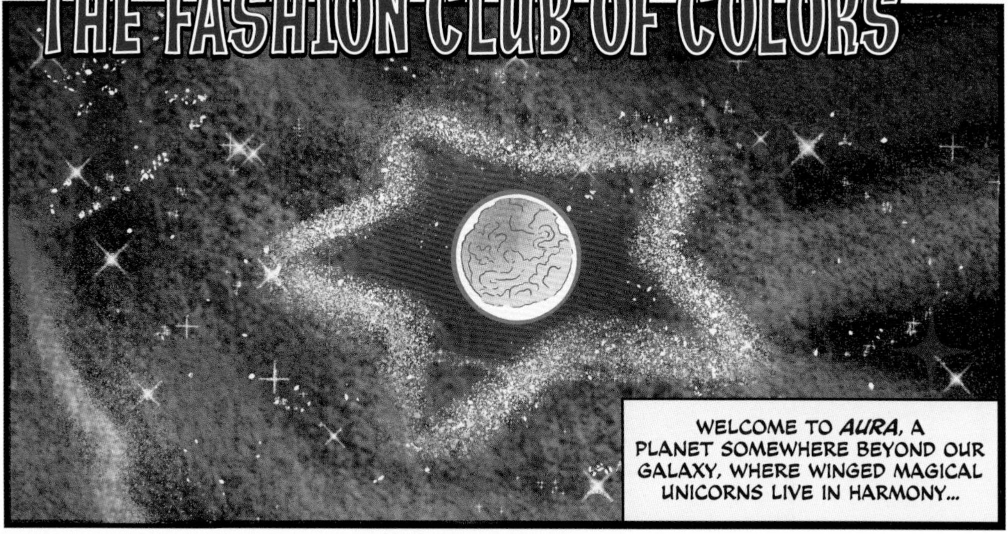
WELCOME TO *AURA*, A PLANET SOMEWHERE BEYOND OUR GALAXY, WHERE WINGED MAGICAL UNICORNS LIVE IN HARMONY...

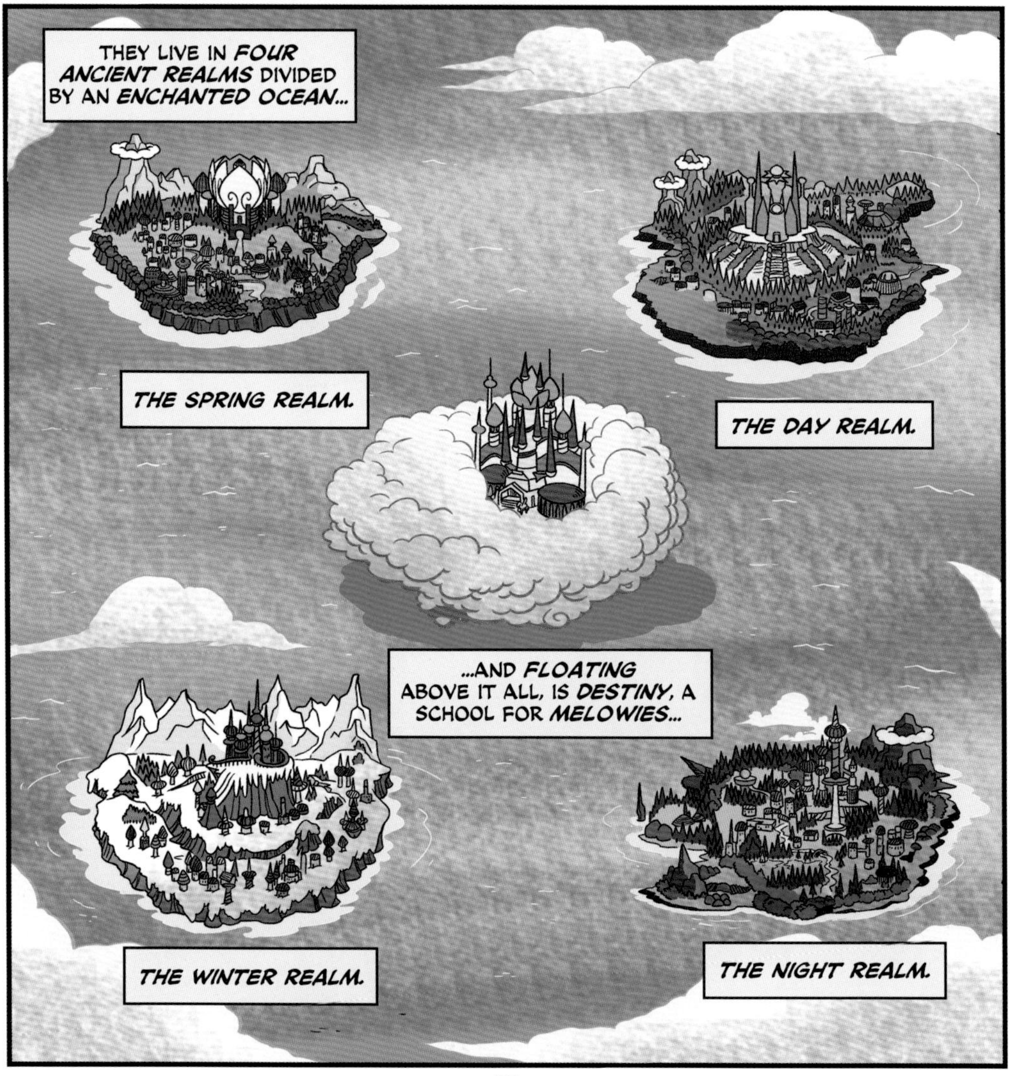
THEY LIVE IN *FOUR ANCIENT REALMS* DIVIDED BY AN *ENCHANTED OCEAN*...
THE SPRING REALM.
THE DAY REALM.
...AND *FLOATING* ABOVE IT ALL, IS *DESTINY*, A SCHOOL FOR *MELOWIES*...
THE WINTER REALM.
THE NIGHT REALM.

MELOWIES ARE *FEMALE PEGASUS* BORN WITH A SPECIAL SYMBOL ON THEIR WINGS INDICATING THAT THEY HAVE A HIDDEN POWER...

...BUT THEY ARE ALSO *TEENAGE GIRLS*...

SELENA! WHAT DO YOU THINK? A HAT MADE FOR A *FASHION QUEEN* OR WHAT?

THAT HAT WAS MADE FOR *YOU*, ELECTRA!

WHAT DO YOU THINK? A GOOD LOOK FOR ME?

WOW. YOU SHOULD TRY OUT FOR THE *FASHION CLUB* WITH ME!

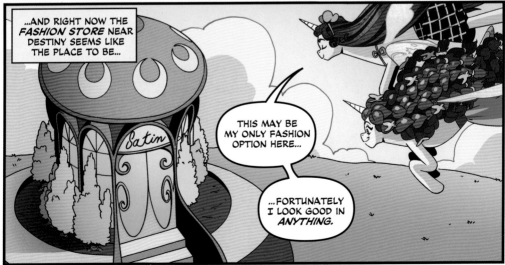

...AND RIGHT NOW THE *FASHION STORE* NEAR DESTINY SEEMS LIKE THE PLACE TO BE...

THIS MAY BE MY ONLY FASHION OPTION HERE...

...FORTUNATELY I LOOK GOOD IN *ANYTHING.*

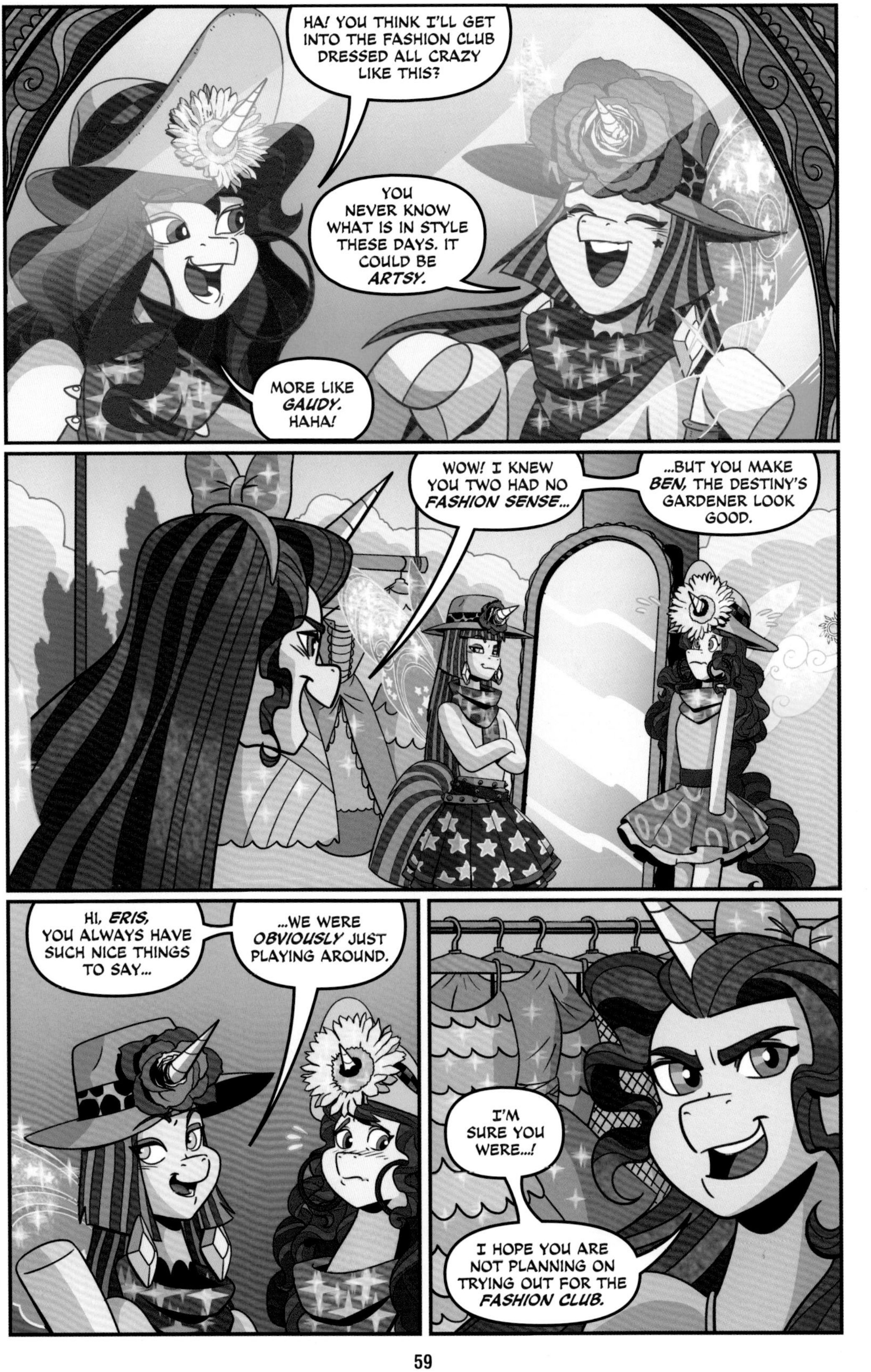
HA! YOU THINK I'LL GET INTO THE FASHION CLUB DRESSED ALL CRAZY LIKE THIS?
YOU NEVER KNOW WHAT IS IN STYLE THESE DAYS. IT COULD BE *ARTSY.*
MORE LIKE *GAUDY.* HAHA!
WOW! I KNEW YOU TWO HAD NO *FASHION SENSE*...
...BUT YOU MAKE *BEN,* THE DESTINY'S GARDENER LOOK GOOD.
HI, *ERIS,* YOU ALWAYS HAVE SUCH NICE THINGS TO SAY...
...WE WERE *OBVIOUSLY* JUST PLAYING AROUND.
I'M SURE YOU WERE...!
I HOPE YOU ARE NOT PLANNING ON TRYING OUT FOR THE *FASHION CLUB.*

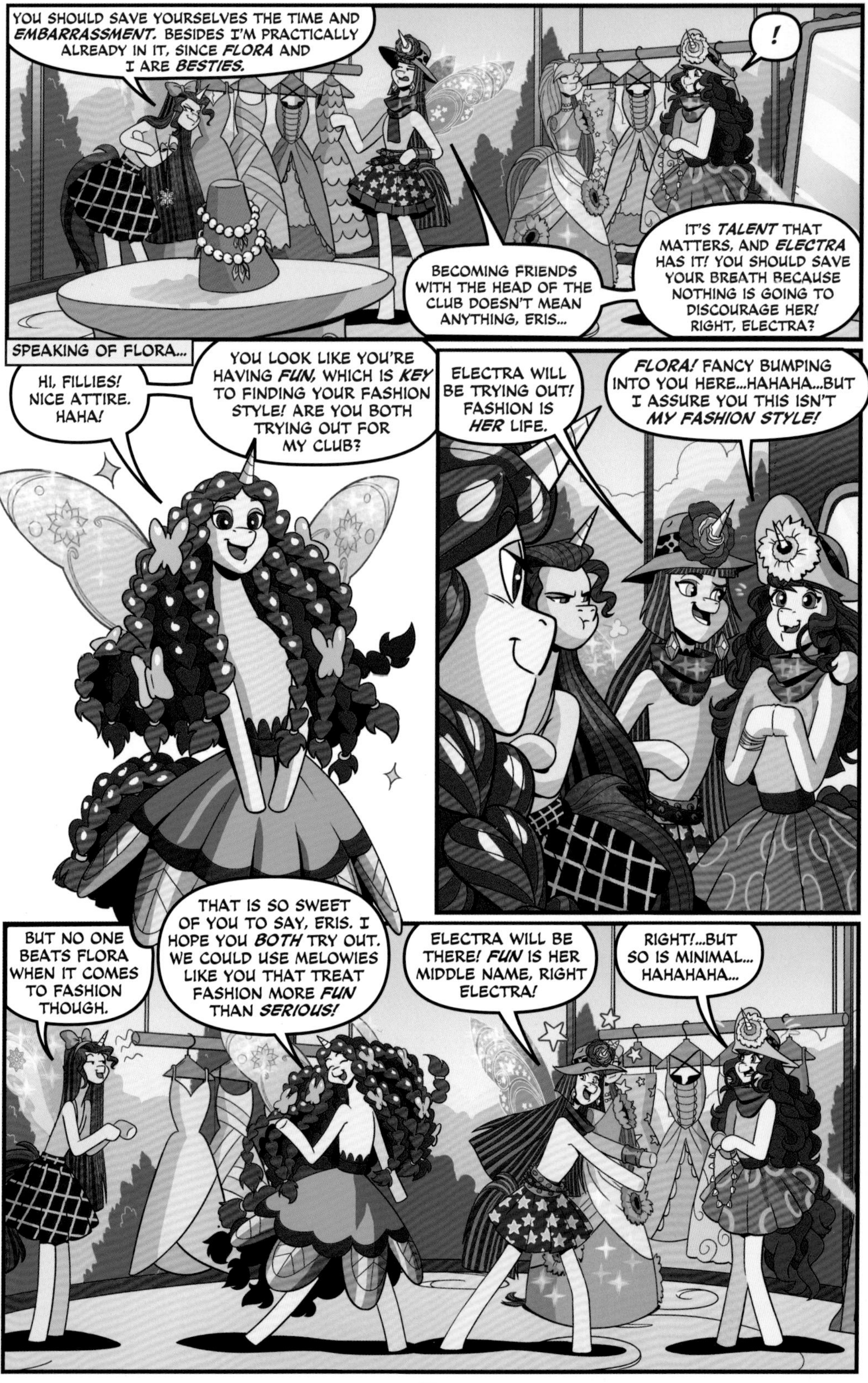
YOU SHOULD SAVE YOURSELVES THE TIME AND EMBARRASSMENT. BESIDES I'M PRACTICALLY ALREADY IN IT, SINCE FLORA AND I ARE BESTIES.
!
BECOMING FRIENDS WITH THE HEAD OF THE CLUB DOESN'T MEAN ANYTHING, ERIS...
IT'S TALENT THAT MATTERS, AND ELECTRA HAS IT! YOU SHOULD SAVE YOUR BREATH BECAUSE NOTHING IS GOING TO DISCOURAGE HER! RIGHT, ELECTRA?
SPEAKING OF FLORA...
HI, FILLIES! NICE ATTIRE. HAHA!
YOU LOOK LIKE YOU'RE HAVING FUN, WHICH IS KEY TO FINDING YOUR FASHION STYLE! ARE YOU BOTH TRYING OUT FOR MY CLUB?
ELECTRA WILL BE TRYING OUT! FASHION IS HER LIFE.
FLORA! FANCY BUMPING INTO YOU HERE...HAHAHA...BUT I ASSURE YOU THIS ISN'T MY FASHION STYLE!
BUT NO ONE BEATS FLORA WHEN IT COMES TO FASHION THOUGH.
THAT IS SO SWEET OF YOU TO SAY, ERIS. I HOPE YOU BOTH TRY OUT. WE COULD USE MELOWIES LIKE YOU THAT TREAT FASHION MORE FUN THAN SERIOUS!
ELECTRA WILL BE THERE! FUN IS HER MIDDLE NAME, RIGHT ELECTRA!
RIGHT!...BUT SO IS MINIMAL... HAHAHAHA...

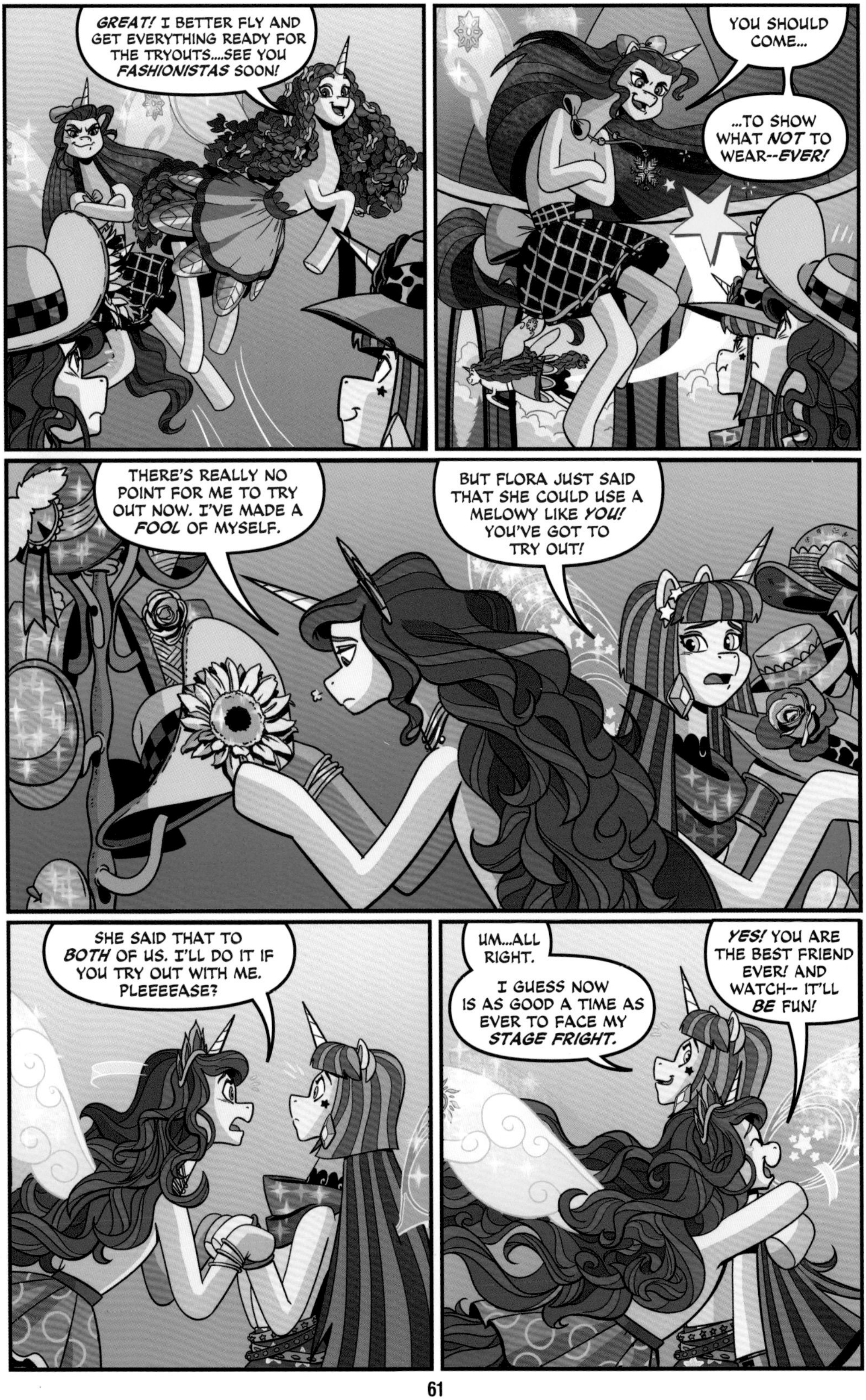
GREAT! I BETTER FLY AND GET EVERYTHING READY FOR THE TRYOUTS....SEE YOU FASHIONISTAS SOON!
YOU SHOULD COME...
...TO SHOW WHAT NOT TO WEAR--EVER!
THERE'S REALLY NO POINT FOR ME TO TRY OUT NOW. I'VE MADE A FOOL OF MYSELF.
BUT FLORA JUST SAID THAT SHE COULD USE A MELOWY LIKE YOU! YOU'VE GOT TO TRY OUT!
SHE SAID THAT TO BOTH OF US. I'LL DO IT IF YOU TRY OUT WITH ME. PLEEEEASE?
UM...ALL RIGHT.
I GUESS NOW IS AS GOOD A TIME AS EVER TO FACE MY STAGE FRIGHT.
YES! YOU ARE THE BEST FRIEND EVER! AND WATCH-- IT'LL BE FUN!

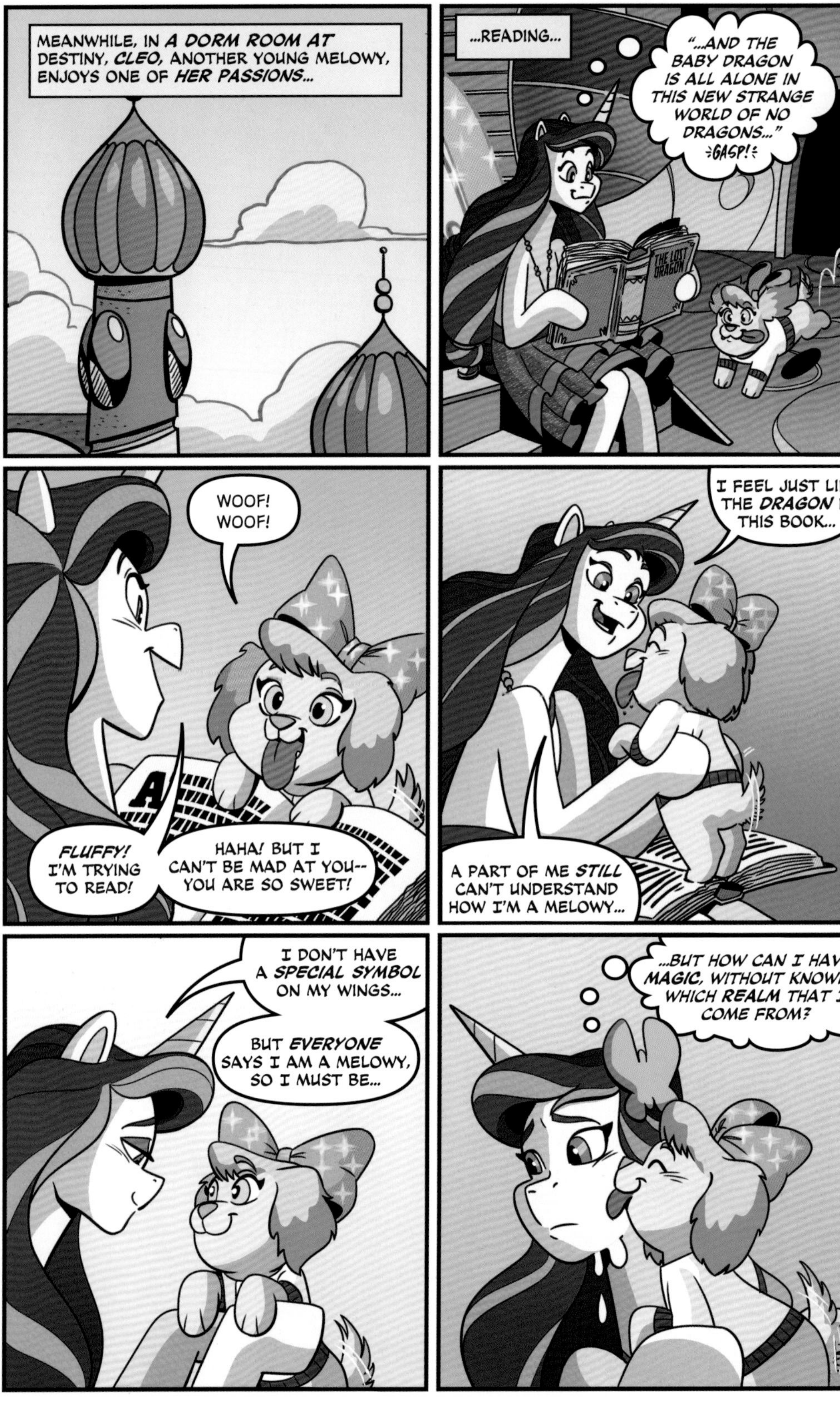

MEANWHILE, IN A DORM ROOM AT DESTINY, CLEO, ANOTHER YOUNG MELOWY, ENJOYS ONE OF HER PASSIONS...
...READING...
"...AND THE BABY DRAGON IS ALL ALONE IN THIS NEW STRANGE WORLD OF NO DRAGONS..." GASP!
THE LOST DRAGON
WOOF! WOOF!
FLUFFY! I'M TRYING TO READ!
HAHA! BUT I CAN'T BE MAD AT YOU-- YOU ARE SO SWEET!
I FEEL JUST LIKE THE DRAGON IN THIS BOOK...
A PART OF ME STILL CAN'T UNDERSTAND HOW I'M A MELOWY...
I DON'T HAVE A SPECIAL SYMBOL ON MY WINGS...
BUT EVERYONE SAYS I AM A MELOWY, SO I MUST BE...
...BUT HOW CAN I HAVE MAGIC, WITHOUT KNOWING WHICH REALM THAT I COME FROM?

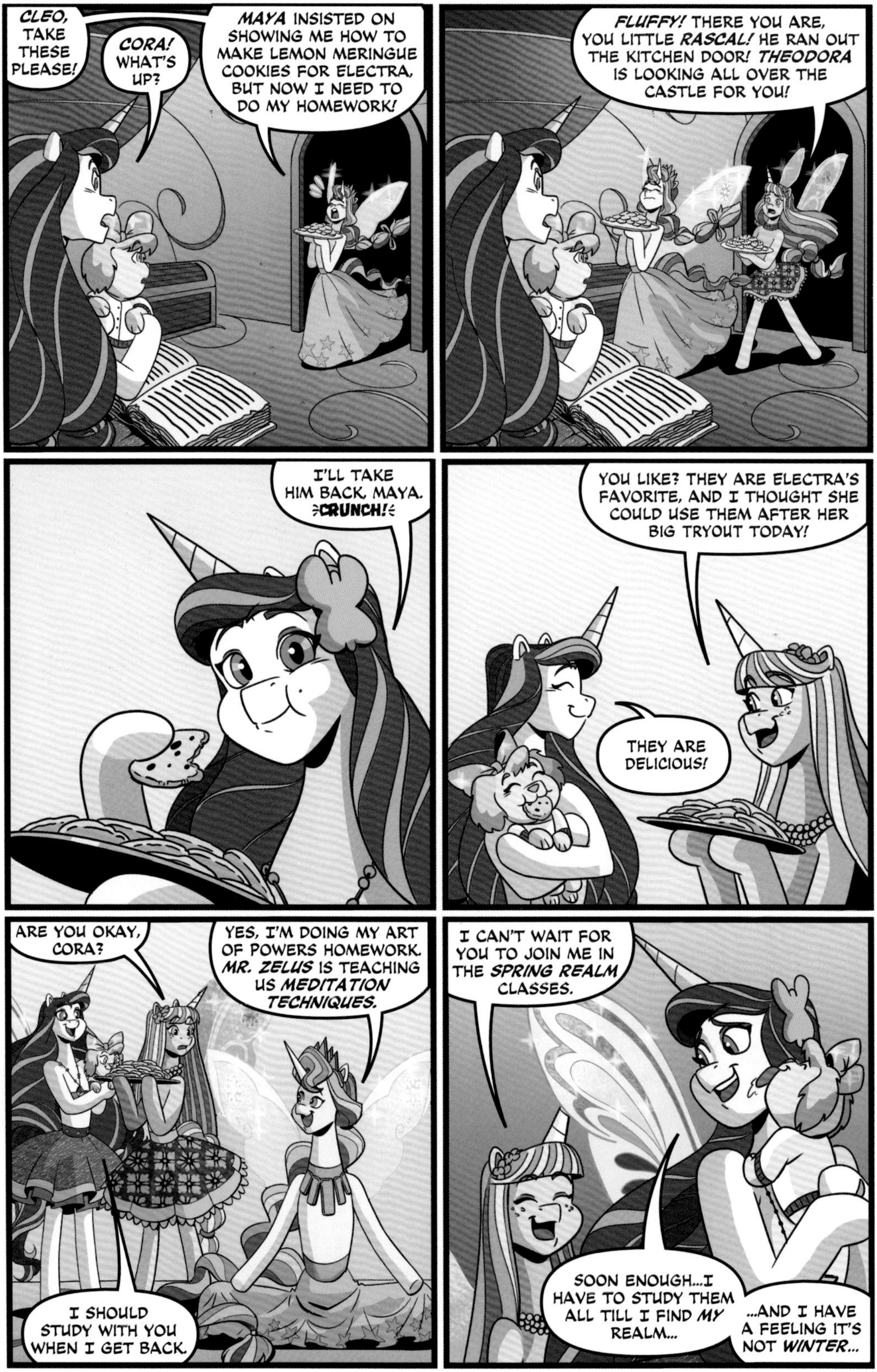
CLEO, TAKE THESE PLEASE!
CORA! WHAT'S UP?
MAYA INSISTED ON SHOWING ME HOW TO MAKE LEMON MERINGUE COOKIES FOR ELECTRA, BUT NOW I NEED TO DO MY HOMEWORK!
FLUFFY! THERE YOU ARE, YOU LITTLE RASCAL! HE RAN OUT THE KITCHEN DOOR! THEODORA IS LOOKING ALL OVER THE CASTLE FOR YOU!
I'LL TAKE HIM BACK, MAYA. CRUNCH!
YOU LIKE? THEY ARE ELECTRA'S FAVORITE, AND I THOUGHT SHE COULD USE THEM AFTER HER BIG TRYOUT TODAY!
THEY ARE DELICIOUS!
ARE YOU OKAY, CORA?
YES, I'M DOING MY ART OF POWERS HOMEWORK. MR. ZELUS IS TEACHING US MEDITATION TECHNIQUES.
I SHOULD STUDY WITH YOU WHEN I GET BACK.
I CAN'T WAIT FOR YOU TO JOIN ME IN THE SPRING REALM CLASSES.
SOON ENOUGH...I HAVE TO STUDY THEM ALL TILL I FIND MY REALM...
...AND I HAVE A FEELING IT'S NOT WINTER...

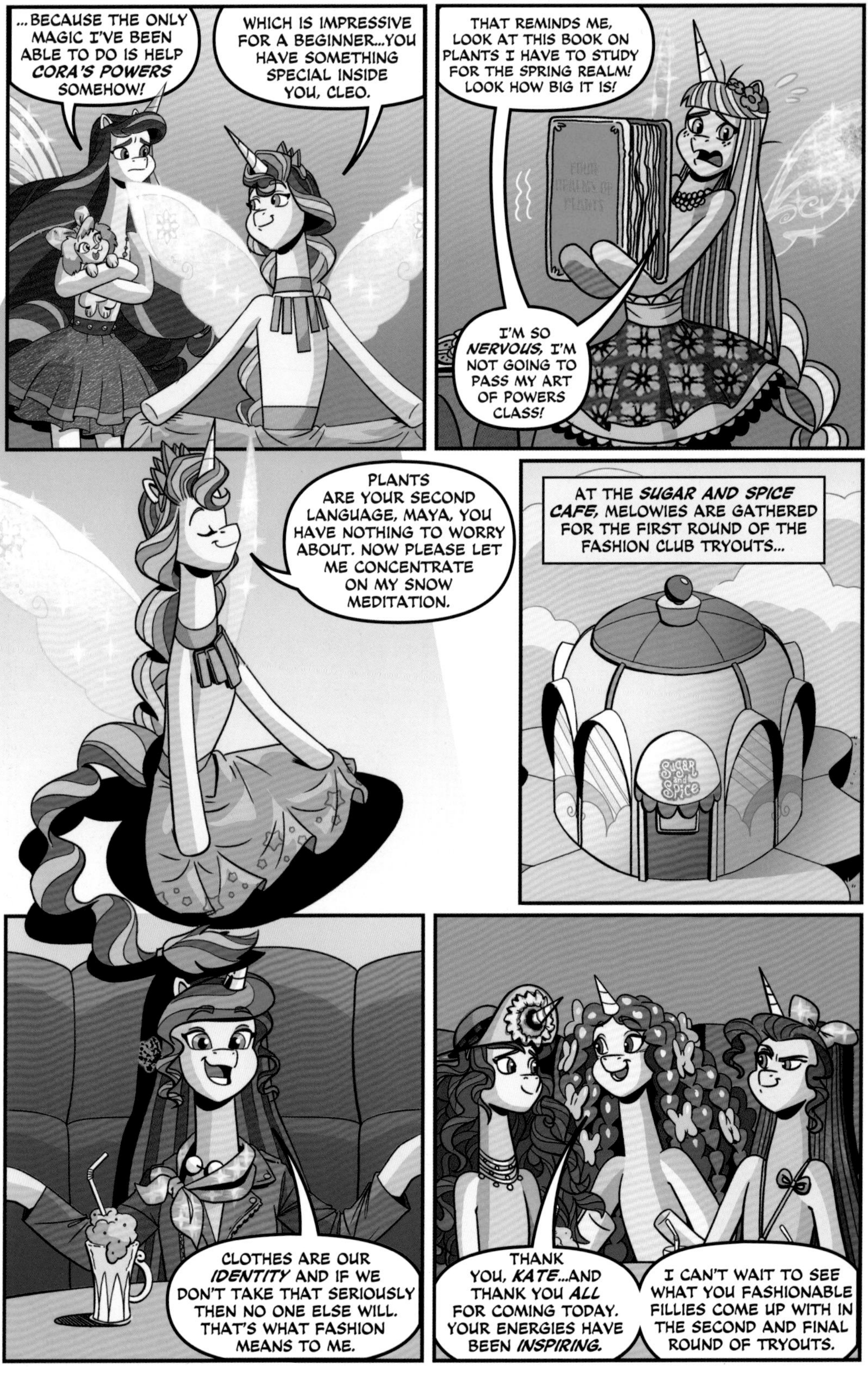
...BECAUSE THE ONLY MAGIC I'VE BEEN ABLE TO DO IS HELP *CORA'S POWERS* SOMEHOW!
WHICH IS IMPRESSIVE FOR A BEGINNER...YOU HAVE SOMETHING SPECIAL INSIDE YOU, CLEO.
THAT REMINDS ME, LOOK AT THIS BOOK ON PLANTS I HAVE TO STUDY FOR THE SPRING REALM! LOOK HOW BIG IT IS!
I'M SO *NERVOUS,* I'M NOT GOING TO PASS MY ART OF POWERS CLASS!
PLANTS ARE YOUR SECOND LANGUAGE, MAYA, YOU HAVE NOTHING TO WORRY ABOUT. NOW PLEASE LET ME CONCENTRATE ON MY SNOW MEDITATION.
AT THE *SUGAR AND SPICE CAFE,* MELOWIES ARE GATHERED FOR THE FIRST ROUND OF THE FASHION CLUB TRYOUTS...
SUGAR and SPICE
CLOTHES ARE OUR *IDENTITY* AND IF WE DON'T TAKE THAT SERIOUSLY THEN NO ONE ELSE WILL. THAT'S WHAT FASHION MEANS TO ME.
THANK YOU, *KATE*...AND THANK YOU *ALL* FOR COMING TODAY. YOUR ENERGIES HAVE BEEN *INSPIRING.*
I CAN'T WAIT TO SEE WHAT YOU FASHIONABLE FILLIES COME UP WITH IN THE SECOND AND FINAL ROUND OF TRYOUTS.

LET'S MEET BACK HERE THE SAME TIME TOMORROW. JUST BRING ALONG YOUR SKETCH PADS AND YOUR *PASSION FOR FASHION!*

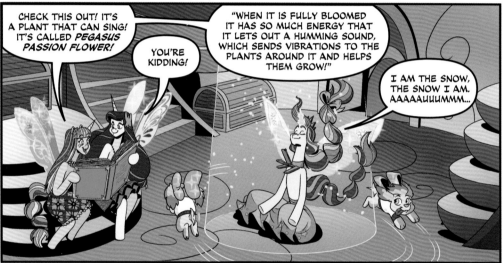

CHECK THIS OUT! IT'S A PLANT THAT CAN SING! IT'S CALLED *PEGASUS PASSION FLOWER!*

YOU'RE KIDDING!

"WHEN IT IS FULLY BLOOMED IT HAS SO MUCH ENERGY THAT IT LETS OUT A HUMMING SOUND, WHICH SENDS VIBRATIONS TO THE PLANTS AROUND IT AND HELPS THEM GROW!"

I AM THE SNOW, THE SNOW I AM. AAAAAUUUMMM...

I WONDER WHERE YOU FIND THEM...?

I DON'T KNOW, BUT IT SAYS THAT THEY AREN'T FROM ANY SPECIFIC REALM. THEY ARE SPREAD OUT ALL OVER AURA... *NO KNOWN ORIGIN.*

FOUR REALMS OF PLANTS

WE'RE *BACK!* JUST FINISHED THE FIRST SET OF TRYOUTS!

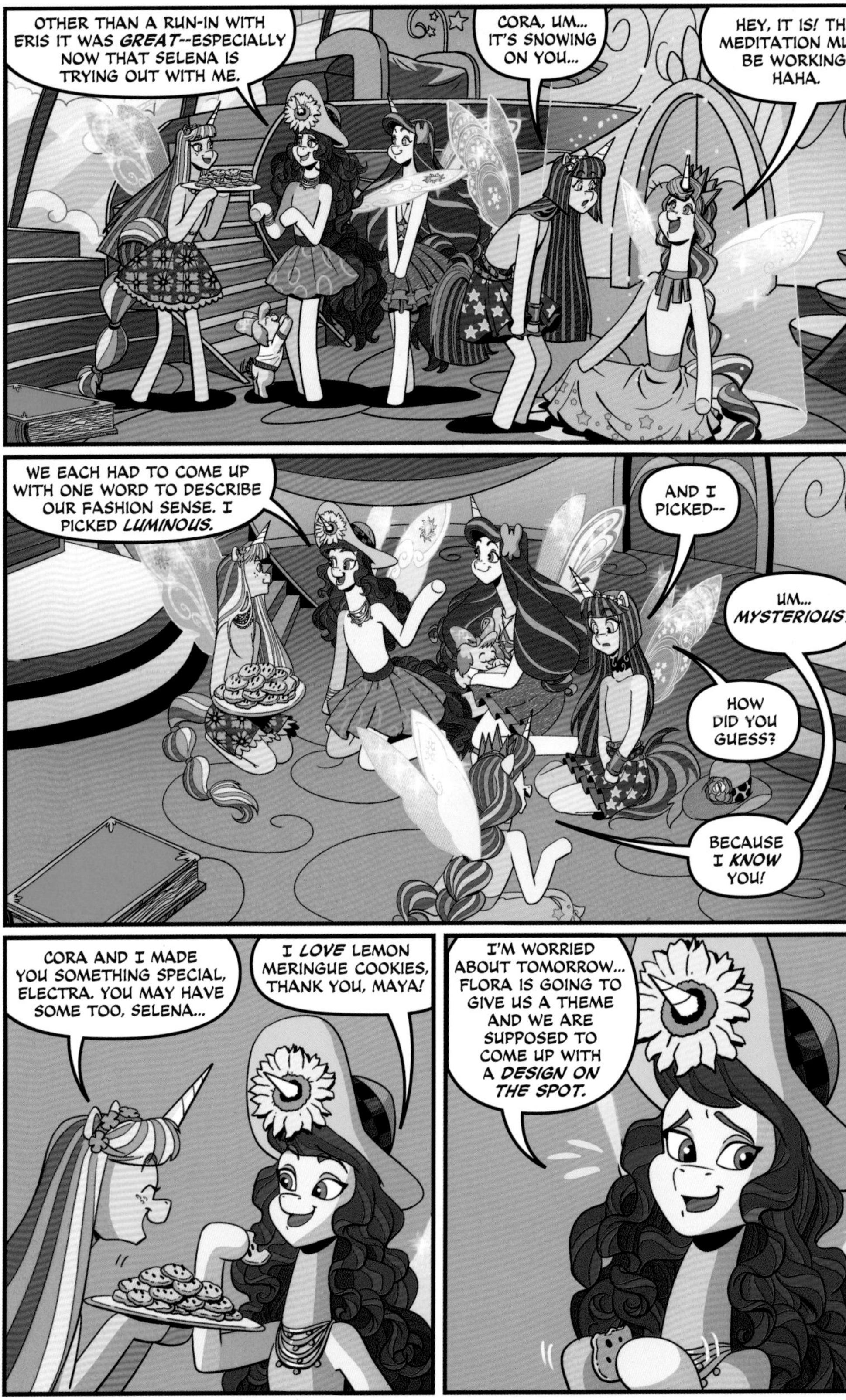
OTHER THAN A RUN-IN WITH ERIS IT WAS GREAT--ESPECIALLY NOW THAT SELENA IS TRYING OUT WITH ME.
CORA, UM... IT'S SNOWING ON YOU...
HEY, IT IS! THE MEDITATION MUST BE WORKING. HAHA.
WE EACH HAD TO COME UP WITH ONE WORD TO DESCRIBE OUR FASHION SENSE. I PICKED LUMINOUS.
AND I PICKED--
UM... MYSTERIOUS?
HOW DID YOU GUESS?
BECAUSE I KNOW YOU!
CORA AND I MADE YOU SOMETHING SPECIAL, ELECTRA. YOU MAY HAVE SOME TOO, SELENA...
I LOVE LEMON MERINGUE COOKIES, THANK YOU, MAYA!
I'M WORRIED ABOUT TOMORROW... FLORA IS GOING TO GIVE US A THEME AND WE ARE SUPPOSED TO COME UP WITH A DESIGN ON THE SPOT.

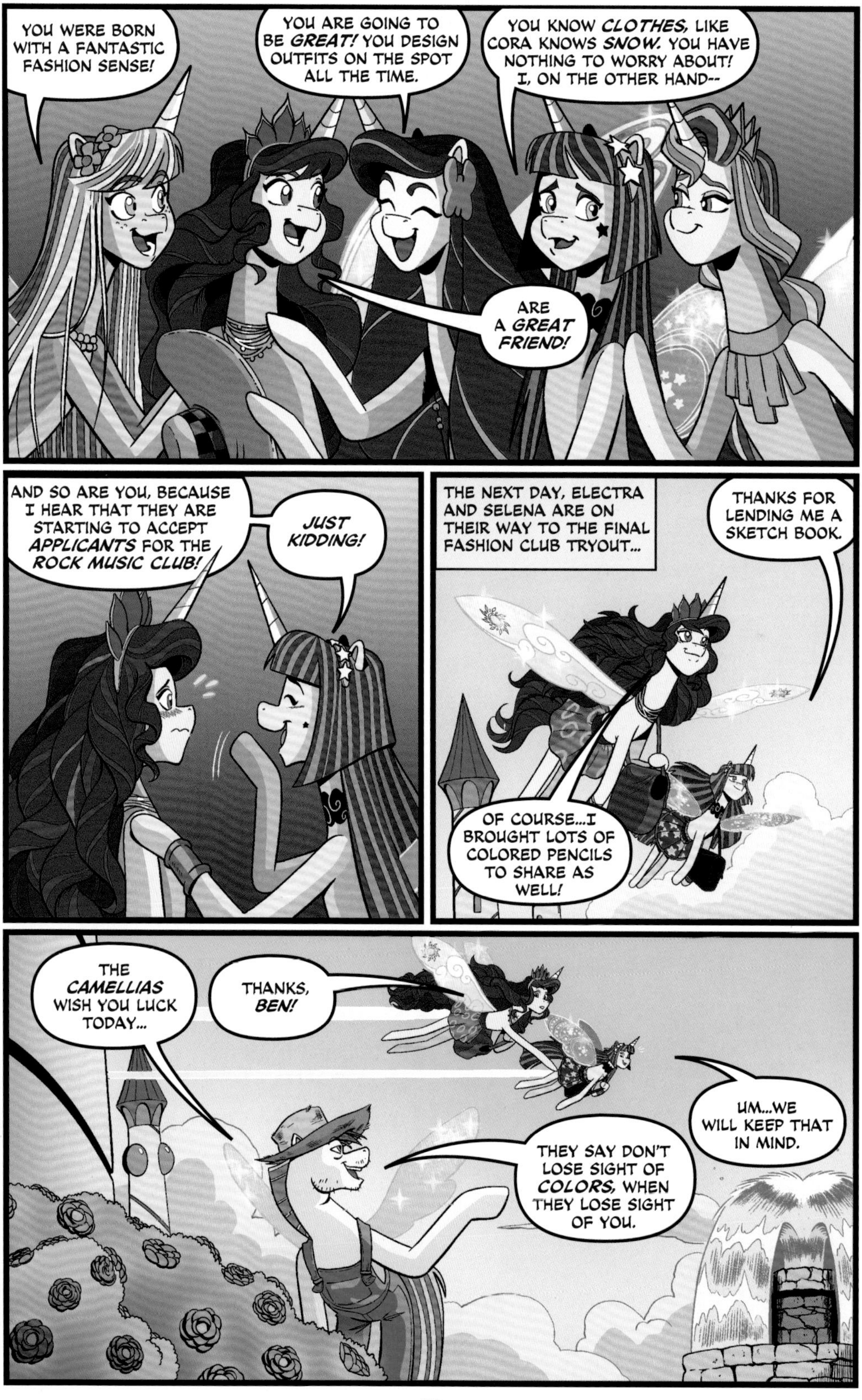
YOU WERE BORN WITH A FANTASTIC FASHION SENSE!
YOU ARE GOING TO BE GREAT! YOU DESIGN OUTFITS ON THE SPOT ALL THE TIME.
YOU KNOW CLOTHES, LIKE CORA KNOWS SNOW. YOU HAVE NOTHING TO WORRY ABOUT! I, ON THE OTHER HAND--
ARE A GREAT FRIEND!
AND SO ARE YOU, BECAUSE I HEAR THAT THEY ARE STARTING TO ACCEPT APPLICANTS FOR THE ROCK MUSIC CLUB!
JUST KIDDING!
THE NEXT DAY, ELECTRA AND SELENA ARE ON THEIR WAY TO THE FINAL FASHION CLUB TRYOUT...
THANKS FOR LENDING ME A SKETCH BOOK.
OF COURSE...I BROUGHT LOTS OF COLORED PENCILS TO SHARE AS WELL!
THE CAMELLIAS WISH YOU LUCK TODAY...
THANKS, BEN!
THEY SAY DON'T LOSE SIGHT OF COLORS, WHEN THEY LOSE SIGHT OF YOU.
UM...WE WILL KEEP THAT IN MIND.

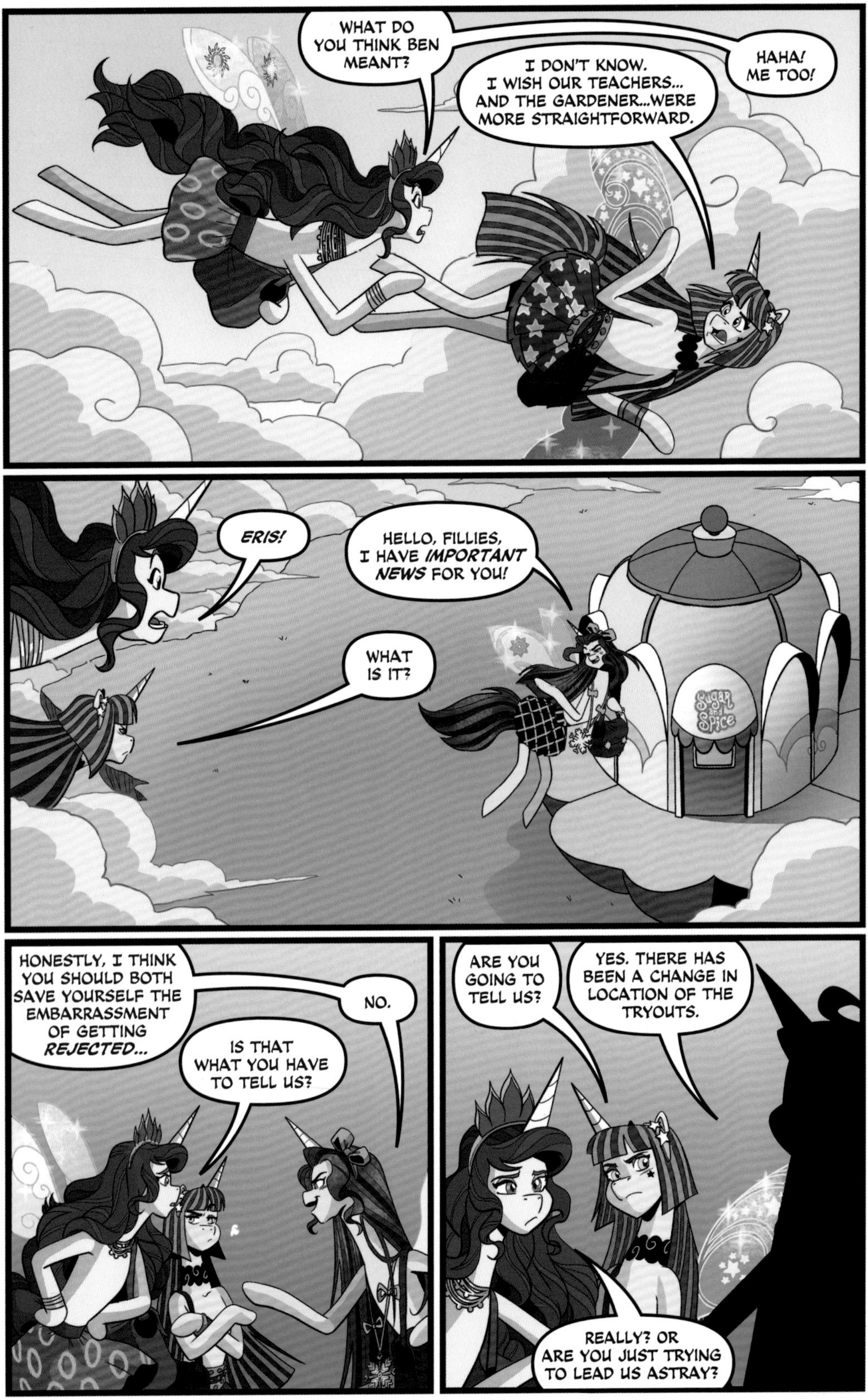
WHAT DO YOU THINK BEN MEANT?
I DON'T KNOW. I WISH OUR TEACHERS... AND THE GARDENER...WERE MORE STRAIGHTFORWARD.
HAHA! ME TOO!
ERIS!
HELLO, FILLIES, I HAVE ***IMPORTANT NEWS*** FOR YOU!
WHAT IS IT?
Sugar and Spice
HONESTLY, I THINK YOU SHOULD BOTH SAVE YOURSELF THE EMBARRASSMENT OF GETTING ***REJECTED...***
NO.
IS THAT WHAT YOU HAVE TO TELL US?
ARE YOU GOING TO TELL US?
YES. THERE HAS BEEN A CHANGE IN LOCATION OF THE TRYOUTS.
REALLY? OR ARE YOU JUST TRYING TO LEAD US ASTRAY?

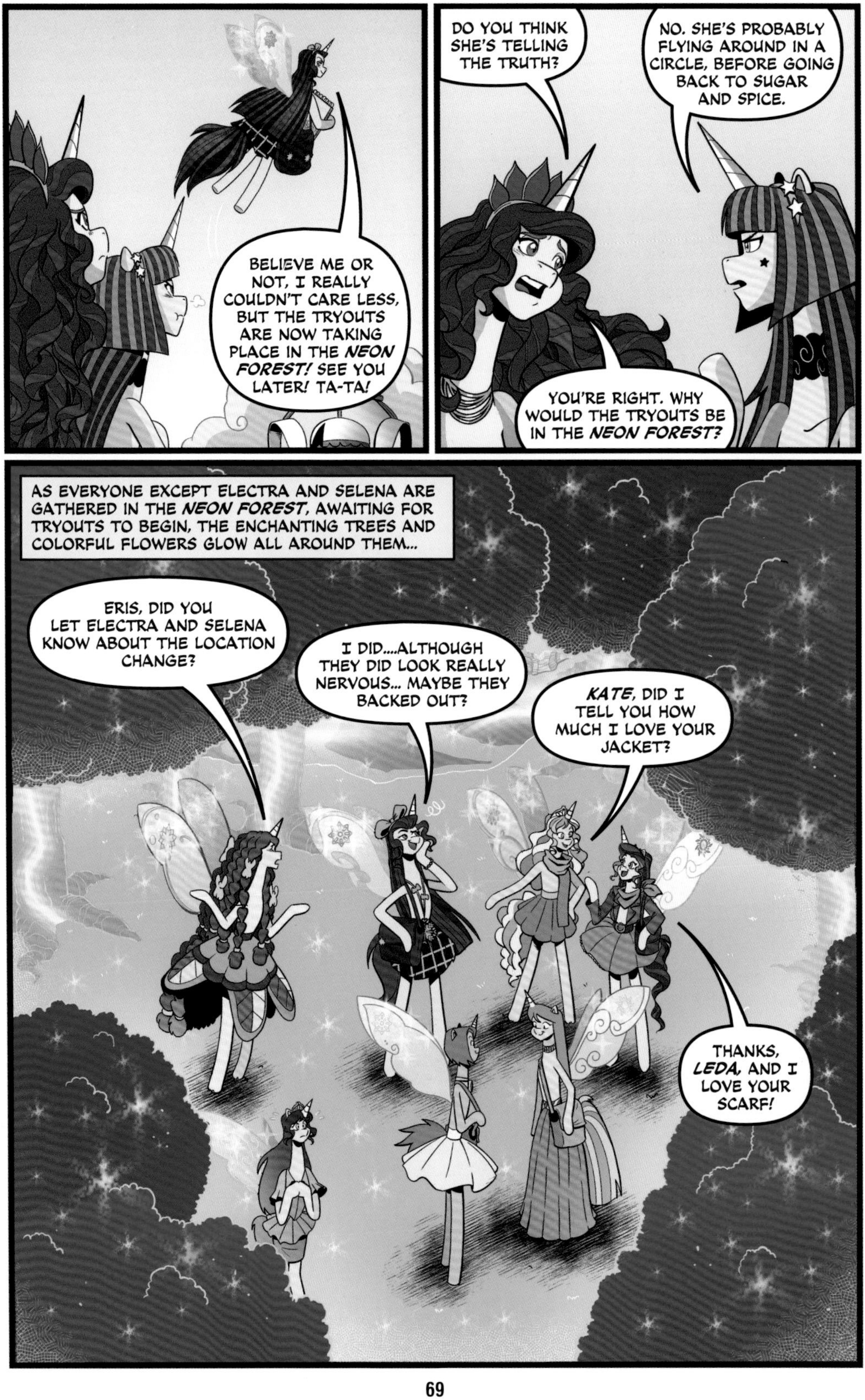

BELIEVE ME OR NOT, I REALLY COULDN'T CARE LESS, BUT THE TRYOUTS ARE NOW TAKING PLACE IN THE *NEON FOREST!* SEE YOU LATER! TA-TA!
DO YOU THINK SHE'S TELLING THE TRUTH?
NO. SHE'S PROBABLY FLYING AROUND IN A CIRCLE, BEFORE GOING BACK TO SUGAR AND SPICE.
YOU'RE RIGHT. WHY WOULD THE TRYOUTS BE IN THE *NEON FOREST?*
AS EVERYONE EXCEPT ELECTRA AND SELENA ARE GATHERED IN THE *NEON FOREST*, AWAITING FOR TRYOUTS TO BEGIN, THE ENCHANTING TREES AND COLORFUL FLOWERS GLOW ALL AROUND THEM...
ERIS, DID YOU LET ELECTRA AND SELENA KNOW ABOUT THE LOCATION CHANGE?
I DID....ALTHOUGH THEY DID LOOK REALLY NERVOUS... MAYBE THEY BACKED OUT?
KATE, DID I TELL YOU HOW MUCH I LOVE YOUR JACKET?
THANKS, *LEDA*, AND I LOVE YOUR SCARF!

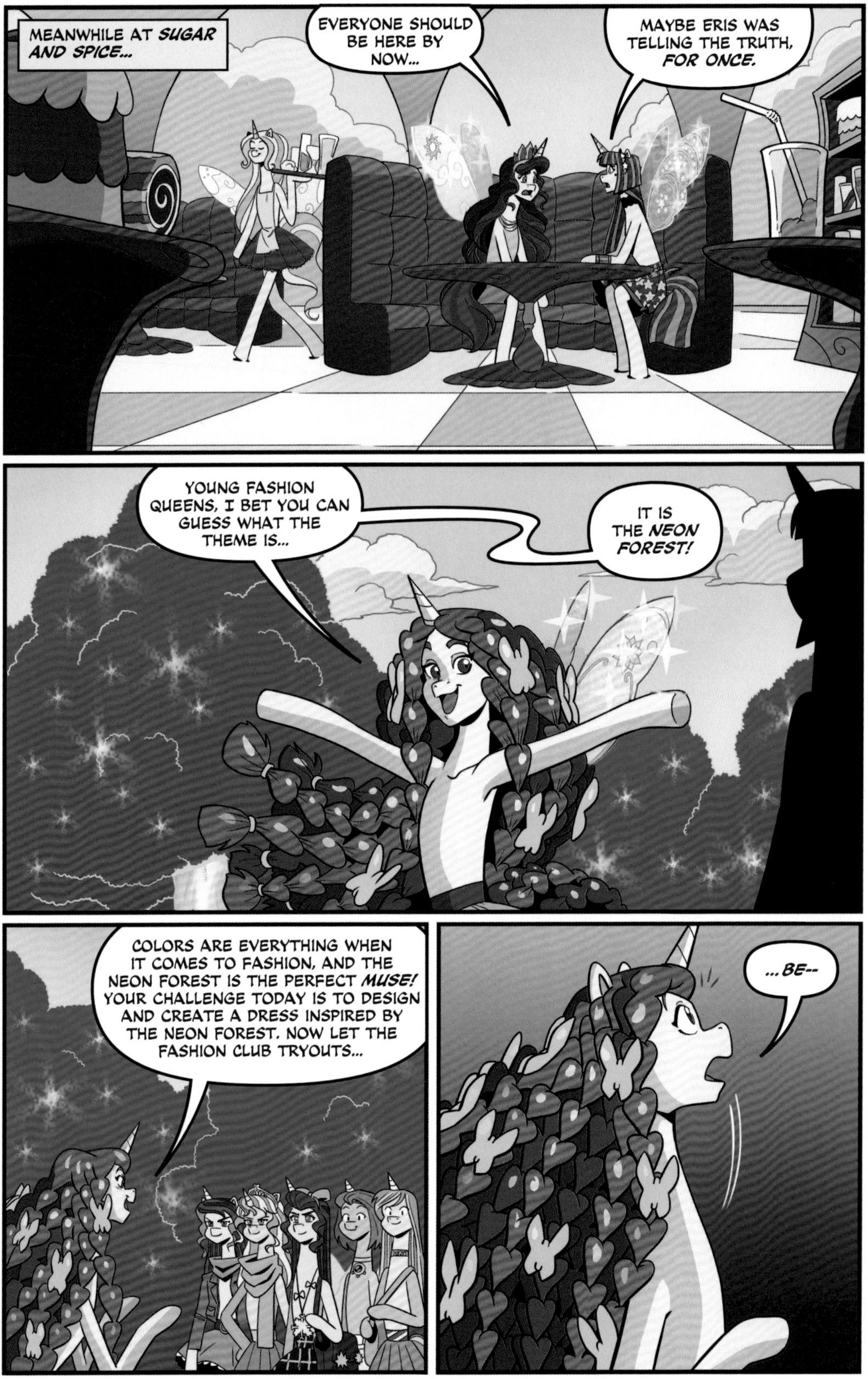
MEANWHILE AT SUGAR AND SPICE...
EVERYONE SHOULD BE HERE BY NOW...
MAYBE ERIS WAS TELLING THE TRUTH, FOR ONCE.
YOUNG FASHION QUEENS, I BET YOU CAN GUESS WHAT THE THEME IS...
IT IS THE NEON FOREST!
COLORS ARE EVERYTHING WHEN IT COMES TO FASHION, AND THE NEON FOREST IS THE PERFECT MUSE! YOUR CHALLENGE TODAY IS TO DESIGN AND CREATE A DRESS INSPIRED BY THE NEON FOREST. NOW LET THE FASHION CLUB TRYOUTS...
...BE--

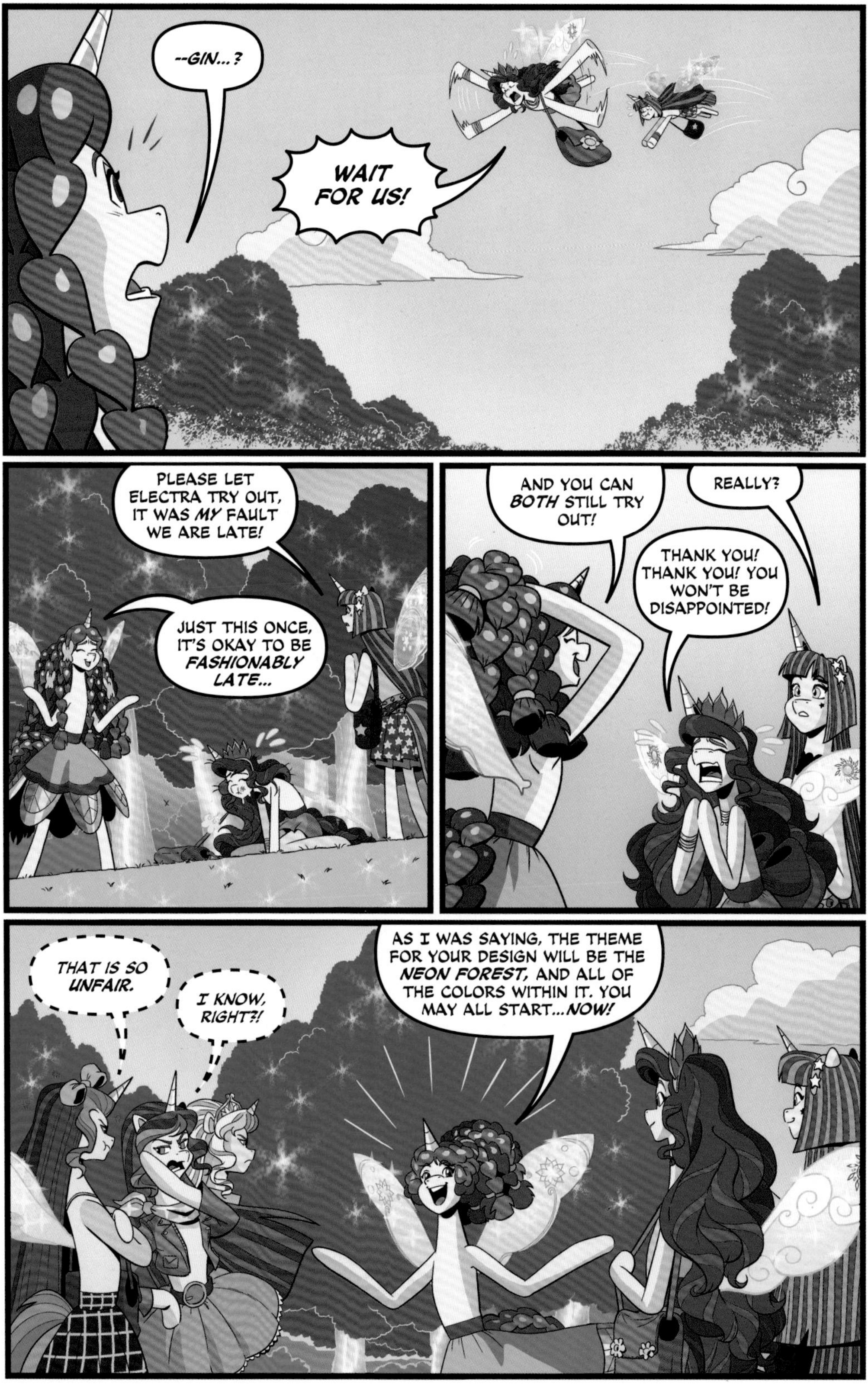
--GIN...?
WAIT FOR US!
PLEASE LET ELECTRA TRY OUT, IT WAS MY FAULT WE ARE LATE!
JUST THIS ONCE, IT'S OKAY TO BE FASHIONABLY LATE...
AND YOU CAN BOTH STILL TRY OUT!
REALLY?
THANK YOU! THANK YOU! YOU WON'T BE DISAPPOINTED!
THAT IS SO UNFAIR.
I KNOW, RIGHT?!
AS I WAS SAYING, THE THEME FOR YOUR DESIGN WILL BE THE NEON FOREST, AND ALL OF THE COLORS WITHIN IT. YOU MAY ALL START...NOW!

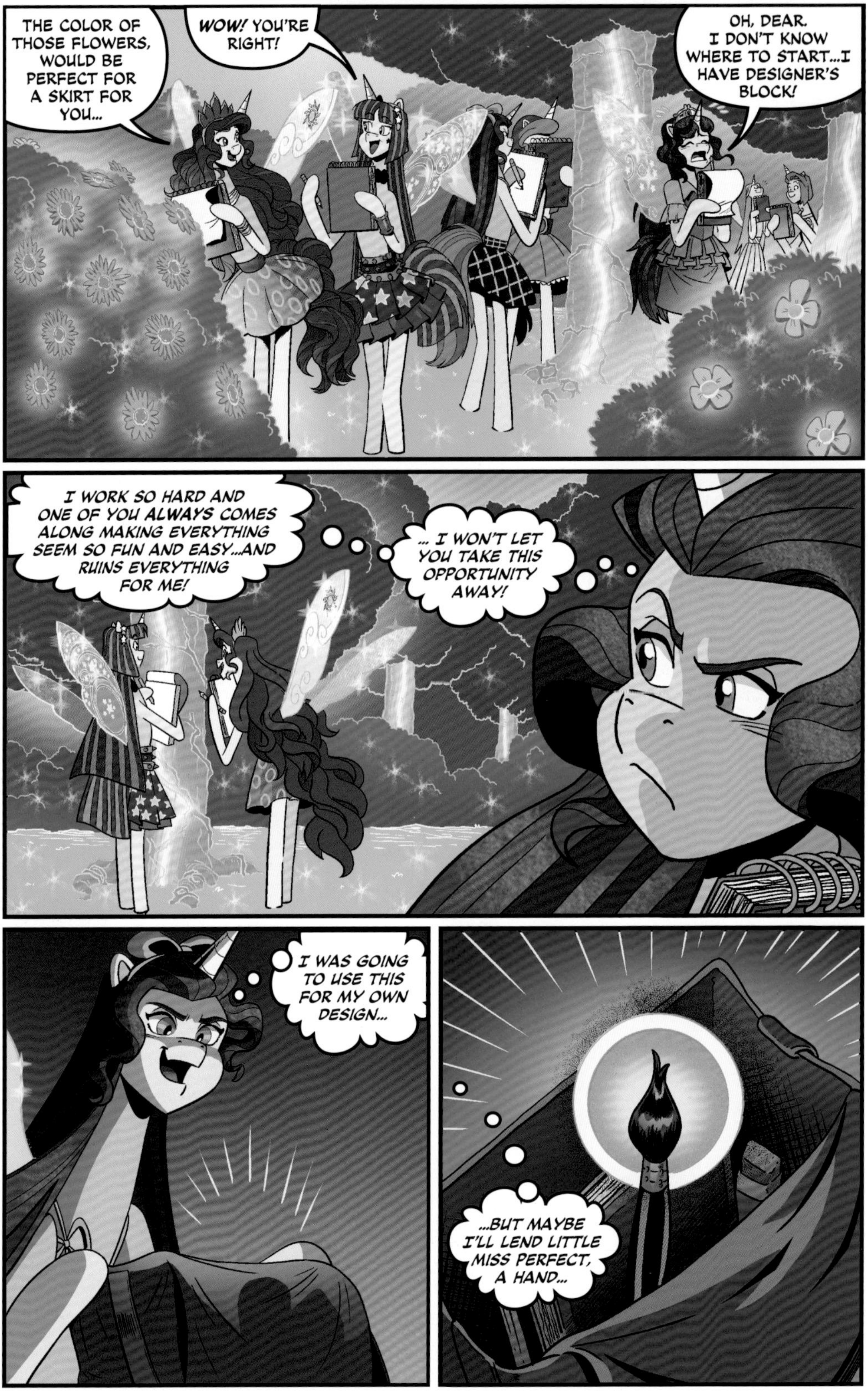
THE COLOR OF THOSE FLOWERS, WOULD BE PERFECT FOR A SKIRT FOR YOU...
WOW! YOU'RE RIGHT!
OH, DEAR. I DON'T KNOW WHERE TO START...I HAVE DESIGNER'S BLOCK!
I WORK SO HARD AND ONE OF YOU ALWAYS COMES ALONG MAKING EVERYTHING SEEM SO FUN AND EASY...AND RUINS EVERYTHING FOR ME!
... I WON'T LET YOU TAKE THIS OPPORTUNITY AWAY!
I WAS GOING TO USE THIS FOR MY OWN DESIGN...
...BUT MAYBE I'LL LEND LITTLE MISS PERFECT, A HAND...

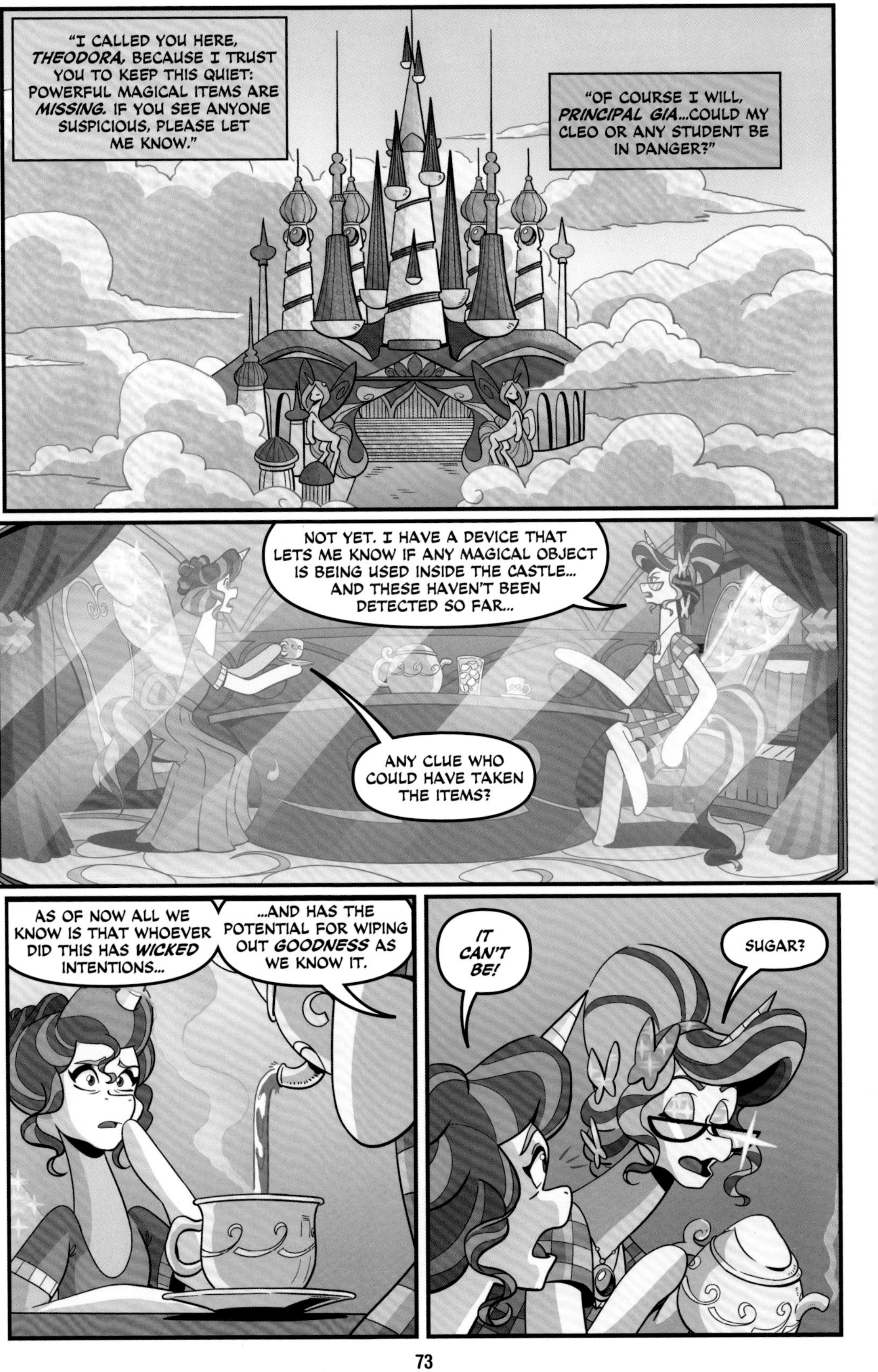
"I CALLED YOU HERE, THEODORA, BECAUSE I TRUST YOU TO KEEP THIS QUIET: POWERFUL MAGICAL ITEMS ARE MISSING. IF YOU SEE ANYONE SUSPICIOUS, PLEASE LET ME KNOW."
"OF COURSE I WILL, PRINCIPAL GIA...COULD MY CLEO OR ANY STUDENT BE IN DANGER?"
NOT YET. I HAVE A DEVICE THAT LETS ME KNOW IF ANY MAGICAL OBJECT IS BEING USED INSIDE THE CASTLE... AND THESE HAVEN'T BEEN DETECTED SO FAR...
ANY CLUE WHO COULD HAVE TAKEN THE ITEMS?
AS OF NOW ALL WE KNOW IS THAT WHOEVER DID THIS HAS WICKED INTENTIONS...
...AND HAS THE POTENTIAL FOR WIPING OUT GOODNESS AS WE KNOW IT.
IT CAN'T BE!
SUGAR?

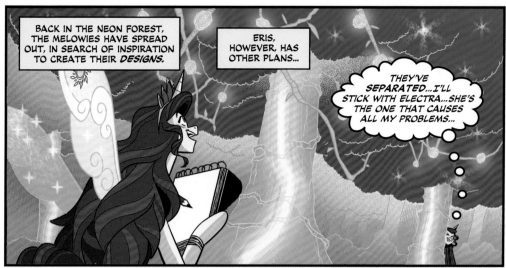

BACK IN THE NEON FOREST, THE MELOWIES HAVE SPREAD OUT, IN SEARCH OF INSPIRATION TO CREATE THEIR *DESIGNS*.

ERIS, HOWEVER, HAS OTHER PLANS...

THEY'VE *SEPARATED*...I'LL STICK WITH ELECTRA...SHE'S THE ONE THAT CAUSES ALL MY PROBLEMS...

THESE ARE GOING TO BE *PERFECT* FOR MY DRESS!

THEY WON'T BE PERFECT... FOR LONG!

I HAVE TO BE QUICK-- NO ONE MUST SEE ME...

TIME TO SEE IF THIS REALLY IS A MAGICAL PAINTBRUSH...
GASP! IT WORKED!
THESE YELLOW BELLS WILL BE PERFECT WITH THE PINK AND GOLD DRESS! AND THIS VINE I CAN USE TO MAKE A HEADPIECE.
WHEW! I JUST MADE IT! ANOTHER SECOND AND SHE WOULD'VE SPOTTED ME!
WHAT HAPPENED HERE?

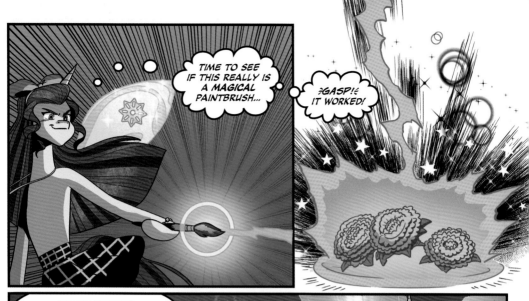

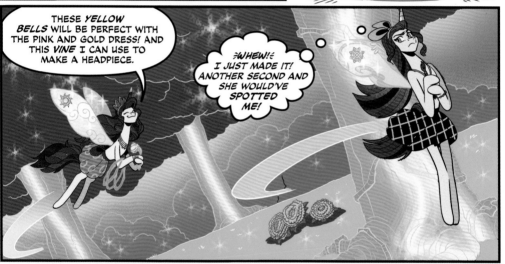

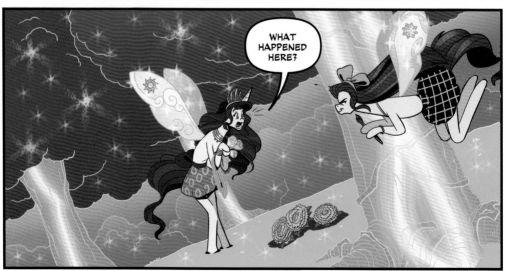

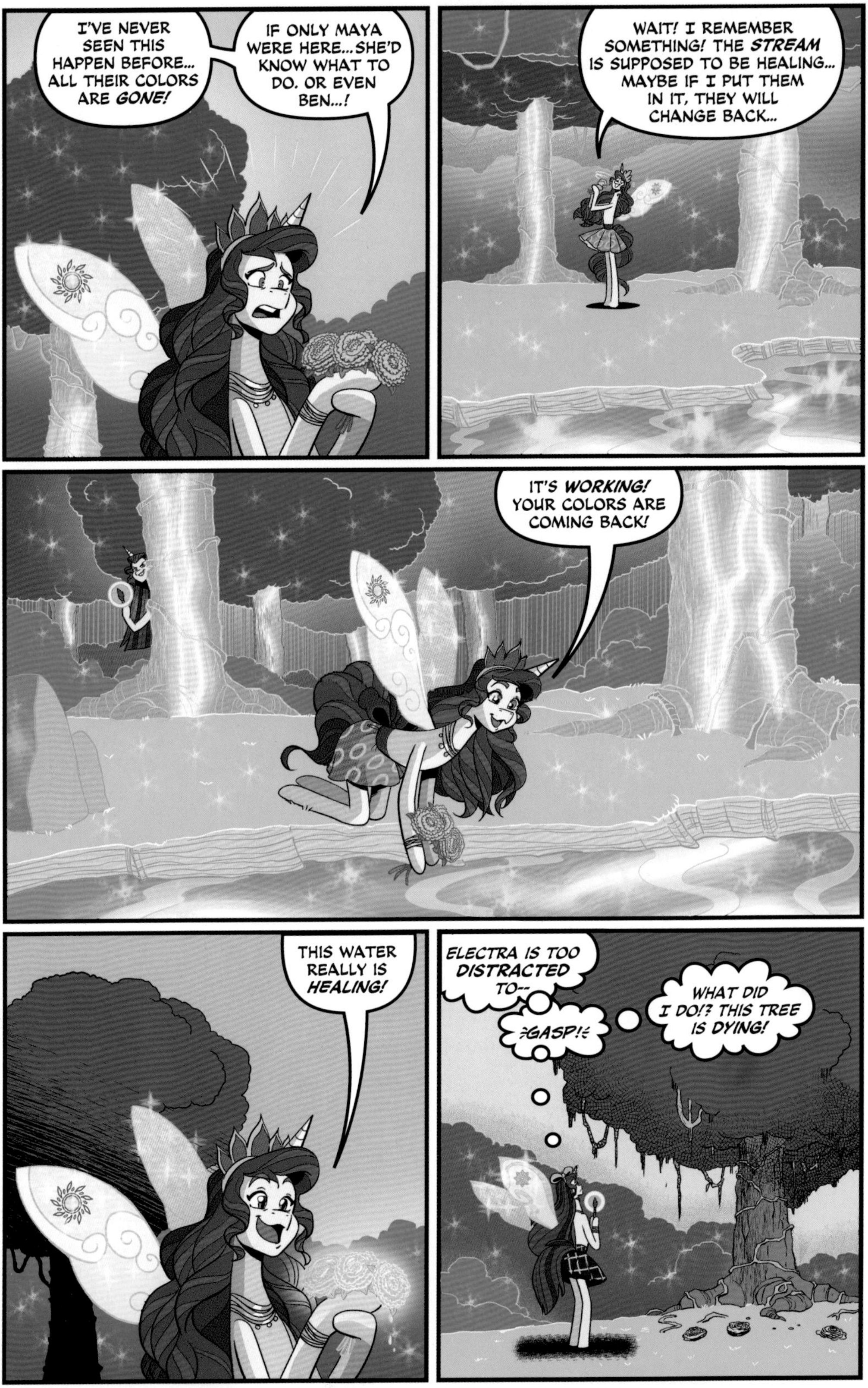

I'VE NEVER SEEN THIS HAPPEN BEFORE... ALL THEIR COLORS ARE GONE!
IF ONLY MAYA WERE HERE...SHE'D KNOW WHAT TO DO. OR EVEN BEN...!
WAIT! I REMEMBER SOMETHING! THE STREAM IS SUPPOSED TO BE HEALING... MAYBE IF I PUT THEM IN IT, THEY WILL CHANGE BACK...
IT'S WORKING! YOUR COLORS ARE COMING BACK!
THIS WATER REALLY IS HEALING!
ELECTRA IS TOO DISTRACTED TO--
GASP!
WHAT DID I DO!? THIS TREE IS DYING!

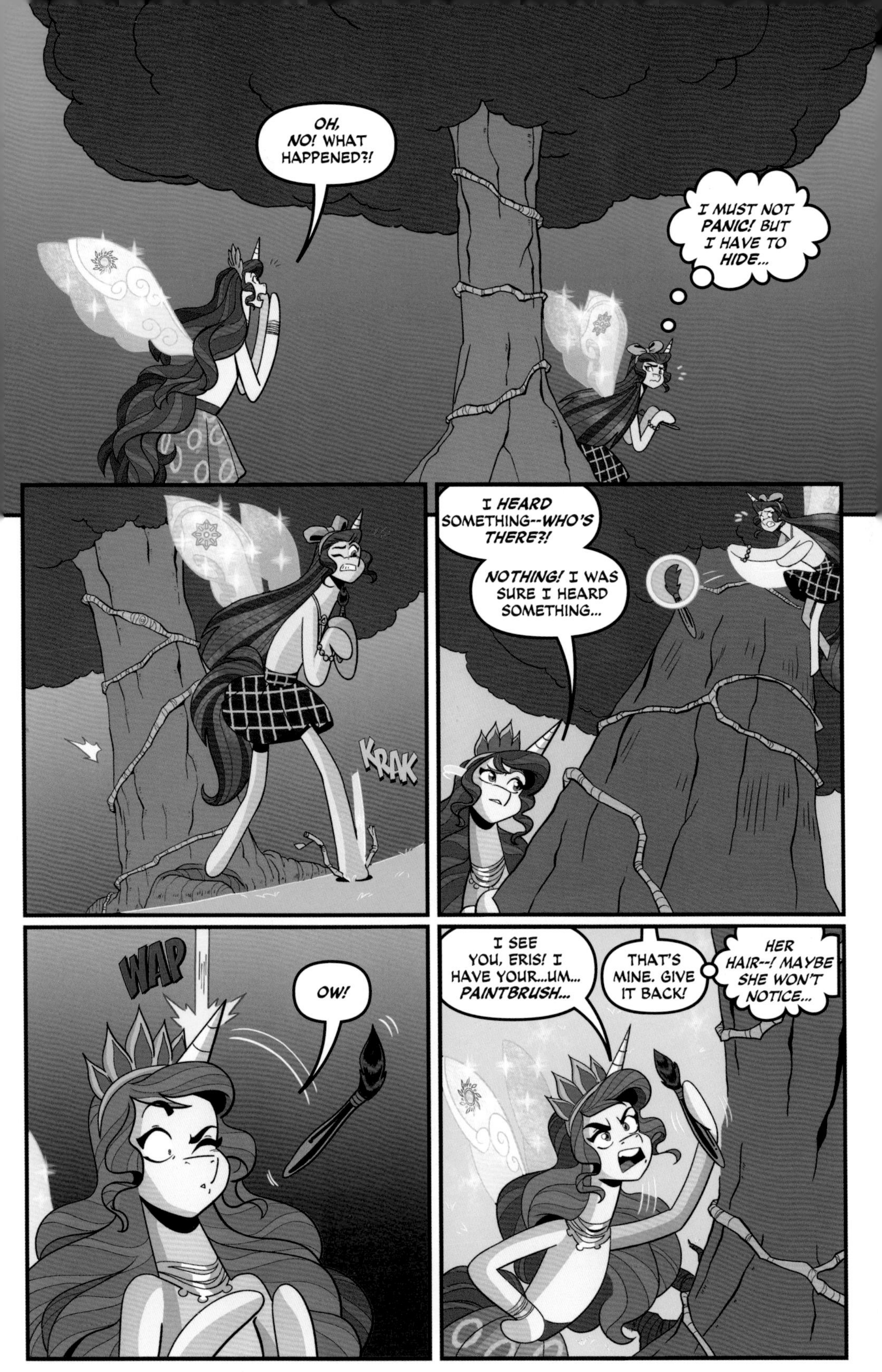
OH, NO! WHAT HAPPENED?!
I MUST NOT PANIC! BUT I HAVE TO HIDE...
KRAK
I HEARD SOMETHING--WHO'S THERE?!
NOTHING! I WAS SURE I HEARD SOMETHING...
WAP
OW!
I SEE YOU, ERIS! I HAVE YOUR...UM... PAINTBRUSH...
THAT'S MINE. GIVE IT BACK!
HER HAIR--! MAYBE SHE WON'T NOTICE...

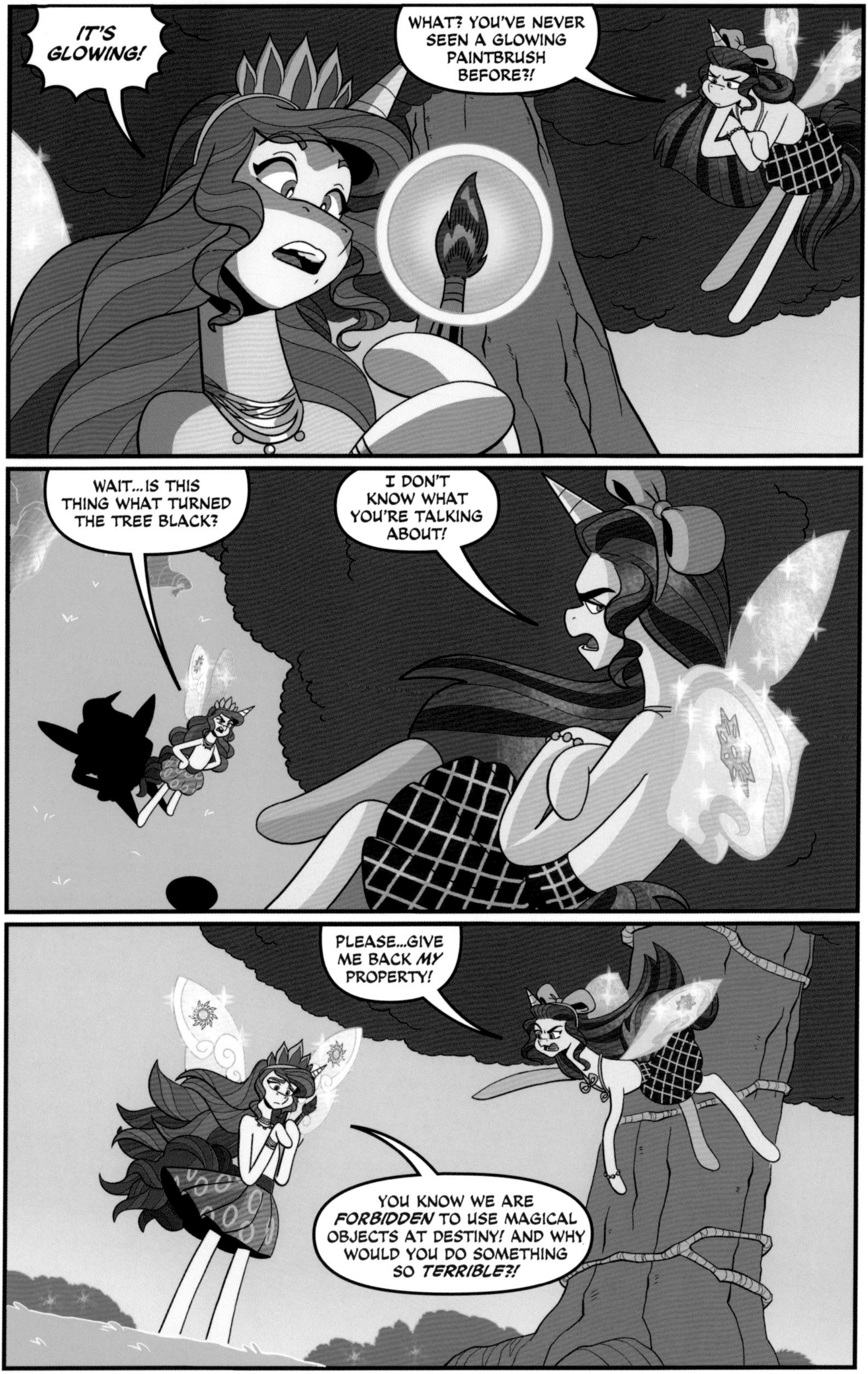
IT'S GLOWING!
WHAT? YOU'VE NEVER SEEN A GLOWING PAINTBRUSH BEFORE?!
WAIT...IS THIS THING WHAT TURNED THE TREE BLACK?
I DON'T KNOW WHAT YOU'RE TALKING ABOUT!
PLEASE...GIVE ME BACK MY PROPERTY!
YOU KNOW WE ARE FORBIDDEN TO USE MAGICAL OBJECTS AT DESTINY! AND WHY WOULD YOU DO SOMETHING SO TERRIBLE?!

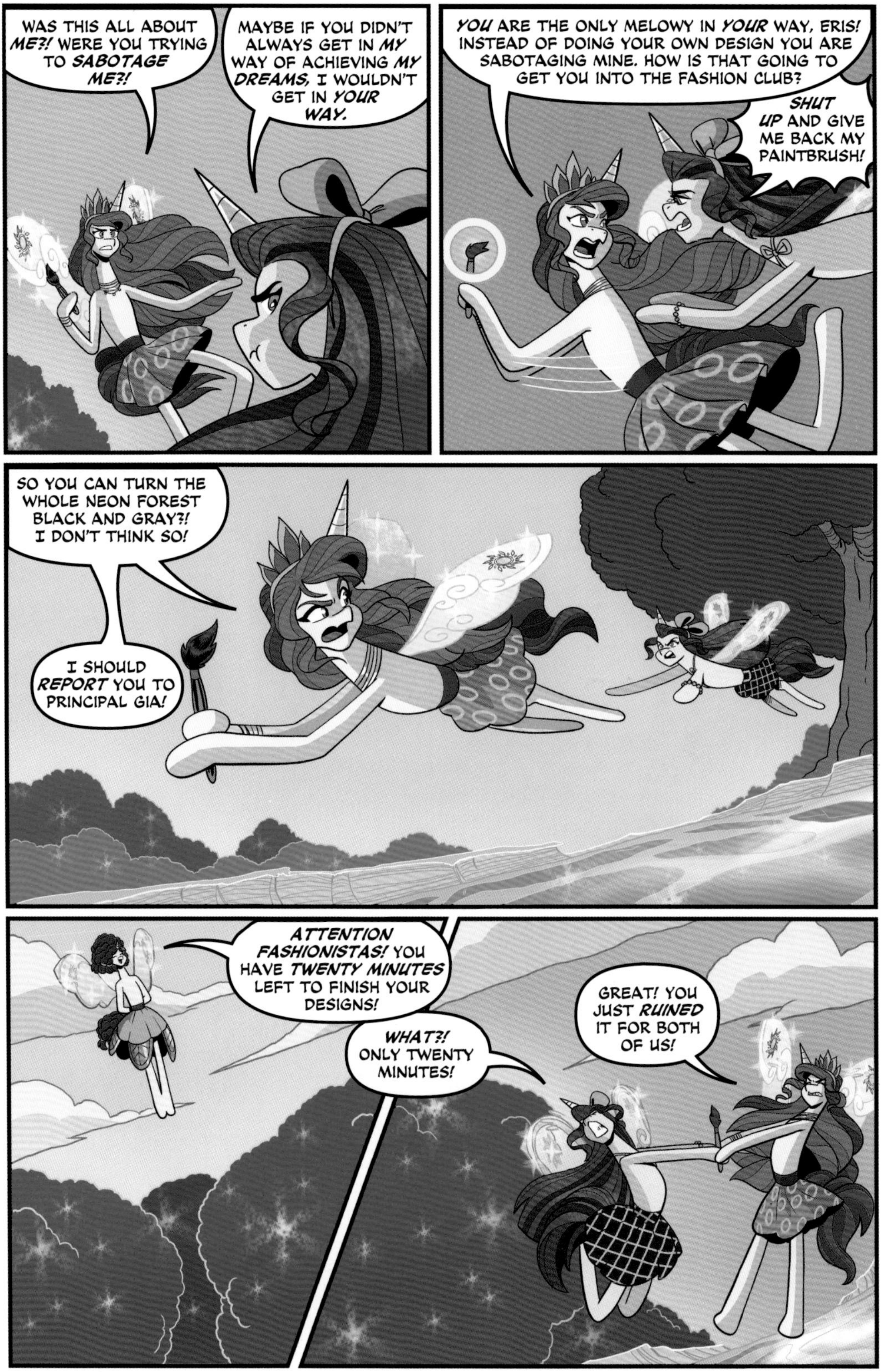
WAS THIS ALL ABOUT ME?! WERE YOU TRYING TO SABOTAGE ME?!
MAYBE IF YOU DIDN'T ALWAYS GET IN MY WAY OF ACHIEVING MY DREAMS, I WOULDN'T GET IN YOUR WAY.
YOU ARE THE ONLY MELOWY IN YOUR WAY, ERIS! INSTEAD OF DOING YOUR OWN DESIGN YOU ARE SABOTAGING MINE. HOW IS THAT GOING TO GET YOU INTO THE FASHION CLUB?
SHUT UP AND GIVE ME BACK MY PAINTBRUSH!
SO YOU CAN TURN THE WHOLE NEON FOREST BLACK AND GRAY?! I DON'T THINK SO!
I SHOULD REPORT YOU TO PRINCIPAL GIA!
ATTENTION FASHIONISTAS! YOU HAVE TWENTY MINUTES LEFT TO FINISH YOUR DESIGNS!
WHAT?! ONLY TWENTY MINUTES!
GREAT! YOU JUST RUINED IT FOR BOTH OF US!

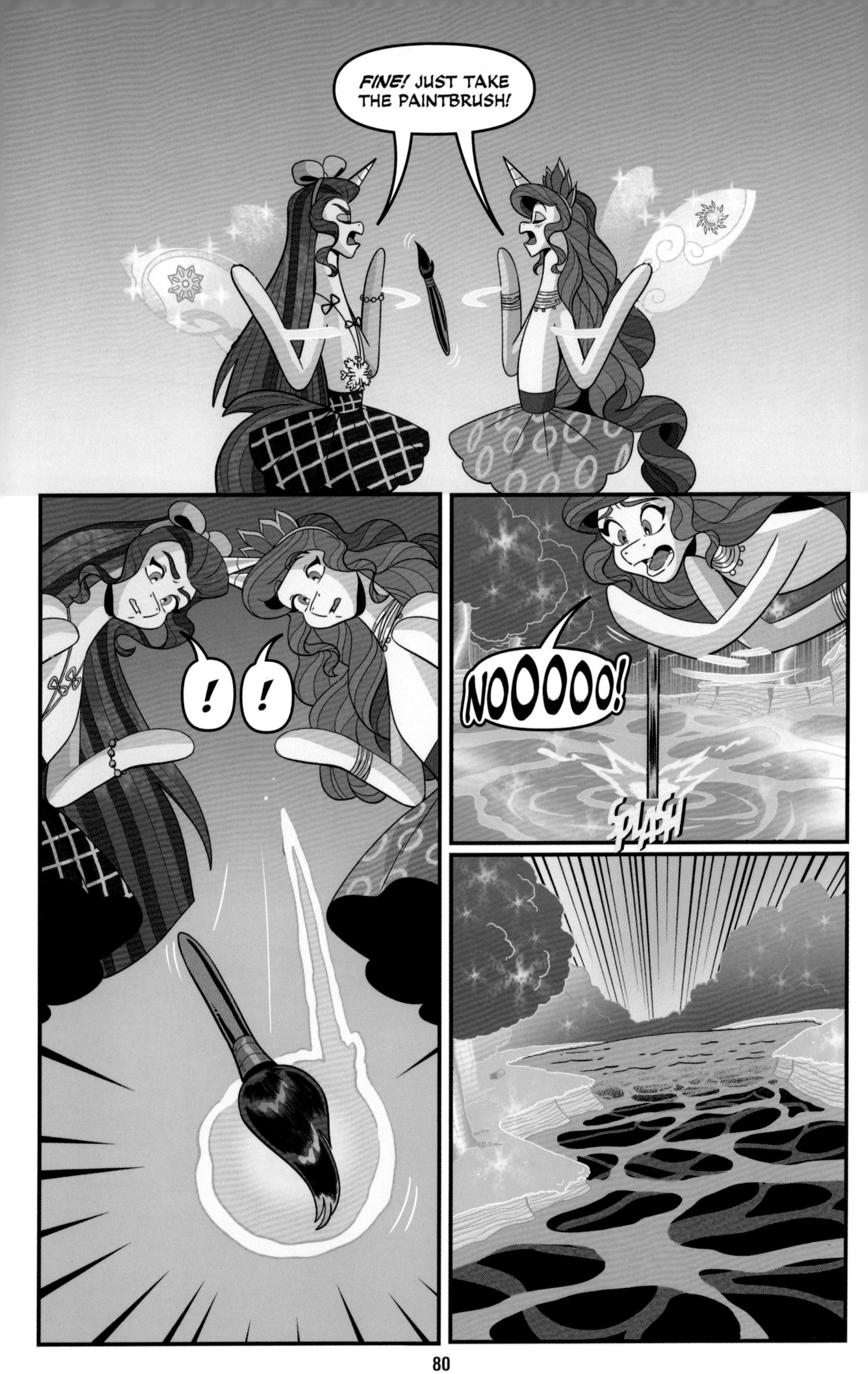
FINE! JUST TAKE THE PAINTBRUSH!
!
!
NOOOOO!
SPLASH

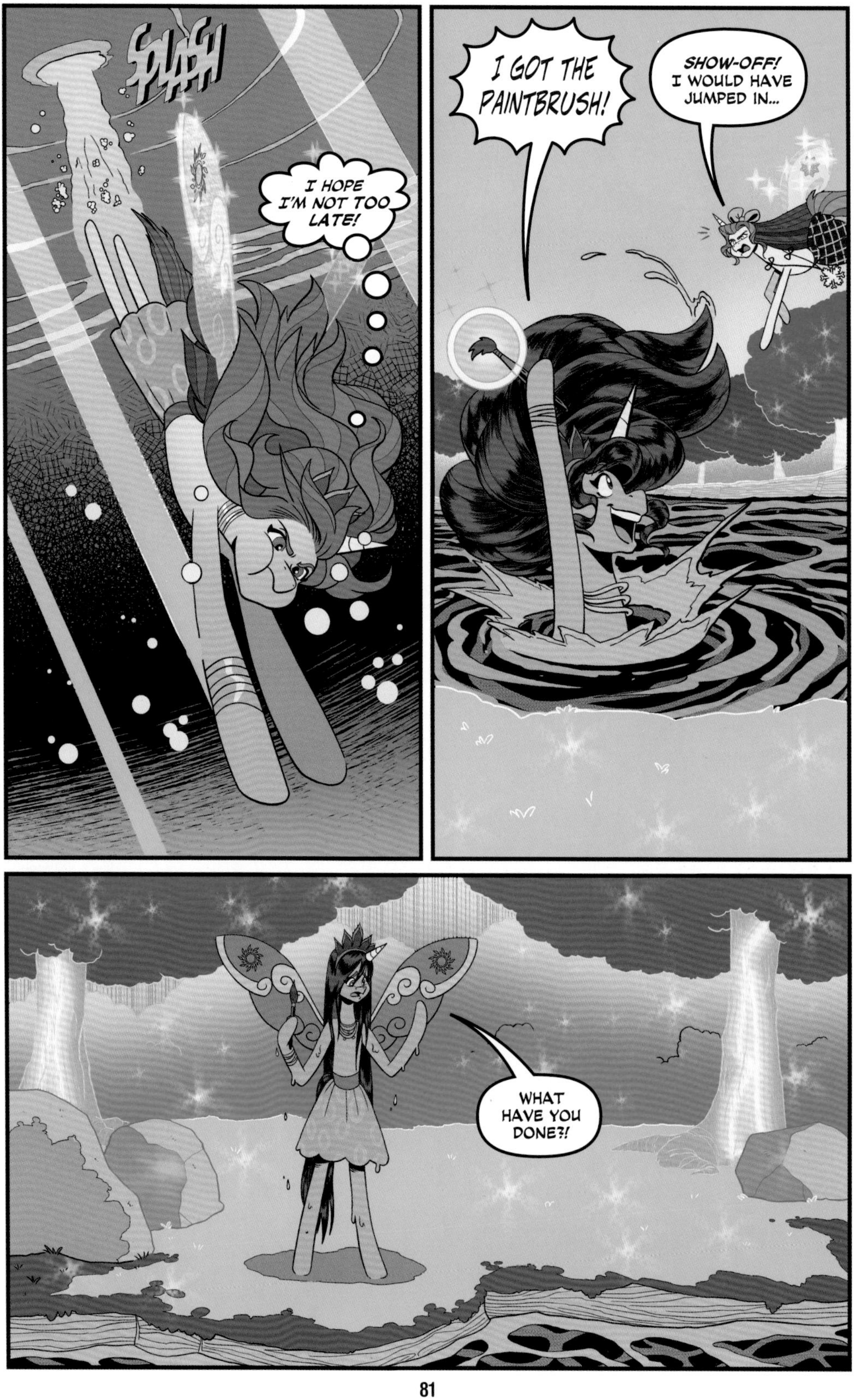
SPLASH
I HOPE I'M NOT TOO LATE!
I GOT THE PAINTBRUSH!
SHOW-OFF! I WOULD HAVE JUMPED IN...
WHAT HAVE YOU DONE?!

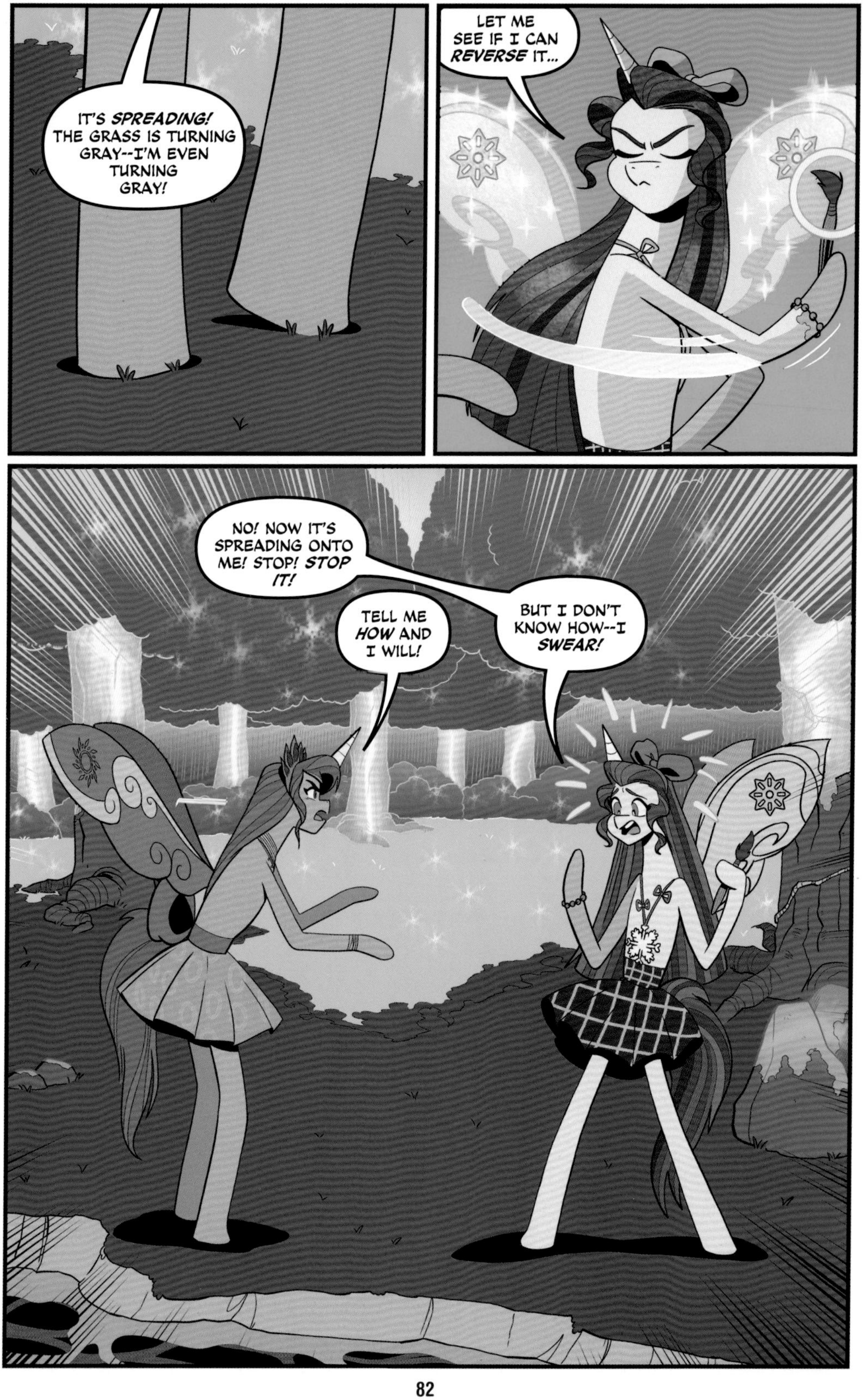
IT'S SPREADING! THE GRASS IS TURNING GRAY--I'M EVEN TURNING GRAY!
LET ME SEE IF I CAN REVERSE IT...
NO! NOW IT'S SPREADING ONTO ME! STOP! STOP IT!
BUT I DON'T KNOW HOW--I SWEAR!
TELL ME HOW AND I WILL!

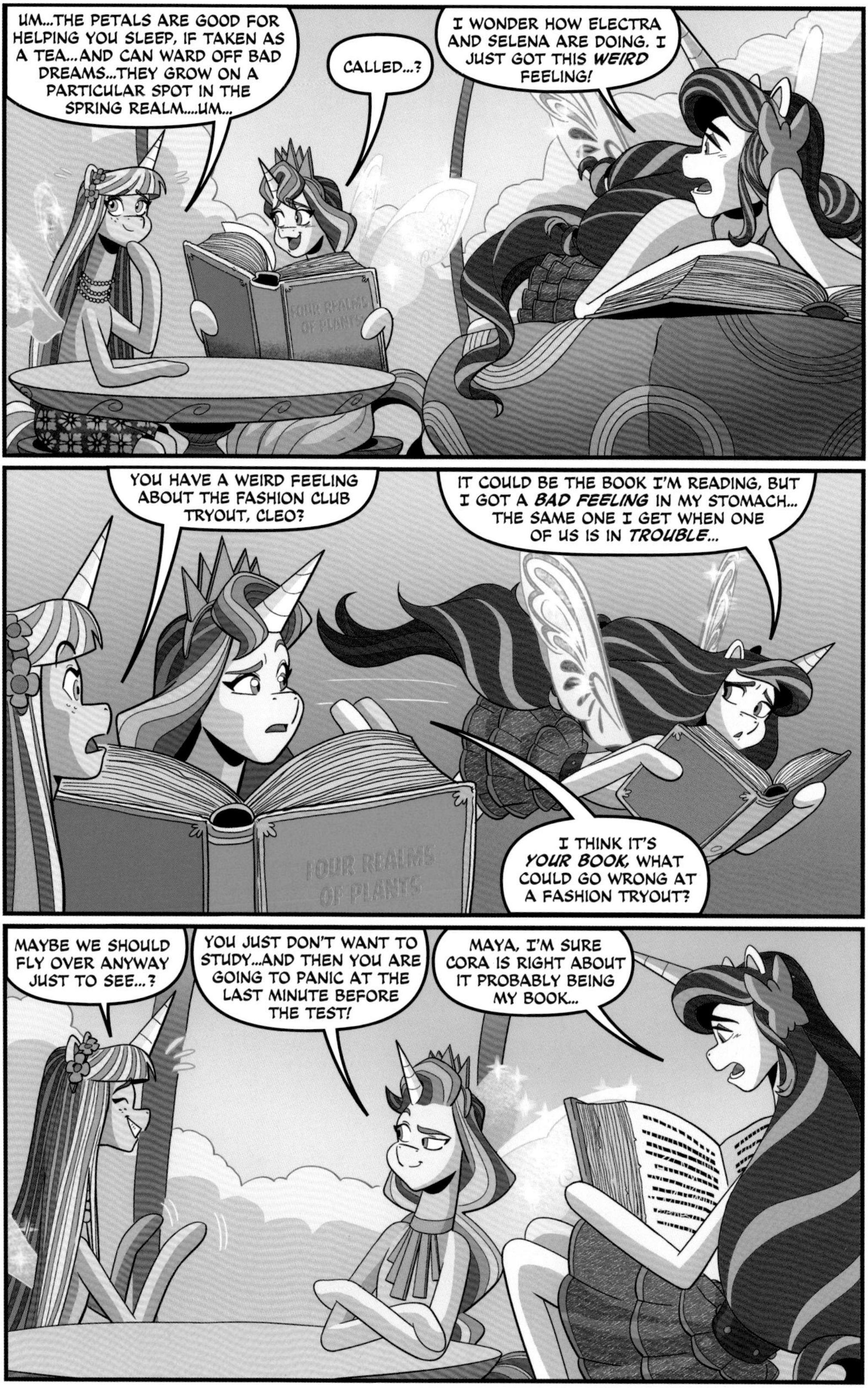
UM...THE PETALS ARE GOOD FOR HELPING YOU SLEEP, IF TAKEN AS A TEA...AND CAN WARD OFF BAD DREAMS...THEY GROW ON A PARTICULAR SPOT IN THE SPRING REALM....UM...
CALLED...?
I WONDER HOW ELECTRA AND SELENA ARE DOING. I JUST GOT THIS *WEIRD* FEELING!
FOUR REALMS OF PLANTS
YOU HAVE A WEIRD FEELING ABOUT THE FASHION CLUB TRYOUT, CLEO?
IT COULD BE THE BOOK I'M READING, BUT I GOT A *BAD FEELING* IN MY STOMACH... THE SAME ONE I GET WHEN ONE OF US IS IN *TROUBLE*...
I THINK IT'S *YOUR BOOK*, WHAT COULD GO WRONG AT A FASHION TRYOUT?
FOUR REALMS OF PLANTS
MAYBE WE SHOULD FLY OVER ANYWAY JUST TO SEE...?
YOU JUST DON'T WANT TO STUDY...AND THEN YOU ARE GOING TO PANIC AT THE LAST MINUTE BEFORE THE TEST!
MAYA, I'M SURE CORA IS RIGHT ABOUT IT PROBABLY BEING MY BOOK...

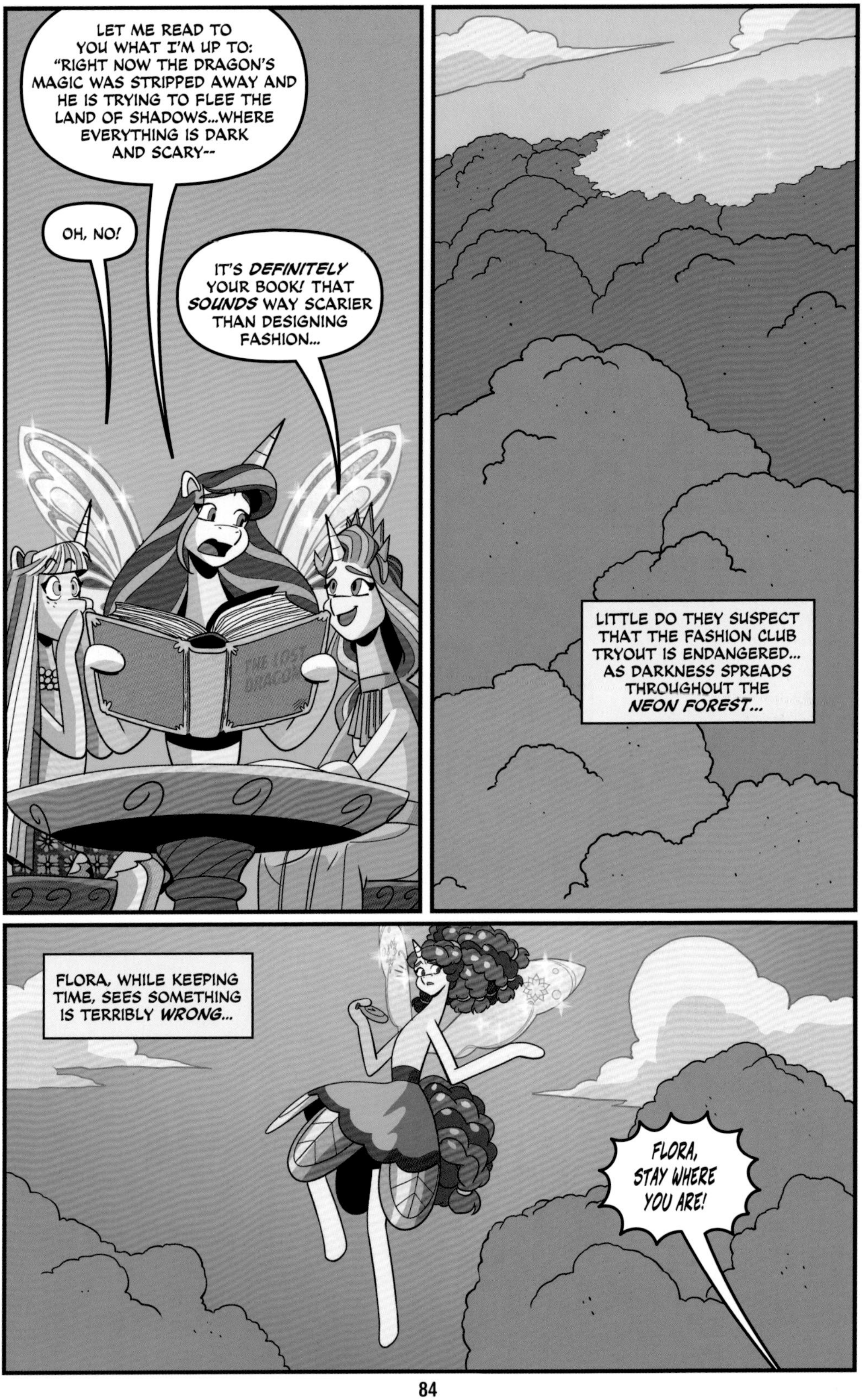
LET ME READ TO YOU WHAT I'M UP TO: "RIGHT NOW THE DRAGON'S MAGIC WAS STRIPPED AWAY AND HE IS TRYING TO FLEE THE LAND OF SHADOWS...WHERE EVERYTHING IS DARK AND SCARY--
OH, NO!
IT'S *DEFINITELY* YOUR BOOK! THAT *SOUNDS* WAY SCARIER THAN DESIGNING FASHION...
THE LOST DRAGON
LITTLE DO THEY SUSPECT THAT THE FASHION CLUB TRYOUT IS ENDANGERED... AS DARKNESS SPREADS THROUGHOUT THE *NEON FOREST*...
FLORA, WHILE KEEPING TIME, SEES SOMETHING IS TERRIBLY *WRONG*...
FLORA, STAY WHERE YOU ARE!

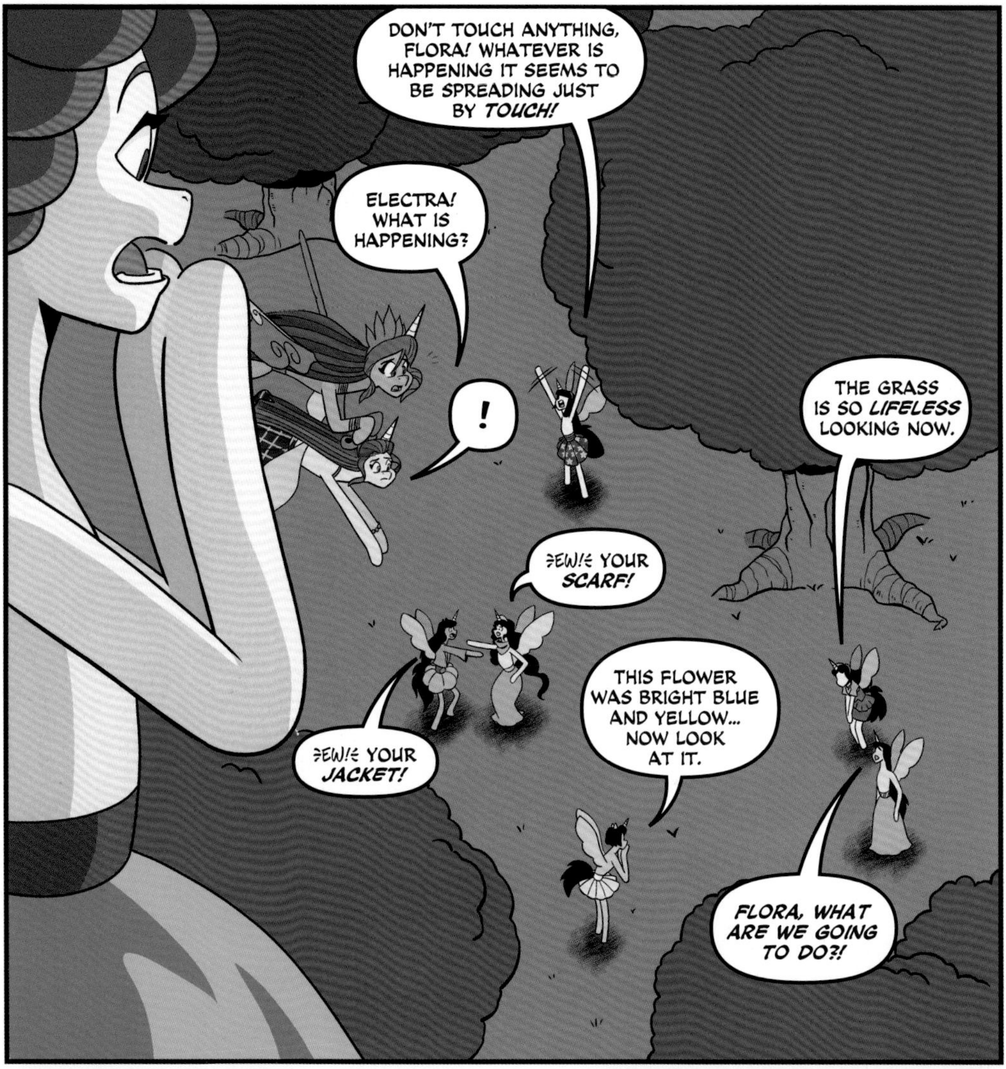
DON'T TOUCH ANYTHING, FLORA! WHATEVER IS HAPPENING IT SEEMS TO BE SPREADING JUST BY *TOUCH!*
ELECTRA! WHAT IS HAPPENING?
!
THE GRASS IS SO *LIFELESS* LOOKING NOW.
EW! YOUR *SCARF!*
EW! YOUR *JACKET!*
THIS FLOWER WAS BRIGHT BLUE AND YELLOW... NOW LOOK AT IT.
FLORA, WHAT ARE WE GOING TO DO?!

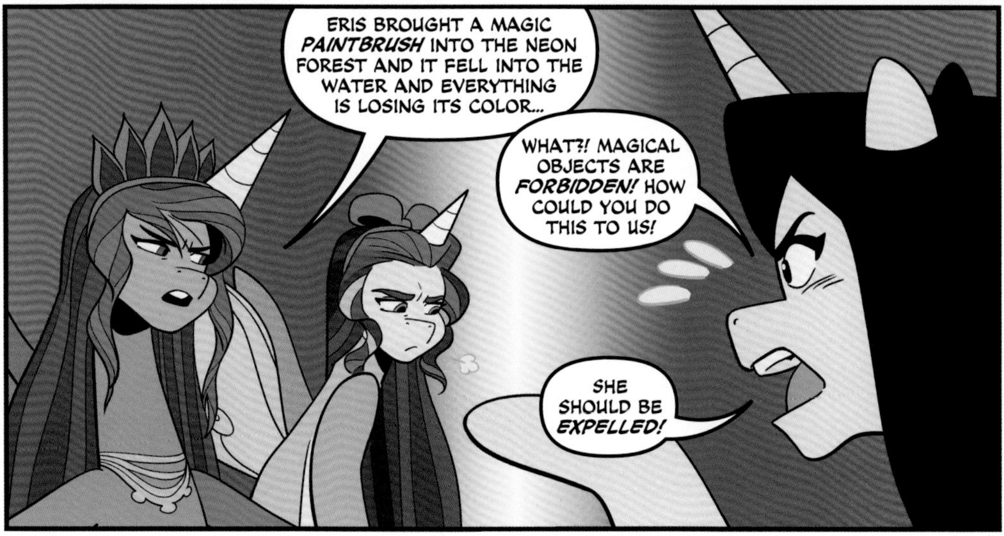
ERIS BROUGHT A MAGIC *PAINTBRUSH* INTO THE NEON FOREST AND IT FELL INTO THE WATER AND EVERYTHING IS LOSING ITS COLOR...
WHAT?! MAGICAL OBJECTS ARE *FORBIDDEN!* HOW COULD YOU DO THIS TO US!
SHE SHOULD BE *EXPELLED!*

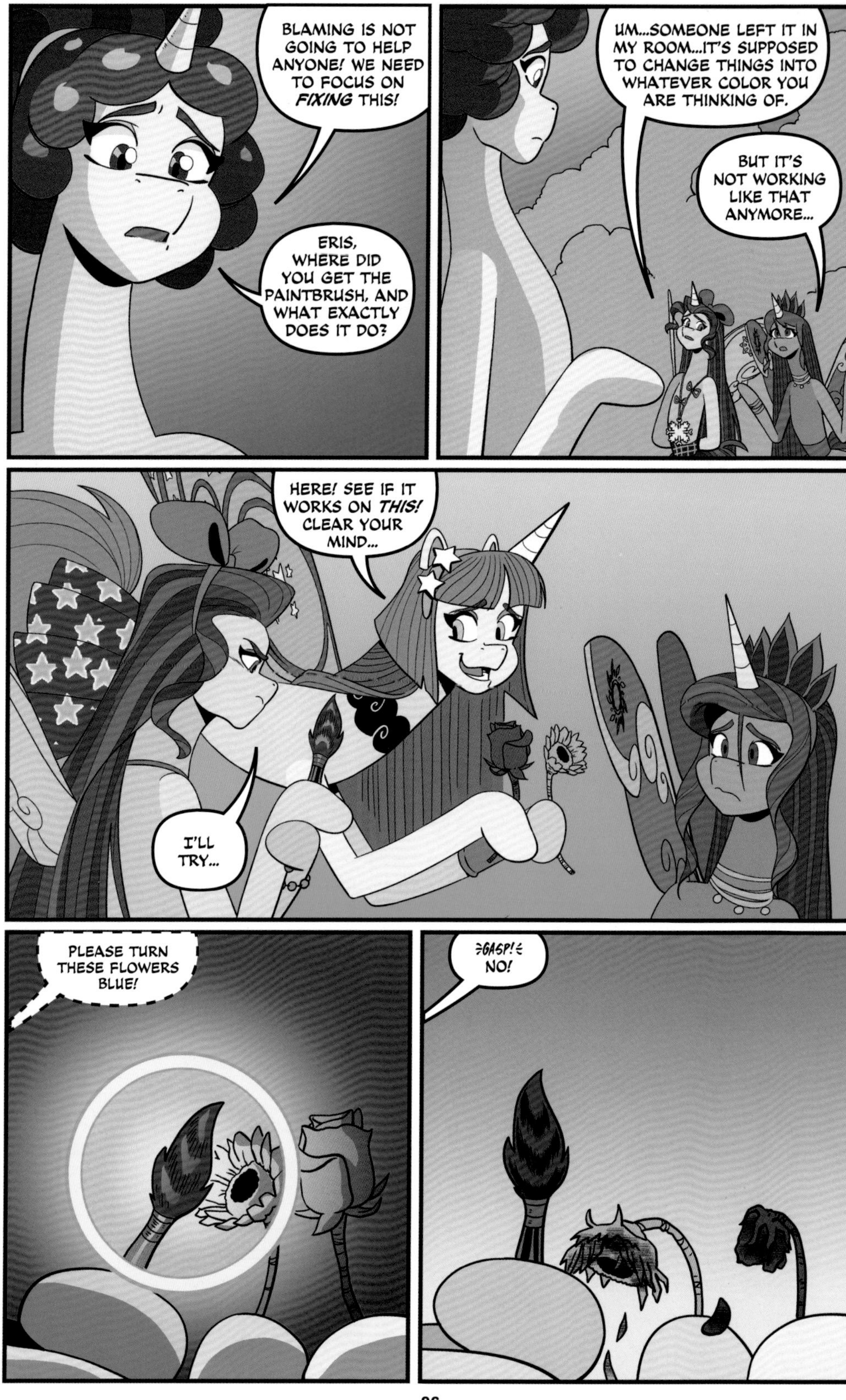
BLAMING IS NOT GOING TO HELP ANYONE! WE NEED TO FOCUS ON *FIXING* THIS!
ERIS, WHERE DID YOU GET THE PAINTBRUSH, AND WHAT EXACTLY DOES IT DO?
UM...SOMEONE LEFT IT IN MY ROOM...IT'S SUPPOSED TO CHANGE THINGS INTO WHATEVER COLOR YOU ARE THINKING OF.
BUT IT'S NOT WORKING LIKE THAT ANYMORE...
HERE! SEE IF IT WORKS ON *THIS!* CLEAR YOUR MIND...
I'LL TRY...
PLEASE TURN THESE FLOWERS BLUE!
GASP! NO!

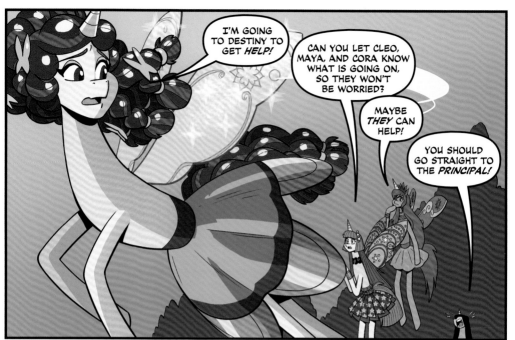

I'M GOING TO DESTINY TO GET *HELP!*

CAN YOU LET CLEO, MAYA, AND CORA KNOW WHAT IS GOING ON, SO THEY WON'T BE WORRIED?

MAYBE *THEY* CAN HELP!

YOU SHOULD GO STRAIGHT TO THE *PRINCIPAL!*

DO NOT *PANIC!* I PROMISE A *SOLUTION* IS COMING SOON!

SOON...

CORA WAS RIGHT, THIS BOOK WAS PRETTY SCARY...

MAYBE MY NEXT BOOK WILL BE ABOUT SOMETHING *HAPPIER...*

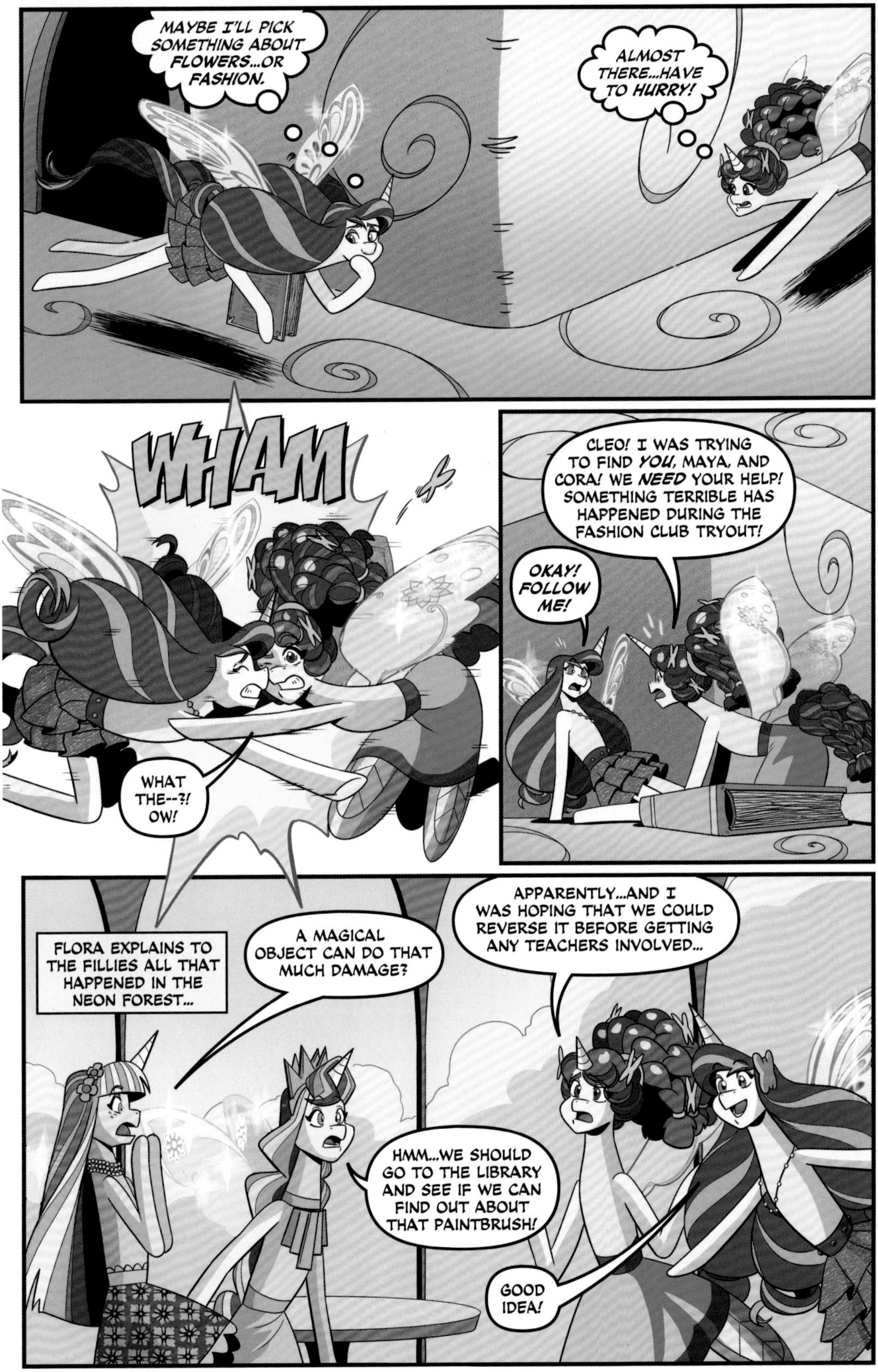
MAYBE I'LL PICK SOMETHING ABOUT FLOWERS...OR FASHION.
ALMOST THERE...HAVE TO HURRY!
WHAM
WHAT THE--?! OW!
CLEO! I WAS TRYING TO FIND YOU, MAYA, AND CORA! WE NEED YOUR HELP! SOMETHING TERRIBLE HAS HAPPENED DURING THE FASHION CLUB TRYOUT!
OKAY! FOLLOW ME!
FLORA EXPLAINS TO THE FILLIES ALL THAT HAPPENED IN THE NEON FOREST...
A MAGICAL OBJECT CAN DO THAT MUCH DAMAGE?
APPARENTLY...AND I WAS HOPING THAT WE COULD REVERSE IT BEFORE GETTING ANY TEACHERS INVOLVED...
HMM...WE SHOULD GO TO THE LIBRARY AND SEE IF WE CAN FIND OUT ABOUT THAT PAINTBRUSH!
GOOD IDEA!

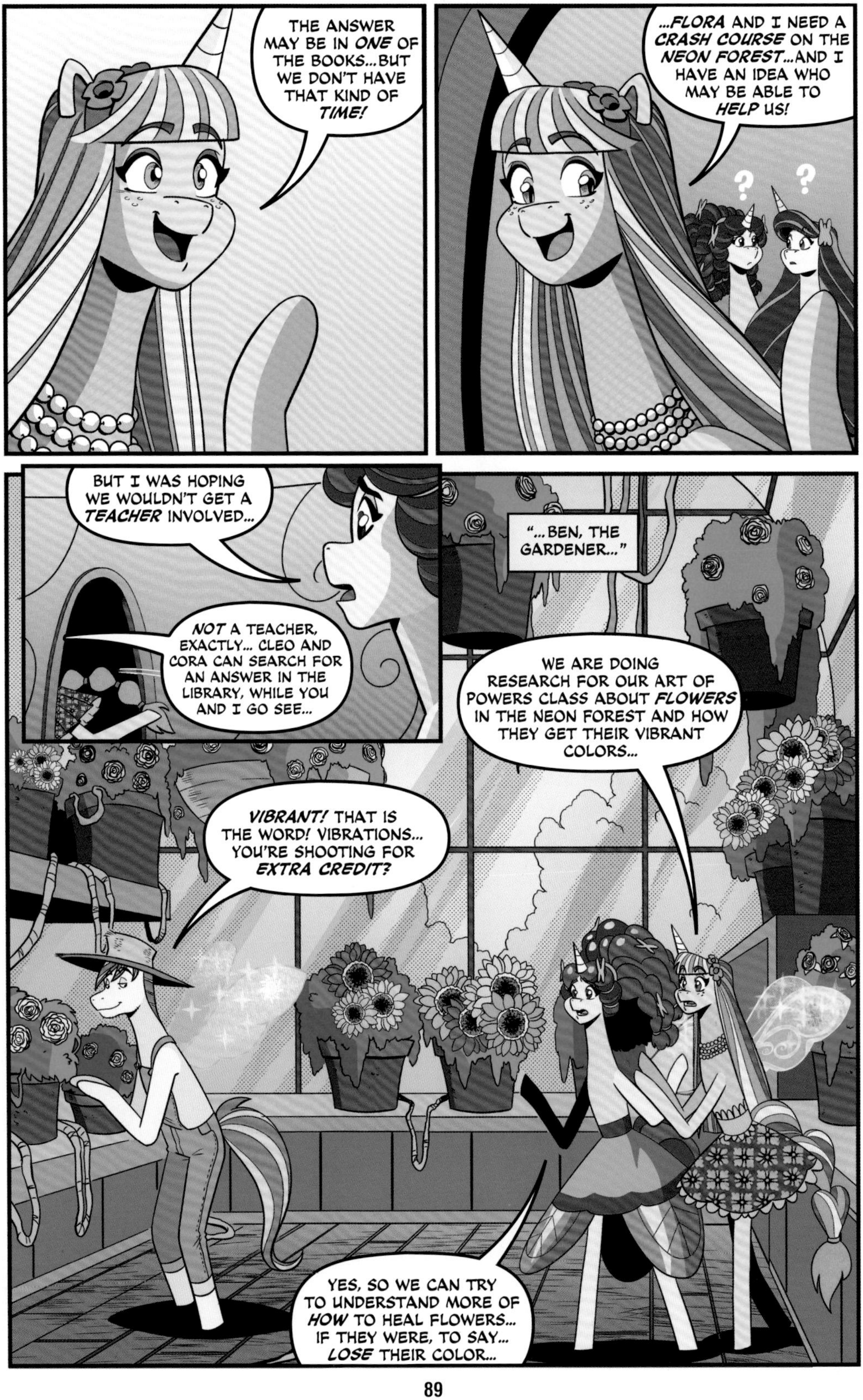
THE ANSWER MAY BE IN ONE OF THE BOOKS...BUT WE DON'T HAVE THAT KIND OF TIME!
...FLORA AND I NEED A CRASH COURSE ON THE NEON FOREST...AND I HAVE AN IDEA WHO MAY BE ABLE TO HELP US!
?
?
BUT I WAS HOPING WE WOULDN'T GET A TEACHER INVOLVED...
NOT A TEACHER, EXACTLY... CLEO AND CORA CAN SEARCH FOR AN ANSWER IN THE LIBRARY, WHILE YOU AND I GO SEE...
"...BEN, THE GARDENER..."
WE ARE DOING RESEARCH FOR OUR ART OF POWERS CLASS ABOUT FLOWERS IN THE NEON FOREST AND HOW THEY GET THEIR VIBRANT COLORS...
VIBRANT! THAT IS THE WORD! VIBRATIONS... YOU'RE SHOOTING FOR EXTRA CREDIT?
YES, SO WE CAN TRY TO UNDERSTAND MORE OF HOW TO HEAL FLOWERS... IF THEY WERE, TO SAY... LOSE THEIR COLOR...

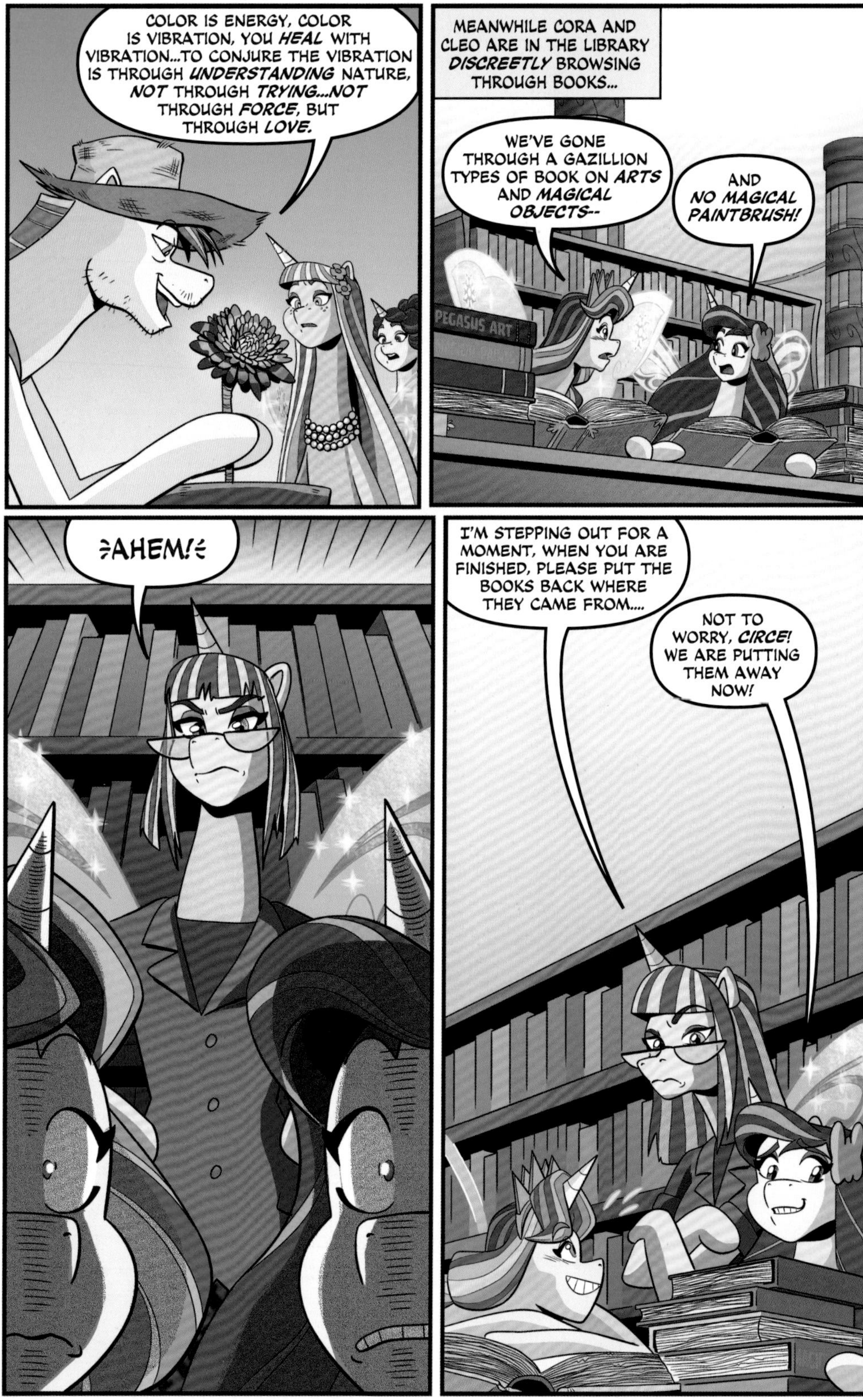
COLOR IS ENERGY, COLOR IS VIBRATION, YOU HEAL WITH VIBRATION...TO CONJURE THE VIBRATION IS THROUGH UNDERSTANDING NATURE, NOT THROUGH TRYING...NOT THROUGH FORCE, BUT THROUGH LOVE.
MEANWHILE CORA AND CLEO ARE IN THE LIBRARY DISCREETLY BROWSING THROUGH BOOKS...
WE'VE GONE THROUGH A GAZILLION TYPES OF BOOK ON ARTS AND MAGICAL OBJECTS--
AND NO MAGICAL PAINTBRUSH!
PEGASUS ART
AHEM!
I'M STEPPING OUT FOR A MOMENT, WHEN YOU ARE FINISHED, PLEASE PUT THE BOOKS BACK WHERE THEY CAME FROM....
NOT TO WORRY, CIRCE! WE ARE PUTTING THEM AWAY NOW!

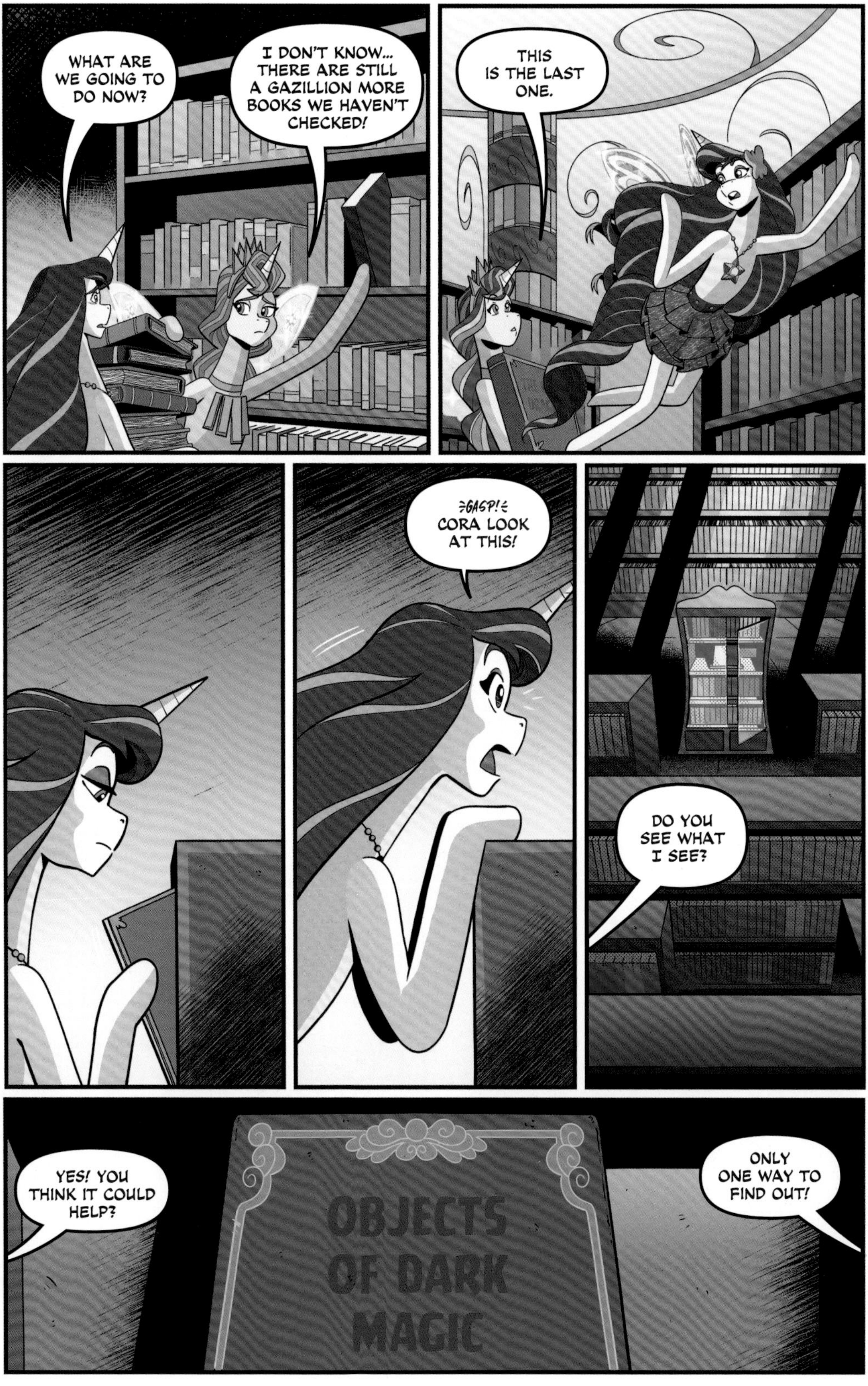
WHAT ARE WE GOING TO DO NOW?
I DON'T KNOW... THERE ARE STILL A GAZILLION MORE BOOKS WE HAVEN'T CHECKED!
THIS IS THE LAST ONE.
GASP! CORA LOOK AT THIS!
DO YOU SEE WHAT I SEE?
YES! YOU THINK IT COULD HELP?
ONLY ONE WAY TO FIND OUT!
OBJECTS OF DARK MAGIC

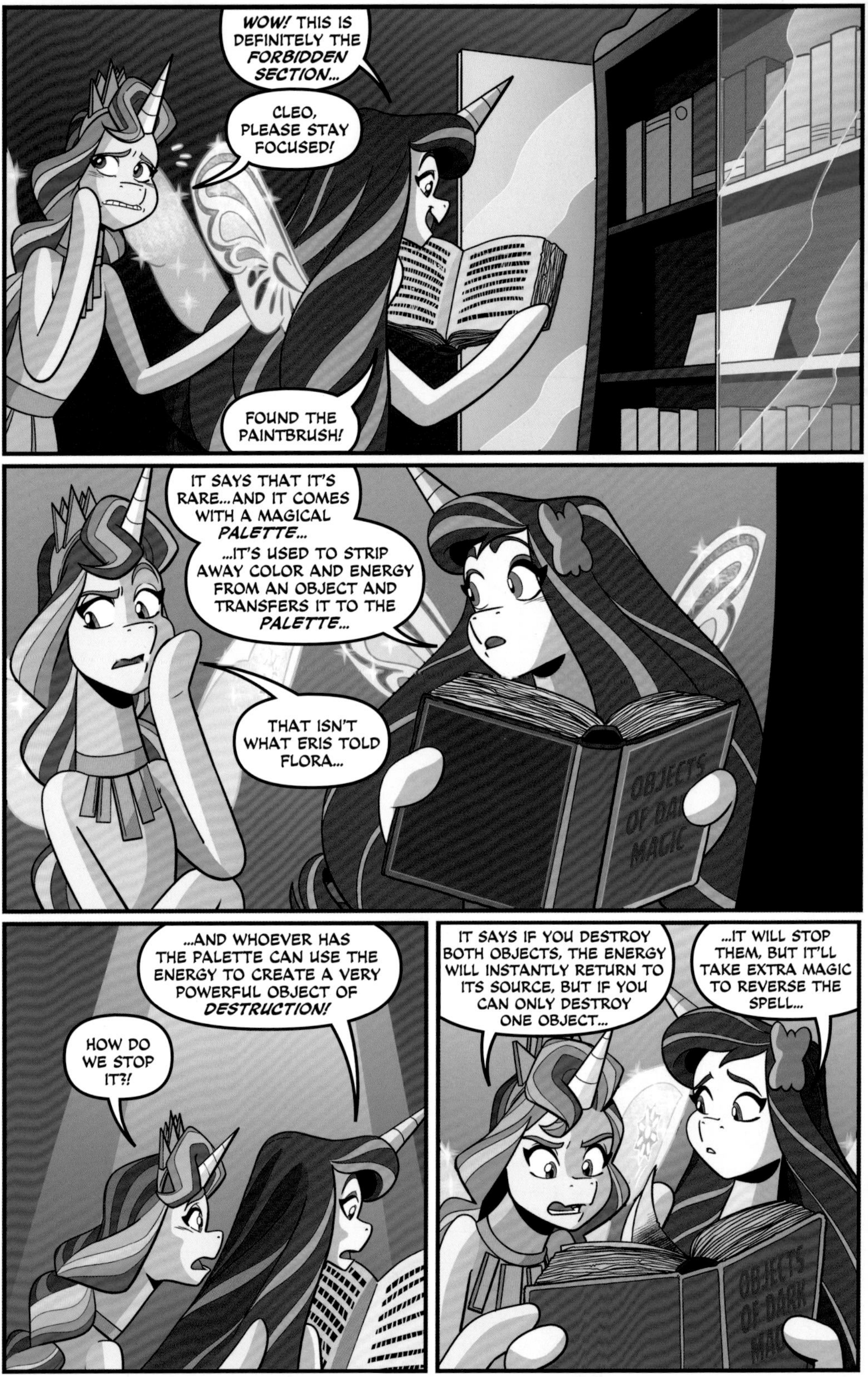
WOW! THIS IS DEFINITELY THE FORBIDDEN SECTION...
CLEO, PLEASE STAY FOCUSED!
FOUND THE PAINTBRUSH!
IT SAYS THAT IT'S RARE...AND IT COMES WITH A MAGICAL PALETTE...
...IT'S USED TO STRIP AWAY COLOR AND ENERGY FROM AN OBJECT AND TRANSFERS IT TO THE PALETTE...
THAT ISN'T WHAT ERIS TOLD FLORA...
OBJECTS OF DARK MAGIC
...AND WHOEVER HAS THE PALETTE CAN USE THE ENERGY TO CREATE A VERY POWERFUL OBJECT OF DESTRUCTION!
HOW DO WE STOP IT?!
IT SAYS IF YOU DESTROY BOTH OBJECTS, THE ENERGY WILL INSTANTLY RETURN TO ITS SOURCE, BUT IF YOU CAN ONLY DESTROY ONE OBJECT...
...IT WILL STOP THEM, BUT IT'LL TAKE EXTRA MAGIC TO REVERSE THE SPELL...

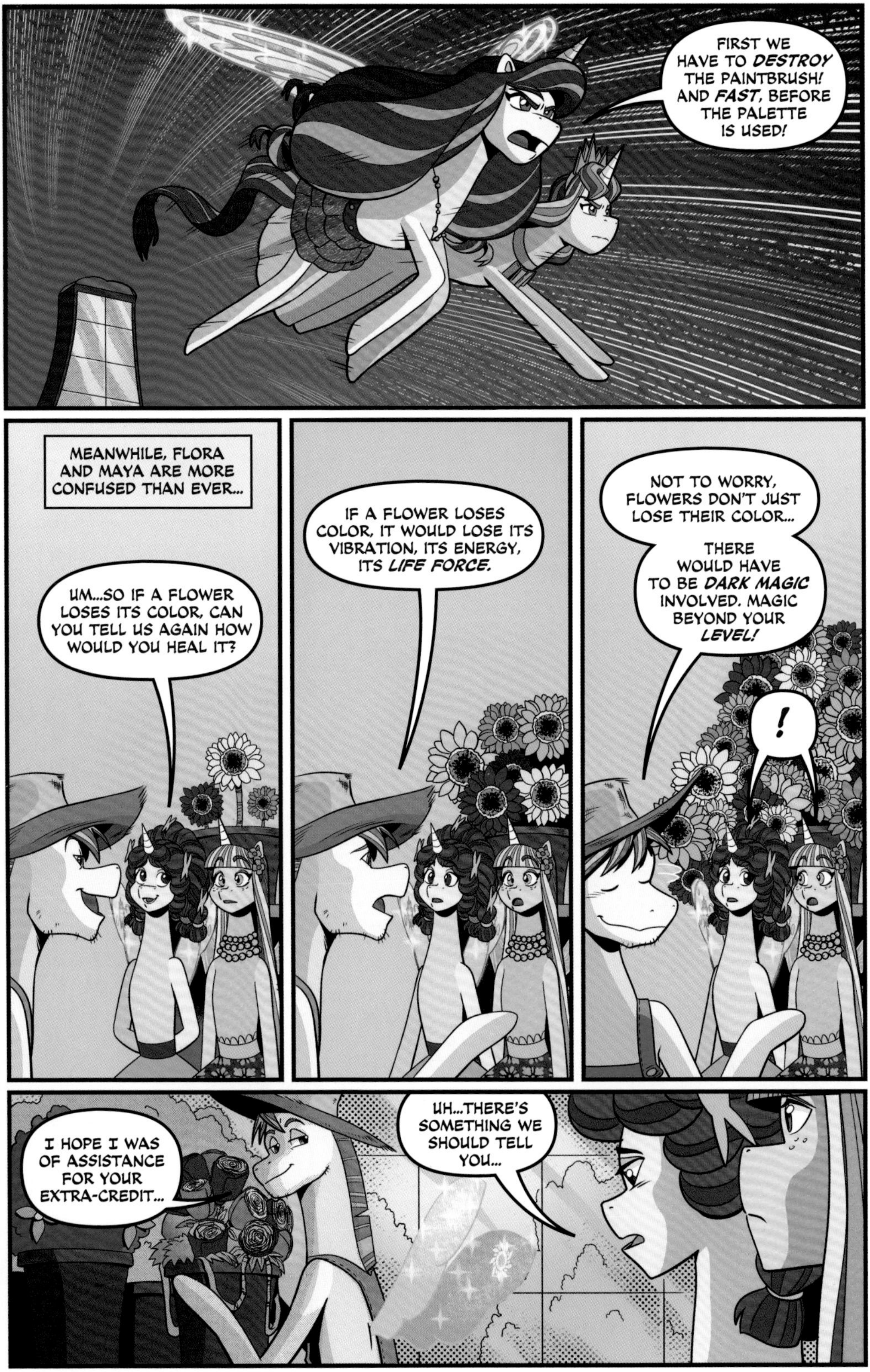

FIRST WE HAVE TO *DESTROY* THE PAINTBRUSH! AND *FAST*, BEFORE THE PALETTE IS USED!
MEANWHILE, FLORA AND MAYA ARE MORE CONFUSED THAN EVER...
UM...SO IF A FLOWER LOSES ITS COLOR, CAN YOU TELL US AGAIN HOW WOULD YOU HEAL IT?
IF A FLOWER LOSES COLOR, IT WOULD LOSE ITS VIBRATION, ITS ENERGY, ITS *LIFE FORCE.*
NOT TO WORRY, FLOWERS DON'T JUST LOSE THEIR COLOR...
THERE WOULD HAVE TO BE *DARK MAGIC* INVOLVED. MAGIC BEYOND YOUR *LEVEL!*
!
I HOPE I WAS OF ASSISTANCE FOR YOUR EXTRA-CREDIT...
UH...THERE'S SOMETHING WE SHOULD TELL YOU...

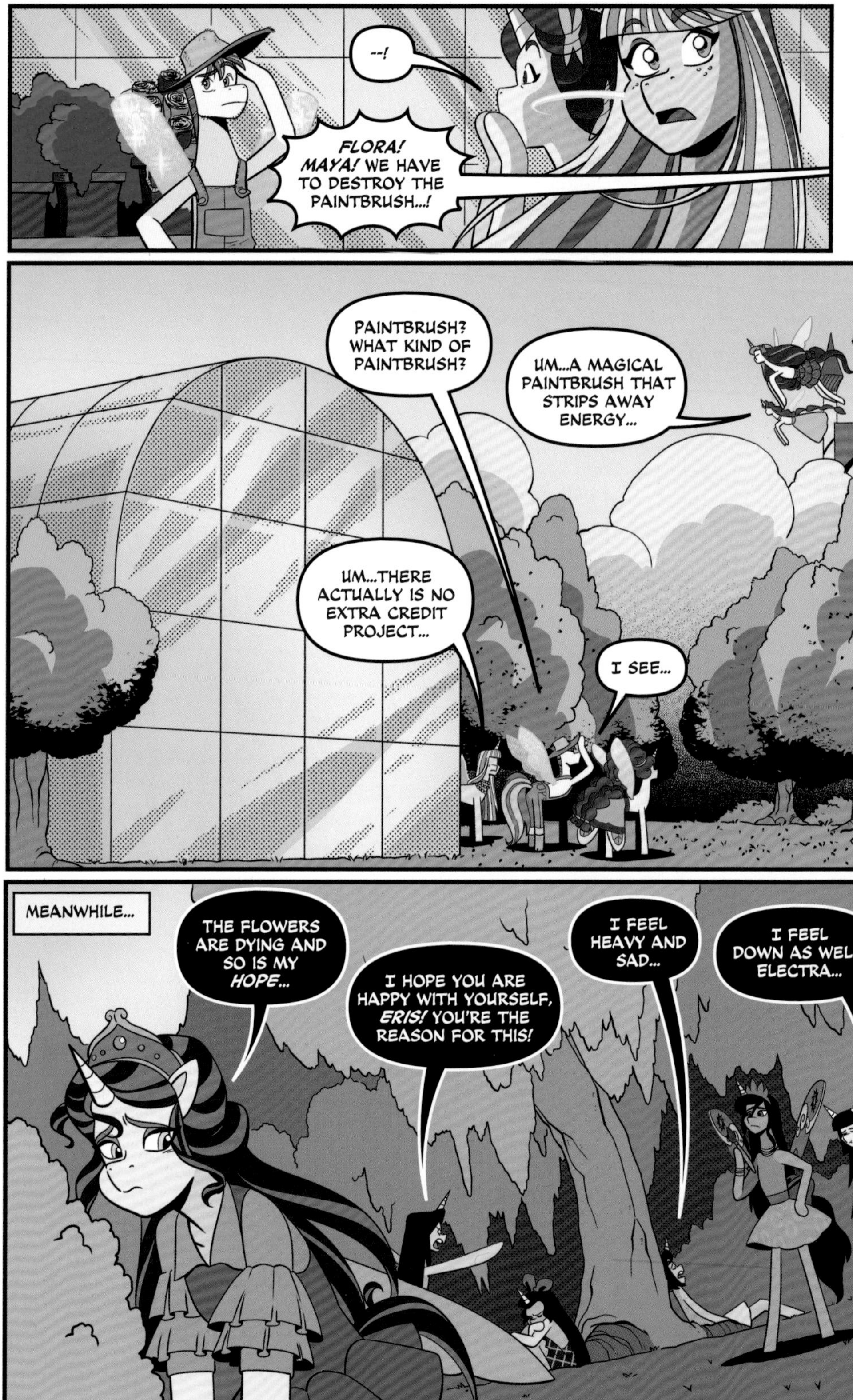
--!
FLORA! MAYA! WE HAVE TO DESTROY THE PAINTBRUSH...!
PAINTBRUSH? WHAT KIND OF PAINTBRUSH?
UM...A MAGICAL PAINTBRUSH THAT STRIPS AWAY ENERGY...
UM...THERE ACTUALLY IS NO EXTRA CREDIT PROJECT...
I SEE...
MEANWHILE...
THE FLOWERS ARE DYING AND SO IS MY HOPE...
I HOPE YOU ARE HAPPY WITH YOURSELF, ERIS! YOU'RE THE REASON FOR THIS!
I FEEL HEAVY AND SAD...
I FEEL DOWN AS WELL, ELECTRA...

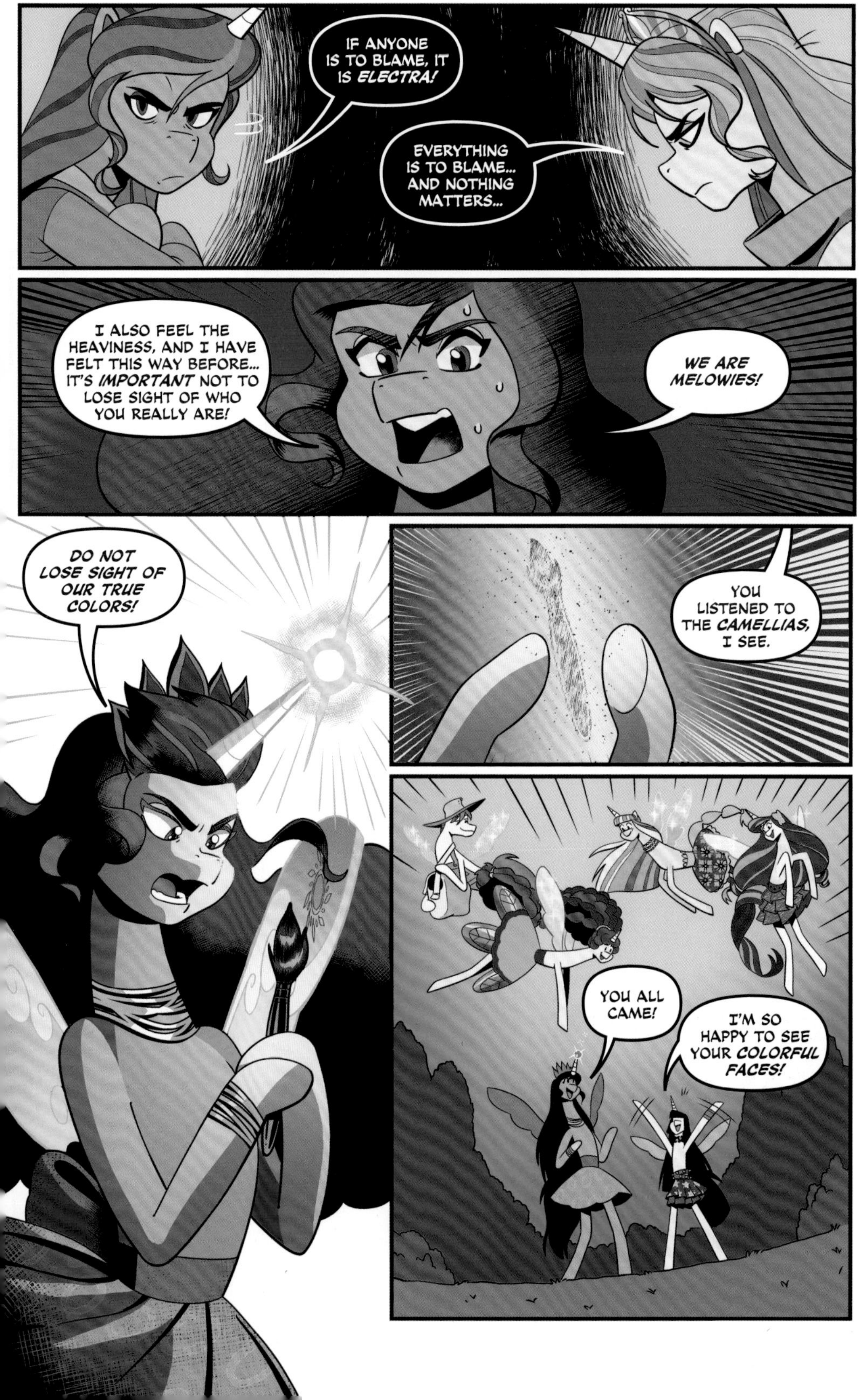
IF ANYONE IS TO BLAME, IT IS *ELECTRA!*
EVERYTHING IS TO BLAME... AND NOTHING MATTERS...
I ALSO FEEL THE HEAVINESS, AND I HAVE FELT THIS WAY BEFORE... IT'S *IMPORTANT* NOT TO LOSE SIGHT OF WHO YOU REALLY ARE!
WE ARE MELOWIES!
DO NOT LOSE SIGHT OF OUR TRUE COLORS!
YOU LISTENED TO THE *CAMELLIAS,* I SEE.
YOU ALL CAME!
I'M SO HAPPY TO SEE YOUR *COLORFUL FACES!*

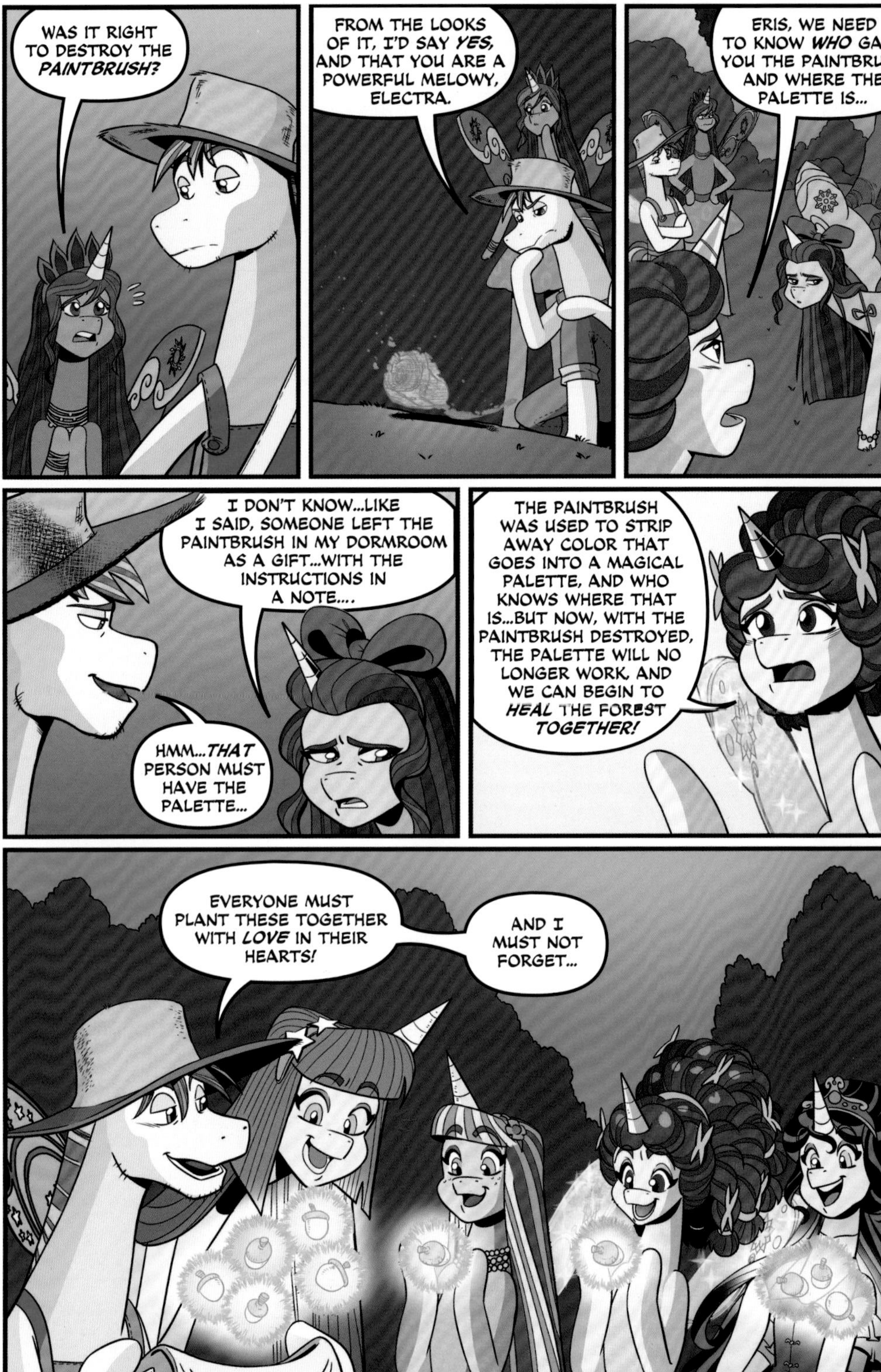
WAS IT RIGHT TO DESTROY THE PAINTBRUSH?
FROM THE LOOKS OF IT, I'D SAY YES, AND THAT YOU ARE A POWERFUL MELOWY, ELECTRA.
ERIS, WE NEED TO KNOW WHO GAVE YOU THE PAINTBRUSH AND WHERE THE PALETTE IS...
I DON'T KNOW...LIKE I SAID, SOMEONE LEFT THE PAINTBRUSH IN MY DORMROOM AS A GIFT...WITH THE INSTRUCTIONS IN A NOTE....
HMM...THAT PERSON MUST HAVE THE PALETTE...
THE PAINTBRUSH WAS USED TO STRIP AWAY COLOR THAT GOES INTO A MAGICAL PALETTE, AND WHO KNOWS WHERE THAT IS...BUT NOW, WITH THE PAINTBRUSH DESTROYED, THE PALETTE WILL NO LONGER WORK, AND WE CAN BEGIN TO HEAL THE FOREST TOGETHER!
EVERYONE MUST PLANT THESE TOGETHER WITH LOVE IN THEIR HEARTS!
AND I MUST NOT FORGET...

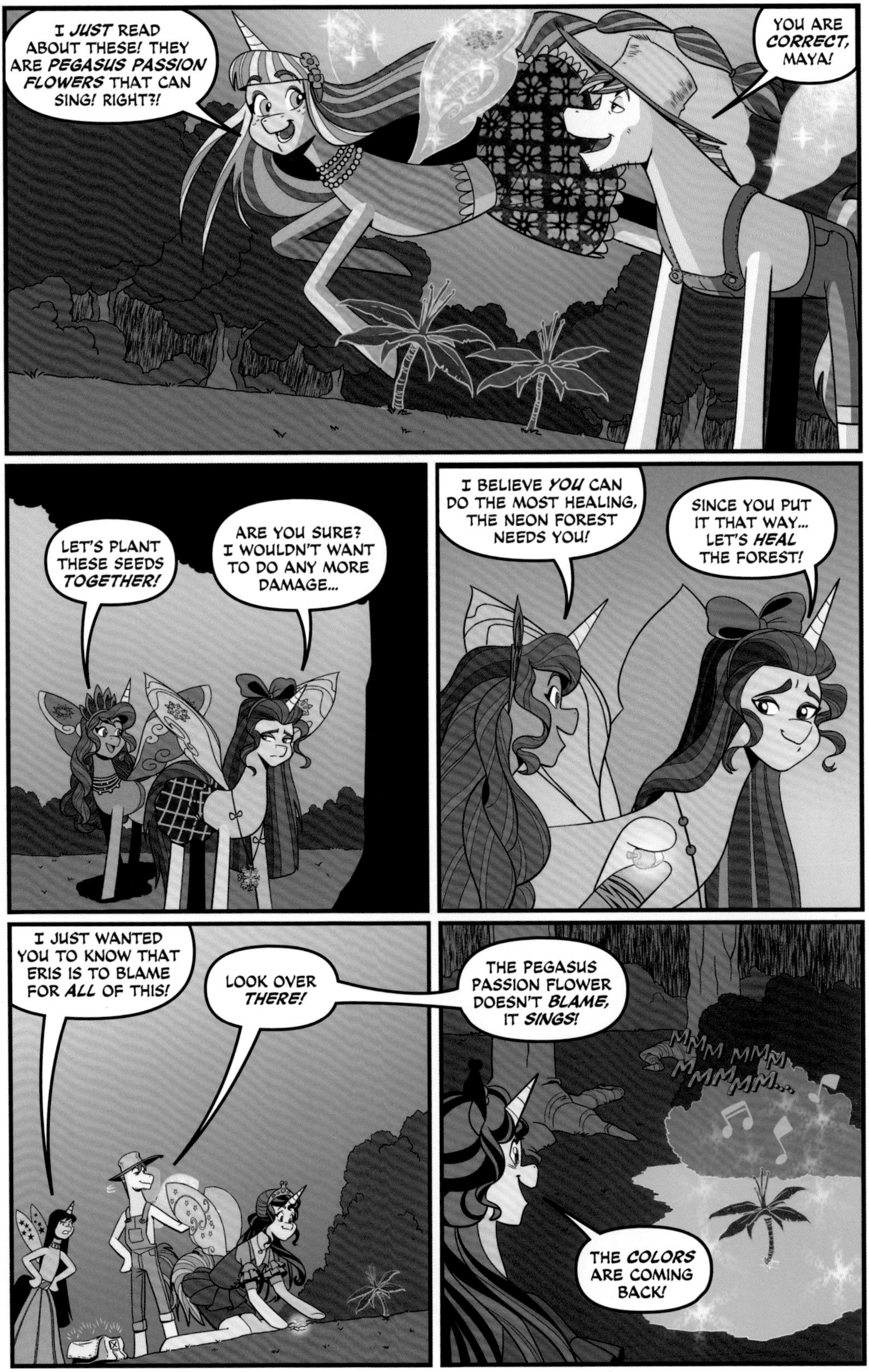
I JUST READ ABOUT THESE! THEY ARE PEGASUS PASSION FLOWERS THAT CAN SING! RIGHT?!
YOU ARE CORRECT, MAYA!
LET'S PLANT THESE SEEDS TOGETHER!
ARE YOU SURE? I WOULDN'T WANT TO DO ANY MORE DAMAGE...
I BELIEVE YOU CAN DO THE MOST HEALING, THE NEON FOREST NEEDS YOU!
SINCE YOU PUT IT THAT WAY... LET'S HEAL THE FOREST!
I JUST WANTED YOU TO KNOW THAT ERIS IS TO BLAME FOR ALL OF THIS!
LOOK OVER THERE!
THE PEGASUS PASSION FLOWER DOESN'T BLAME, IT SINGS!
MMM MMM MMMMM...
THE COLORS ARE COMING BACK!

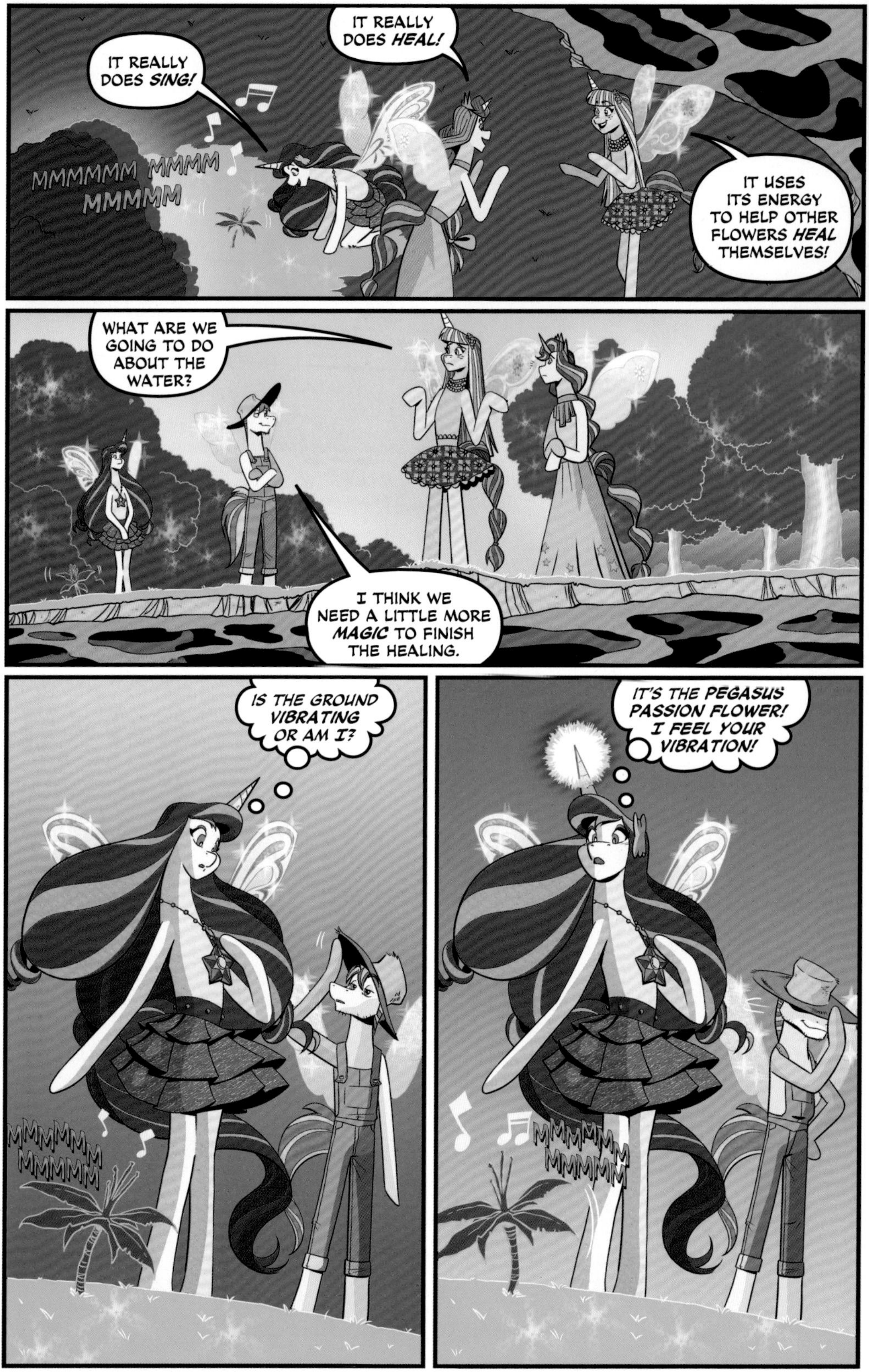
IT REALLY DOES SING!
MMMMMM MMMM MMMMM
IT REALLY DOES HEAL!
IT USES ITS ENERGY TO HELP OTHER FLOWERS HEAL THEMSELVES!
WHAT ARE WE GOING TO DO ABOUT THE WATER?
I THINK WE NEED A LITTLE MORE MAGIC TO FINISH THE HEALING.
IS THE GROUND VIBRATING OR AM I?
MMMMMM MMMMM
IT'S THE PEGASUS PASSION FLOWER! I FEEL YOUR VIBRATION!
MMMMMM MMMMM

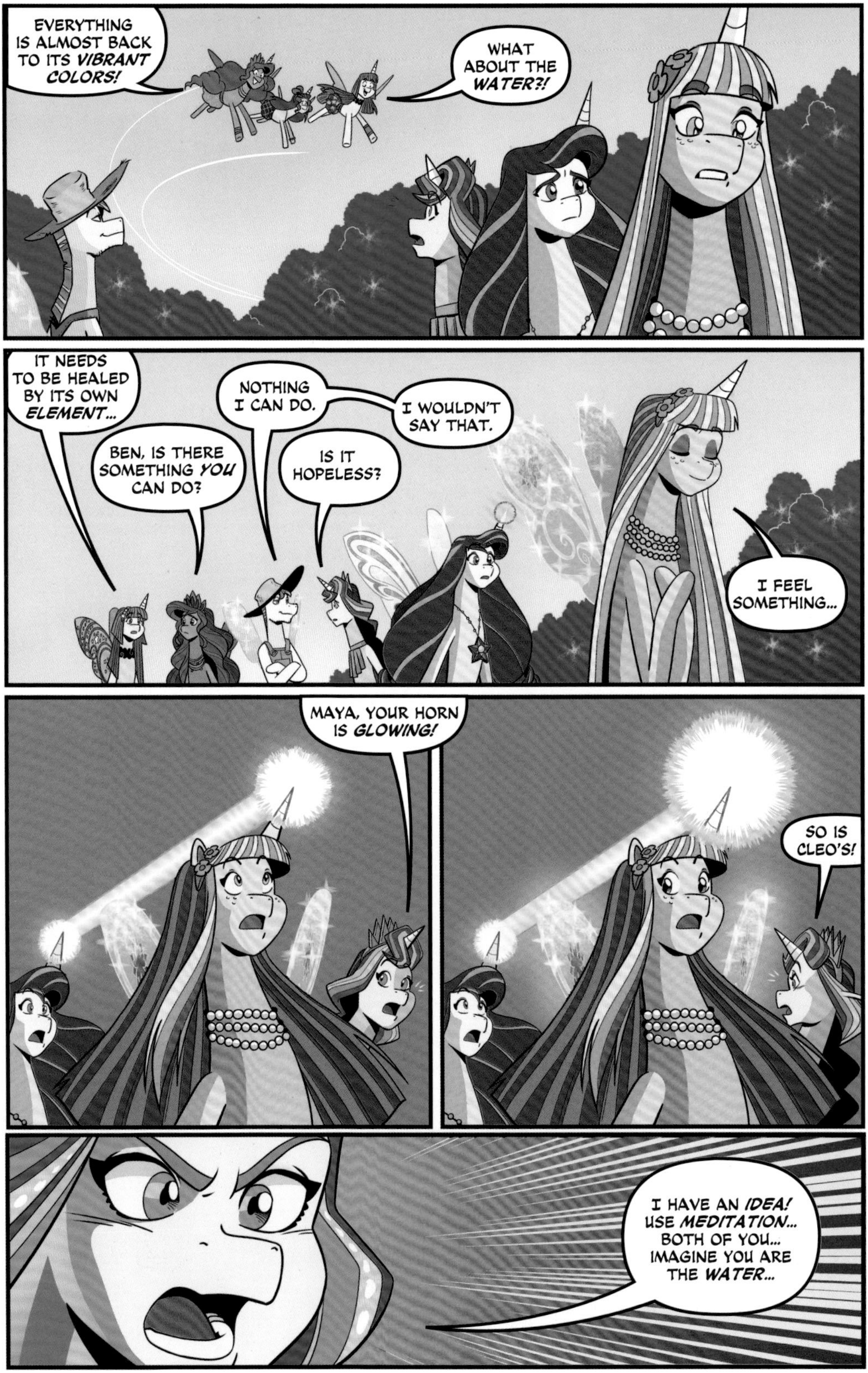
EVERYTHING IS ALMOST BACK TO ITS VIBRANT COLORS!
WHAT ABOUT THE WATER?!
IT NEEDS TO BE HEALED BY ITS OWN ELEMENT...
BEN, IS THERE SOMETHING YOU CAN DO?
NOTHING I CAN DO.
IS IT HOPELESS?
I WOULDN'T SAY THAT.
I FEEL SOMETHING...
MAYA, YOUR HORN IS GLOWING!
SO IS CLEO'S!
I HAVE AN IDEA! USE MEDITATION... BOTH OF YOU... IMAGINE YOU ARE THE WATER...

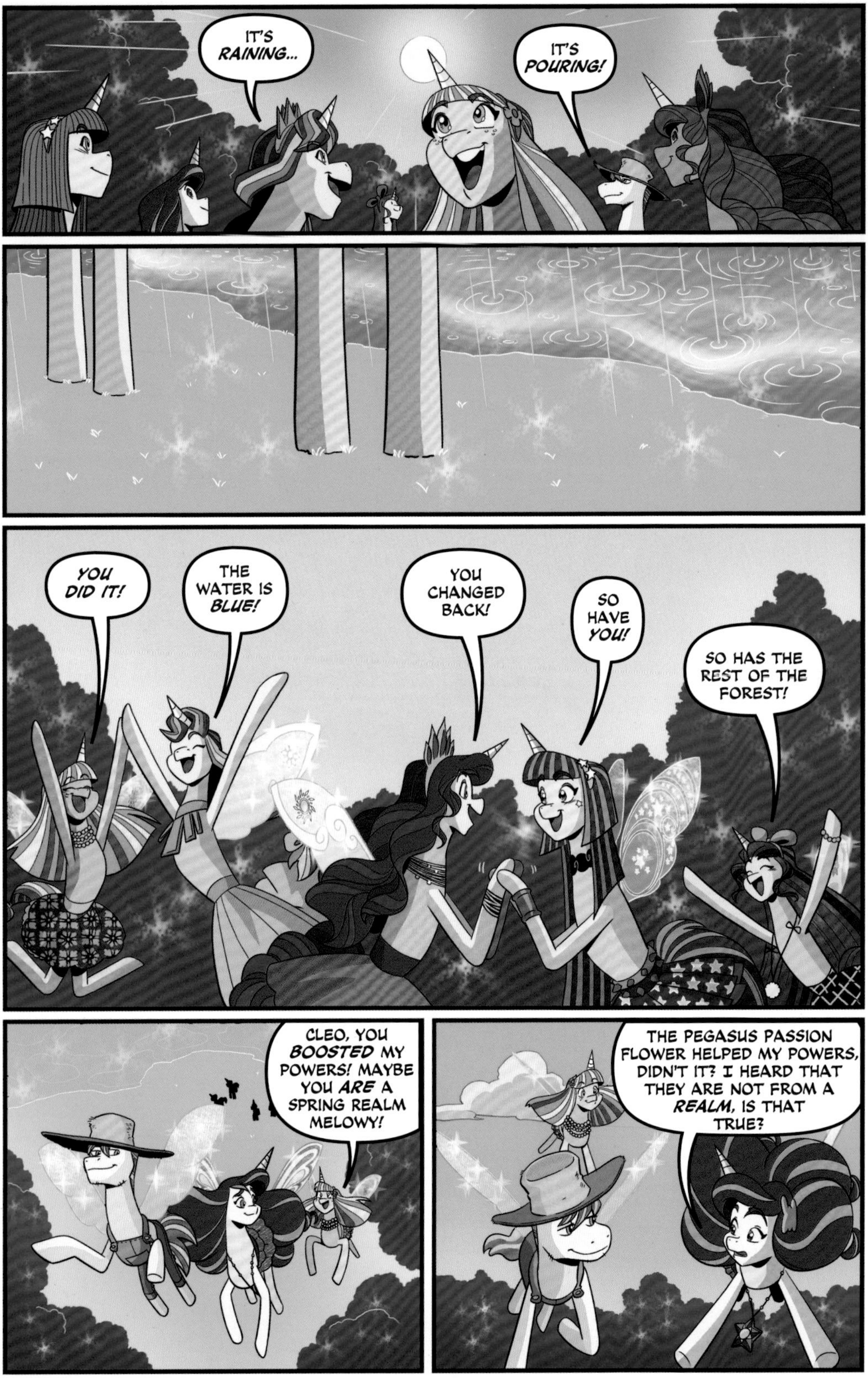
IT'S RAINING...
IT'S POURING!
YOU DID IT!
THE WATER IS BLUE!
YOU CHANGED BACK!
SO HAVE YOU!
SO HAS THE REST OF THE FOREST!
CLEO, YOU BOOSTED MY POWERS! MAYBE YOU ARE A SPRING REALM MELOWY!
THE PEGASUS PASSION FLOWER HELPED MY POWERS, DIDN'T IT? I HEARD THAT THEY ARE NOT FROM A REALM, IS THAT TRUE?

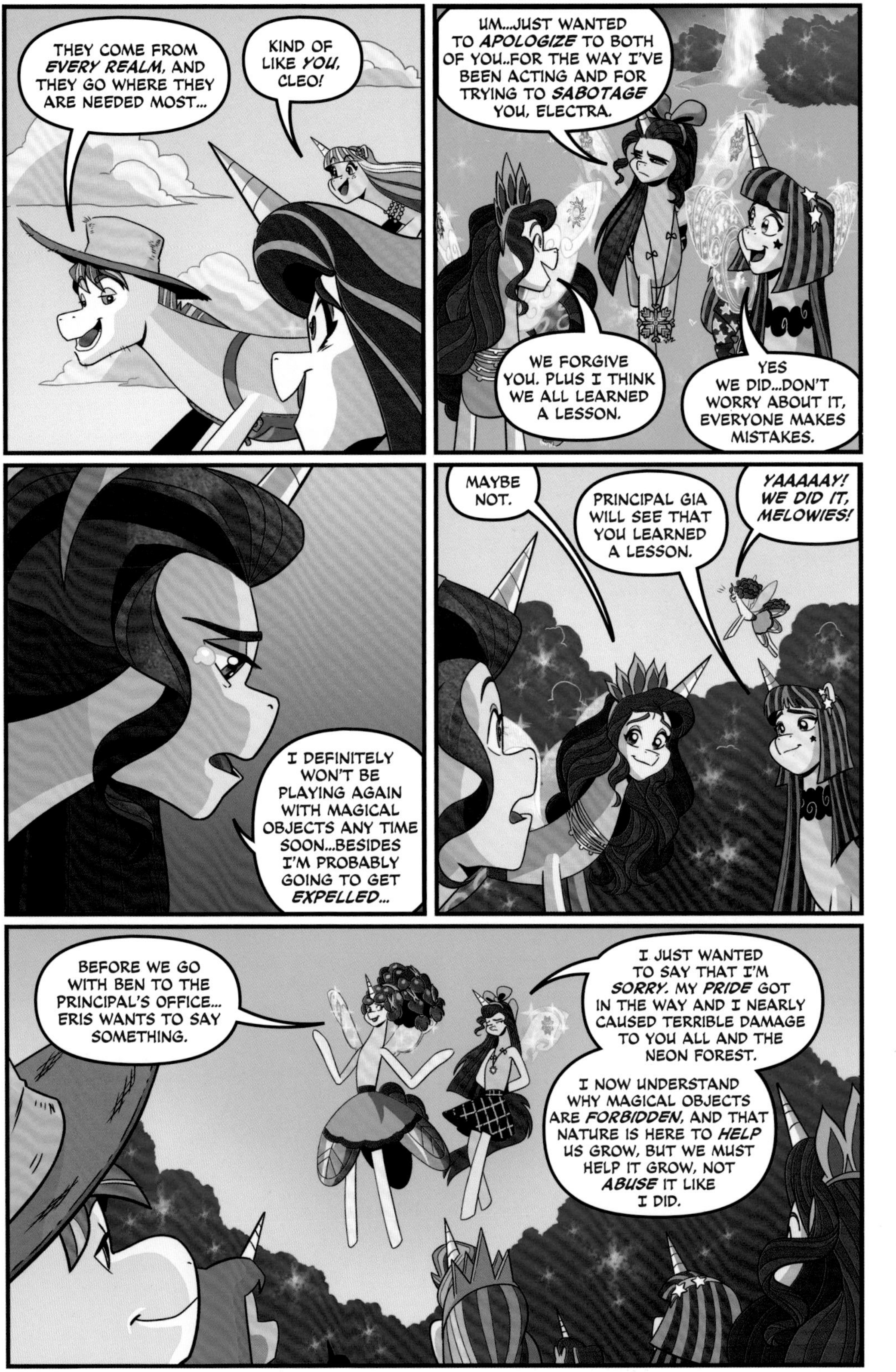

THEY COME FROM EVERY REALM, AND THEY GO WHERE THEY ARE NEEDED MOST...
KIND OF LIKE YOU, CLEO!
UM...JUST WANTED TO APOLOGIZE TO BOTH OF YOU..FOR THE WAY I'VE BEEN ACTING AND FOR TRYING TO SABOTAGE YOU, ELECTRA.
WE FORGIVE YOU. PLUS I THINK WE ALL LEARNED A LESSON.
YES WE DID...DON'T WORRY ABOUT IT, EVERYONE MAKES MISTAKES.
I DEFINITELY WON'T BE PLAYING AGAIN WITH MAGICAL OBJECTS ANY TIME SOON...BESIDES I'M PROBABLY GOING TO GET EXPELLED...
MAYBE NOT.
PRINCIPAL GIA WILL SEE THAT YOU LEARNED A LESSON.
YAAAAAY! WE DID IT, MELOWIES!
BEFORE WE GO WITH BEN TO THE PRINCIPAL'S OFFICE... ERIS WANTS TO SAY SOMETHING.
I JUST WANTED TO SAY THAT I'M SORRY. MY PRIDE GOT IN THE WAY AND I NEARLY CAUSED TERRIBLE DAMAGE TO YOU ALL AND THE NEON FOREST.
I NOW UNDERSTAND WHY MAGICAL OBJECTS ARE FORBIDDEN, AND THAT NATURE IS HERE TO HELP US GROW, BUT WE MUST HELP IT GROW, NOT ABUSE IT LIKE I DID.

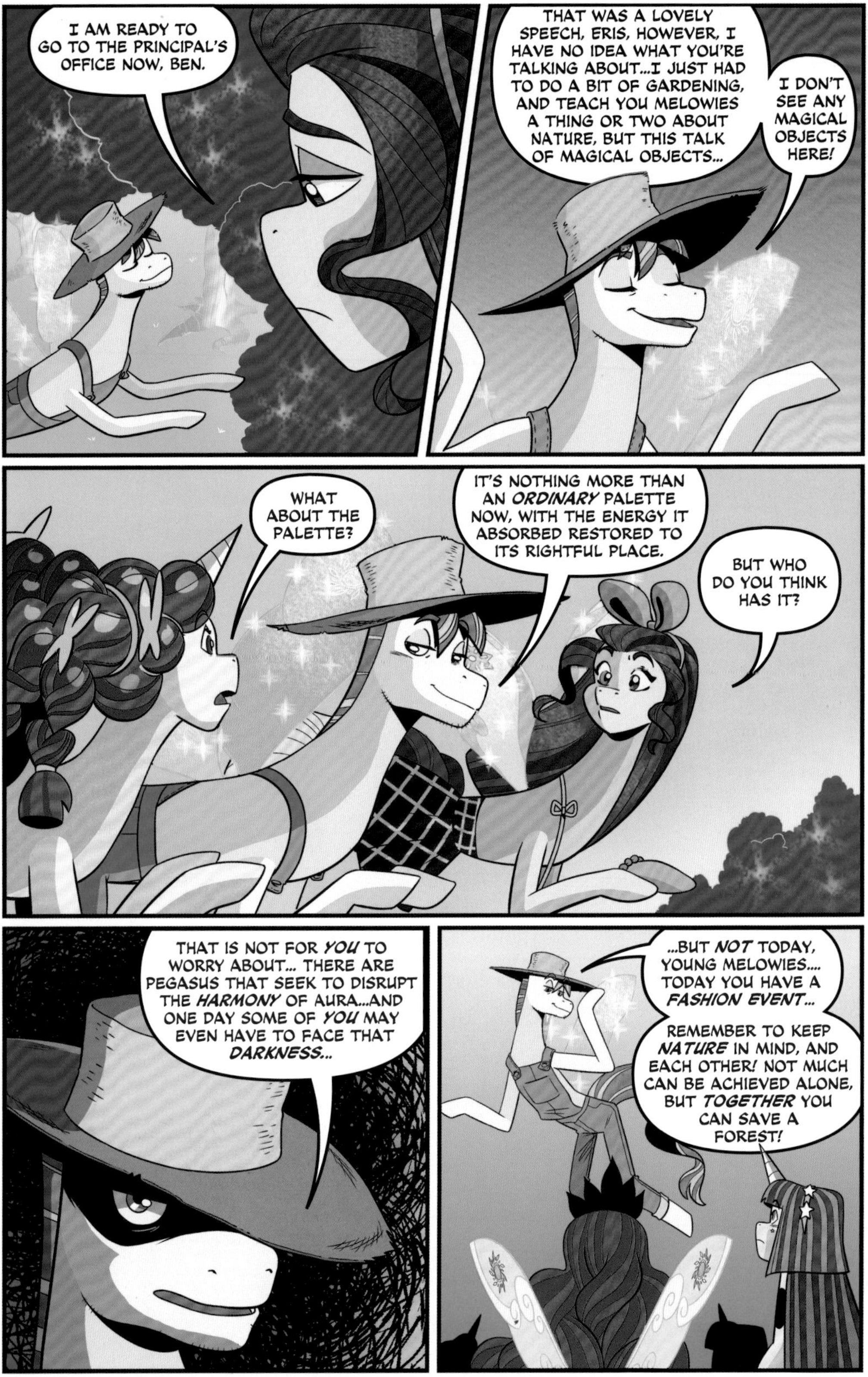
I AM READY TO GO TO THE PRINCIPAL'S OFFICE NOW, BEN.
THAT WAS A LOVELY SPEECH, ERIS, HOWEVER, I HAVE NO IDEA WHAT YOU'RE TALKING ABOUT...I JUST HAD TO DO A BIT OF GARDENING, AND TEACH YOU MELOWIES A THING OR TWO ABOUT NATURE, BUT THIS TALK OF MAGICAL OBJECTS...
I DON'T SEE ANY MAGICAL OBJECTS HERE!
WHAT ABOUT THE PALETTE?
IT'S NOTHING MORE THAN AN *ORDINARY* PALETTE NOW, WITH THE ENERGY IT ABSORBED RESTORED TO ITS RIGHTFUL PLACE.
BUT WHO DO YOU THINK HAS IT?
THAT IS NOT FOR *YOU* TO WORRY ABOUT... THERE ARE PEGASUS THAT SEEK TO DISRUPT THE *HARMONY* OF AURA...AND ONE DAY SOME OF *YOU* MAY EVEN HAVE TO FACE THAT *DARKNESS...*
...BUT *NOT* TODAY, YOUNG MELOWIES.... TODAY YOU HAVE A *FASHION EVENT*...
REMEMBER TO KEEP *NATURE* IN MIND, AND EACH OTHER! NOT MUCH CAN BE ACHIEVED ALONE, BUT *TOGETHER* YOU CAN SAVE A FOREST!

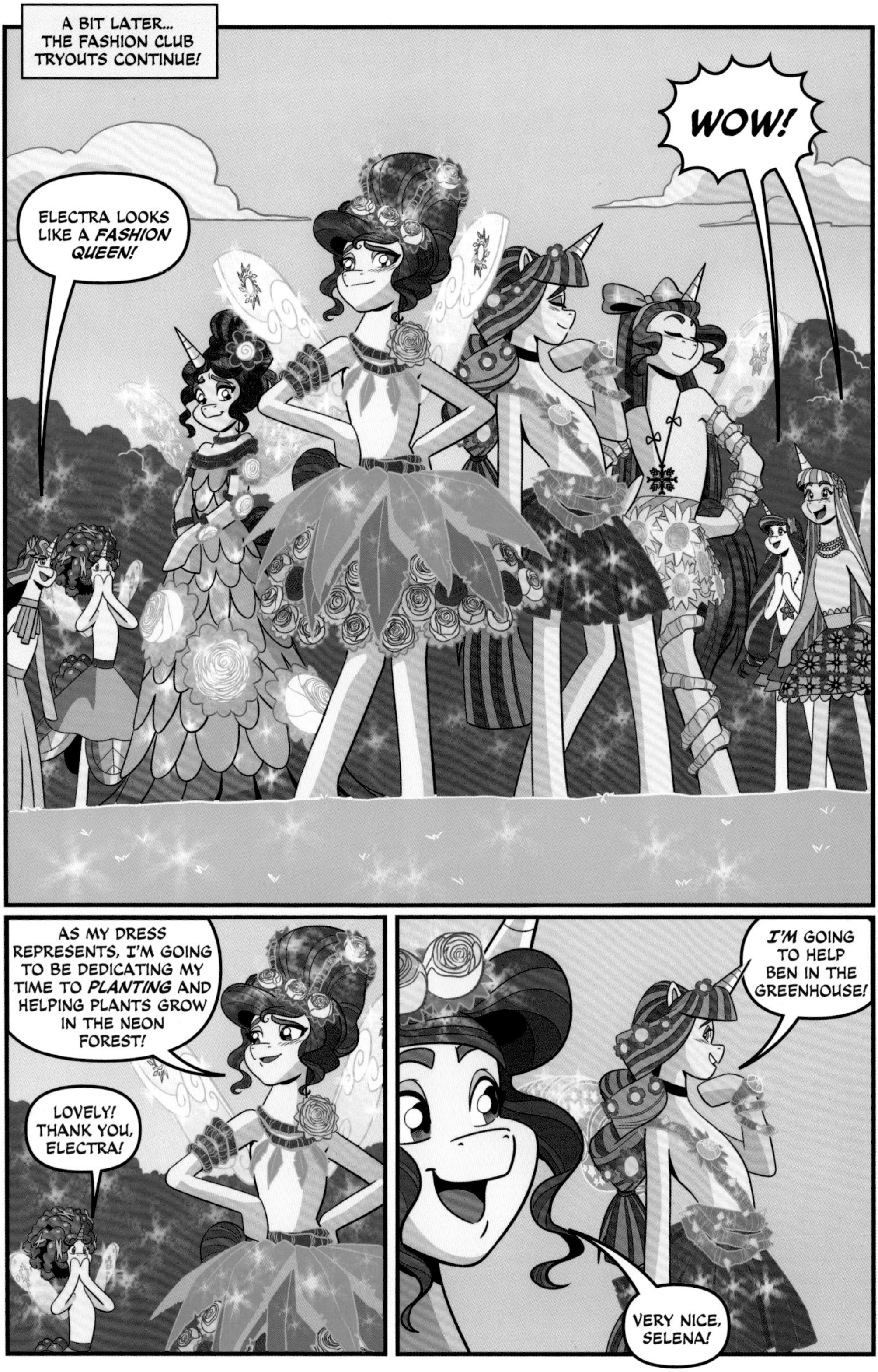
A BIT LATER... THE FASHION CLUB TRYOUTS CONTINUE!
WOW!
ELECTRA LOOKS LIKE A *FASHION QUEEN!*
AS MY DRESS REPRESENTS, I'M GOING TO BE DEDICATING MY TIME TO *PLANTING* AND HELPING PLANTS GROW IN THE NEON FOREST!
LOVELY! THANK YOU, ELECTRA!
I'M GOING TO HELP BEN IN THE GREENHOUSE!
VERY NICE, SELENA!

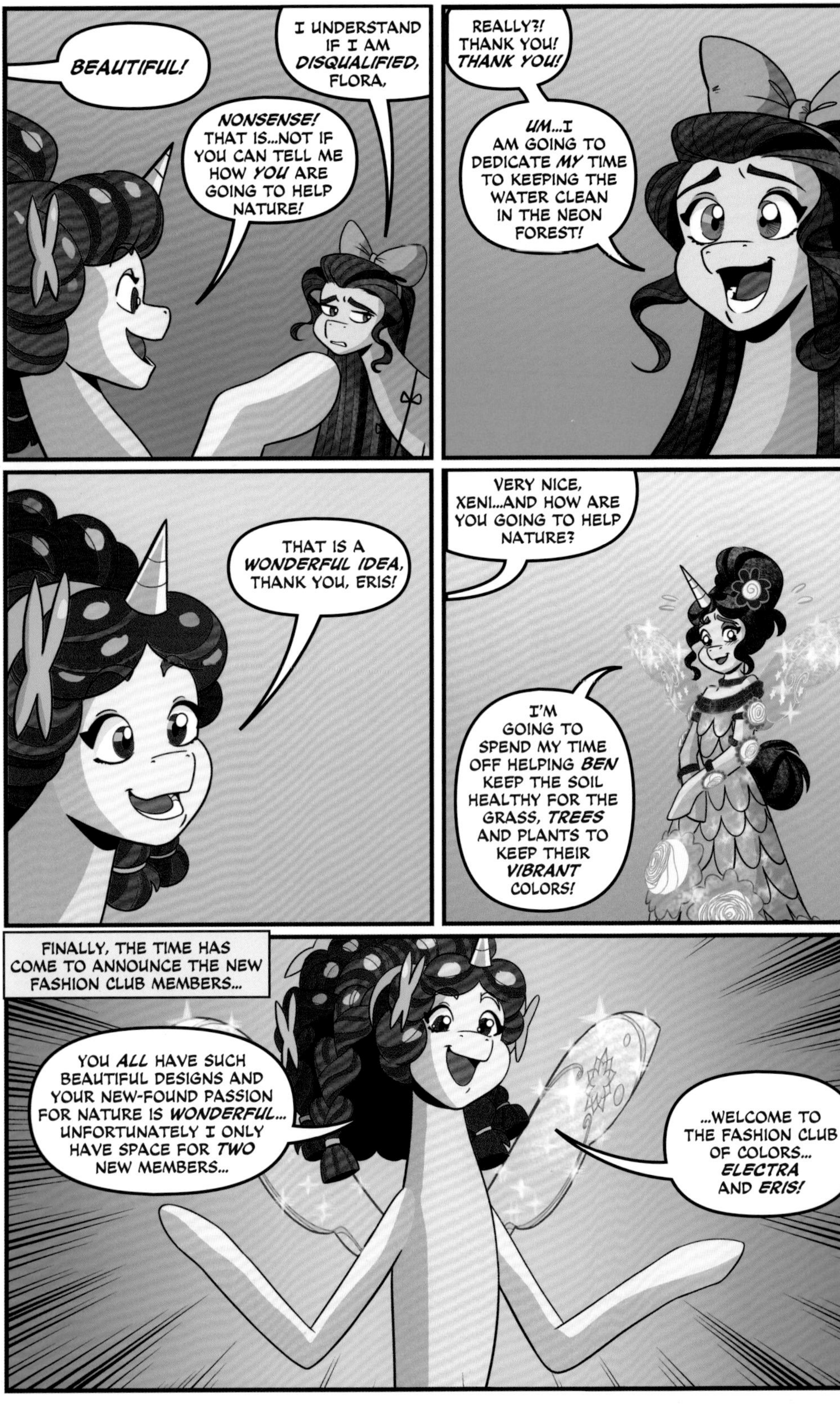
BEAUTIFUL!
I UNDERSTAND IF I AM DISQUALIFIED, FLORA,
NONSENSE! THAT IS...NOT IF YOU CAN TELL ME HOW YOU ARE GOING TO HELP NATURE!
REALLY?! THANK YOU! THANK YOU!
UM...I AM GOING TO DEDICATE MY TIME TO KEEPING THE WATER CLEAN IN THE NEON FOREST!
THAT IS A WONDERFUL IDEA, THANK YOU, ERIS!
VERY NICE, XENI...AND HOW ARE YOU GOING TO HELP NATURE?
I'M GOING TO SPEND MY TIME OFF HELPING BEN KEEP THE SOIL HEALTHY FOR THE GRASS, TREES AND PLANTS TO KEEP THEIR VIBRANT COLORS!
FINALLY, THE TIME HAS COME TO ANNOUNCE THE NEW FASHION CLUB MEMBERS...
YOU ALL HAVE SUCH BEAUTIFUL DESIGNS AND YOUR NEW-FOUND PASSION FOR NATURE IS WONDERFUL... UNFORTUNATELY I ONLY HAVE SPACE FOR TWO NEW MEMBERS...
...WELCOME TO THE FASHION CLUB OF COLORS... ELECTRA AND ERIS!

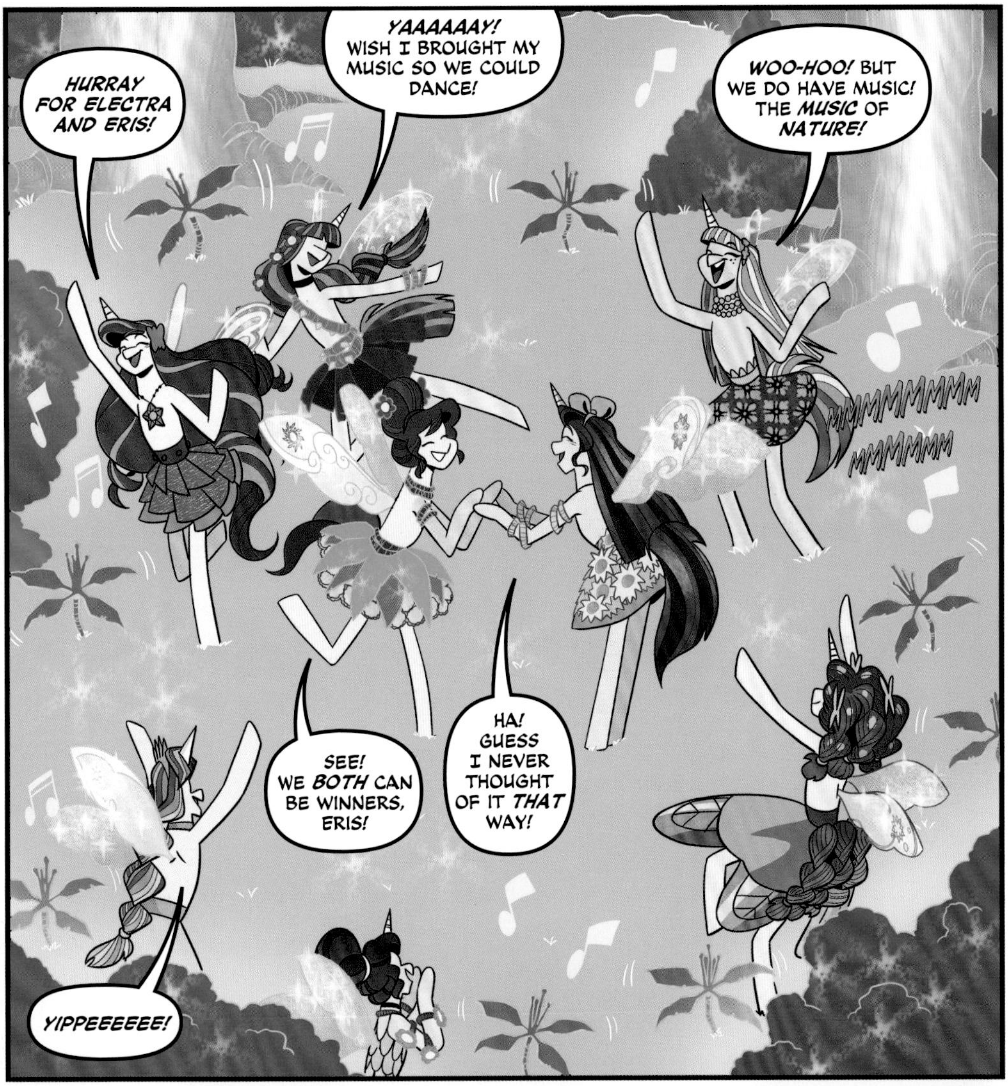
HURRAY FOR ELECTRA AND ERIS!
YAAAAAAY! WISH I BROUGHT MY MUSIC SO WE COULD DANCE!
WOO-HOO! BUT WE DO HAVE MUSIC! THE MUSIC OF NATURE!
MMMMMMMM
MMMMMM
SEE! WE BOTH CAN BE WINNERS, ERIS!
HA! GUESS I NEVER THOUGHT OF IT THAT WAY!
YIPPEEEEEE!

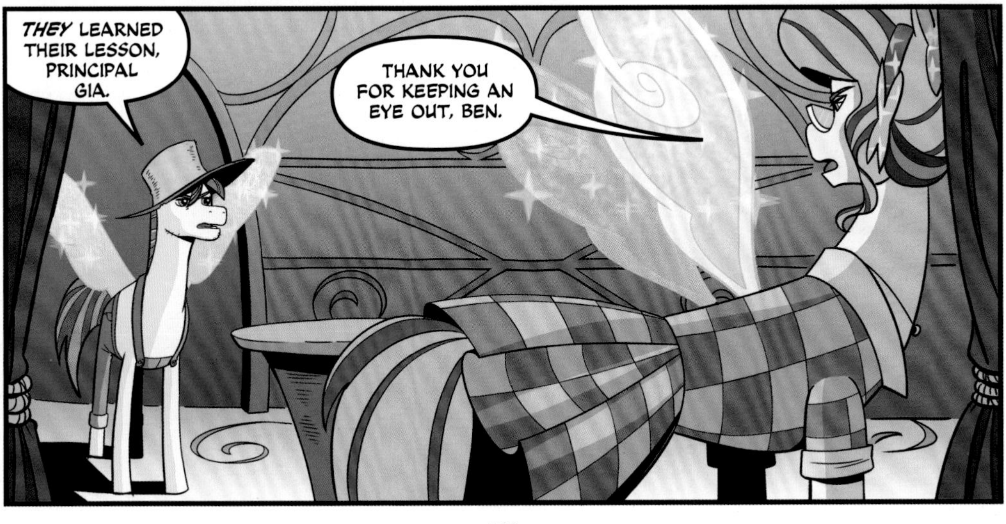
THEY LEARNED THEIR LESSON, PRINCIPAL GIA.
THANK YOU FOR KEEPING AN EYE OUT, BEN.

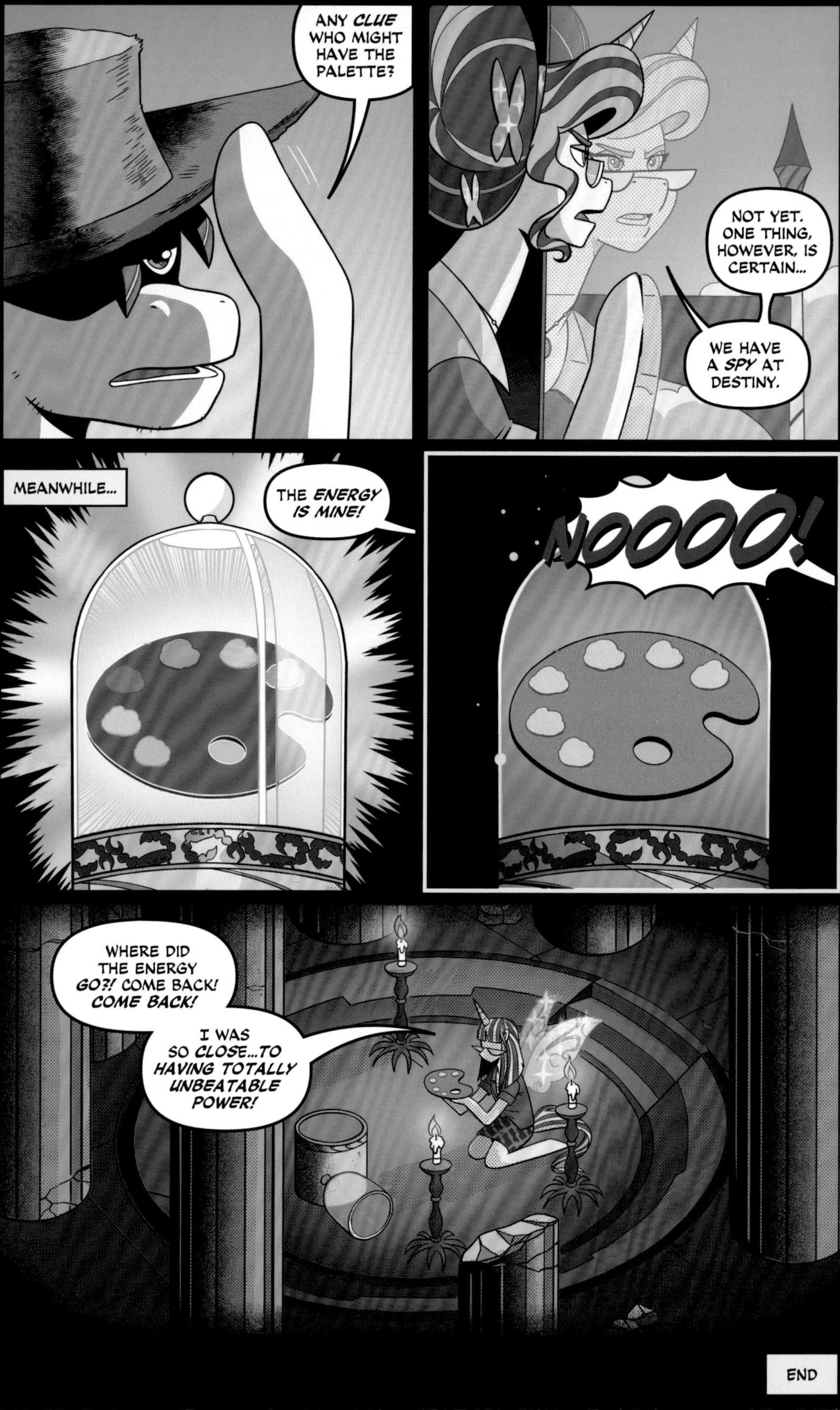
ANY CLUE WHO MIGHT HAVE THE PALETTE?
NOT YET. ONE THING, HOWEVER, IS CERTAIN...
WE HAVE A SPY AT DESTINY.
MEANWHILE...
THE ENERGY IS MINE!
NOOOO!
WHERE DID THE ENERGY GO?! COME BACK! COME BACK!
I WAS SO CLOSE...TO HAVING TOTALLY UNBEATABLE POWER!
END

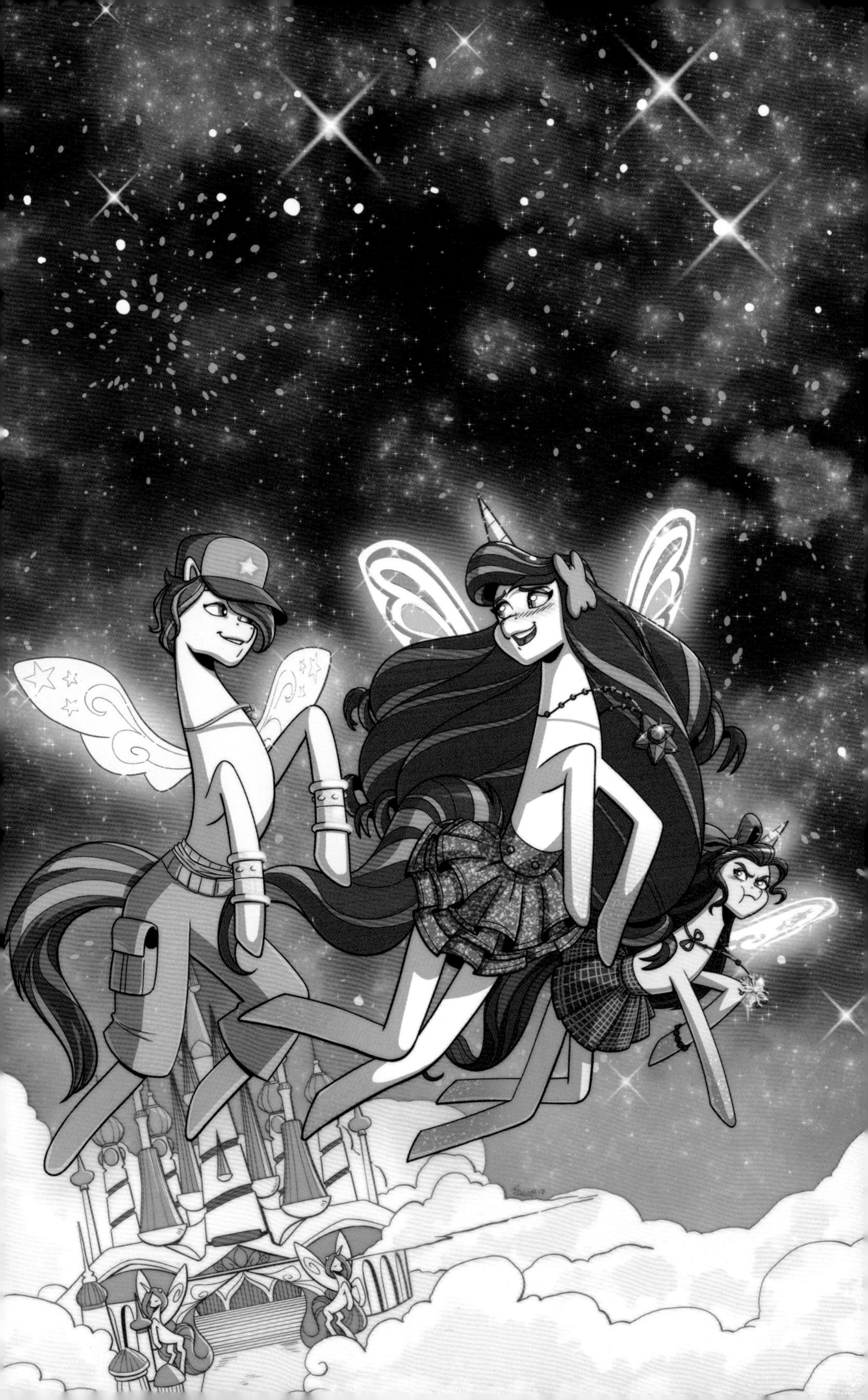

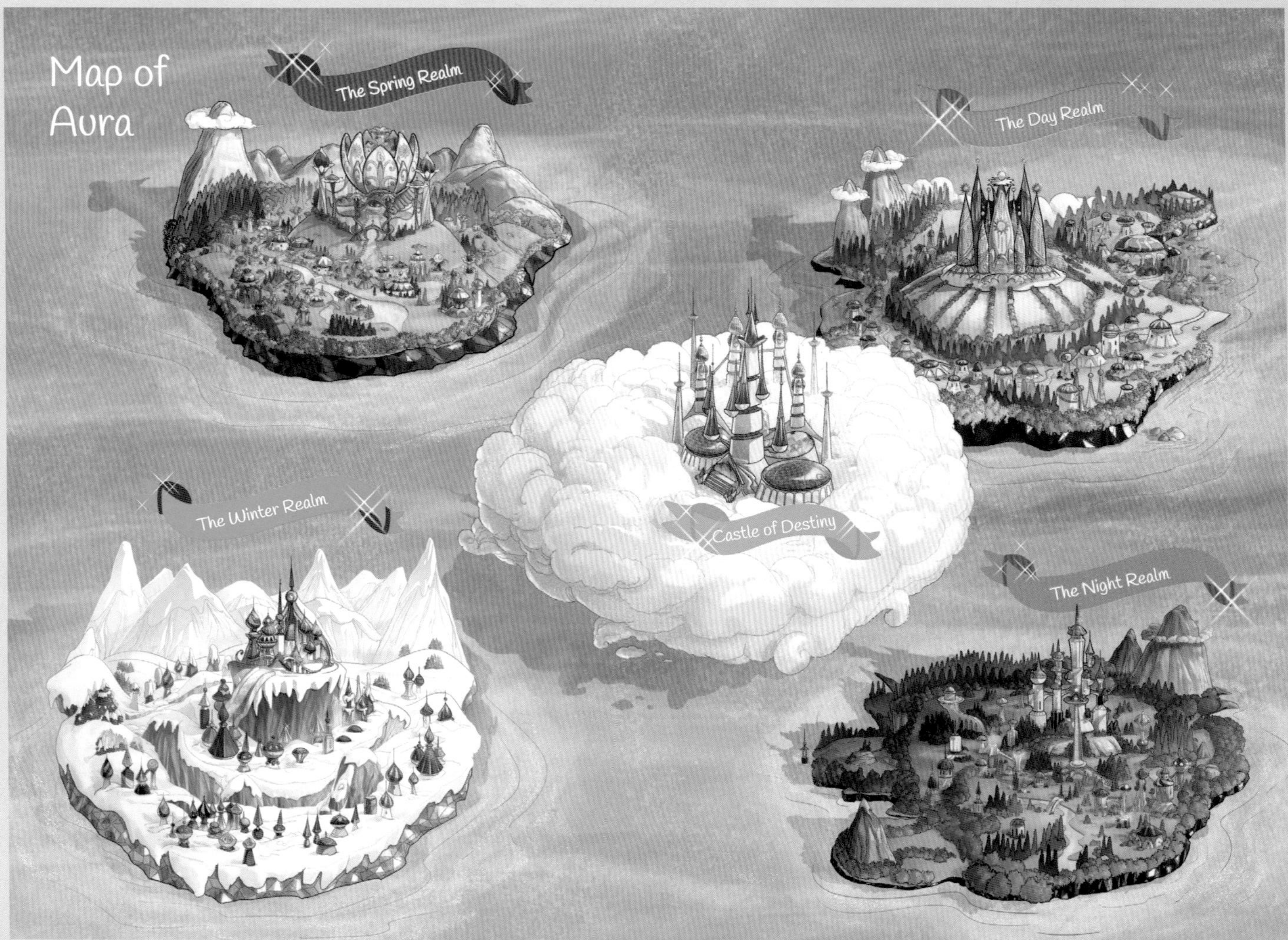
Map of
Aura
The Spring Realm
The Day Realm
The Winter Realm
Castle of Destiny
The Night Realm

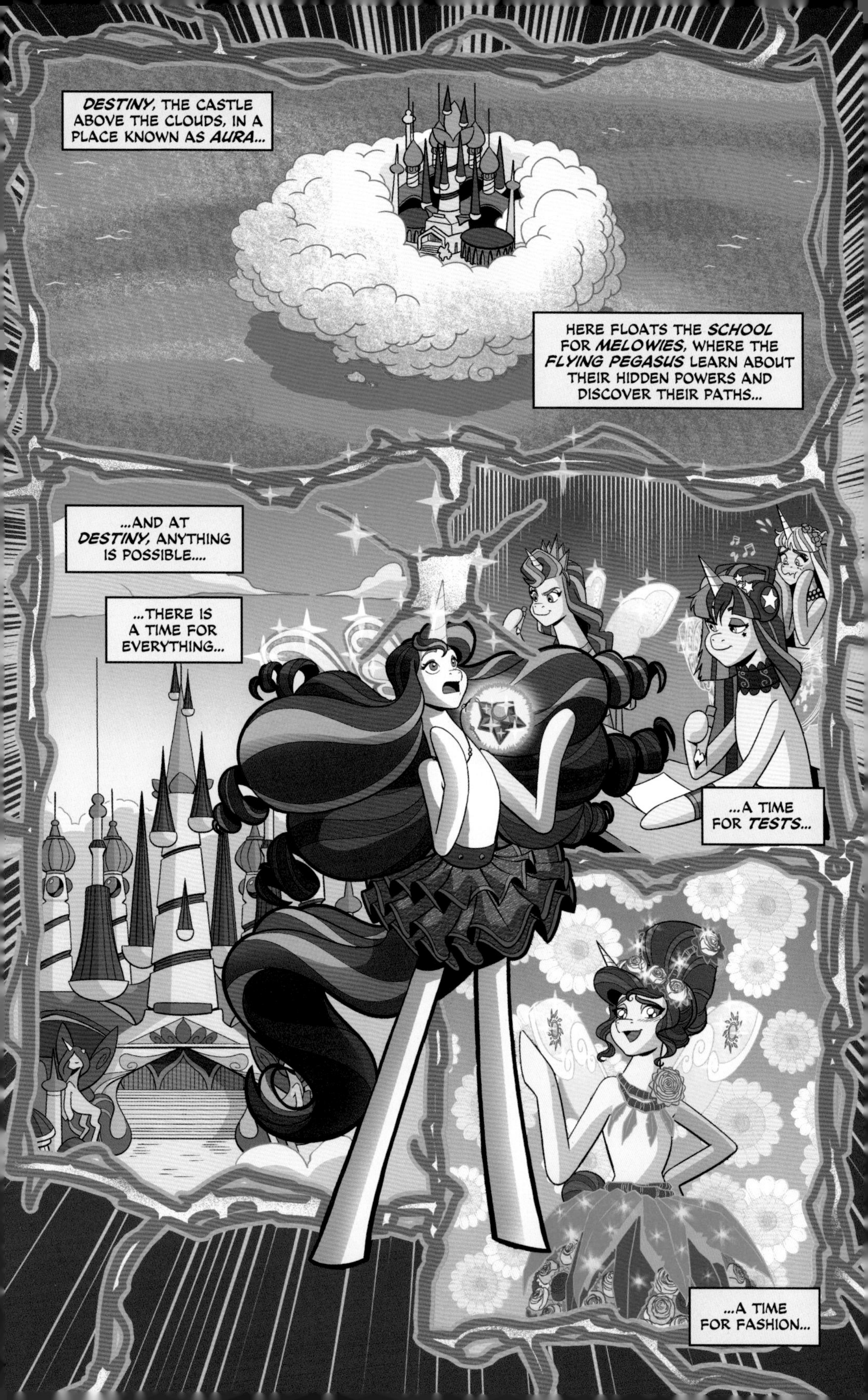

DESTINY, THE CASTLE ABOVE THE CLOUDS, IN A PLACE KNOWN AS *AURA*...
HERE FLOATS THE *SCHOOL* FOR *MELOWIES*, WHERE THE *FLYING PEGASUS* LEARN ABOUT THEIR HIDDEN POWERS AND DISCOVER THEIR PATHS...
...AND AT *DESTINY*, ANYTHING IS POSSIBLE....
...THERE IS A TIME FOR EVERYTHING...
...A TIME FOR *TESTS*...
...A TIME FOR FASHION...

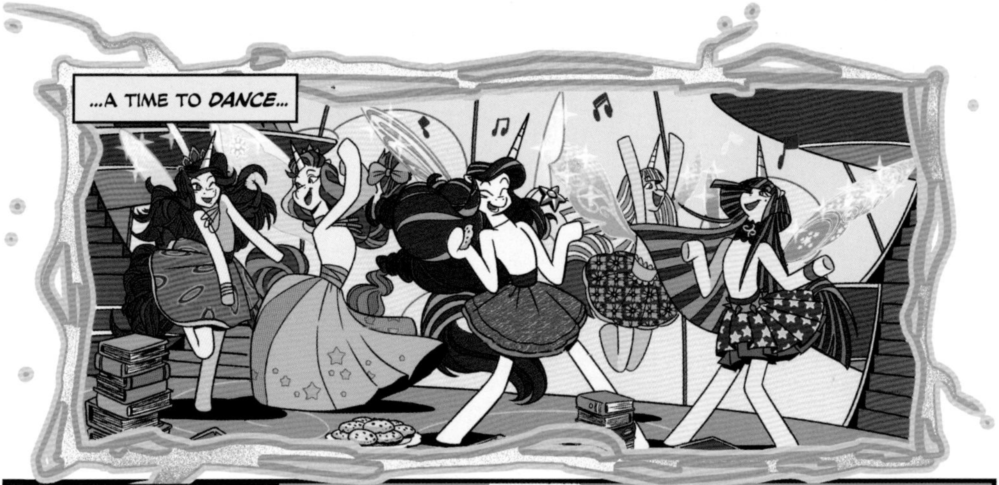
...A TIME TO DANCE...

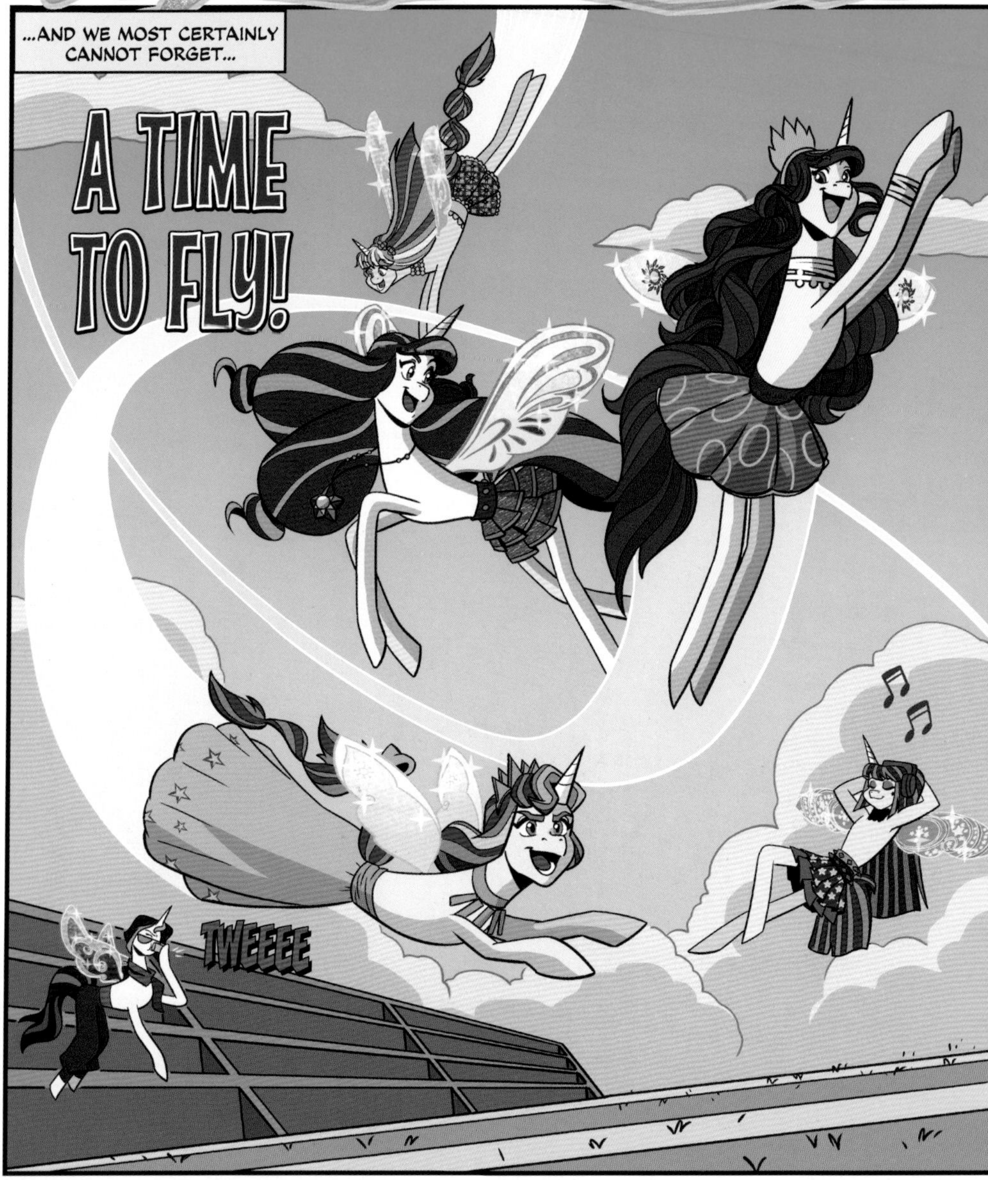
...AND WE MOST CERTAINLY CANNOT FORGET...
A TIME TO FLY!
TWEEEE

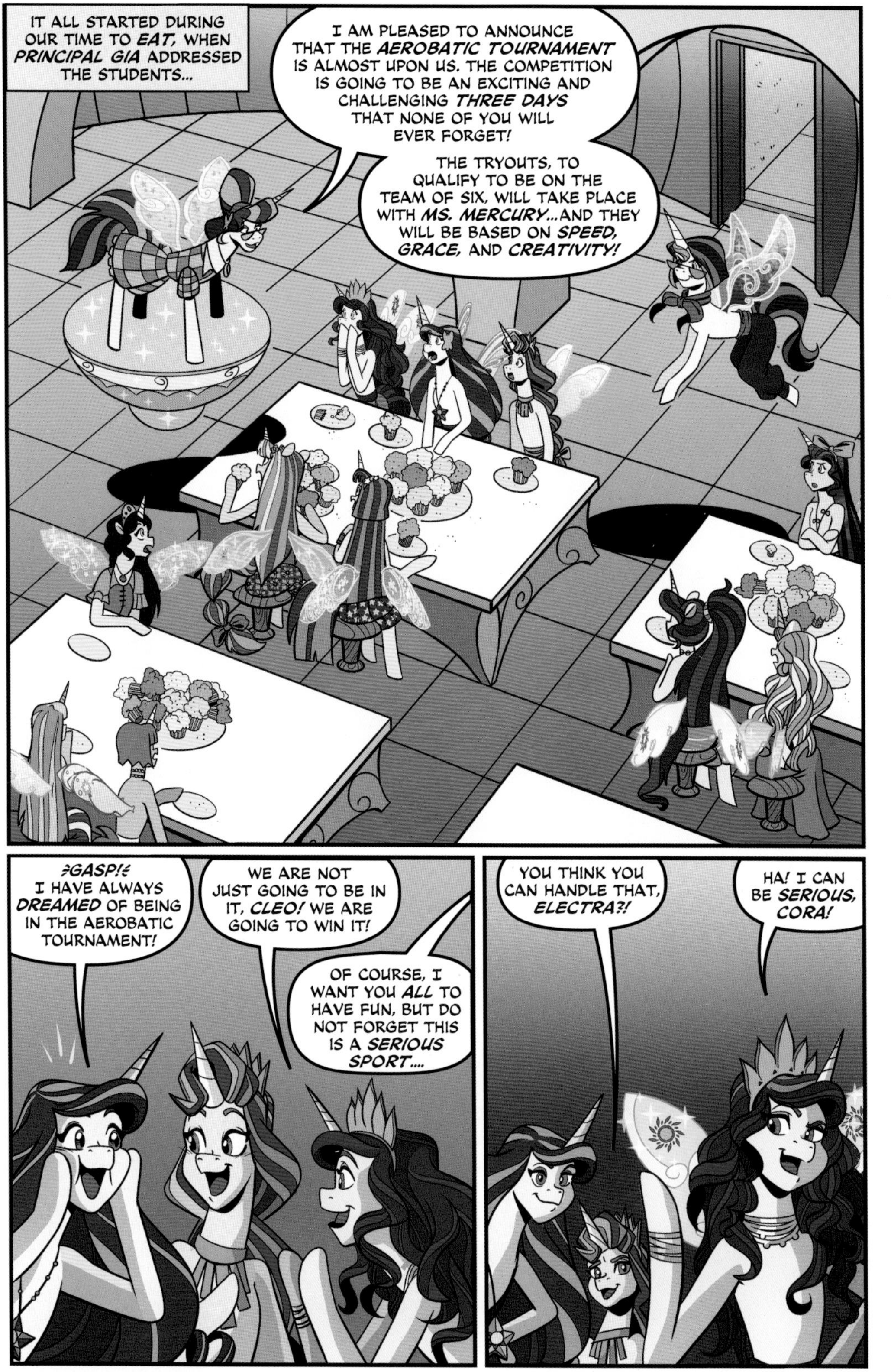
IT ALL STARTED DURING OUR TIME TO EAT, WHEN PRINCIPAL GIA ADDRESSED THE STUDENTS...
I AM PLEASED TO ANNOUNCE THAT THE AEROBATIC TOURNAMENT IS ALMOST UPON US. THE COMPETITION IS GOING TO BE AN EXCITING AND CHALLENGING THREE DAYS THAT NONE OF YOU WILL EVER FORGET!
THE TRYOUTS, TO QUALIFY TO BE ON THE TEAM OF SIX, WILL TAKE PLACE WITH MS. MERCURY...AND THEY WILL BE BASED ON SPEED, GRACE, AND CREATIVITY!
GASP! I HAVE ALWAYS DREAMED OF BEING IN THE AEROBATIC TOURNAMENT!
WE ARE NOT JUST GOING TO BE IN IT, CLEO! WE ARE GOING TO WIN IT!
OF COURSE, I WANT YOU ALL TO HAVE FUN, BUT DO NOT FORGET THIS IS A SERIOUS SPORT....
YOU THINK YOU CAN HANDLE THAT, ELECTRA?!
HA! I CAN BE SERIOUS, CORA!

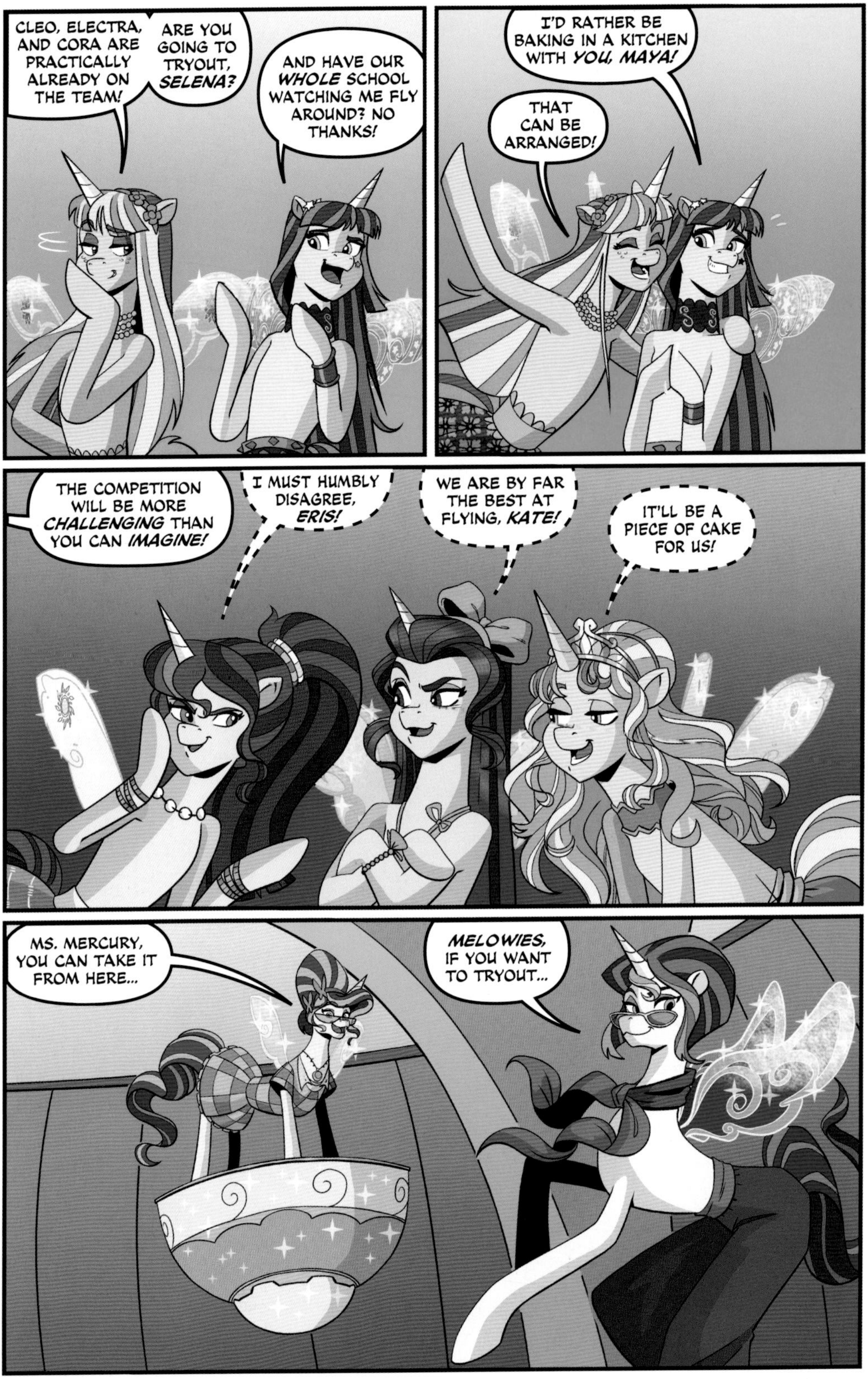
CLEO, ELECTRA, AND CORA ARE PRACTICALLY ALREADY ON THE TEAM!
ARE YOU GOING TO TRYOUT, SELENA?
AND HAVE OUR WHOLE SCHOOL WATCHING ME FLY AROUND? NO THANKS!
I'D RATHER BE BAKING IN A KITCHEN WITH YOU, MAYA!
THAT CAN BE ARRANGED!
THE COMPETITION WILL BE MORE CHALLENGING THAN YOU CAN IMAGINE!
I MUST HUMBLY DISAGREE, ERIS!
WE ARE BY FAR THE BEST AT FLYING, KATE!
IT'LL BE A PIECE OF CAKE FOR US!
MS. MERCURY, YOU CAN TAKE IT FROM HERE...
MELOWIES, IF YOU WANT TO TRYOUT...

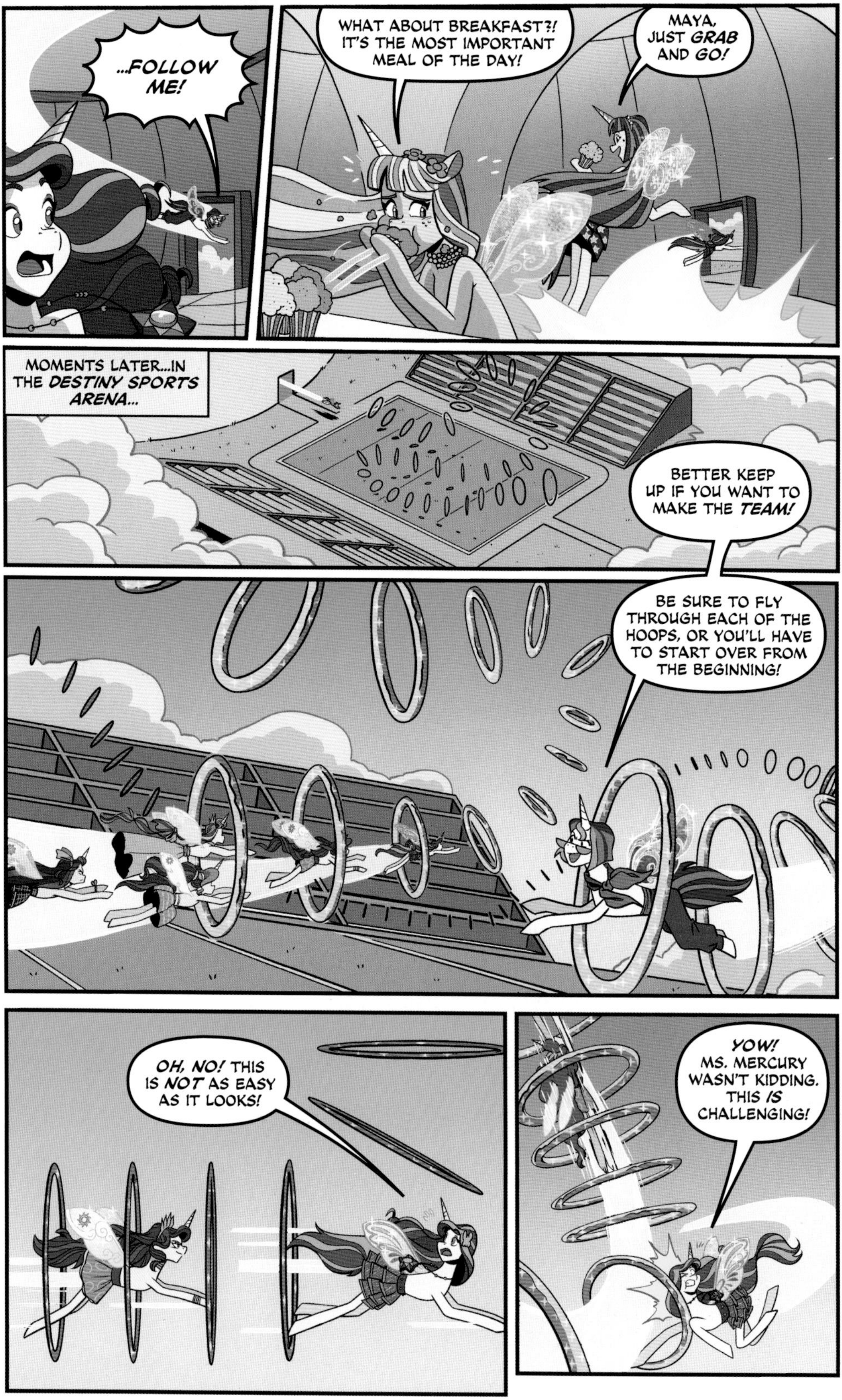
...FOLLOW ME!
WHAT ABOUT BREAKFAST?! IT'S THE MOST IMPORTANT MEAL OF THE DAY!
MAYA, JUST GRAB AND GO!
MOMENTS LATER...IN THE DESTINY SPORTS ARENA...
BETTER KEEP UP IF YOU WANT TO MAKE THE TEAM!
BE SURE TO FLY THROUGH EACH OF THE HOOPS, OR YOU'LL HAVE TO START OVER FROM THE BEGINNING!
OH, NO! THIS IS NOT AS EASY AS IT LOOKS!
YOW! MS. MERCURY WASN'T KIDDING. THIS IS CHALLENGING!

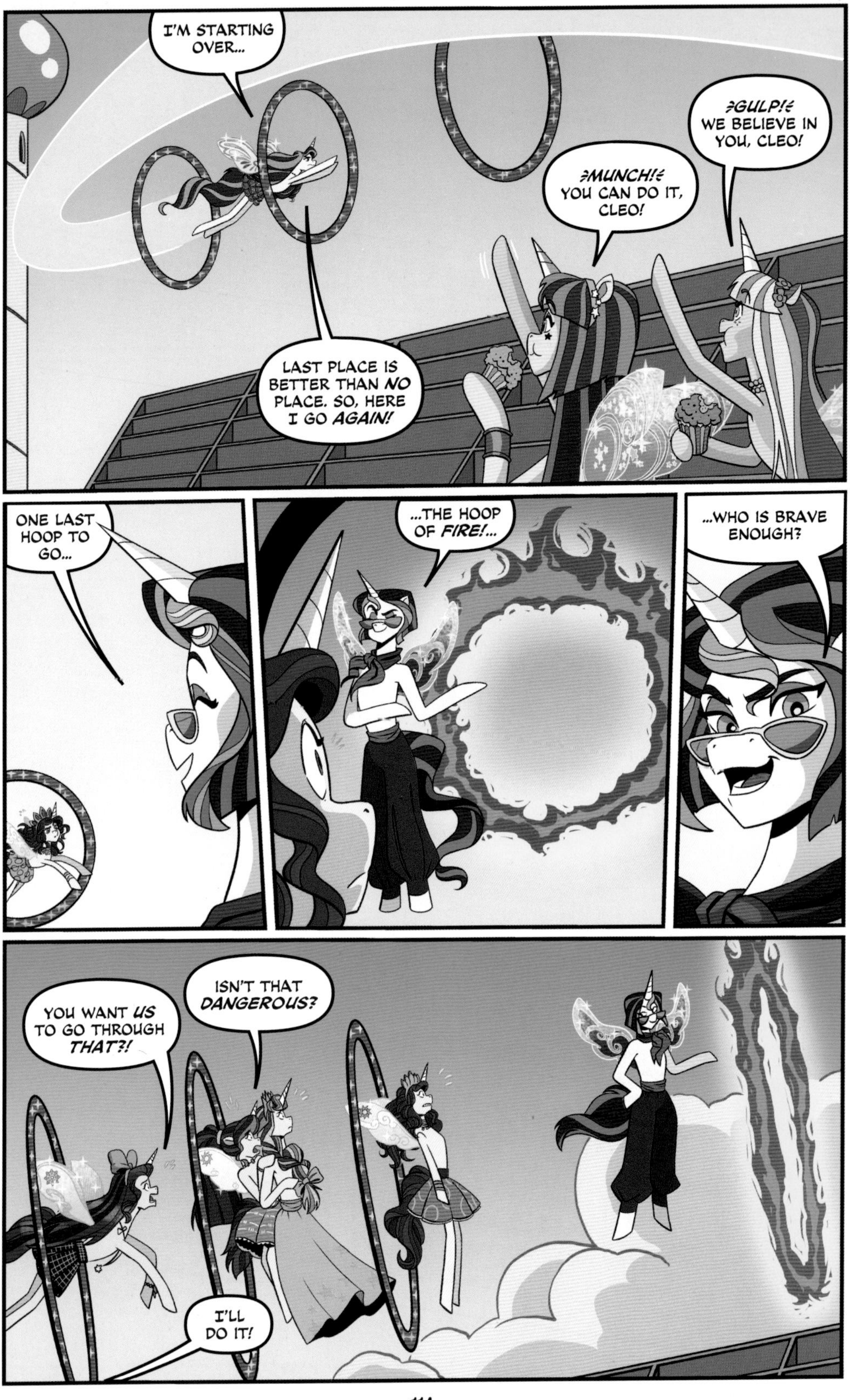
I'M STARTING OVER...
LAST PLACE IS BETTER THAN *NO* PLACE. SO, HERE I GO *AGAIN!*
⋟MUNCH!⋞ YOU CAN DO IT, CLEO!
⋟GULP!⋞ WE BELIEVE IN YOU, CLEO!
ONE LAST HOOP TO GO...
...THE HOOP OF *FIRE!*...
...WHO IS BRAVE ENOUGH?
YOU WANT *US* TO GO THROUGH *THAT?!*
ISN'T THAT *DANGEROUS?*
I'LL DO IT!

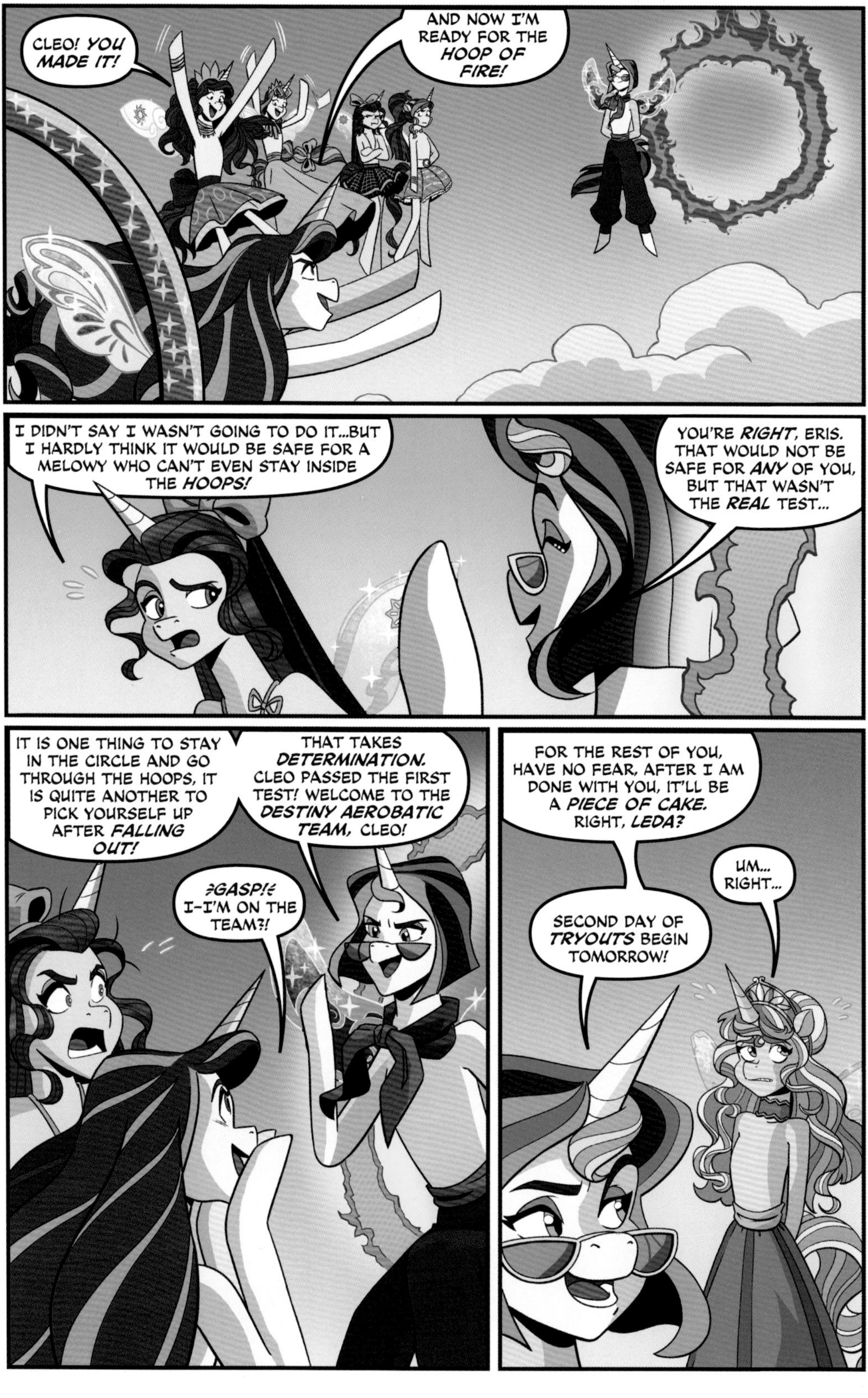
CLEO! YOU MADE IT!
AND NOW I'M READY FOR THE HOOP OF FIRE!
I DIDN'T SAY I WASN'T GOING TO DO IT...BUT I HARDLY THINK IT WOULD BE SAFE FOR A MELOWY WHO CAN'T EVEN STAY INSIDE THE HOOPS!
YOU'RE RIGHT, ERIS. THAT WOULD NOT BE SAFE FOR ANY OF YOU, BUT THAT WASN'T THE REAL TEST...
IT IS ONE THING TO STAY IN THE CIRCLE AND GO THROUGH THE HOOPS, IT IS QUITE ANOTHER TO PICK YOURSELF UP AFTER FALLING OUT!
THAT TAKES DETERMINATION. CLEO PASSED THE FIRST TEST! WELCOME TO THE DESTINY AEROBATIC TEAM, CLEO!
GASP! I-I'M ON THE TEAM?!
FOR THE REST OF YOU, HAVE NO FEAR, AFTER I AM DONE WITH YOU, IT'LL BE A PIECE OF CAKE. RIGHT, LEDA?
UM... RIGHT...
SECOND DAY OF TRYOUTS BEGIN TOMORROW!

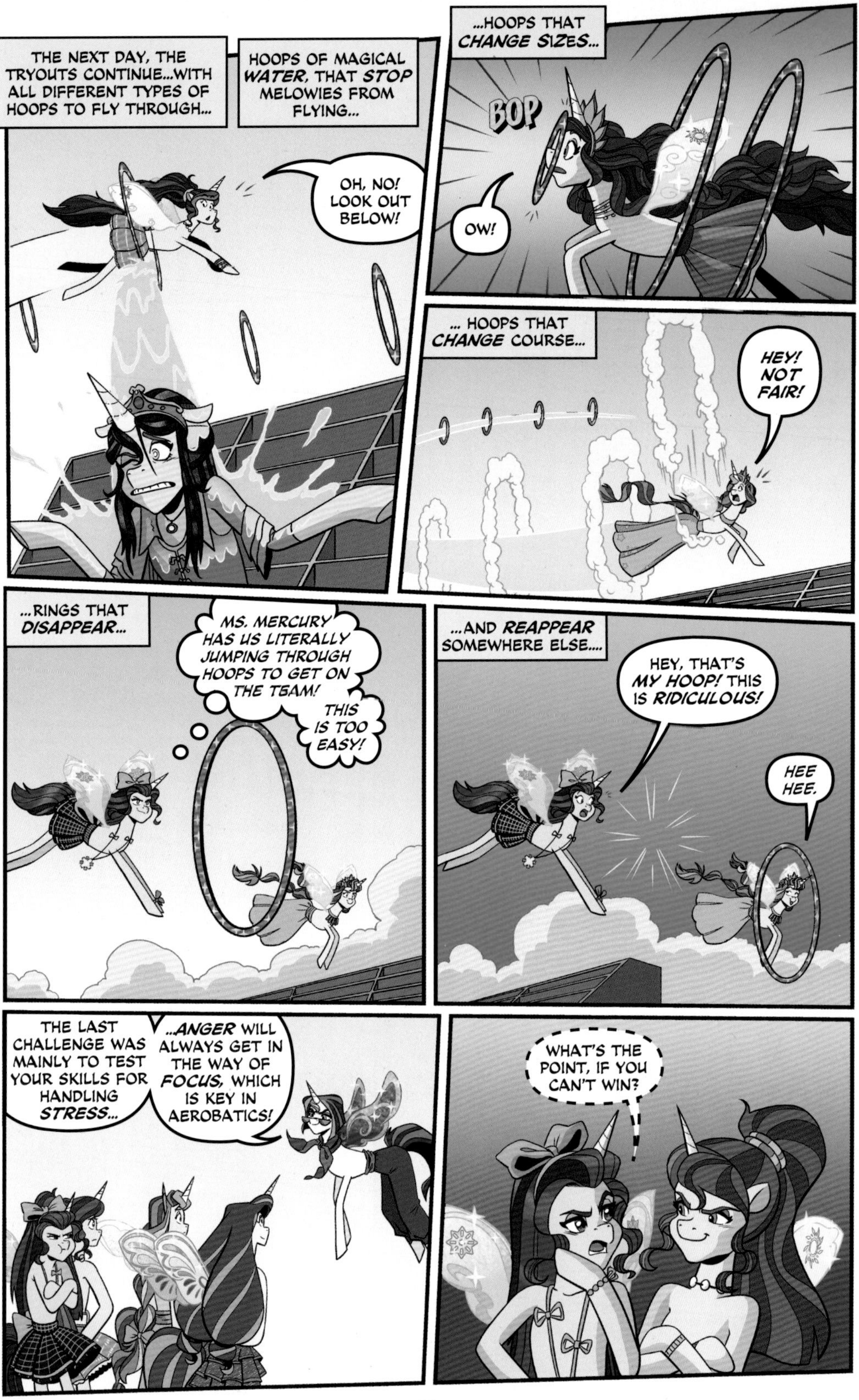
THE NEXT DAY, THE TRYOUTS CONTINUE...WITH ALL DIFFERENT TYPES OF HOOPS TO FLY THROUGH...
HOOPS OF MAGICAL WATER, THAT STOP MELOWIES FROM FLYING...
OH, NO! LOOK OUT BELOW!
...HOOPS THAT CHANGE SIZES...
BOP
OW!
... HOOPS THAT CHANGE COURSE...
HEY! NOT FAIR!
...RINGS THAT DISAPPEAR...
MS. MERCURY HAS US LITERALLY JUMPING THROUGH HOOPS TO GET ON THE TEAM!
THIS IS TOO EASY!
...AND REAPPEAR SOMEWHERE ELSE....
HEY, THAT'S MY HOOP! THIS IS RIDICULOUS!
HEE HEE.
THE LAST CHALLENGE WAS MAINLY TO TEST YOUR SKILLS FOR HANDLING STRESS...
...ANGER WILL ALWAYS GET IN THE WAY OF FOCUS, WHICH IS KEY IN AEROBATICS!
WHAT'S THE POINT, IF YOU CAN'T WIN?

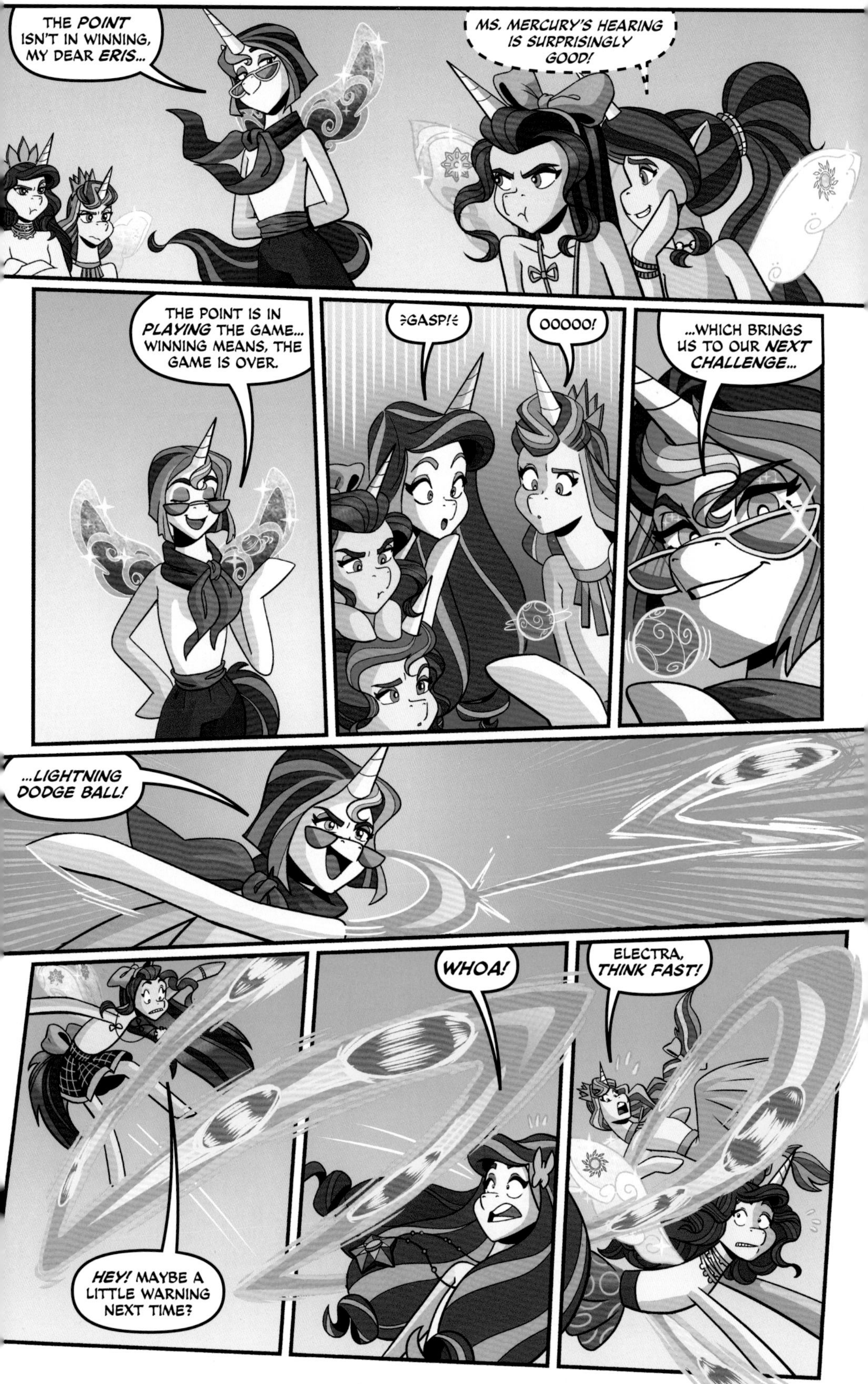
THE POINT ISN'T IN WINNING, MY DEAR ERIS...
MS. MERCURY'S HEARING IS SURPRISINGLY GOOD!
THE POINT IS IN PLAYING THE GAME... WINNING MEANS, THE GAME IS OVER.
GASP!
OOOOO!
...WHICH BRINGS US TO OUR NEXT CHALLENGE...
...LIGHTNING DODGE BALL!
HEY! MAYBE A LITTLE WARNING NEXT TIME?
WHOA!
ELECTRA, THINK FAST!

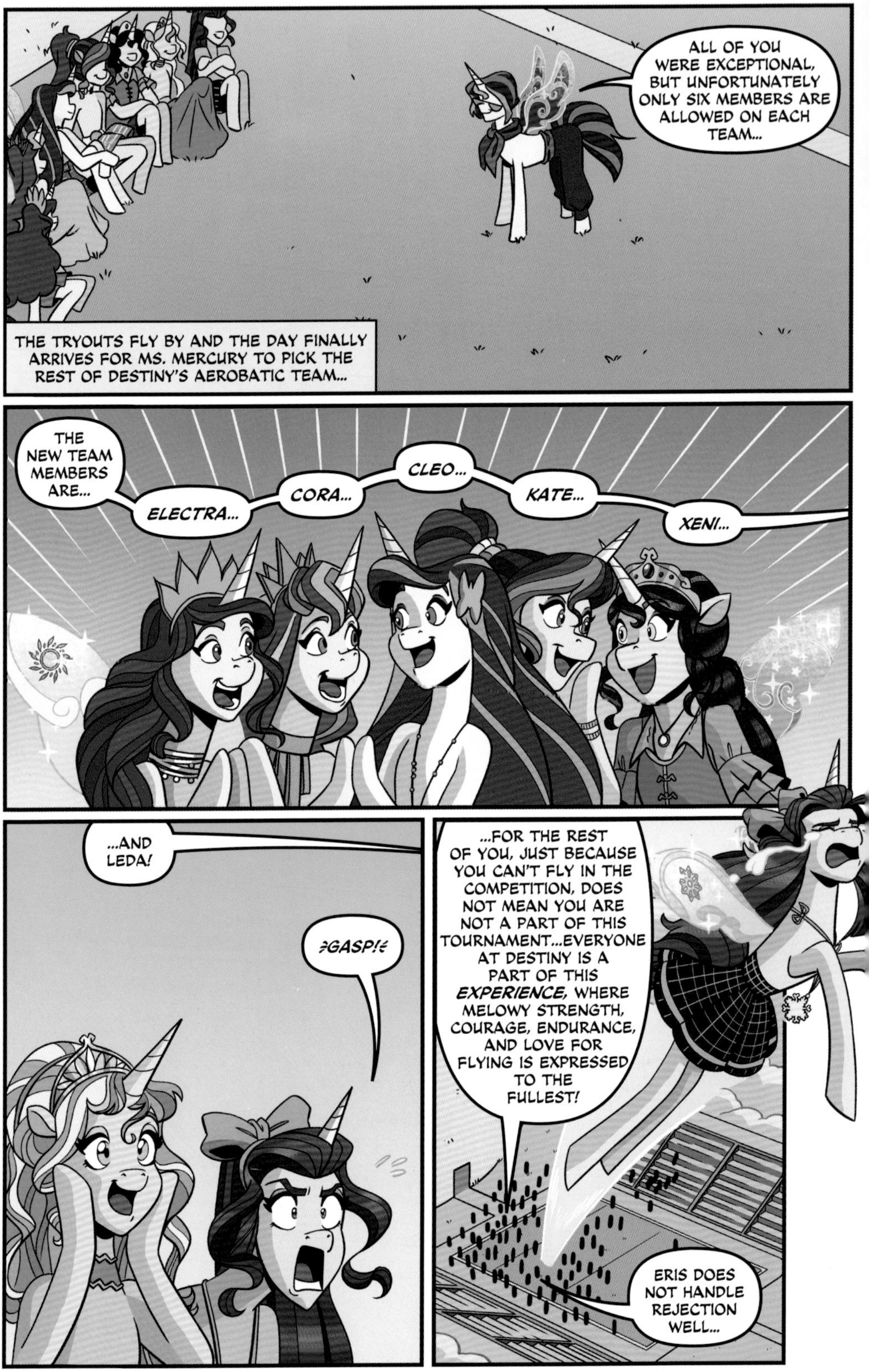
ALL OF YOU WERE EXCEPTIONAL, BUT UNFORTUNATELY ONLY SIX MEMBERS ARE ALLOWED ON EACH TEAM...
THE TRYOUTS FLY BY AND THE DAY FINALLY ARRIVES FOR MS. MERCURY TO PICK THE REST OF DESTINY'S AEROBATIC TEAM...
THE NEW TEAM MEMBERS ARE...
ELECTRA...
CORA...
CLEO...
KATE...
XENI...
...AND LEDA!
GASP!
...FOR THE REST OF YOU, JUST BECAUSE YOU CAN'T FLY IN THE COMPETITION, DOES NOT MEAN YOU ARE NOT A PART OF THIS TOURNAMENT...EVERYONE AT DESTINY IS A PART OF THIS EXPERIENCE, WHERE MELOWY STRENGTH, COURAGE, ENDURANCE, AND LOVE FOR FLYING IS EXPRESSED TO THE FULLEST!
ERIS DOES NOT HANDLE REJECTION WELL...

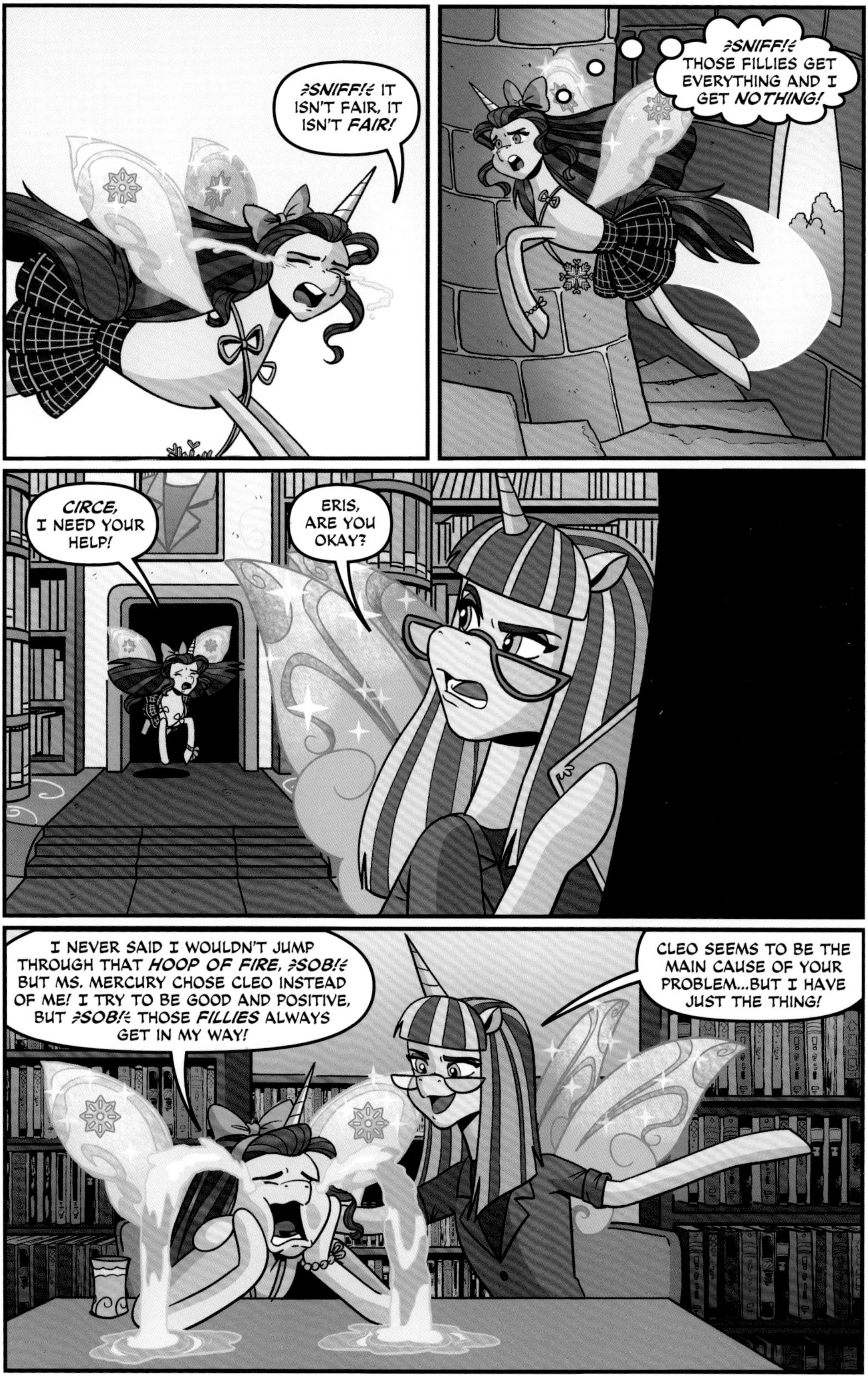

⋛SNIFF!⋚ IT ISN'T FAIR, IT ISN'T FAIR!
⋛SNIFF!⋚ THOSE FILLIES GET EVERYTHING AND I GET NOTHING!
CIRCE, I NEED YOUR HELP!
ERIS, ARE YOU OKAY?
I NEVER SAID I WOULDN'T JUMP THROUGH THAT HOOP OF FIRE, ⋛SOB!⋚ BUT MS. MERCURY CHOSE CLEO INSTEAD OF ME! I TRY TO BE GOOD AND POSITIVE, BUT ⋛SOB!⋚ THOSE FILLIES ALWAYS GET IN MY WAY!
CLEO SEEMS TO BE THE MAIN CAUSE OF YOUR PROBLEM...BUT I HAVE JUST THE THING!

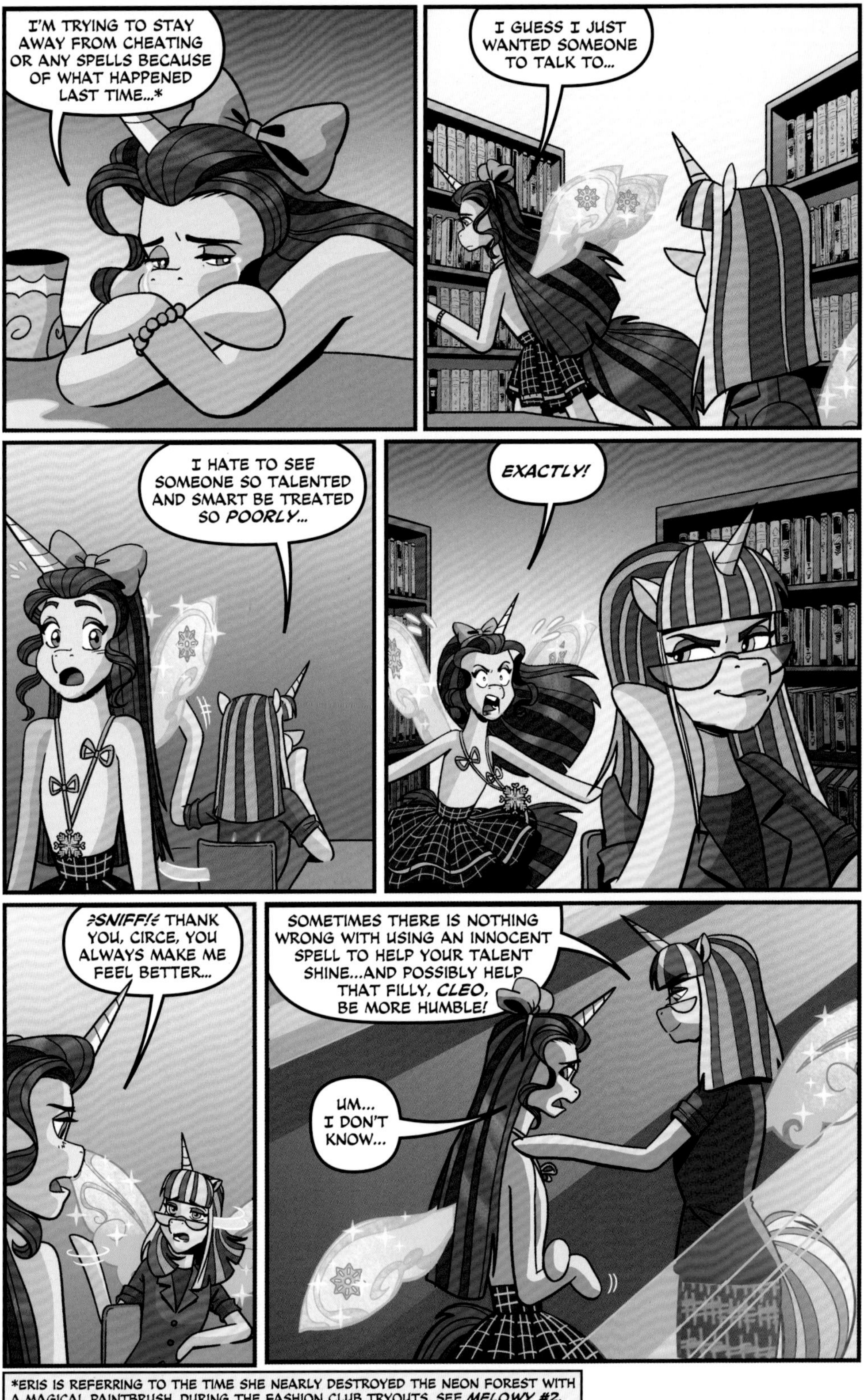
I'M TRYING TO STAY AWAY FROM CHEATING OR ANY SPELLS BECAUSE OF WHAT HAPPENED LAST TIME...*
I GUESS I JUST WANTED SOMEONE TO TALK TO...
I HATE TO SEE SOMEONE SO TALENTED AND SMART BE TREATED SO *POORLY*...
EXACTLY!
SNIFF! THANK YOU, CIRCE, YOU ALWAYS MAKE ME FEEL BETTER...
SOMETIMES THERE IS NOTHING WRONG WITH USING AN INNOCENT SPELL TO HELP YOUR TALENT SHINE...AND POSSIBLY HELP THAT FILLY, *CLEO*, BE MORE HUMBLE!
UM... I DON'T KNOW...

*ERIS IS REFERRING TO THE TIME SHE NEARLY DESTROYED THE NEON FOREST WITH A MAGICAL PAINTBRUSH, DURING THE FASHION CLUB TRYOUTS. SEE ***MELOWY #2.***

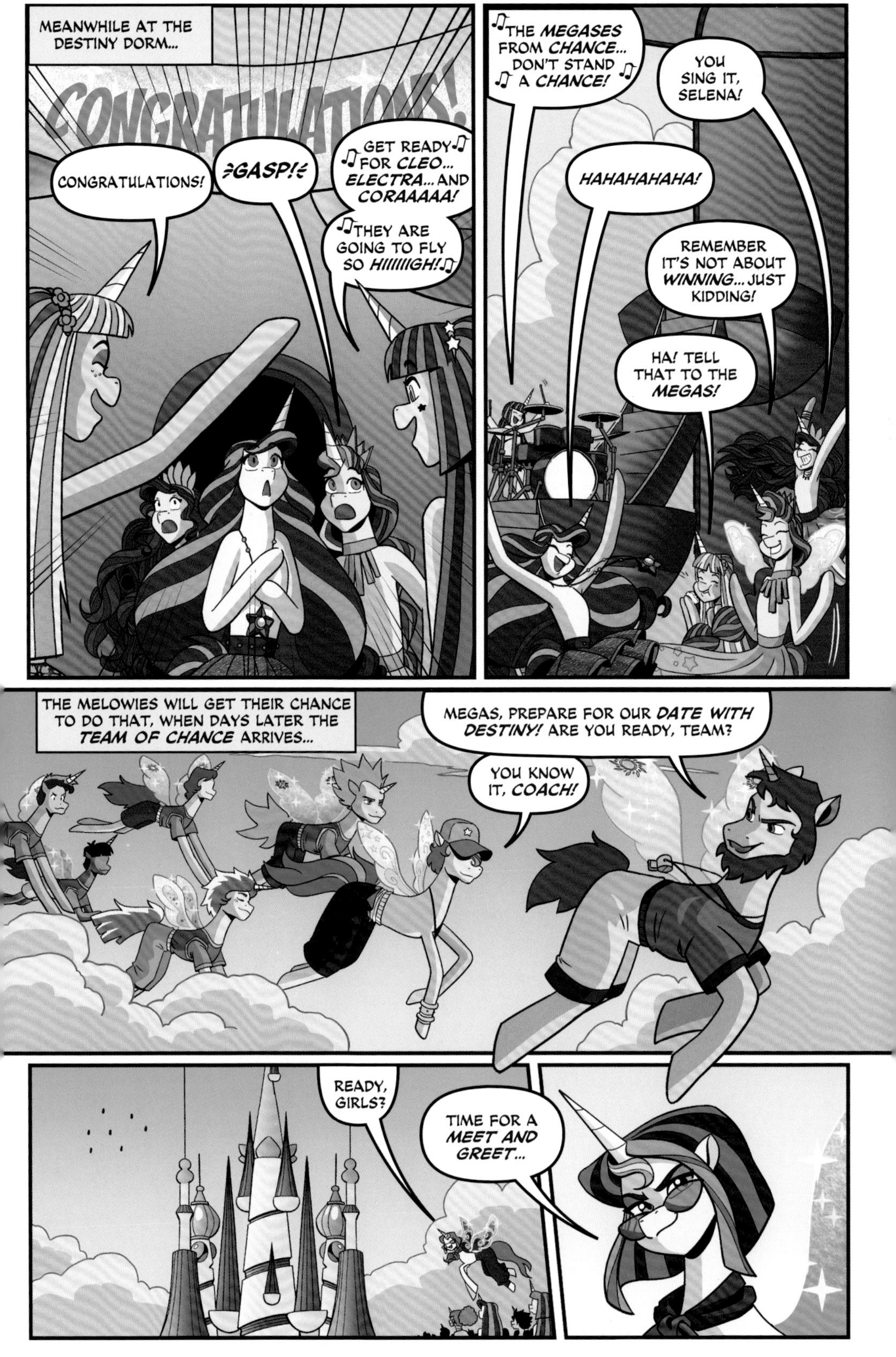
MEANWHILE AT THE DESTINY DORM...
CONGRATULATIONS!
CONGRATULATIONS!
GASP!
♫ GET READY ♫ FOR CLEO... ELECTRA... AND CORAAAAAA!
♫ THEY ARE GOING TO FLY SO HIIIIIGH! ♫
♫ THE MEGASES FROM CHANCE... DON'T STAND ♫ A CHANCE! ♫
YOU SING IT, SELENA!
HAHAHAHAHA!
REMEMBER IT'S NOT ABOUT WINNING... JUST KIDDING!
HA! TELL THAT TO THE MEGAS!
THE MELOWIES WILL GET THEIR CHANCE TO DO THAT, WHEN DAYS LATER THE TEAM OF CHANCE ARRIVES...
MEGAS, PREPARE FOR OUR DATE WITH DESTINY! ARE YOU READY, TEAM?
YOU KNOW IT, COACH!
READY, GIRLS?
TIME FOR A MEET AND GREET...

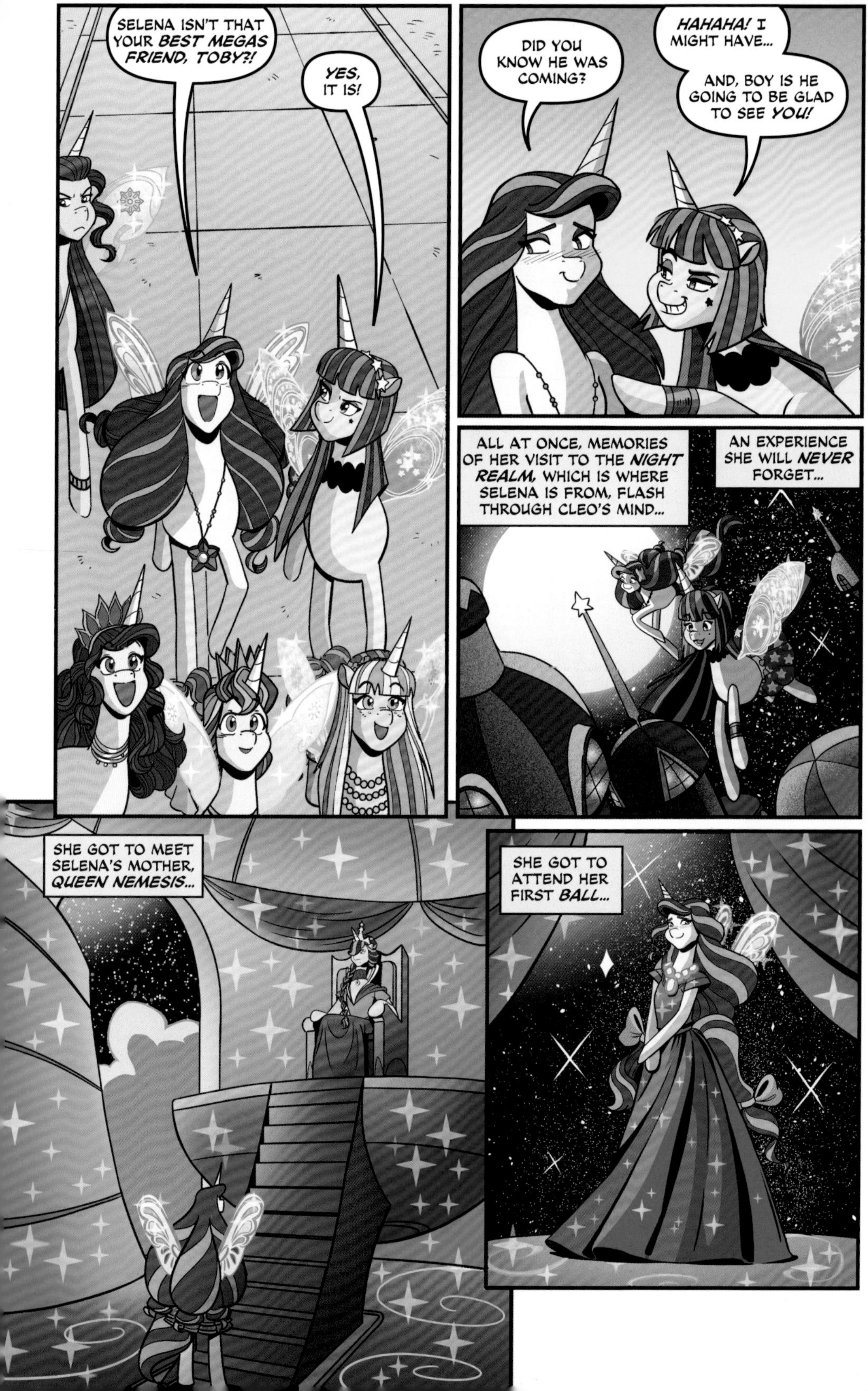
SELENA ISN'T THAT YOUR *BEST MEGAS FRIEND, TOBY?!*
YES, IT IS!
DID YOU KNOW HE WAS COMING?
HAHAHA! I MIGHT HAVE...
AND, BOY IS HE GOING TO BE GLAD TO SEE *YOU!*
ALL AT ONCE, MEMORIES OF HER VISIT TO THE *NIGHT REALM,* WHICH IS WHERE SELENA IS FROM, FLASH THROUGH CLEO'S MIND...
AN EXPERIENCE SHE WILL *NEVER* FORGET...
SHE GOT TO MEET SELENA'S MOTHER, *QUEEN NEMESIS*...
SHE GOT TO ATTEND HER FIRST *BALL*...

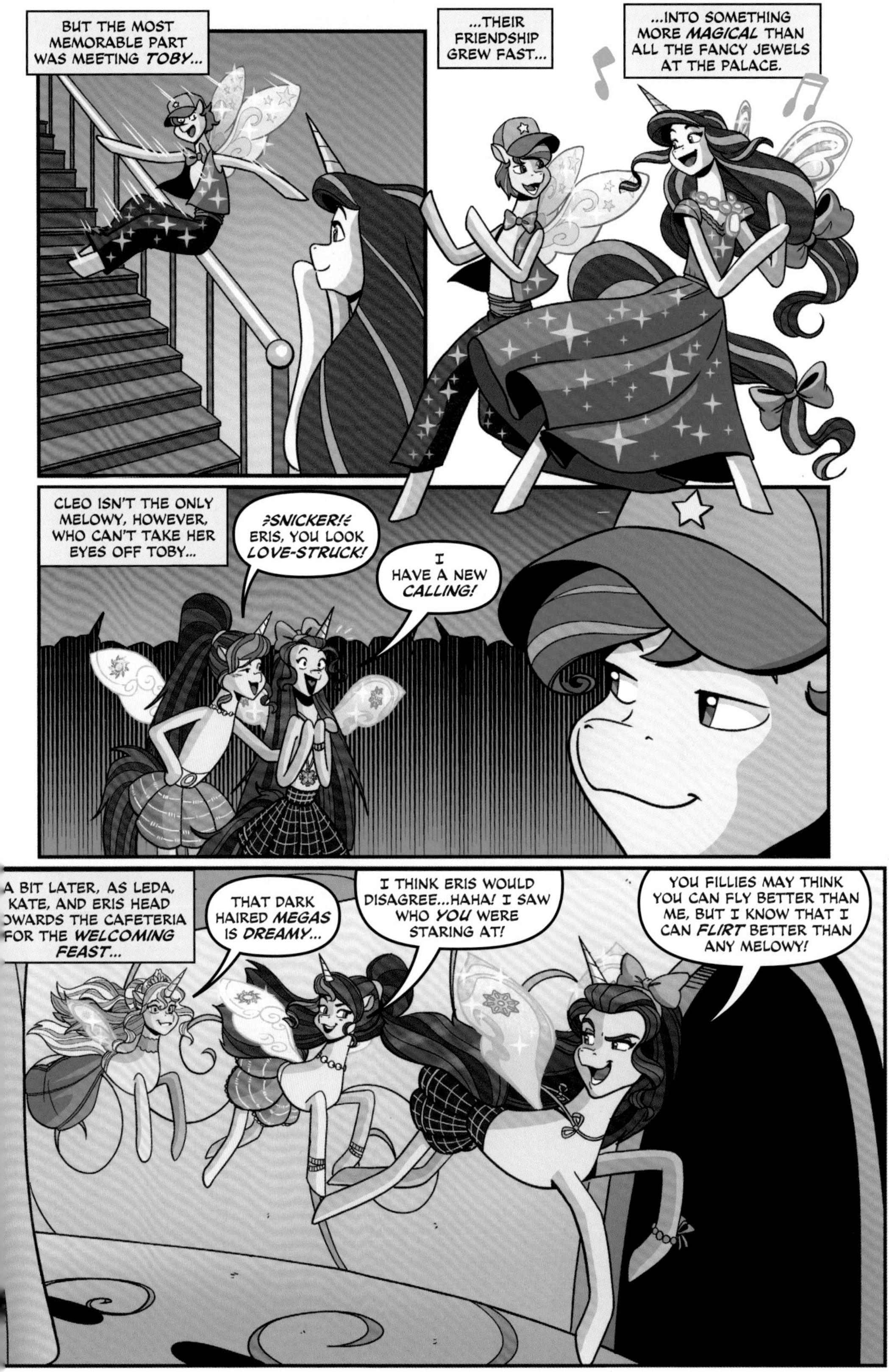
BUT THE MOST MEMORABLE PART WAS MEETING TOBY...
...THEIR FRIENDSHIP GREW FAST...
...INTO SOMETHING MORE MAGICAL THAN ALL THE FANCY JEWELS AT THE PALACE.
CLEO ISN'T THE ONLY MELOWY, HOWEVER, WHO CAN'T TAKE HER EYES OFF TOBY...
⇒SNICKER!⇐ ERIS, YOU LOOK LOVE-STRUCK!
I HAVE A NEW CALLING!
A BIT LATER, AS LEDA, KATE, AND ERIS HEAD TOWARDS THE CAFETERIA FOR THE WELCOMING FEAST...
THAT DARK HAIRED MEGAS IS DREAMY...
I THINK ERIS WOULD DISAGREE...HAHA! I SAW WHO YOU WERE STARING AT!
YOU FILLIES MAY THINK YOU CAN FLY BETTER THAN ME, BUT I KNOW THAT I CAN FLIRT BETTER THAN ANY MELOWY!

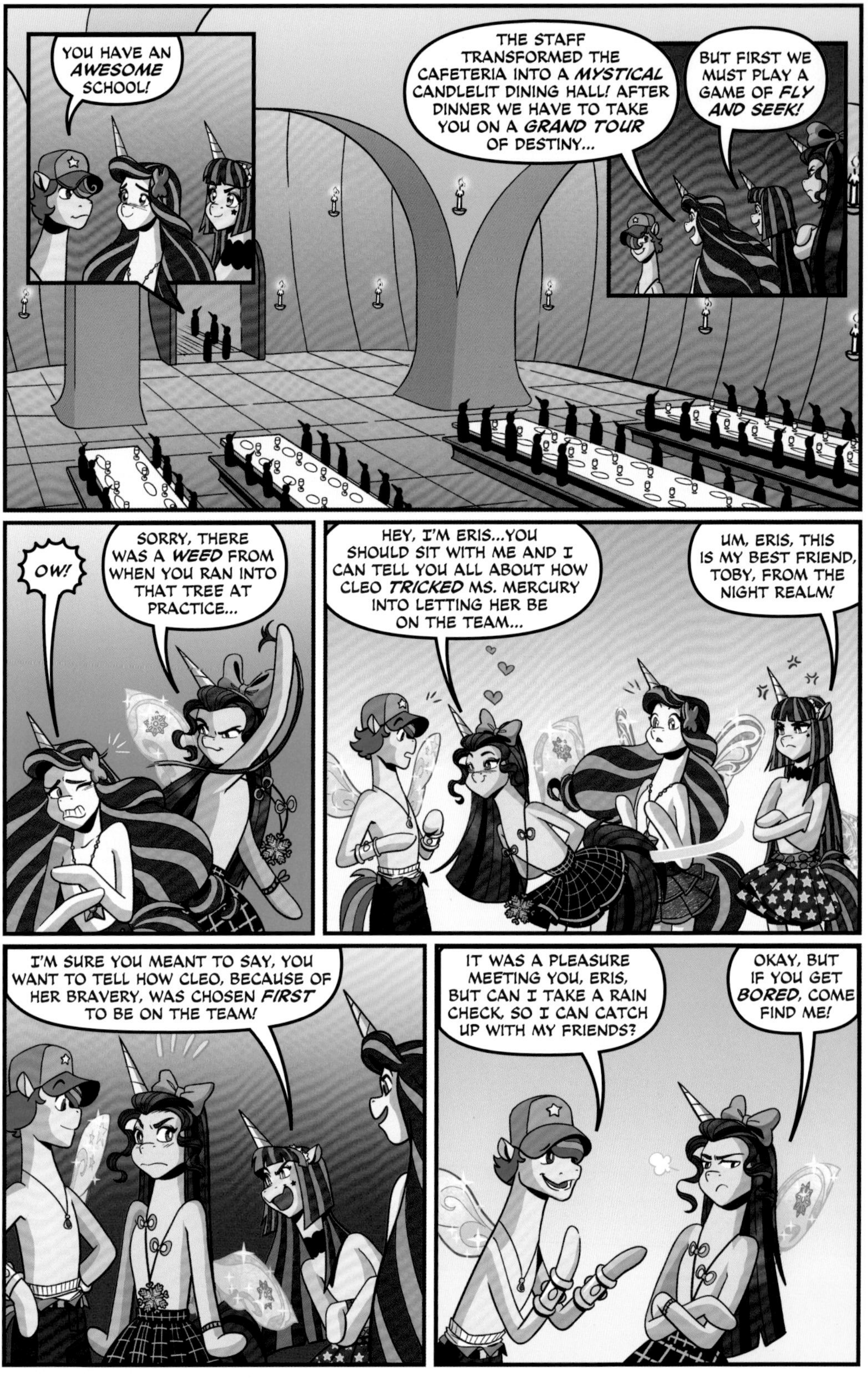

YOU HAVE AN AWESOME SCHOOL!
THE STAFF TRANSFORMED THE CAFETERIA INTO A MYSTICAL CANDLELIT DINING HALL! AFTER DINNER WE HAVE TO TAKE YOU ON A GRAND TOUR OF DESTINY...
BUT FIRST WE MUST PLAY A GAME OF FLY AND SEEK!
OW!
SORRY, THERE WAS A WEED FROM WHEN YOU RAN INTO THAT TREE AT PRACTICE...
HEY, I'M ERIS...YOU SHOULD SIT WITH ME AND I CAN TELL YOU ALL ABOUT HOW CLEO TRICKED MS. MERCURY INTO LETTING HER BE ON THE TEAM...
UM, ERIS, THIS IS MY BEST FRIEND, TOBY, FROM THE NIGHT REALM!
I'M SURE YOU MEANT TO SAY, YOU WANT TO TELL HOW CLEO, BECAUSE OF HER BRAVERY, WAS CHOSEN FIRST TO BE ON THE TEAM!
IT WAS A PLEASURE MEETING YOU, ERIS, BUT CAN I TAKE A RAIN CHECK, SO I CAN CATCH UP WITH MY FRIENDS?
OKAY, BUT IF YOU GET BORED, COME FIND ME!

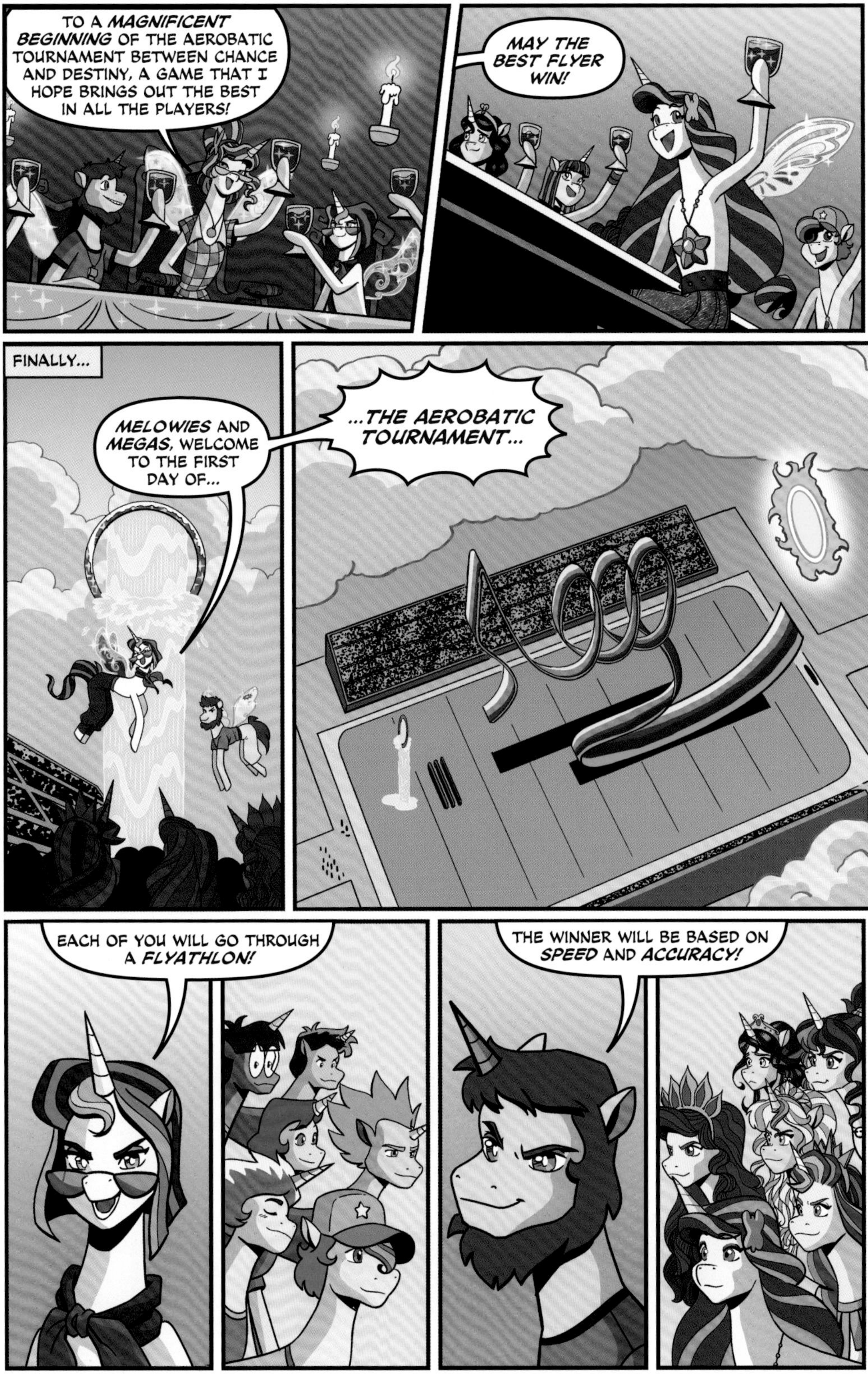
TO A MAGNIFICENT BEGINNING OF THE AEROBATIC TOURNAMENT BETWEEN CHANCE AND DESTINY, A GAME THAT I HOPE BRINGS OUT THE BEST IN ALL THE PLAYERS!
MAY THE BEST FLYER WIN!
FINALLY...
MELOWIES AND MEGAS, WELCOME TO THE FIRST DAY OF...
...THE AEROBATIC TOURNAMENT...
EACH OF YOU WILL GO THROUGH A FLYATHLON!
THE WINNER WILL BE BASED ON SPEED AND ACCURACY!

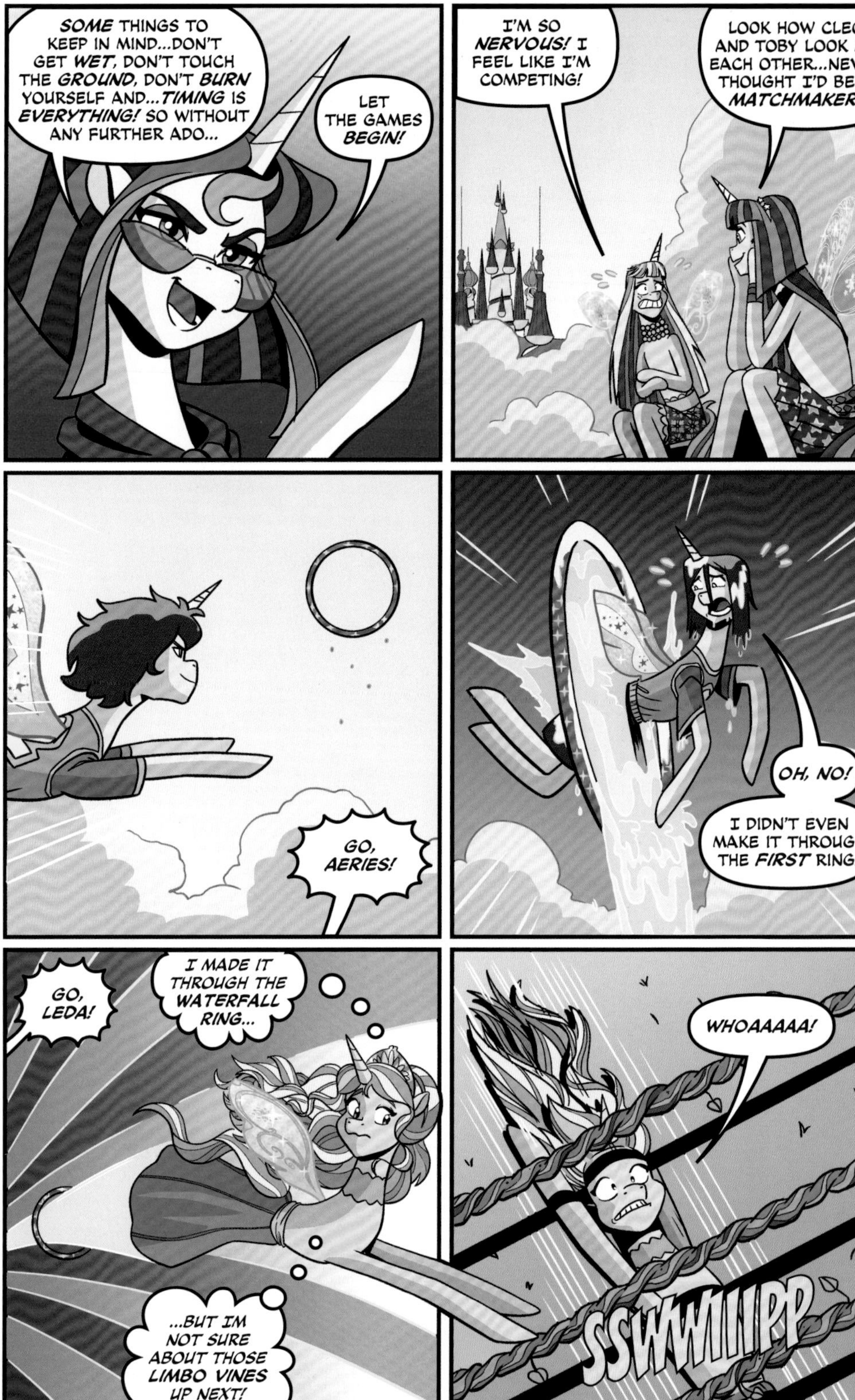
SOME THINGS TO KEEP IN MIND...DON'T GET WET, DON'T TOUCH THE GROUND, DON'T BURN YOURSELF AND...TIMING IS EVERYTHING! SO WITHOUT ANY FURTHER ADO...
LET THE GAMES BEGIN!
I'M SO NERVOUS! I FEEL LIKE I'M COMPETING!
LOOK HOW CLEO AND TOBY LOOK AT EACH OTHER...NEVER THOUGHT I'D BE A MATCHMAKER.
GO, AERIES!
OH, NO!
I DIDN'T EVEN MAKE IT THROUGH THE FIRST RING!
GO, LEDA!
I MADE IT THROUGH THE WATERFALL RING...
...BUT I'M NOT SURE ABOUT THOSE LIMBO VINES UP NEXT!
WHOAAAAA!
SSWWIIIPP

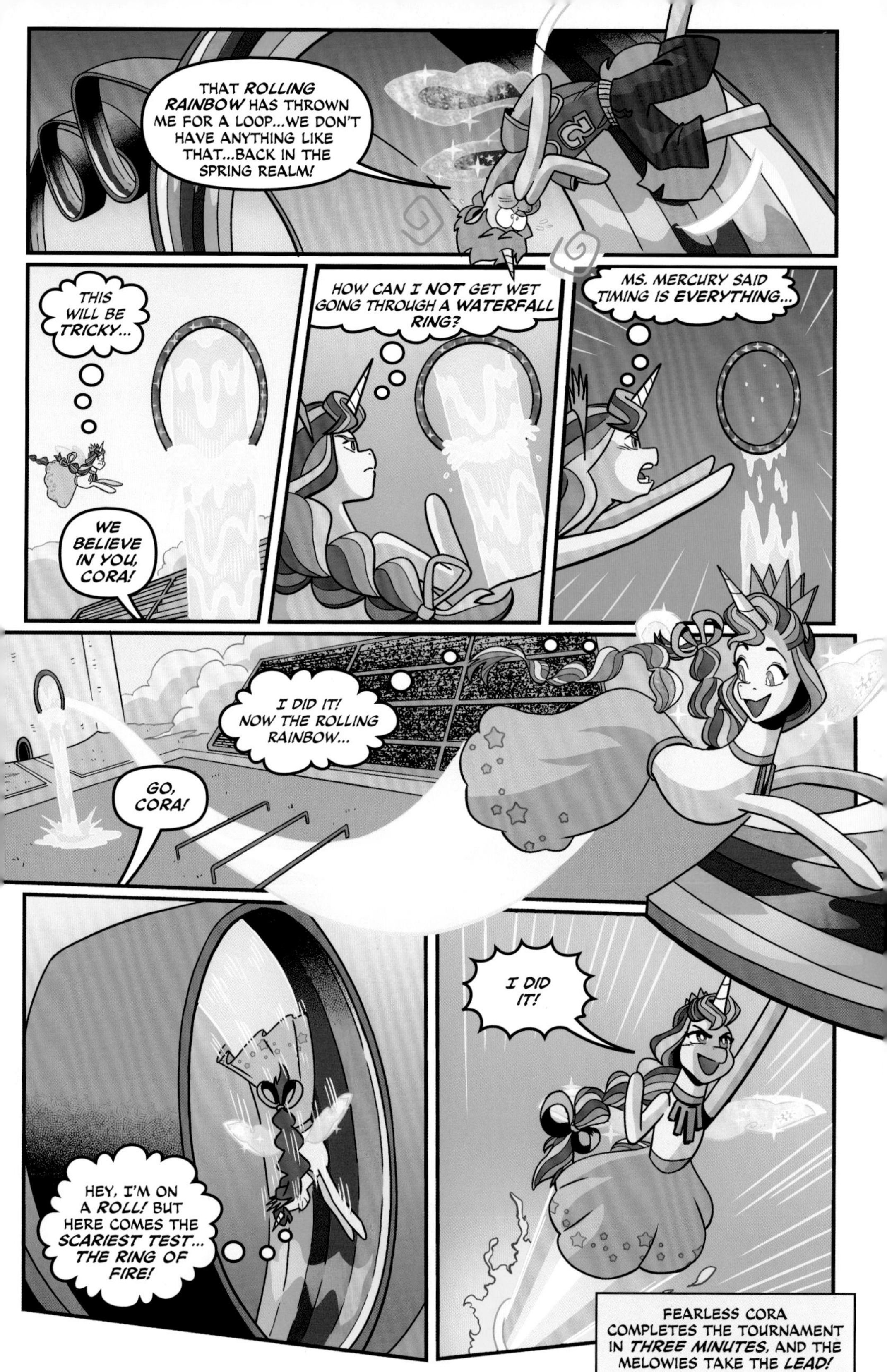
THAT ROLLING RAINBOW HAS THROWN ME FOR A LOOP...WE DON'T HAVE ANYTHING LIKE THAT...BACK IN THE SPRING REALM!
THIS WILL BE TRICKY...
WE BELIEVE IN YOU, CORA!
HOW CAN I NOT GET WET GOING THROUGH A WATERFALL RING?
MS. MERCURY SAID TIMING IS EVERYTHING...
I DID IT! NOW THE ROLLING RAINBOW...
GO, CORA!
HEY, I'M ON A ROLL! BUT HERE COMES THE SCARIEST TEST... THE RING OF FIRE!
I DID IT!
FEARLESS CORA COMPLETES THE TOURNAMENT IN THREE MINUTES, AND THE MELOWIES TAKE THE LEAD!

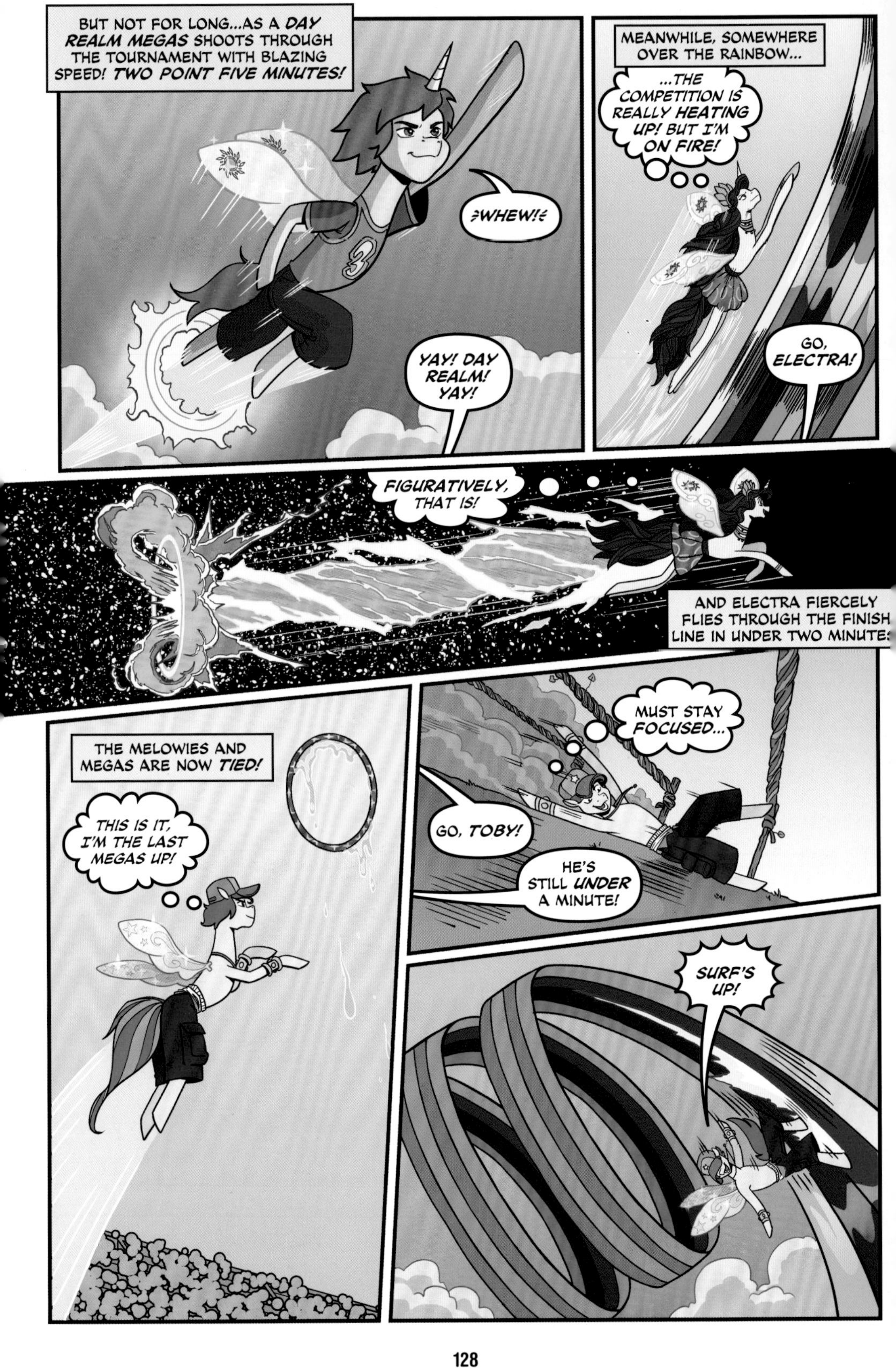
BUT NOT FOR LONG...AS A DAY REALM MEGAS SHOOTS THROUGH THE TOURNAMENT WITH BLAZING SPEED! TWO POINT FIVE MINUTES!
WHEW!
YAY! DAY REALM! YAY!
MEANWHILE, SOMEWHERE OVER THE RAINBOW...
...THE COMPETITION IS REALLY HEATING UP! BUT I'M ON FIRE!
GO, ELECTRA!
FIGURATIVELY, THAT IS!
AND ELECTRA FIERCELY FLIES THROUGH THE FINISH LINE IN UNDER TWO MINUTES
THE MELOWIES AND MEGAS ARE NOW TIED!
THIS IS IT, I'M THE LAST MEGAS UP!
MUST STAY FOCUSED...
GO, TOBY!
HE'S STILL UNDER A MINUTE!
SURF'S UP!

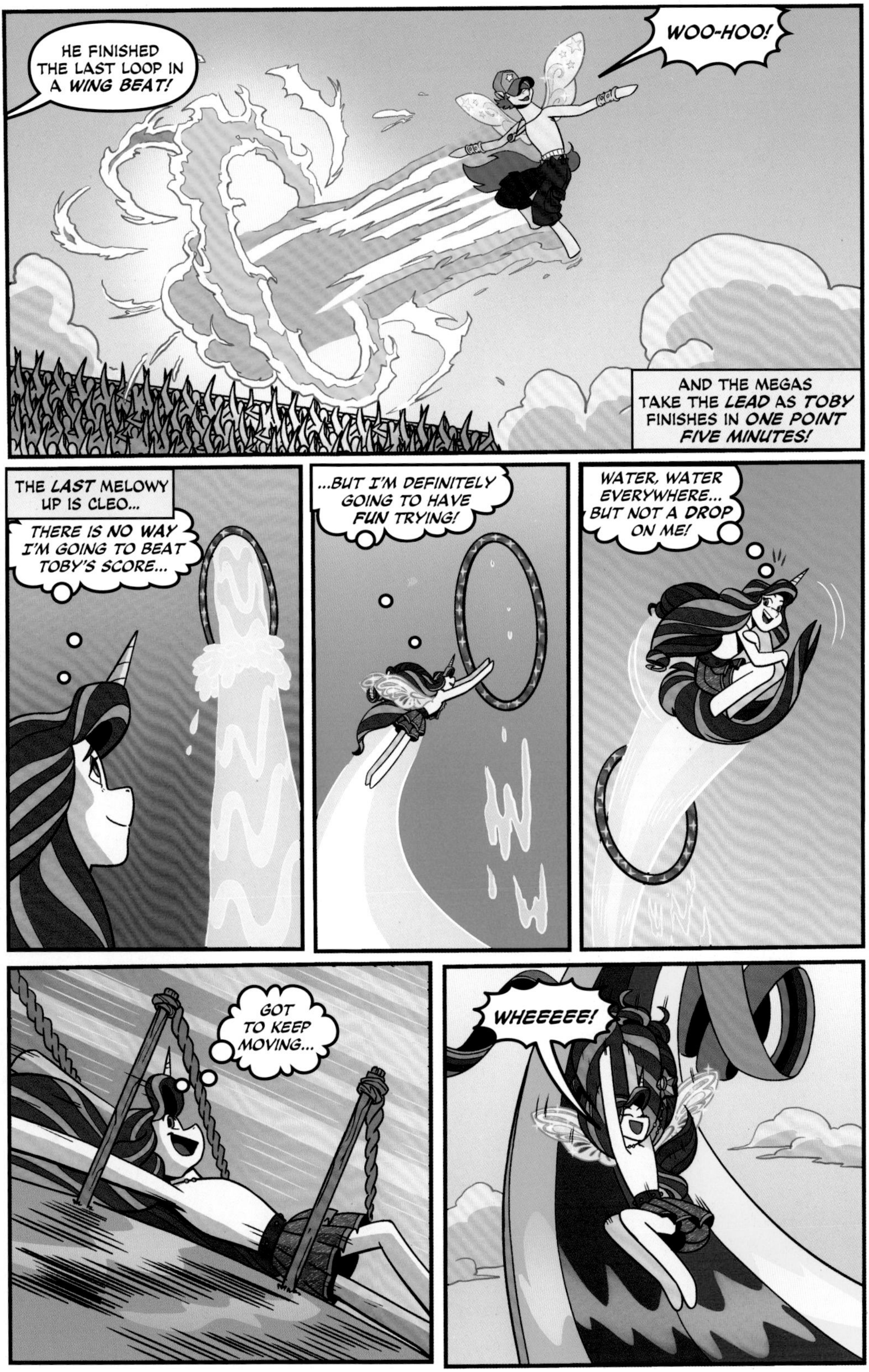
HE FINISHED THE LAST LOOP IN A *WING BEAT!*
WOO-HOO!
AND THE MEGAS TAKE THE *LEAD* AS *TOBY* FINISHES IN *ONE POINT FIVE MINUTES!*
THE *LAST* MELOWY UP IS CLEO...
THERE IS NO WAY I'M GOING TO BEAT TOBY'S SCORE...
...BUT I'M DEFINITELY GOING TO HAVE FUN TRYING!
WATER, WATER EVERYWHERE... BUT NOT A DROP ON ME!
GOT TO KEEP MOVING...
WHEEEEE!

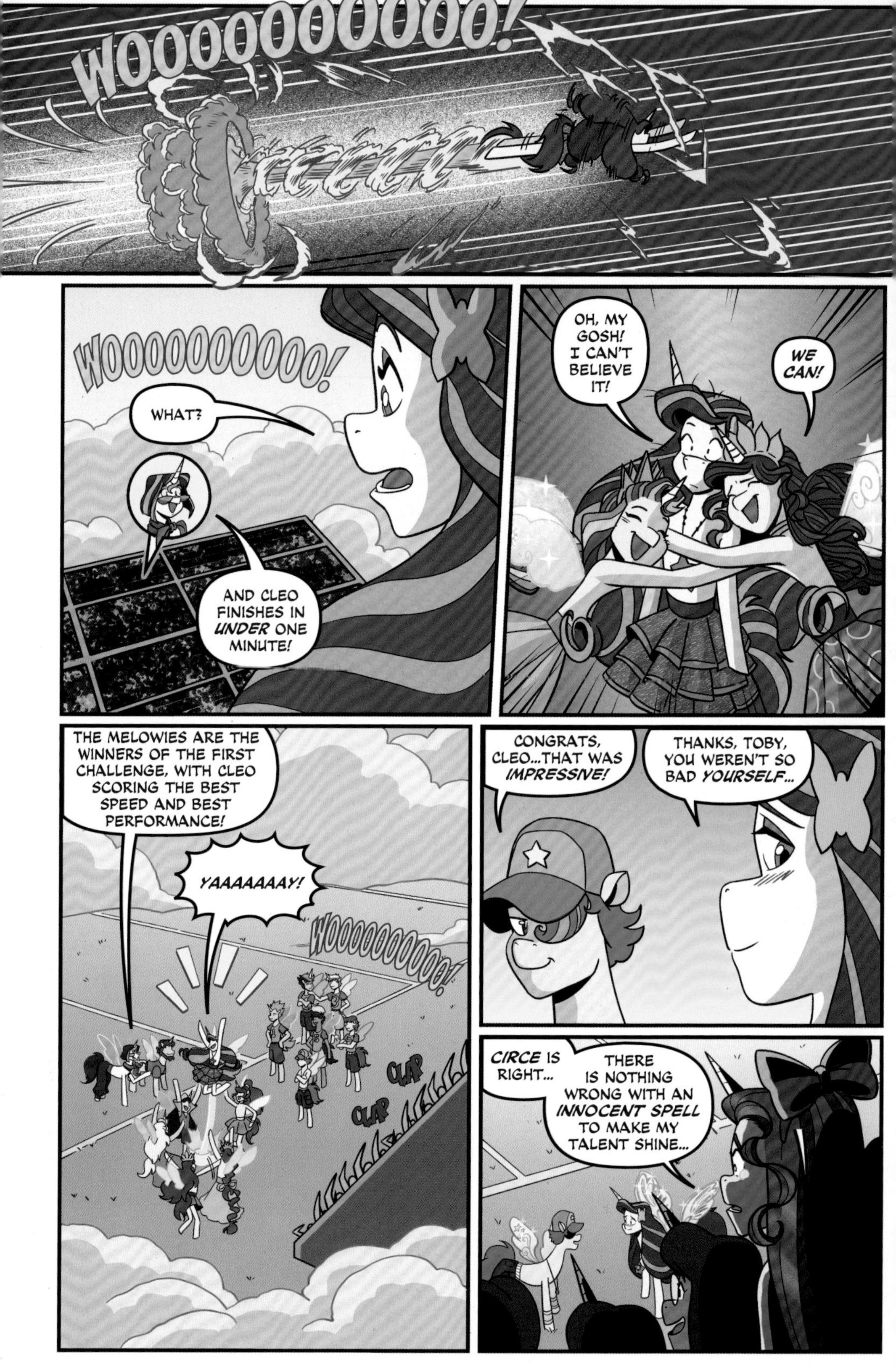
WOOOOOOOOOO!
WOOOOOOOOOOO!
WHAT?
AND CLEO FINISHES IN *UNDER* ONE MINUTE!
OH, MY GOSH! I CAN'T BELIEVE IT!
WE CAN!
THE MELOWIES ARE THE WINNERS OF THE FIRST CHALLENGE, WITH CLEO SCORING THE BEST SPEED AND BEST PERFORMANCE!
YAAAAAAAY!
WOOOOOOOOOOO!
CLAP
CLAP
CONGRATS, CLEO...THAT WAS *IMPRESSIVE!*
THANKS, TOBY, YOU WEREN'T SO BAD *YOURSELF*...
CIRCE IS RIGHT...
THERE IS NOTHING WRONG WITH AN *INNOCENT SPELL* TO MAKE MY TALENT SHINE...

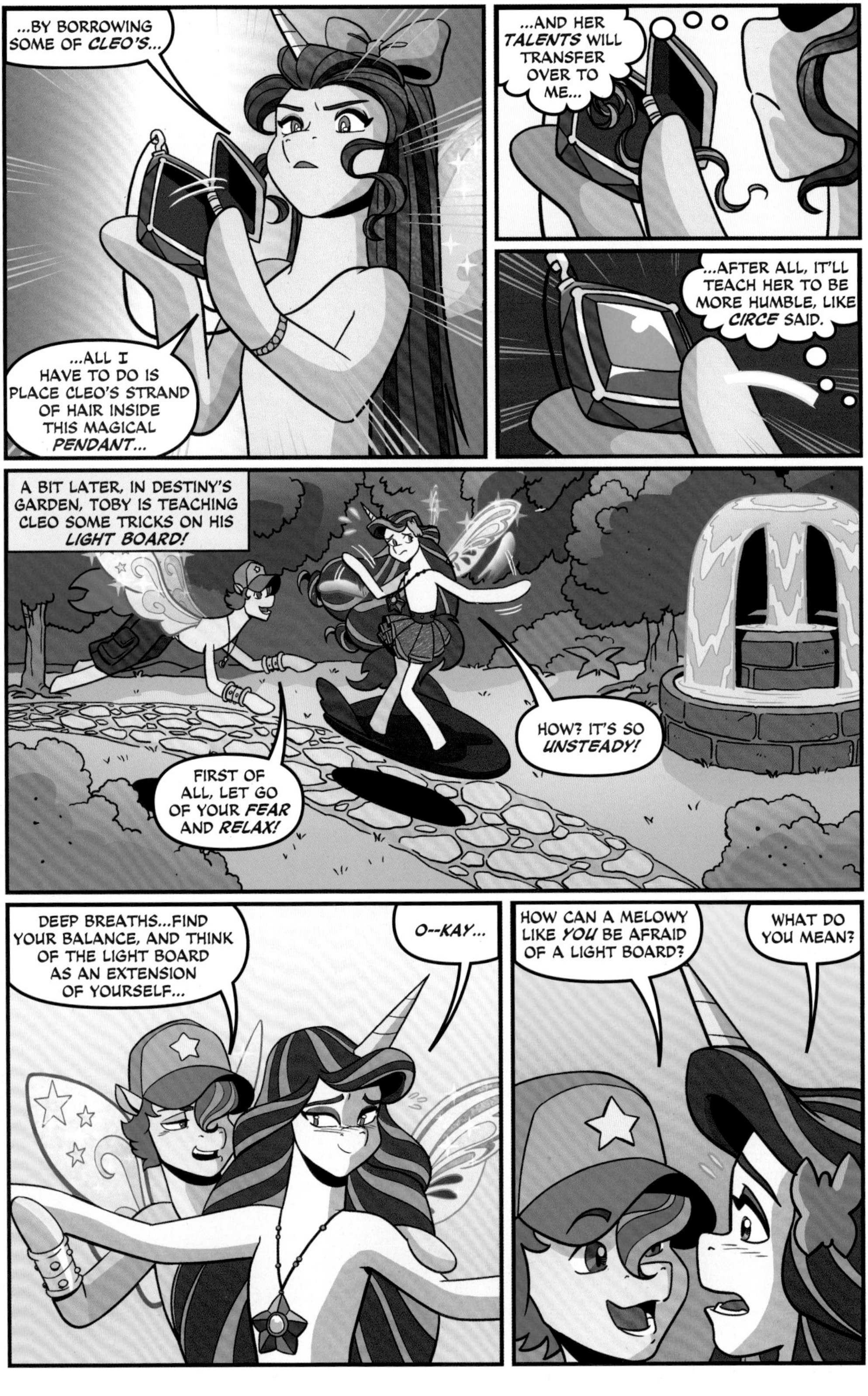
...BY BORROWING SOME OF CLEO'S...
...ALL I HAVE TO DO IS PLACE CLEO'S STRAND OF HAIR INSIDE THIS MAGICAL PENDANT...
...AND HER TALENTS WILL TRANSFER OVER TO ME...
...AFTER ALL, IT'LL TEACH HER TO BE MORE HUMBLE, LIKE CIRCE SAID.
A BIT LATER, IN DESTINY'S GARDEN, TOBY IS TEACHING CLEO SOME TRICKS ON HIS LIGHT BOARD!
HOW? IT'S SO UNSTEADY!
FIRST OF ALL, LET GO OF YOUR FEAR AND RELAX!
DEEP BREATHS...FIND YOUR BALANCE, AND THINK OF THE LIGHT BOARD AS AN EXTENSION OF YOURSELF...
O--KAY...
HOW CAN A MELOWY LIKE YOU BE AFRAID OF A LIGHT BOARD?
WHAT DO YOU MEAN?

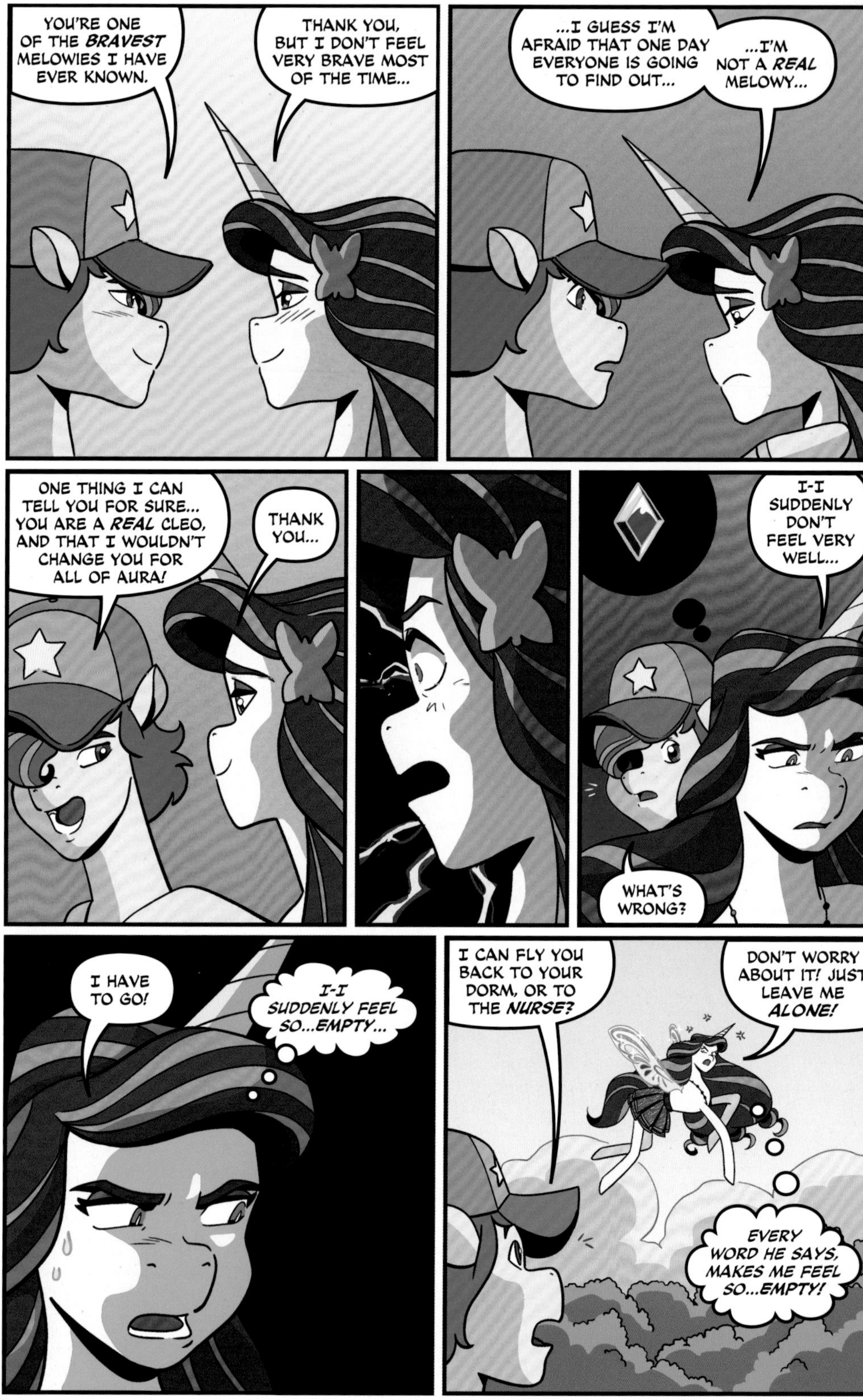
YOU'RE ONE OF THE *BRAVEST* MELOWIES I HAVE EVER KNOWN.
THANK YOU, BUT I DON'T FEEL VERY BRAVE MOST OF THE TIME...
...I GUESS I'M AFRAID THAT ONE DAY EVERYONE IS GOING TO FIND OUT...
...I'M NOT A *REAL* MELOWY...
ONE THING I CAN TELL YOU FOR SURE... YOU ARE A *REAL* CLEO, AND THAT I WOULDN'T CHANGE YOU FOR ALL OF AURA!
THANK YOU...
I-I SUDDENLY DON'T FEEL VERY WELL...
WHAT'S WRONG?
I HAVE TO GO!
I-I SUDDENLY FEEL SO...EMPTY...
I CAN FLY YOU BACK TO YOUR DORM, OR TO THE *NURSE?*
DON'T WORRY ABOUT IT! JUST LEAVE ME *ALONE!*
EVERY WORD HE SAYS, MAKES ME FEEL SO...EMPTY!

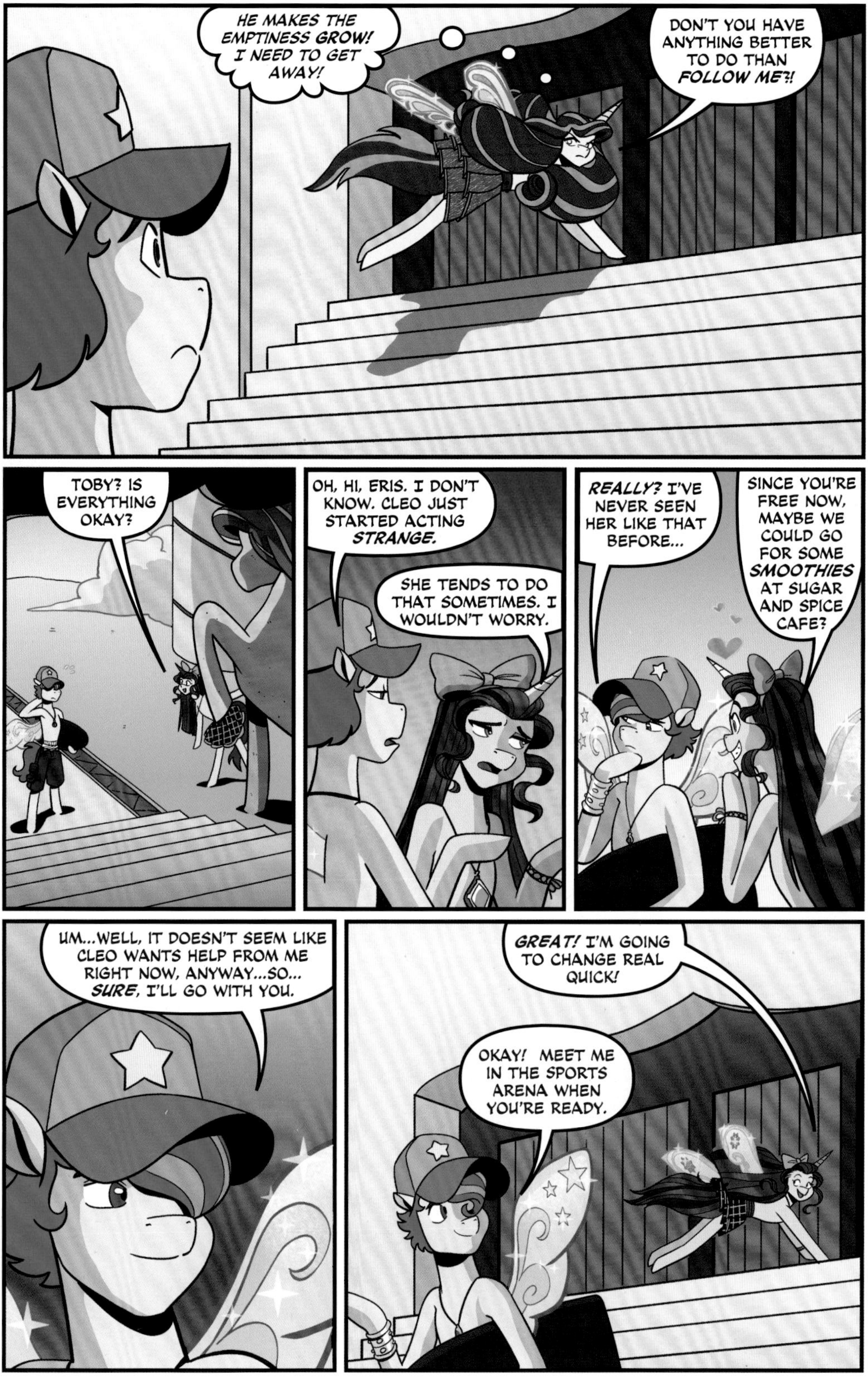
HE MAKES THE EMPTINESS GROW! I NEED TO GET AWAY!
DON'T YOU HAVE ANYTHING BETTER TO DO THAN FOLLOW ME?!
TOBY? IS EVERYTHING OKAY?
OH, HI, ERIS. I DON'T KNOW. CLEO JUST STARTED ACTING STRANGE.
SHE TENDS TO DO THAT SOMETIMES. I WOULDN'T WORRY.
REALLY? I'VE NEVER SEEN HER LIKE THAT BEFORE...
SINCE YOU'RE FREE NOW, MAYBE WE COULD GO FOR SOME SMOOTHIES AT SUGAR AND SPICE CAFE?
UM...WELL, IT DOESN'T SEEM LIKE CLEO WANTS HELP FROM ME RIGHT NOW, ANYWAY...SO... SURE, I'LL GO WITH YOU.
GREAT! I'M GOING TO CHANGE REAL QUICK!
OKAY! MEET ME IN THE SPORTS ARENA WHEN YOU'RE READY.

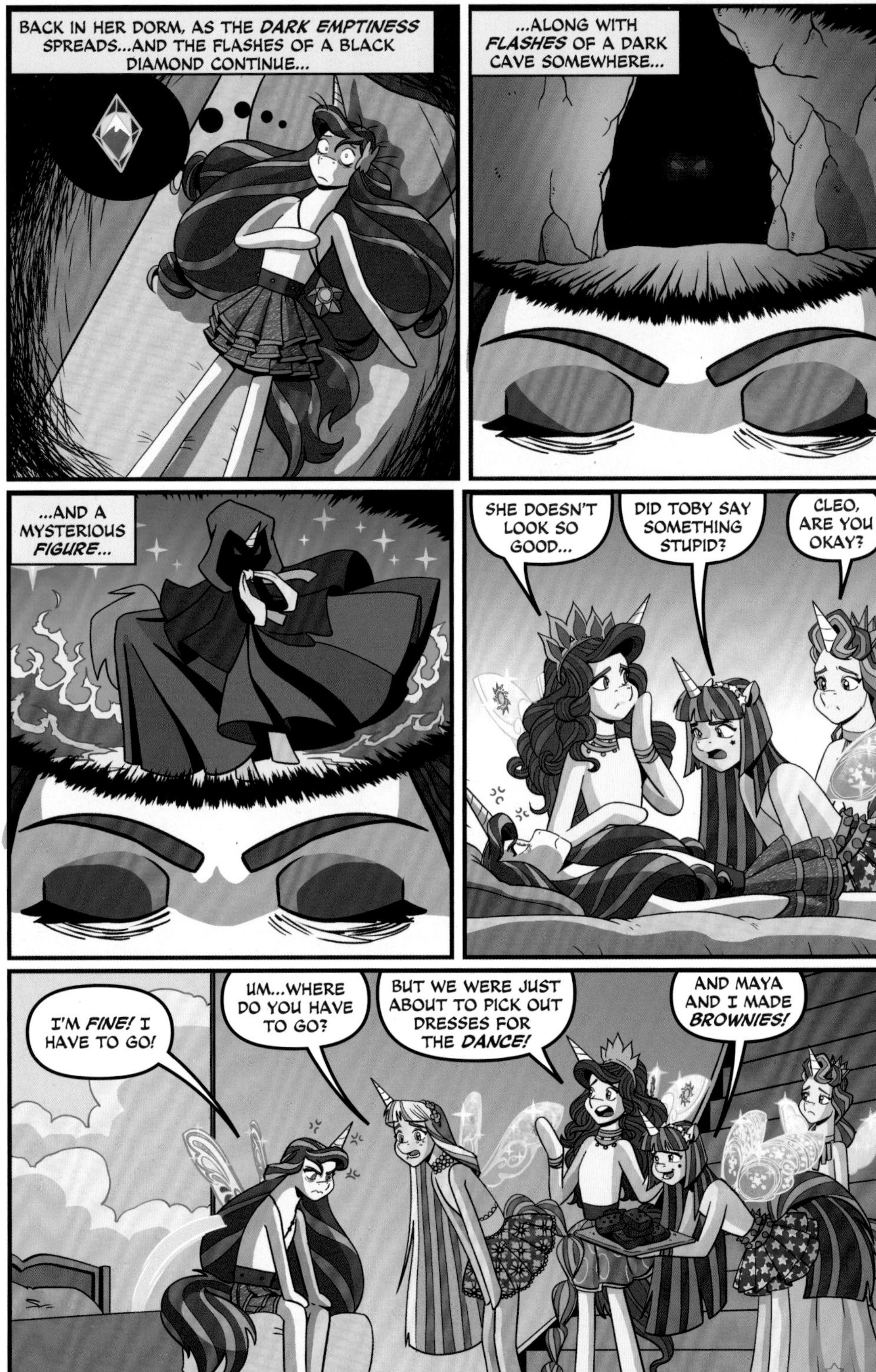

BACK IN HER DORM, AS THE DARK EMPTINESS SPREADS...AND THE FLASHES OF A BLACK DIAMOND CONTINUE...
...ALONG WITH FLASHES OF A DARK CAVE SOMEWHERE...
...AND A MYSTERIOUS FIGURE...
SHE DOESN'T LOOK SO GOOD...
DID TOBY SAY SOMETHING STUPID?
CLEO, ARE YOU OKAY?
I'M FINE! I HAVE TO GO!
UM...WHERE DO YOU HAVE TO GO?
BUT WE WERE JUST ABOUT TO PICK OUT DRESSES FOR THE DANCE!
AND MAYA AND I MADE BROWNIES!

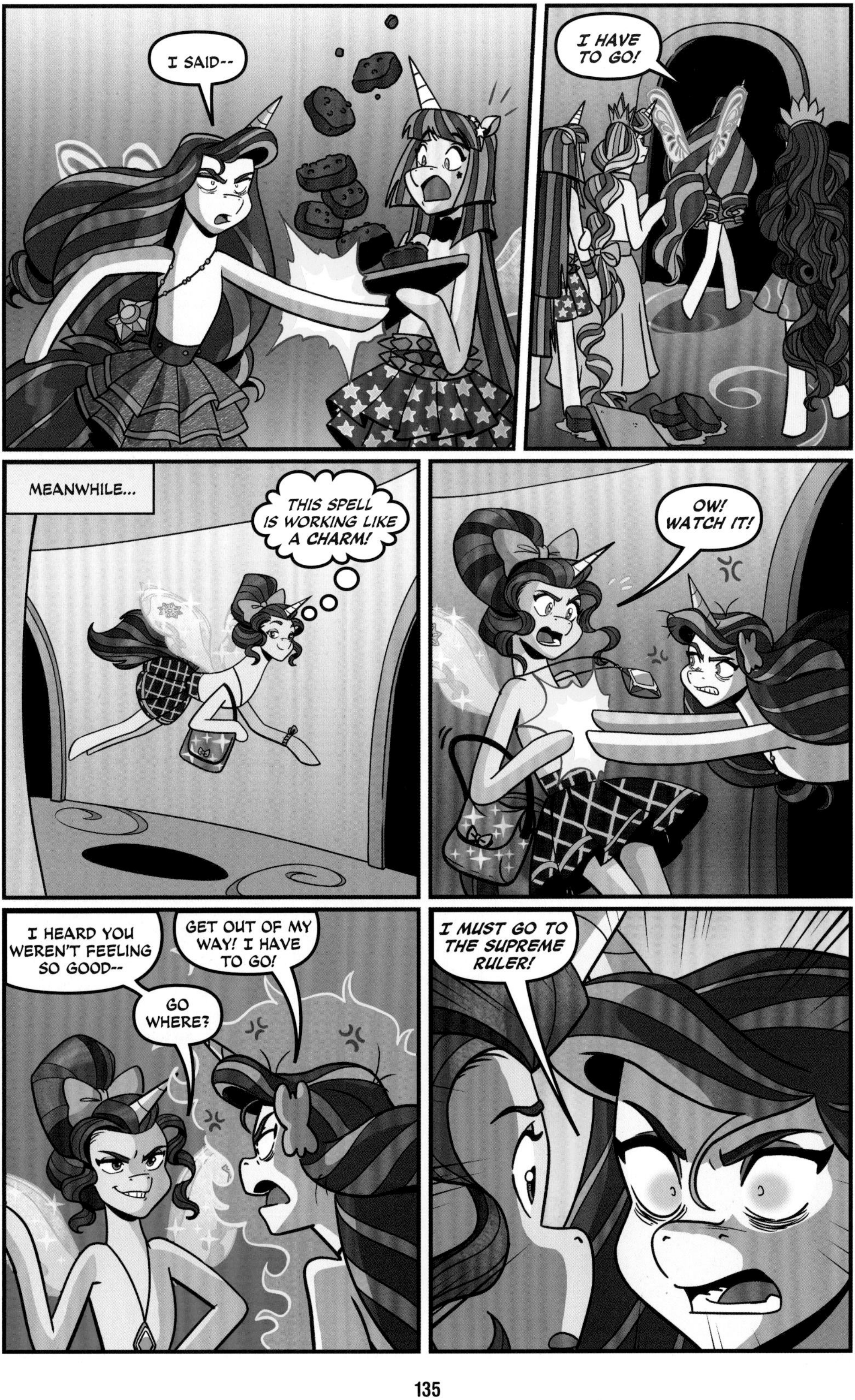
I SAID--
I HAVE TO GO!
MEANWHILE...
THIS SPELL IS WORKING LIKE A CHARM!
OW! WATCH IT!
I HEARD YOU WEREN'T FEELING SO GOOD--
GET OUT OF MY WAY! I HAVE TO GO!
GO WHERE?
I MUST GO TO THE SUPREME RULER!

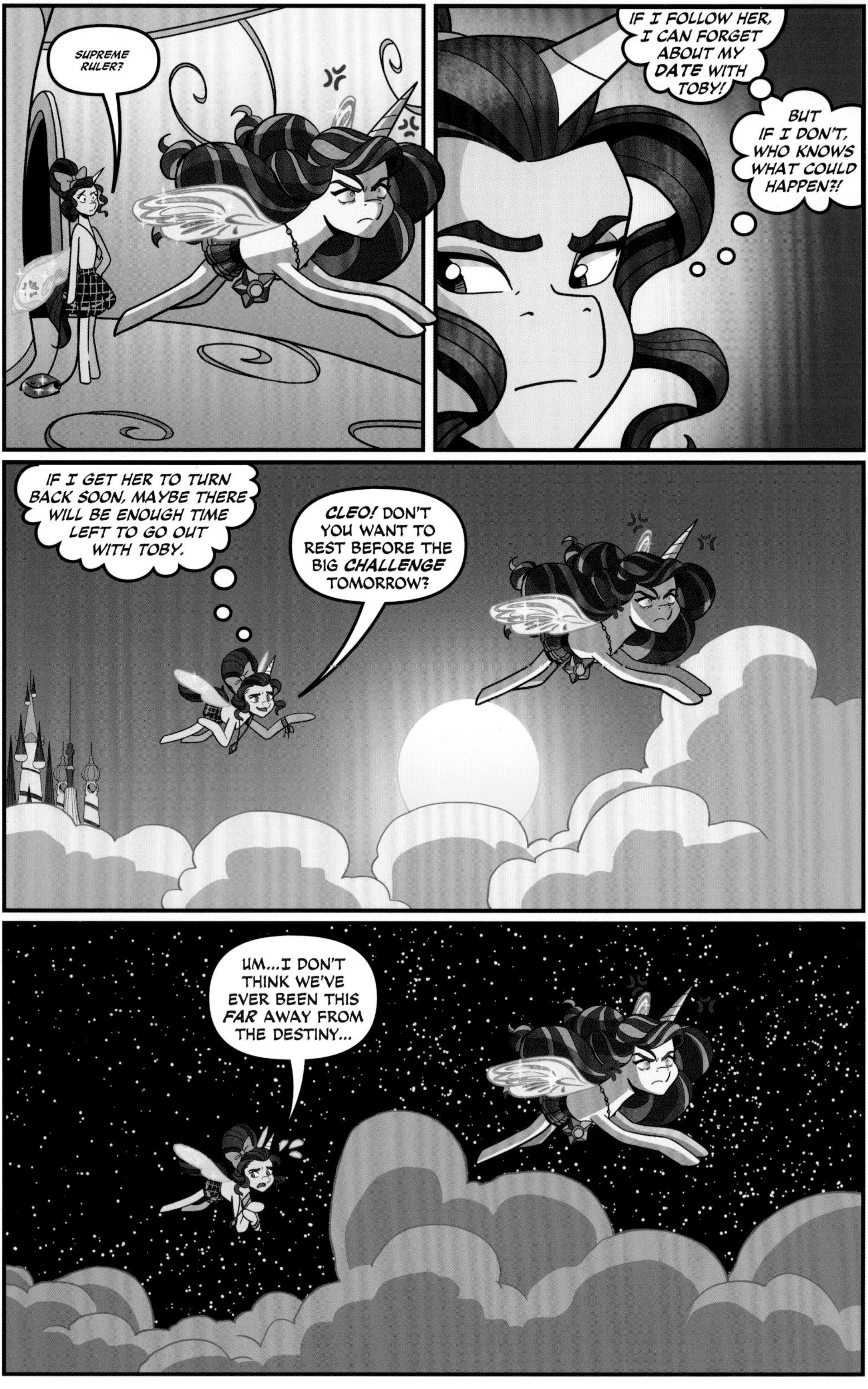
SUPREME RULER?
IF I FOLLOW HER, I CAN FORGET ABOUT MY DATE WITH TOBY!
BUT IF I DON'T, WHO KNOWS WHAT COULD HAPPEN?!
IF I GET HER TO TURN BACK SOON, MAYBE THERE WILL BE ENOUGH TIME LEFT TO GO OUT WITH TOBY.
CLEO! DON'T YOU WANT TO REST BEFORE THE BIG CHALLENGE TOMORROW?
UM...I DON'T THINK WE'VE EVER BEEN THIS FAR AWAY FROM THE DESTINY...

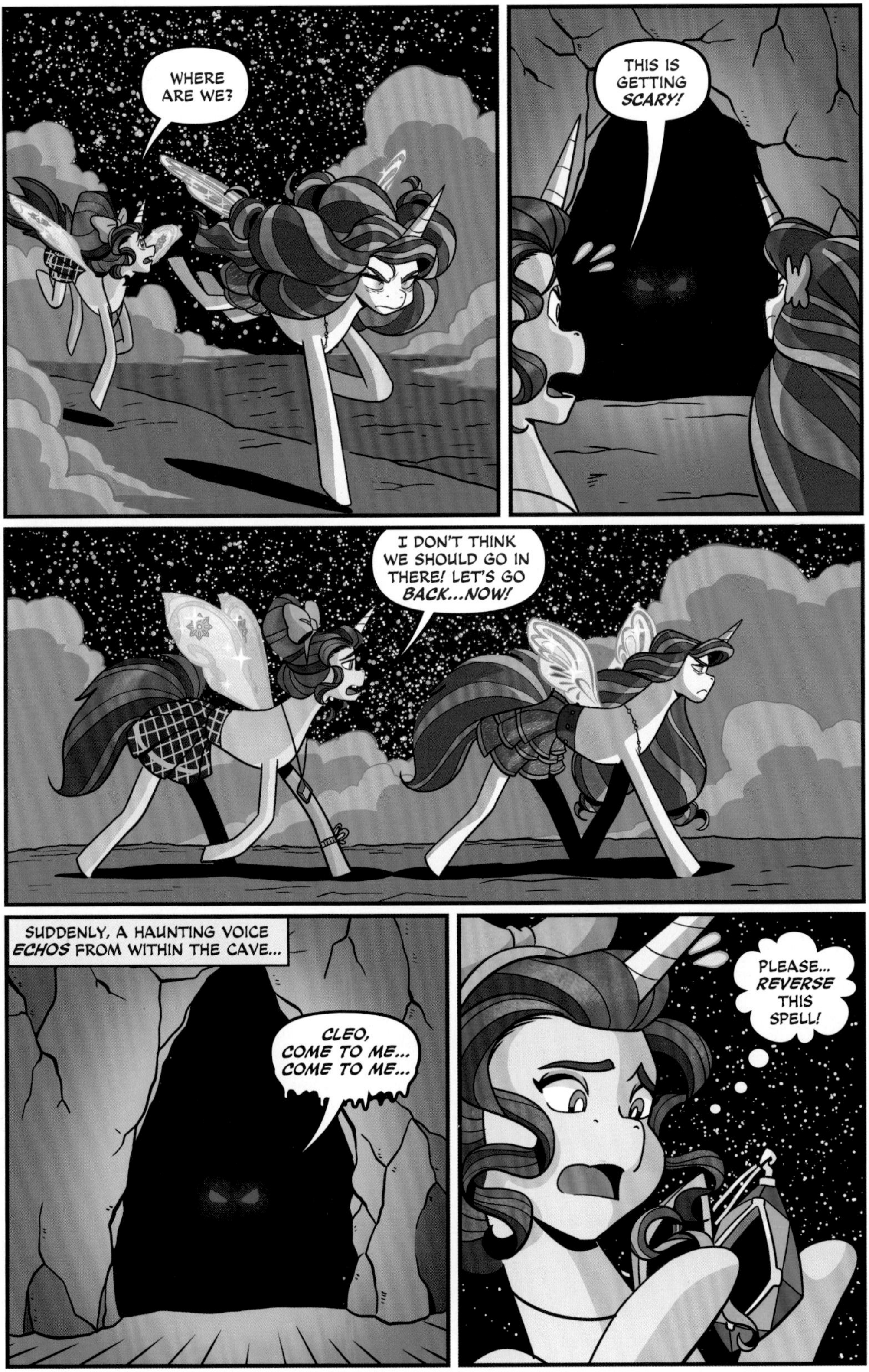
WHERE ARE WE?
THIS IS GETTING SCARY!
I DON'T THINK WE SHOULD GO IN THERE! LET'S GO BACK...NOW!
SUDDENLY, A HAUNTING VOICE ECHOS FROM WITHIN THE CAVE...
CLEO, COME TO ME... COME TO ME...
PLEASE... REVERSE THIS SPELL!

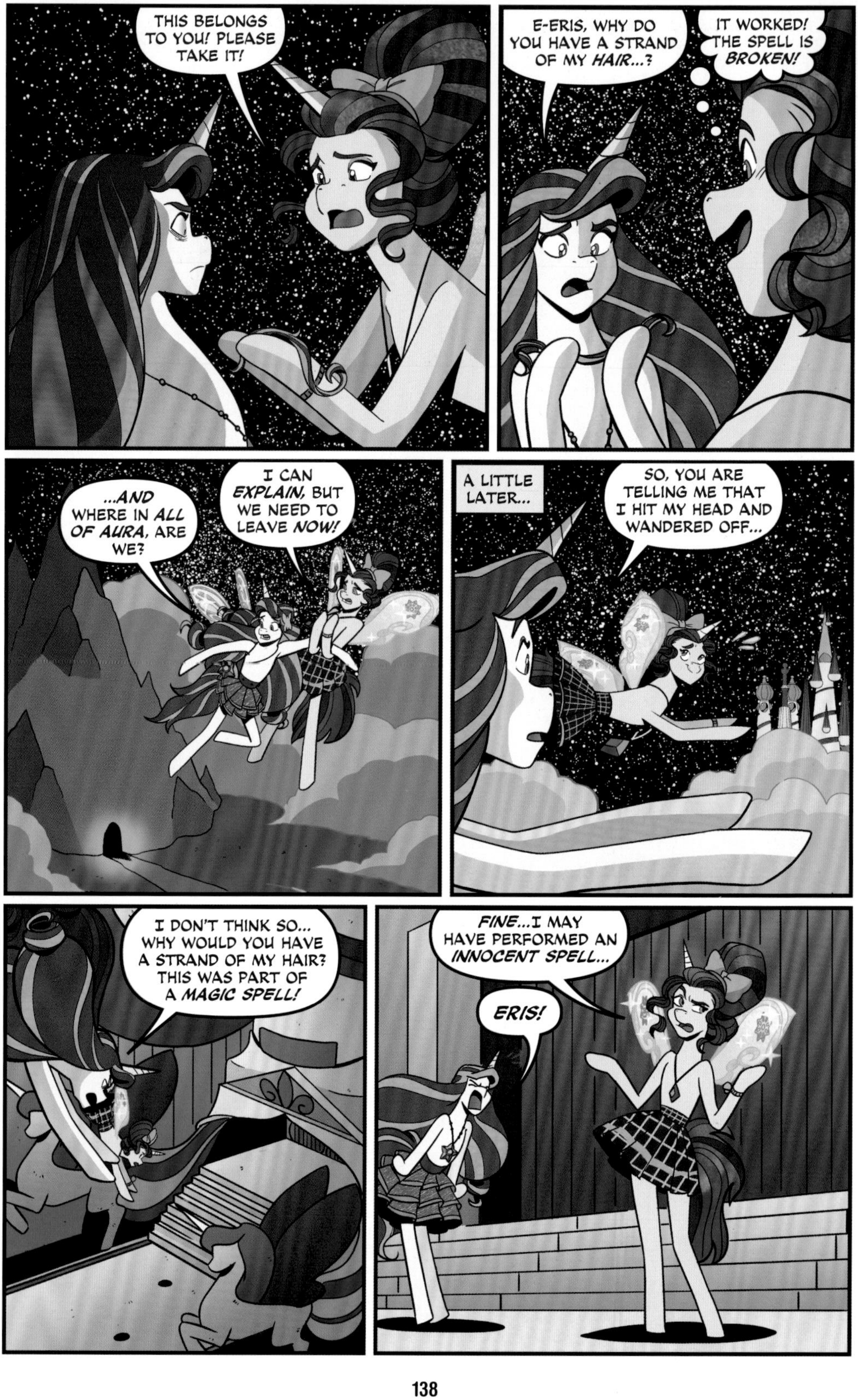
THIS BELONGS TO YOU! PLEASE TAKE IT!
E-ERIS, WHY DO YOU HAVE A STRAND OF MY HAIR...?
IT WORKED! THE SPELL IS BROKEN!
...AND WHERE IN ALL OF AURA, ARE WE?
I CAN EXPLAIN, BUT WE NEED TO LEAVE NOW!
A LITTLE LATER...
SO, YOU ARE TELLING ME THAT I HIT MY HEAD AND WANDERED OFF...
I DON'T THINK SO... WHY WOULD YOU HAVE A STRAND OF MY HAIR? THIS WAS PART OF A MAGIC SPELL!
FINE...I MAY HAVE PERFORMED AN INNOCENT SPELL...
ERIS!

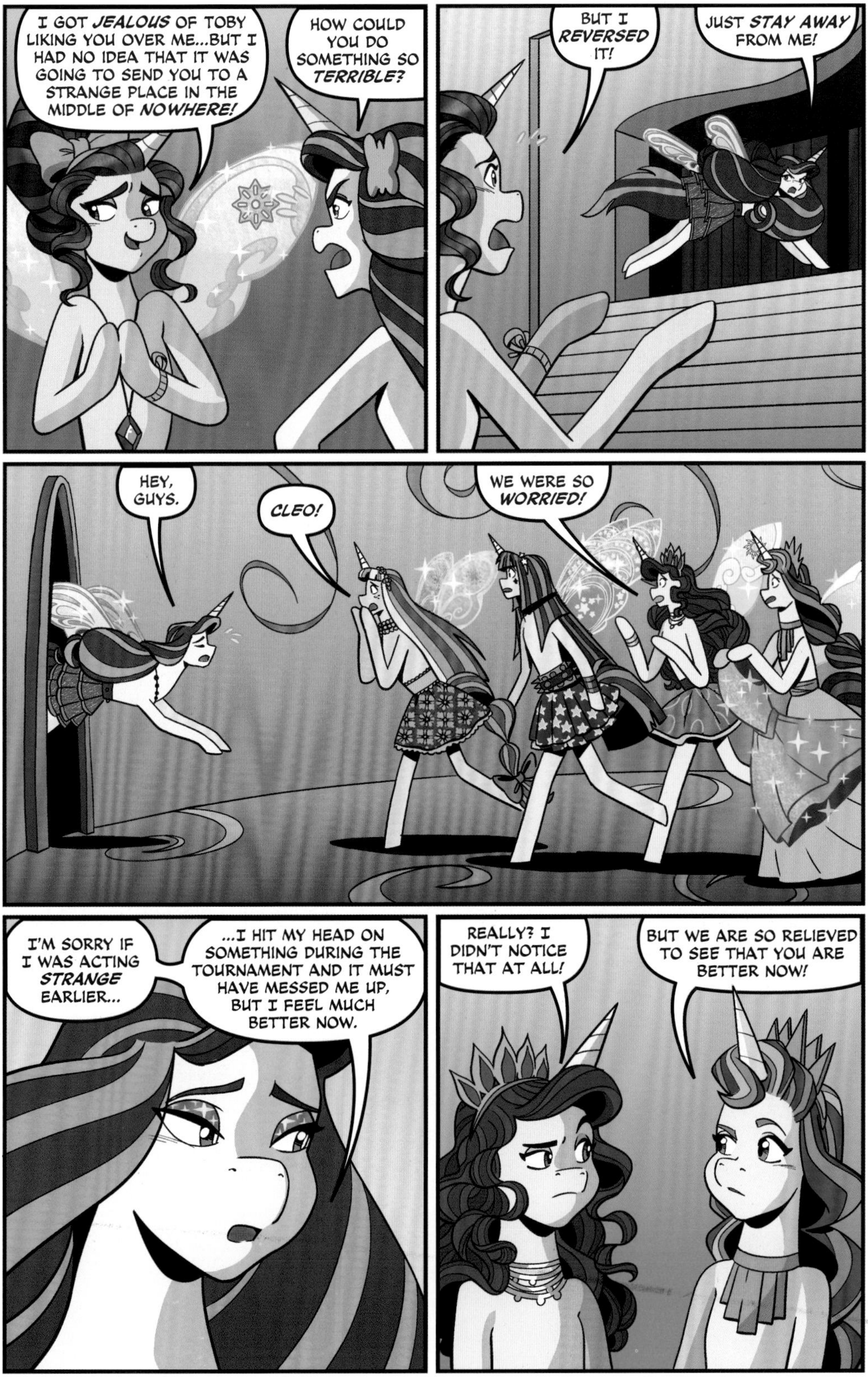
I GOT JEALOUS OF TOBY LIKING YOU OVER ME...BUT I HAD NO IDEA THAT IT WAS GOING TO SEND YOU TO A STRANGE PLACE IN THE MIDDLE OF NOWHERE!
HOW COULD YOU DO SOMETHING SO TERRIBLE?
BUT I REVERSED IT!
JUST STAY AWAY FROM ME!
HEY, GUYS.
CLEO!
WE WERE SO WORRIED!
I'M SORRY IF I WAS ACTING STRANGE EARLIER...
...I HIT MY HEAD ON SOMETHING DURING THE TOURNAMENT AND IT MUST HAVE MESSED ME UP, BUT I FEEL MUCH BETTER NOW.
REALLY? I DIDN'T NOTICE THAT AT ALL!
BUT WE ARE SO RELIEVED TO SEE THAT YOU ARE BETTER NOW!

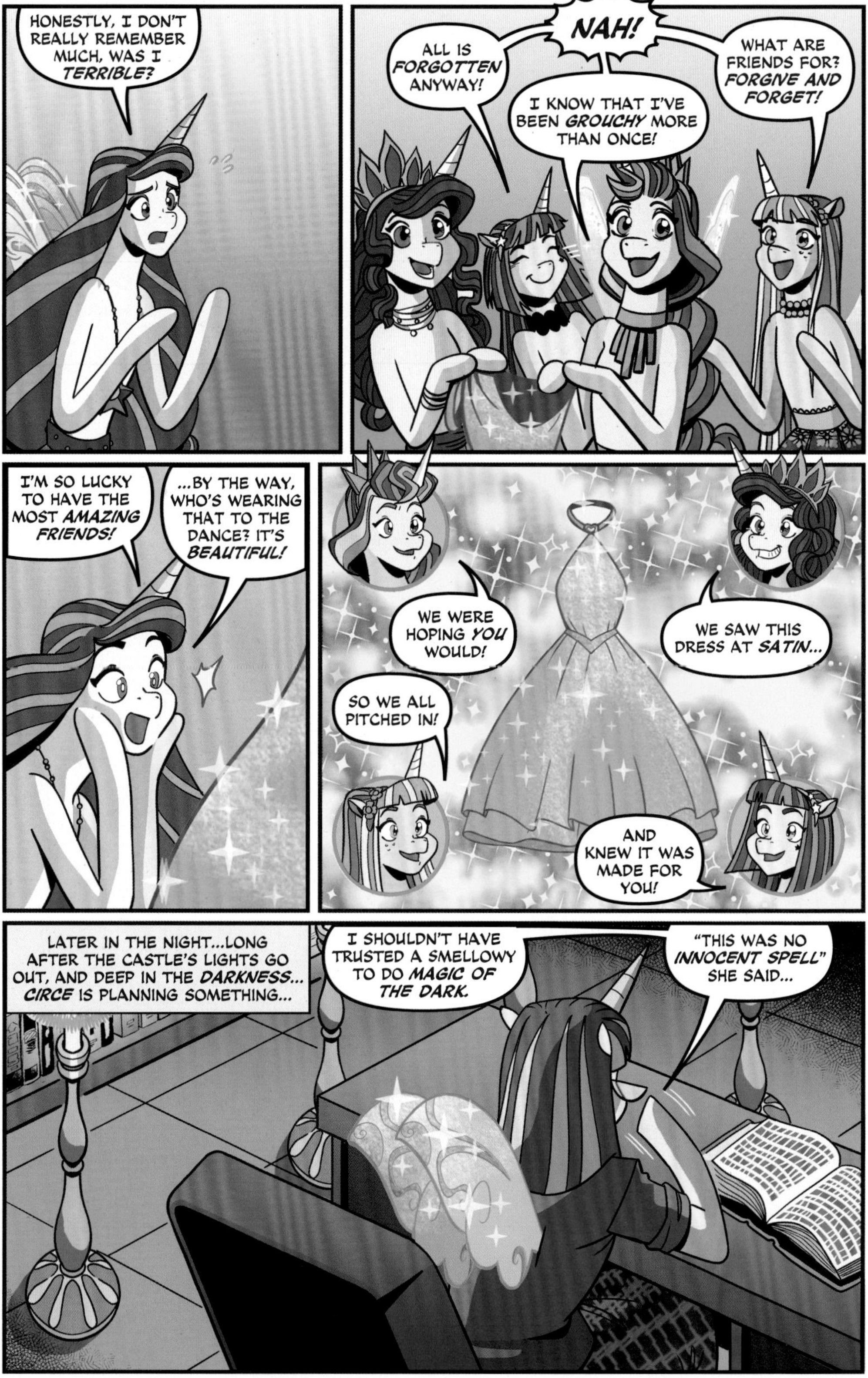
HONESTLY, I DON'T REALLY REMEMBER MUCH, WAS I TERRIBLE?
NAH!
ALL IS FORGOTTEN ANYWAY!
I KNOW THAT I'VE BEEN GROUCHY MORE THAN ONCE!
WHAT ARE FRIENDS FOR? FORGIVE AND FORGET!
I'M SO LUCKY TO HAVE THE MOST AMAZING FRIENDS!
...BY THE WAY, WHO'S WEARING THAT TO THE DANCE? IT'S BEAUTIFUL!
WE WERE HOPING YOU WOULD!
WE SAW THIS DRESS AT SATIN...
SO WE ALL PITCHED IN!
AND KNEW IT WAS MADE FOR YOU!
LATER IN THE NIGHT...LONG AFTER THE CASTLE'S LIGHTS GO OUT, AND DEEP IN THE DARKNESS... CIRCE IS PLANNING SOMETHING...
I SHOULDN'T HAVE TRUSTED A SMELLOWY TO DO MAGIC OF THE DARK.
"THIS WAS NO INNOCENT SPELL" SHE SAID...

IF YOU WANT SOMETHING DONE RIGHT, YOU HAVE TO DO IT *YOURSELF!*

FEAR NOT, *SUPREME RULER...*

CLEO WILL BE *YOURS!*

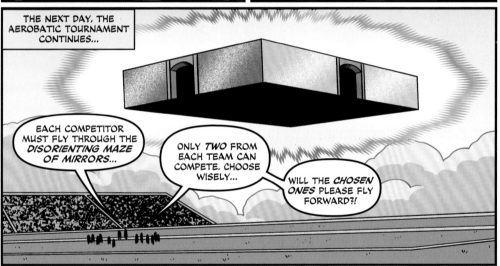

THE NEXT DAY, THE AEROBATIC TOURNAMENT CONTINUES...

EACH COMPETITOR MUST FLY THROUGH THE *DISORIENTING MAZE OF MIRRORS...*

ONLY *TWO* FROM EACH TEAM CAN COMPETE. CHOOSE WISELY...

WILL THE *CHOSEN ONES* PLEASE FLY FORWARD?!

MOMENTS LATER *CLEO, CORA, TOBY,* AND *CLYDE* APPROACH THE MAZE OF GLOWING MIRRORS...

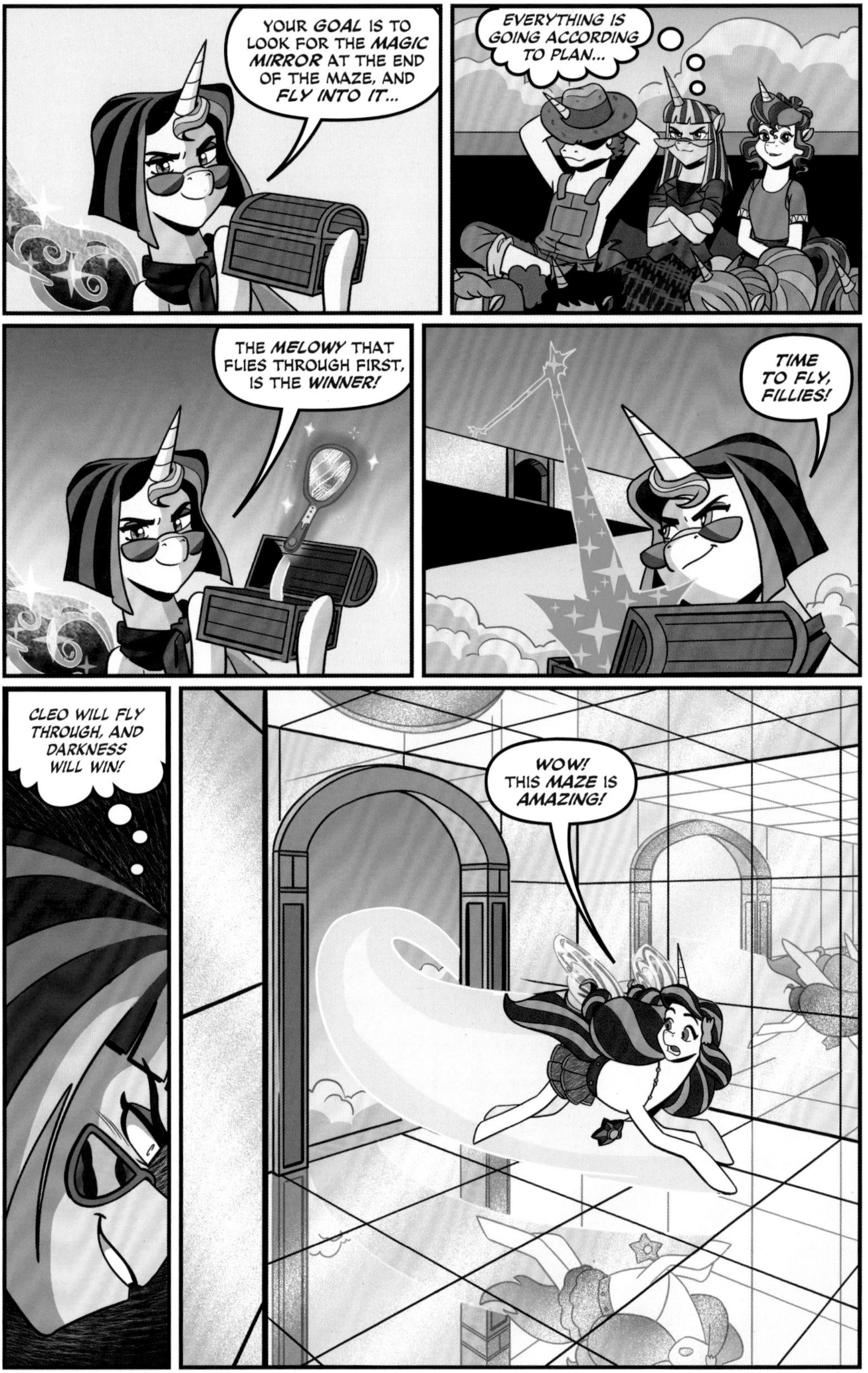
YOUR GOAL IS TO LOOK FOR THE MAGIC MIRROR AT THE END OF THE MAZE, AND FLY INTO IT...
EVERYTHING IS GOING ACCORDING TO PLAN...
THE MELOWY THAT FLIES THROUGH FIRST, IS THE WINNER!
TIME TO FLY, FILLIES!
CLEO WILL FLY THROUGH, AND DARKNESS WILL WIN!
WOW! THIS MAZE IS AMAZING!

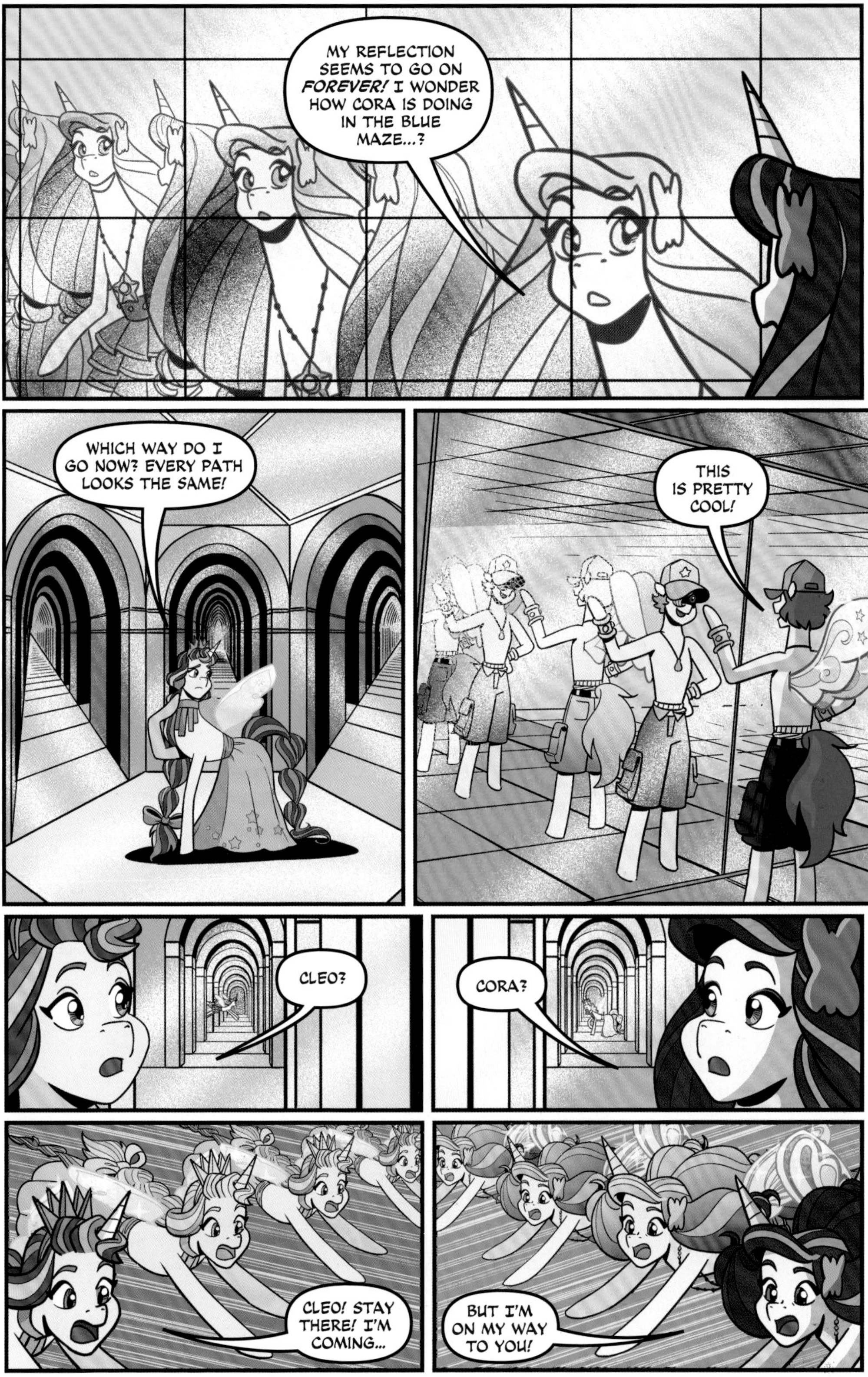
MY REFLECTION SEEMS TO GO ON *FOREVER!* I WONDER HOW CORA IS DOING IN THE BLUE MAZE...?
WHICH WAY DO I GO NOW? EVERY PATH LOOKS THE SAME!
THIS IS PRETTY COOL!
CLEO?
CORA?
CLEO! STAY THERE! I'M COMING...
BUT I'M ON MY WAY TO YOU!

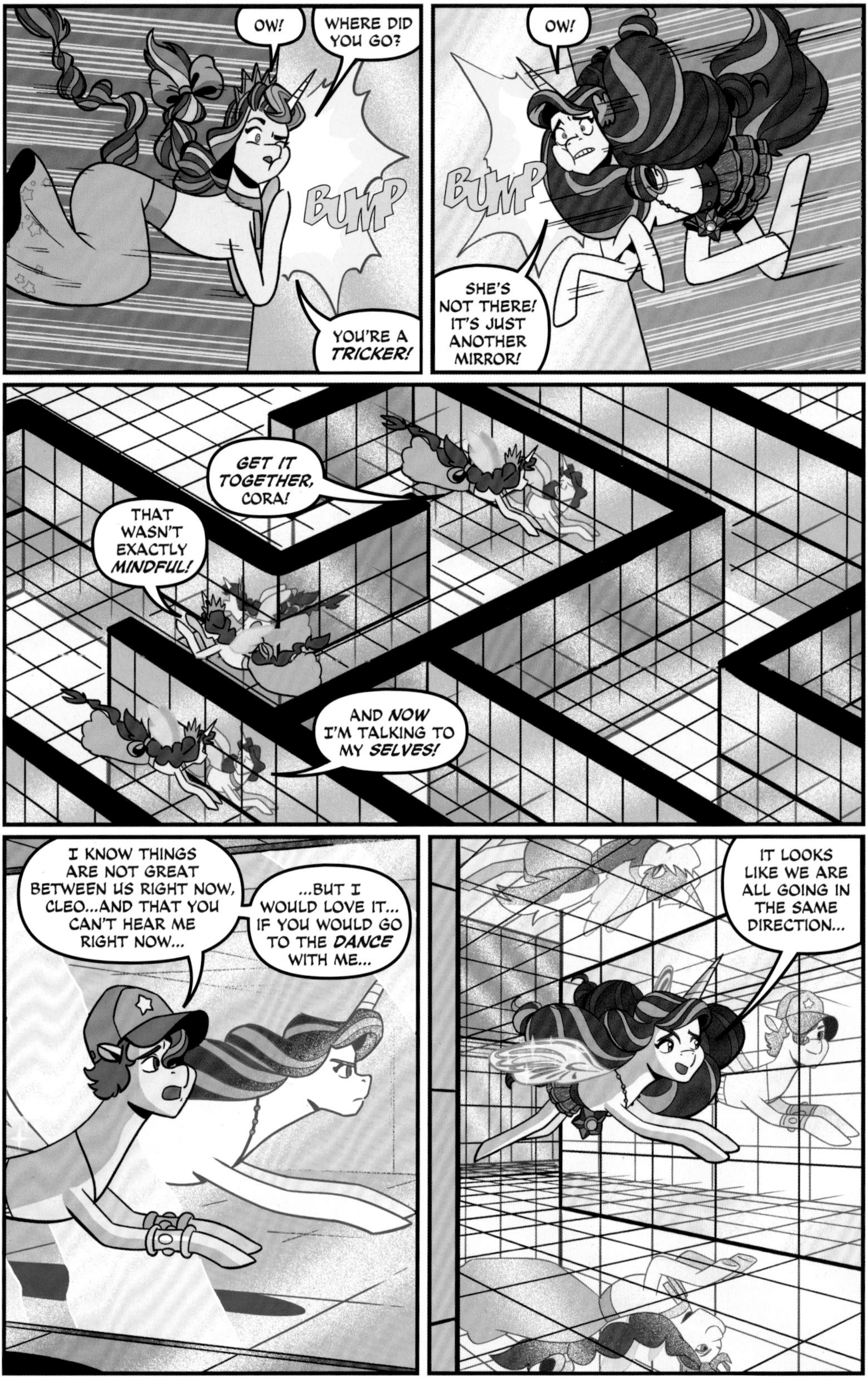
OW!
WHERE DID YOU GO?
BUMP
YOU'RE A *TRICKER!*
OW!
BUMP
SHE'S NOT THERE! IT'S JUST ANOTHER MIRROR!
GET IT TOGETHER, CORA!
THAT WASN'T EXACTLY *MINDFUL!*
AND *NOW* I'M TALKING TO MY *SELVES!*
I KNOW THINGS ARE NOT GREAT BETWEEN US RIGHT NOW, CLEO...AND THAT YOU CAN'T HEAR ME RIGHT NOW...
...BUT I WOULD LOVE IT... IF YOU WOULD GO TO THE *DANCE* WITH ME...
IT LOOKS LIKE WE ARE ALL GOING IN THE SAME DIRECTION...

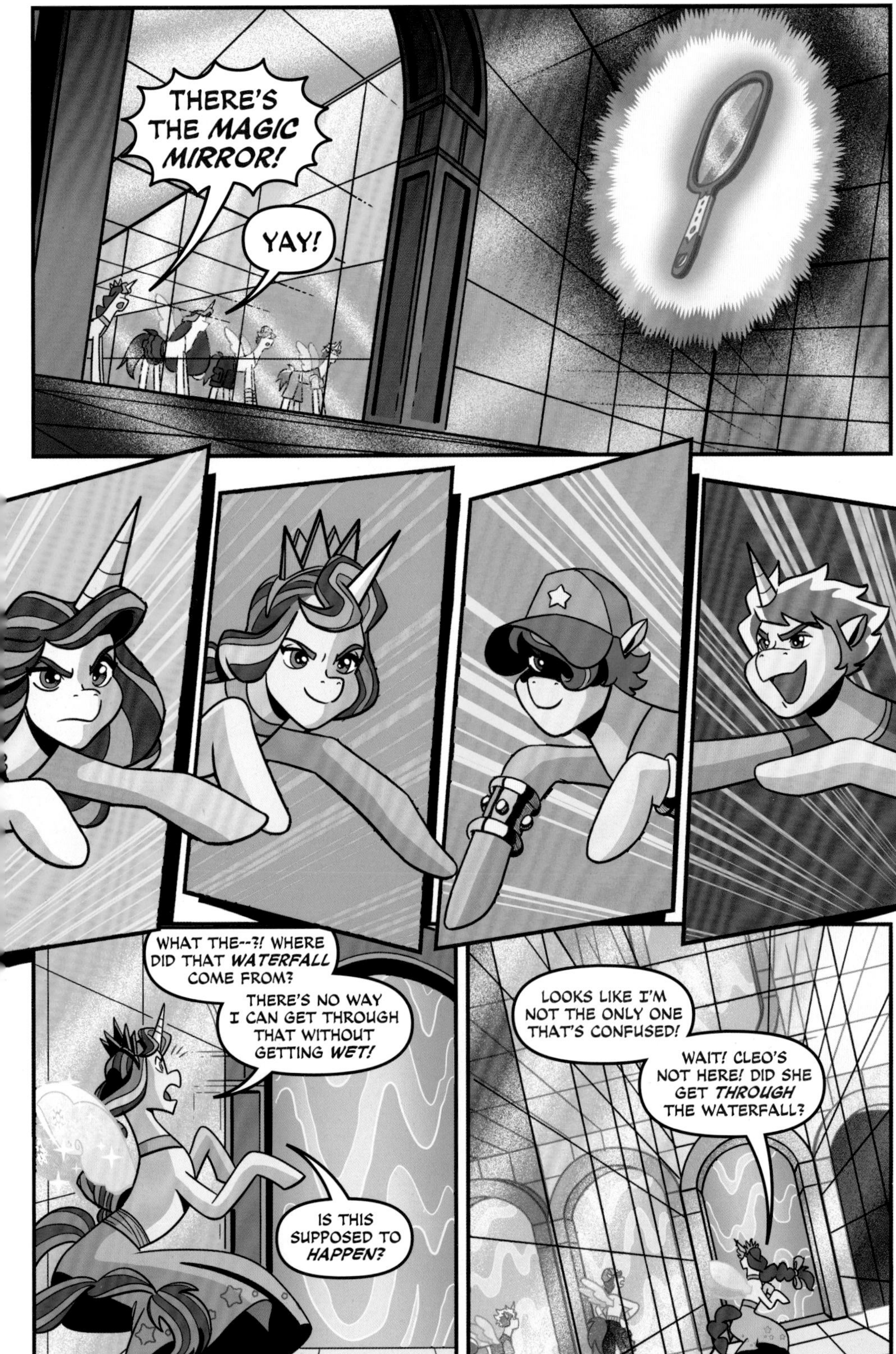
THERE'S THE MAGIC MIRROR!
YAY!
WHAT THE--?! WHERE DID THAT WATERFALL COME FROM?
THERE'S NO WAY I CAN GET THROUGH THAT WITHOUT GETTING WET!
IS THIS SUPPOSED TO HAPPEN?
LOOKS LIKE I'M NOT THE ONLY ONE THAT'S CONFUSED!
WAIT! CLEO'S NOT HERE! DID SHE GET THROUGH THE WATERFALL?

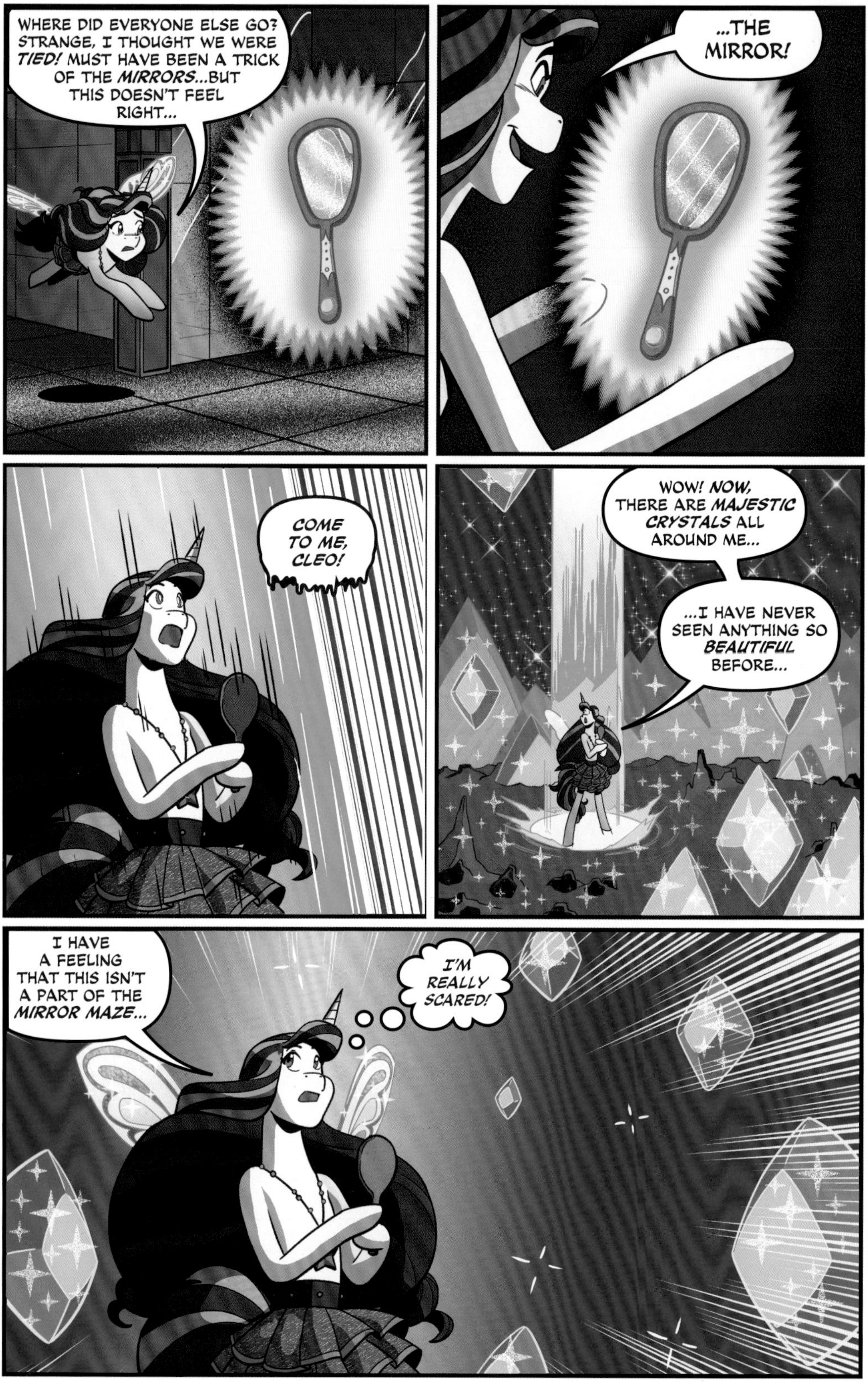
WHERE DID EVERYONE ELSE GO? STRANGE, I THOUGHT WE WERE TIED! MUST HAVE BEEN A TRICK OF THE MIRRORS...BUT THIS DOESN'T FEEL RIGHT...
...THE MIRROR!
COME TO ME, CLEO!
WOW! NOW, THERE ARE MAJESTIC CRYSTALS ALL AROUND ME...
...I HAVE NEVER SEEN ANYTHING SO BEAUTIFUL BEFORE...
I HAVE A FEELING THAT THIS ISN'T A PART OF THE MIRROR MAZE...
I'M REALLY SCARED!

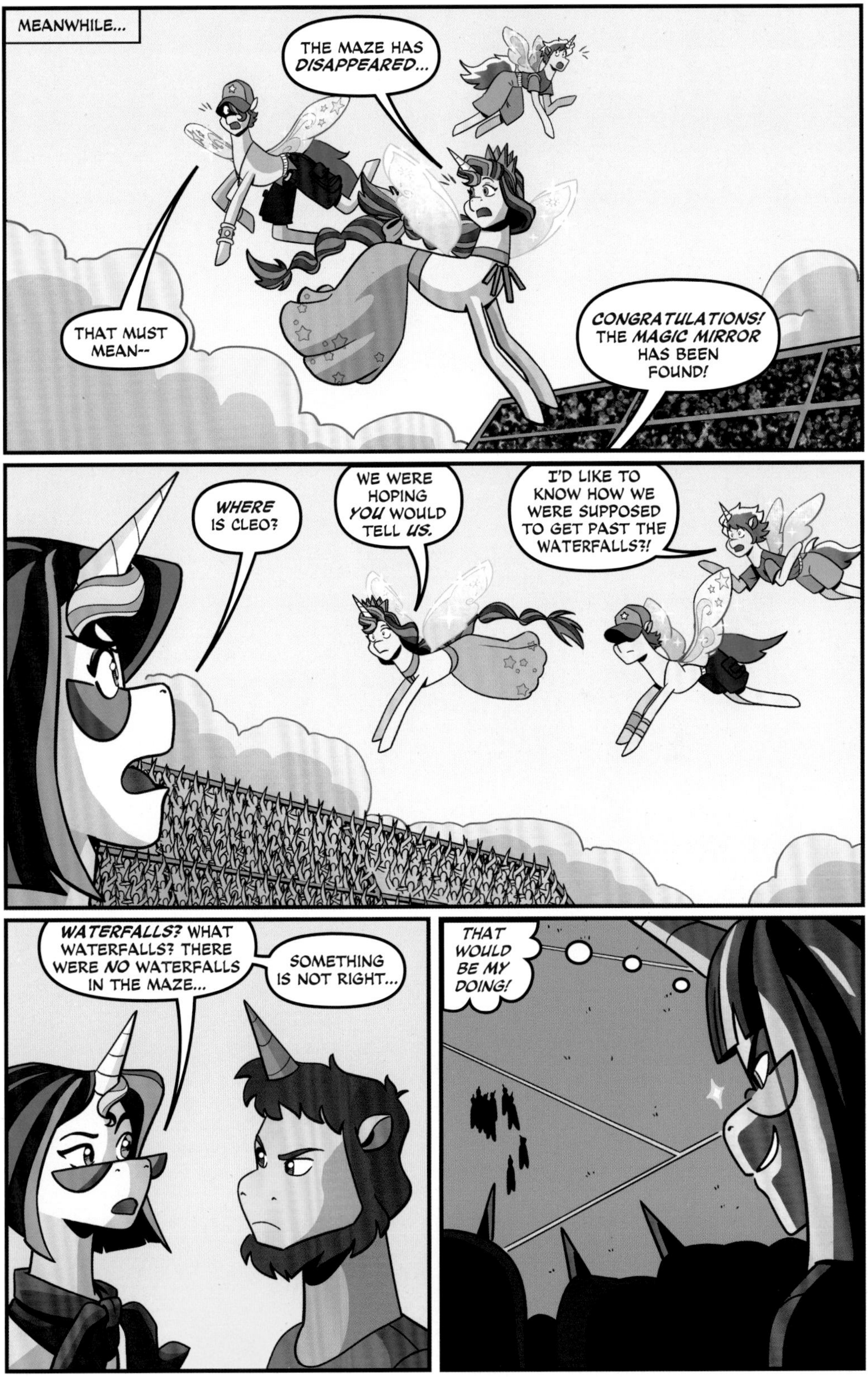
MEANWHILE...
THE MAZE HAS DISAPPEARED...
THAT MUST MEAN--
CONGRATULATIONS! THE MAGIC MIRROR HAS BEEN FOUND!
WHERE IS CLEO?
WE WERE HOPING YOU WOULD TELL US.
I'D LIKE TO KNOW HOW WE WERE SUPPOSED TO GET PAST THE WATERFALLS?!
WATERFALLS? WHAT WATERFALLS? THERE WERE NO WATERFALLS IN THE MAZE...
SOMETHING IS NOT RIGHT...
THAT WOULD BE MY DOING!

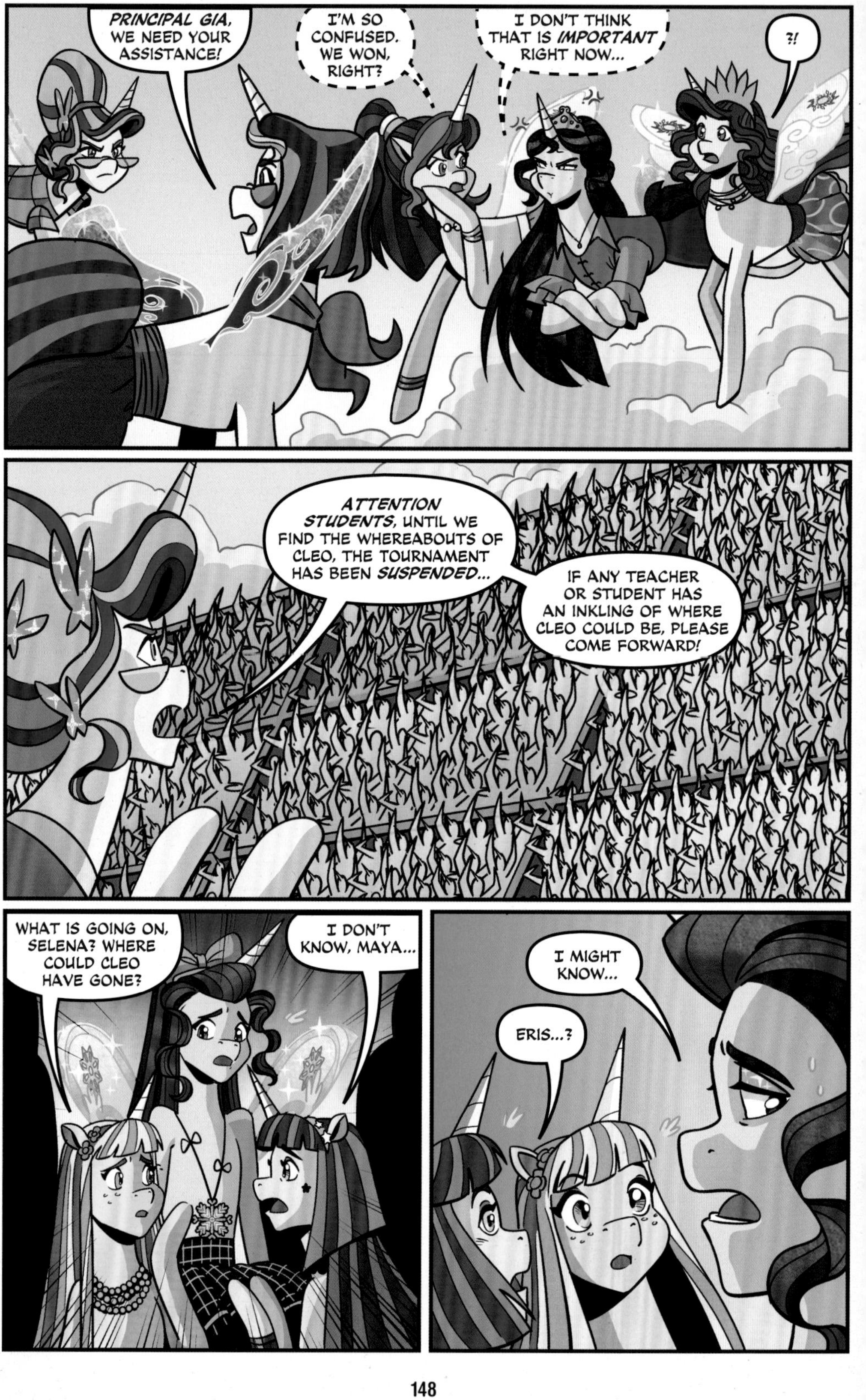
PRINCIPAL GIA, WE NEED YOUR ASSISTANCE!
I'M SO CONFUSED. WE WON, RIGHT?
I DON'T THINK THAT IS IMPORTANT RIGHT NOW...
?!
ATTENTION STUDENTS, UNTIL WE FIND THE WHEREABOUTS OF CLEO, THE TOURNAMENT HAS BEEN SUSPENDED...
IF ANY TEACHER OR STUDENT HAS AN INKLING OF WHERE CLEO COULD BE, PLEASE COME FORWARD!
WHAT IS GOING ON, SELENA? WHERE COULD CLEO HAVE GONE?
I DON'T KNOW, MAYA...
I MIGHT KNOW...
ERIS...?

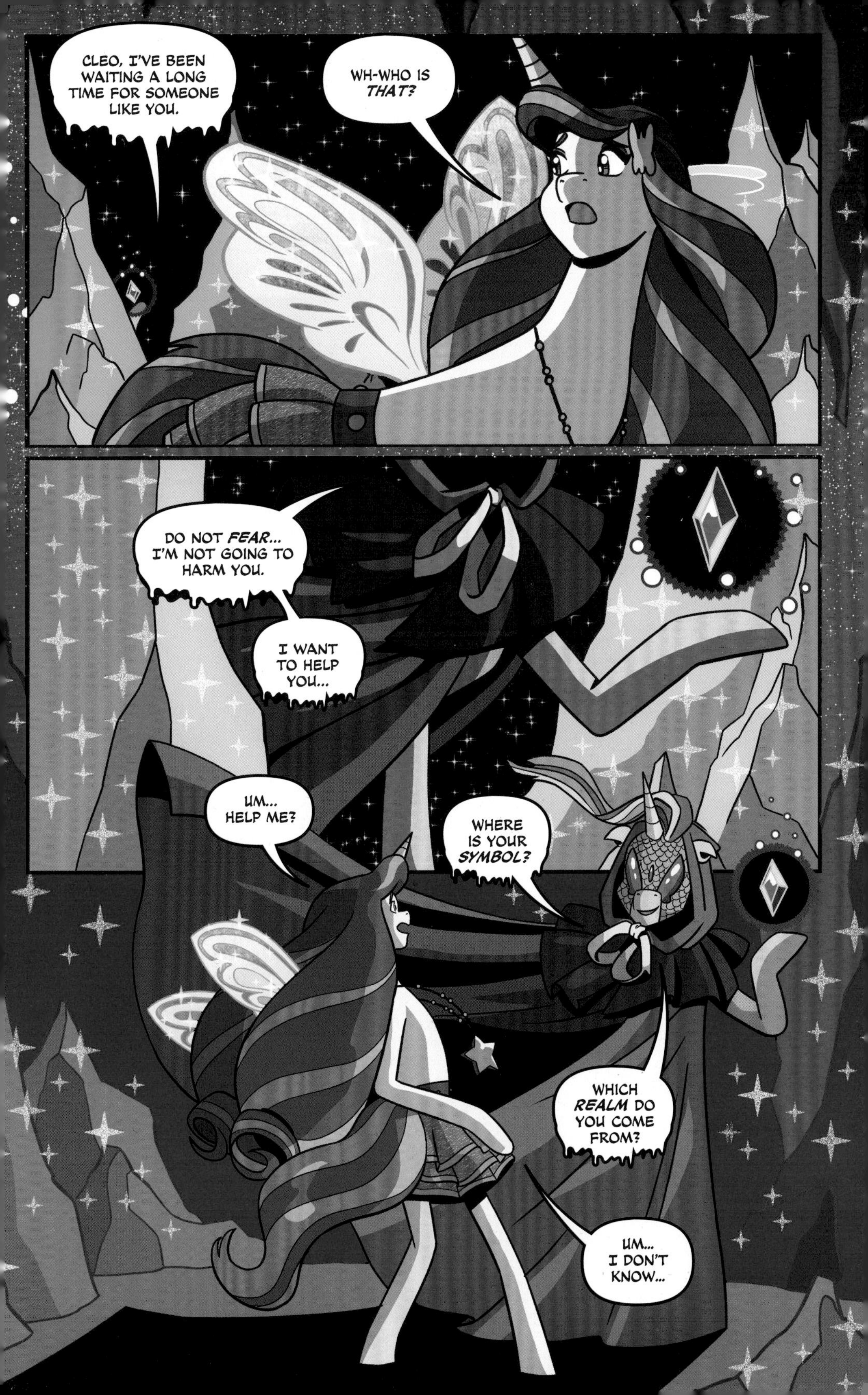
CLEO, I'VE BEEN WAITING A LONG TIME FOR SOMEONE LIKE YOU.
WH-WHO IS *THAT?*
DO NOT *FEAR*... I'M NOT GOING TO HARM YOU.
I WANT TO HELP YOU...
UM... HELP ME?
WHERE IS YOUR *SYMBOL?*
WHICH *REALM* DO YOU COME FROM?
UM... I DON'T KNOW...

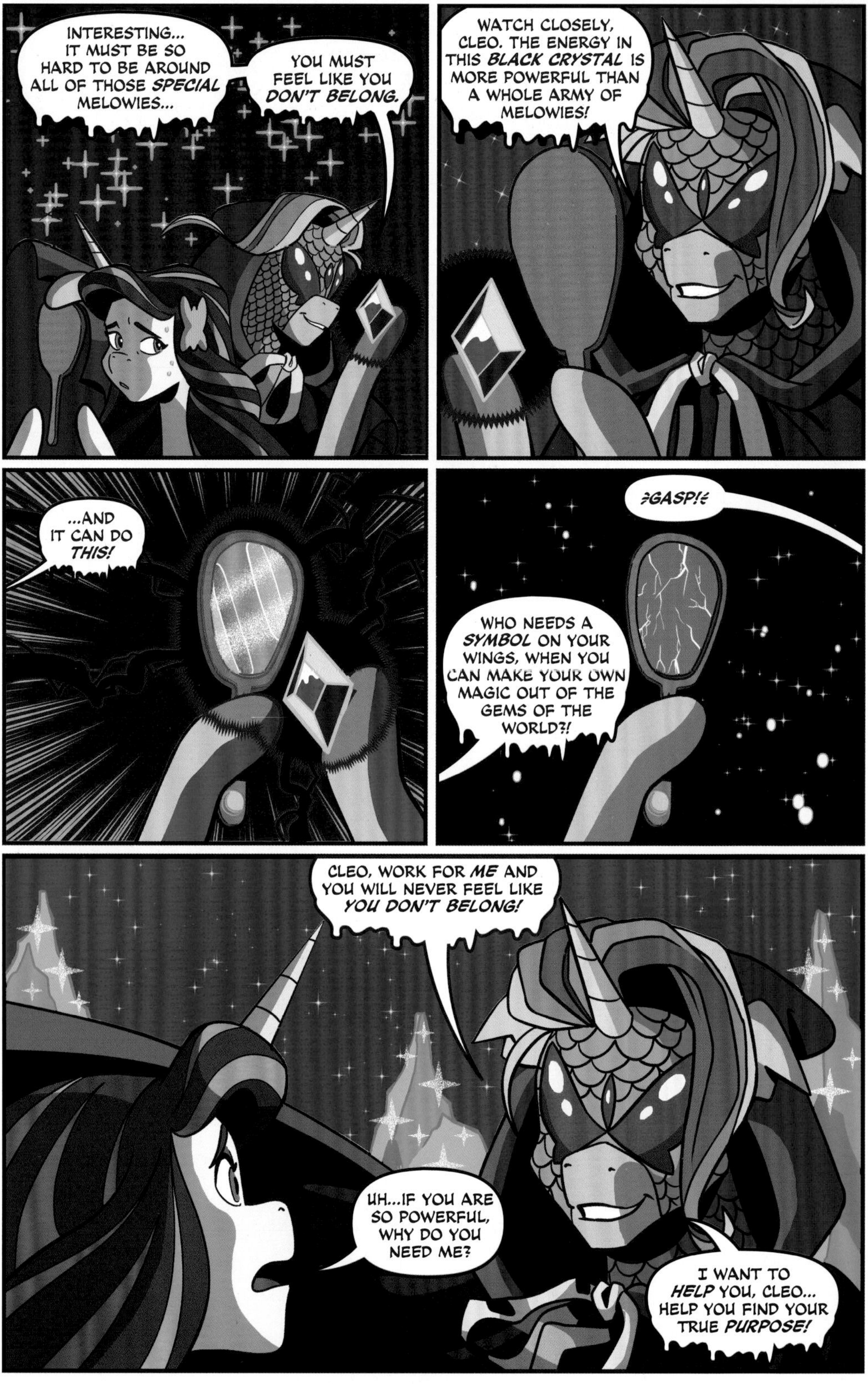
INTERESTING... IT MUST BE SO HARD TO BE AROUND ALL OF THOSE *SPECIAL* MELOWIES...
YOU MUST FEEL LIKE YOU *DON'T BELONG.*
WATCH CLOSELY, CLEO. THE ENERGY IN THIS *BLACK CRYSTAL* IS MORE POWERFUL THAN A WHOLE ARMY OF MELOWIES!
...AND IT CAN DO *THIS!*
GASP!
WHO NEEDS A *SYMBOL* ON YOUR WINGS, WHEN YOU CAN MAKE YOUR OWN MAGIC OUT OF THE GEMS OF THE WORLD?!
CLEO, WORK FOR *ME* AND YOU WILL NEVER FEEL LIKE *YOU DON'T BELONG!*
UH...IF YOU ARE SO POWERFUL, WHY DO YOU NEED ME?
I WANT TO *HELP* YOU, CLEO... HELP YOU FIND YOUR TRUE *PURPOSE!*

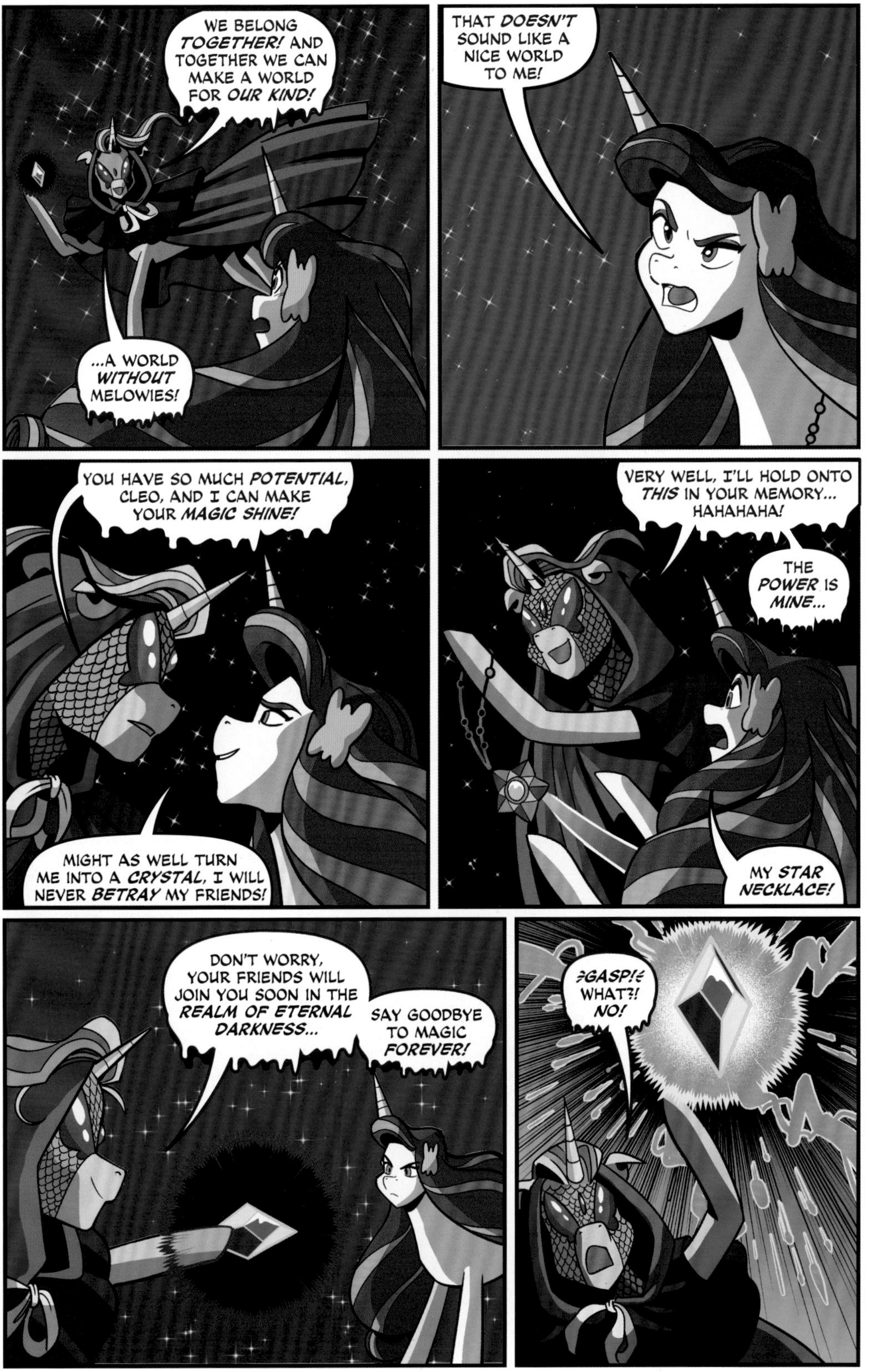
WE BELONG TOGETHER! AND TOGETHER WE CAN MAKE A WORLD FOR OUR KIND!
...A WORLD WITHOUT MELOWIES!
THAT DOESN'T SOUND LIKE A NICE WORLD TO ME!
YOU HAVE SO MUCH POTENTIAL, CLEO, AND I CAN MAKE YOUR MAGIC SHINE!
MIGHT AS WELL TURN ME INTO A CRYSTAL, I WILL NEVER BETRAY MY FRIENDS!
VERY WELL, I'LL HOLD ONTO THIS IN YOUR MEMORY... HAHAHAHA!
THE POWER IS MINE...
MY STAR NECKLACE!
DON'T WORRY, YOUR FRIENDS WILL JOIN YOU SOON IN THE REALM OF ETERNAL DARKNESS...
SAY GOODBYE TO MAGIC FOREVER!
GASP! WHAT?! NO!

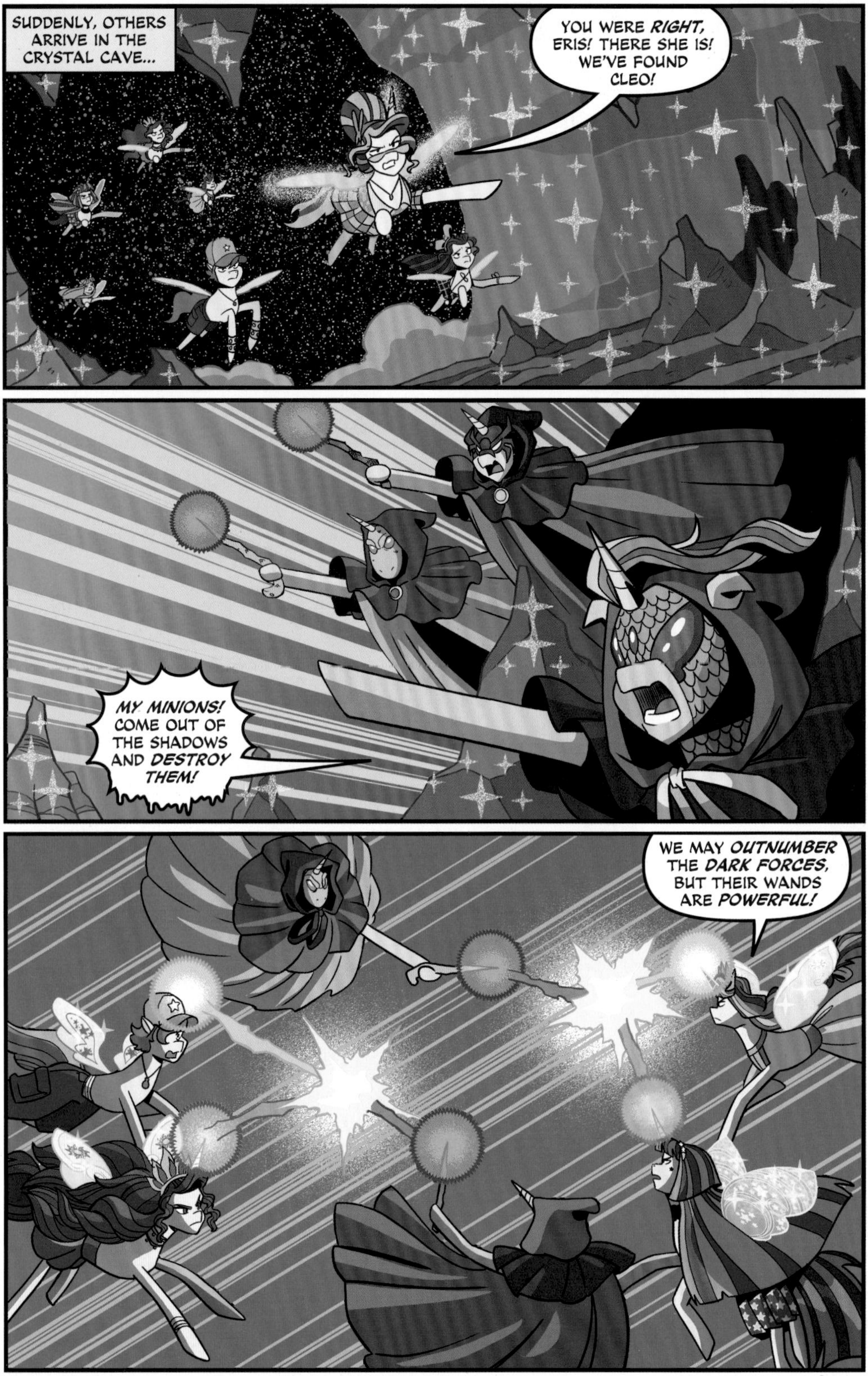
SUDDENLY, OTHERS ARRIVE IN THE CRYSTAL CAVE...
YOU WERE *RIGHT*, ERIS! THERE SHE IS! WE'VE FOUND CLEO!
MY MINIONS! COME OUT OF THE SHADOWS AND *DESTROY THEM!*
WE MAY *OUTNUMBER* THE *DARK FORCES*, BUT THEIR WANDS ARE *POWERFUL!*

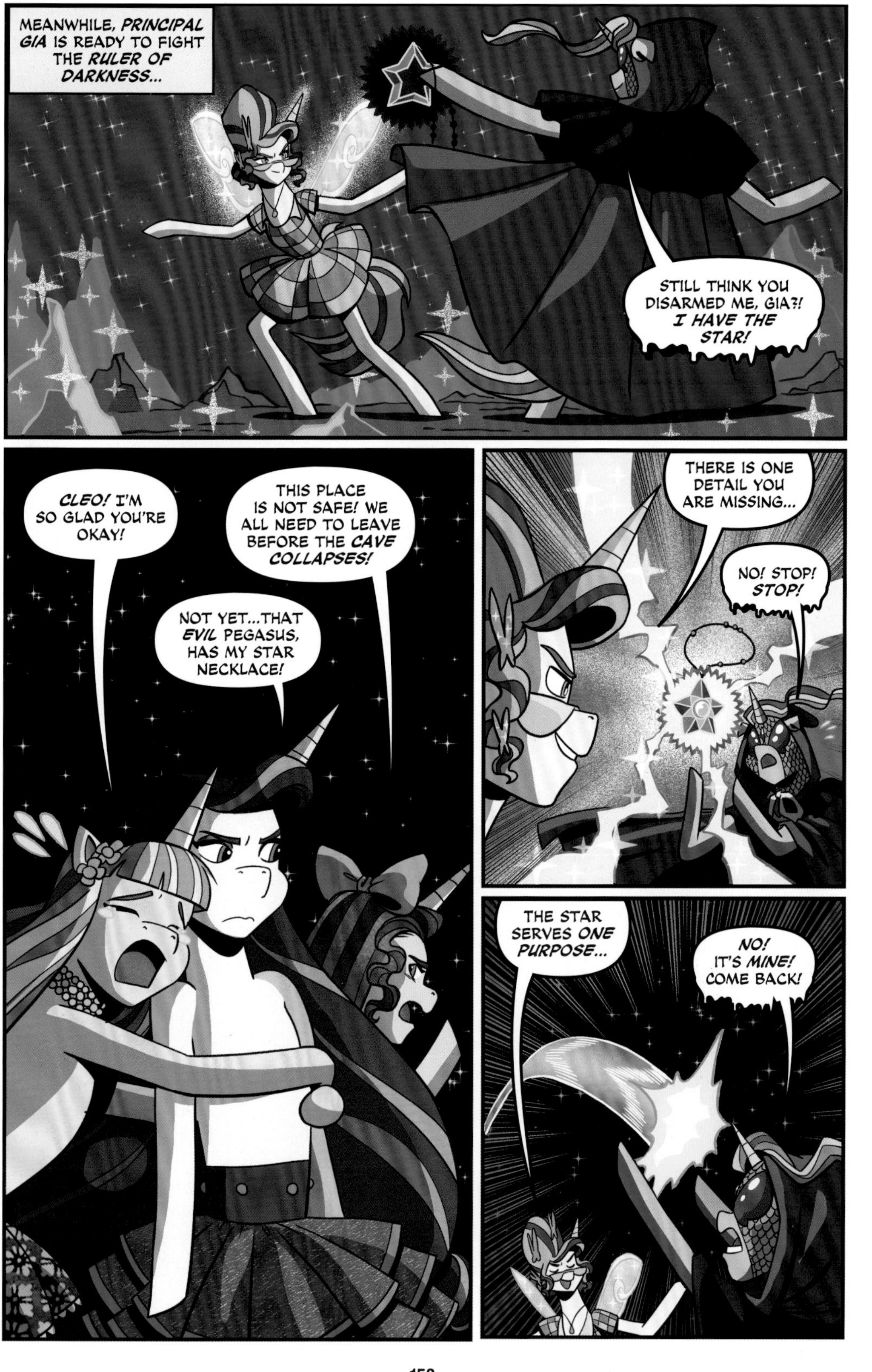
MEANWHILE, PRINCIPAL GIA IS READY TO FIGHT THE RULER OF DARKNESS...
STILL THINK YOU DISARMED ME, GIA?! I HAVE THE STAR!
CLEO! I'M SO GLAD YOU'RE OKAY!
THIS PLACE IS NOT SAFE! WE ALL NEED TO LEAVE BEFORE THE CAVE COLLAPSES!
NOT YET...THAT EVIL PEGASUS, HAS MY STAR NECKLACE!
THERE IS ONE DETAIL YOU ARE MISSING...
NO! STOP! STOP!
THE STAR SERVES ONE PURPOSE...
NO! IT'S MINE! COME BACK!

"...TO PROTECT *THE KEEPER*."

...ME?

I LOVE WHEN THIS HAPPENS!

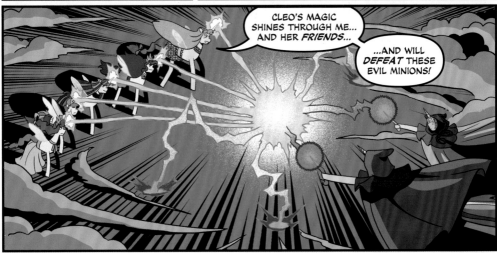

CLEO'S MAGIC SHINES THROUGH ME... AND HER *FRIENDS*...

...AND WILL *DEFEAT* THESE EVIL MINIONS!

THE *SUPREME RULER* HAS *VANISHED!*

KRESH

KRESH

RUMMBLE

KRRK KKRK

WHERE DID THE *MINIONS* GO?!

IT'S TIME TO FLY OUT, THE CAVE IS *COLLAPSING!*

RUMBLE

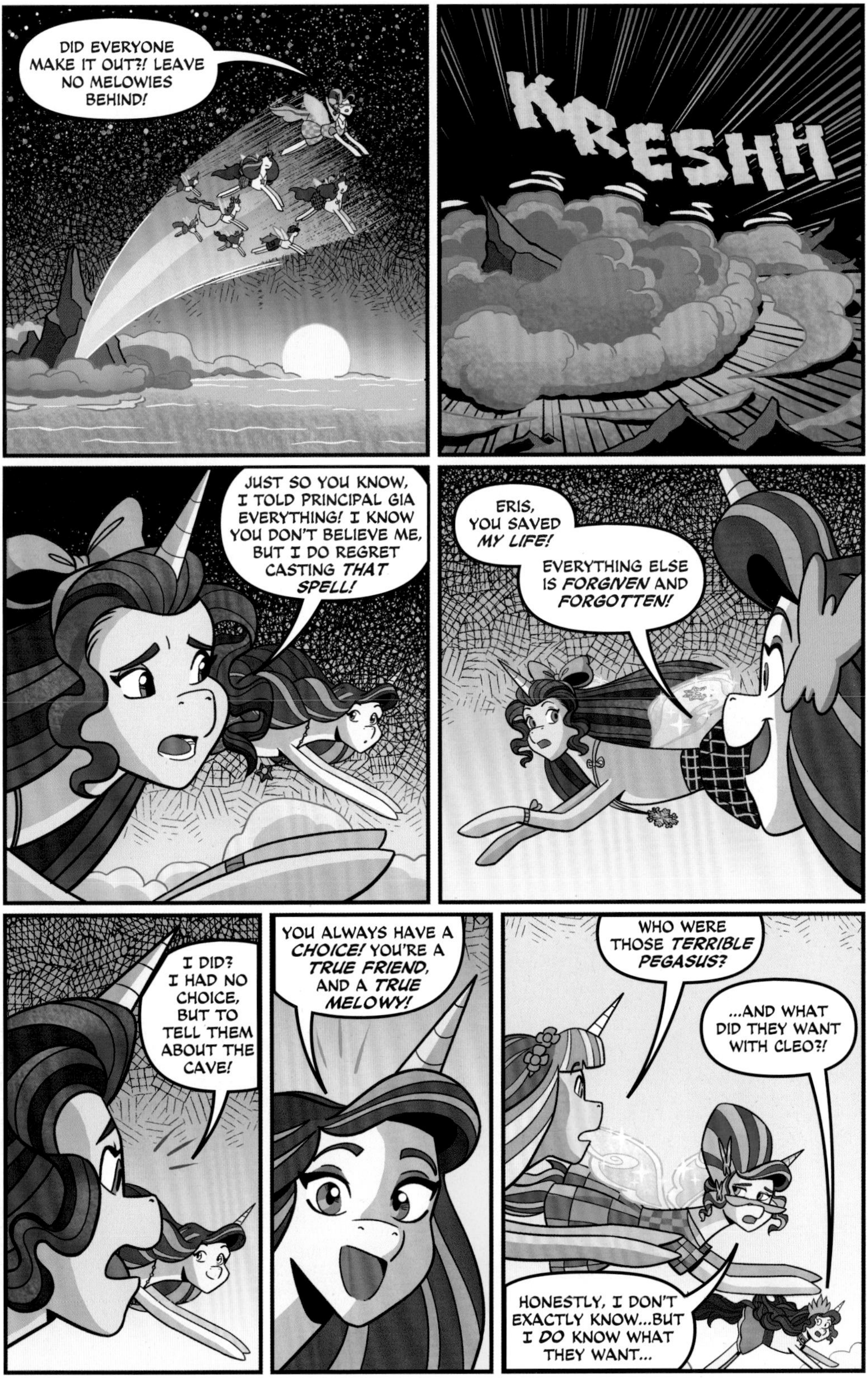
DID EVERYONE MAKE IT OUT?! LEAVE NO MELOWIES BEHIND!
KRESHH
JUST SO YOU KNOW, I TOLD PRINCIPAL GIA EVERYTHING! I KNOW YOU DON'T BELIEVE ME, BUT I DO REGRET CASTING THAT SPELL!
ERIS, YOU SAVED MY LIFE!
EVERYTHING ELSE IS FORGIVEN AND FORGOTTEN!
I DID? I HAD NO CHOICE, BUT TO TELL THEM ABOUT THE CAVE!
YOU ALWAYS HAVE A CHOICE! YOU'RE A TRUE FRIEND, AND A TRUE MELOWY!
WHO WERE THOSE TERRIBLE PEGASUS?
...AND WHAT DID THEY WANT WITH CLEO?!
HONESTLY, I DON'T EXACTLY KNOW...BUT I DO KNOW WHAT THEY WANT...

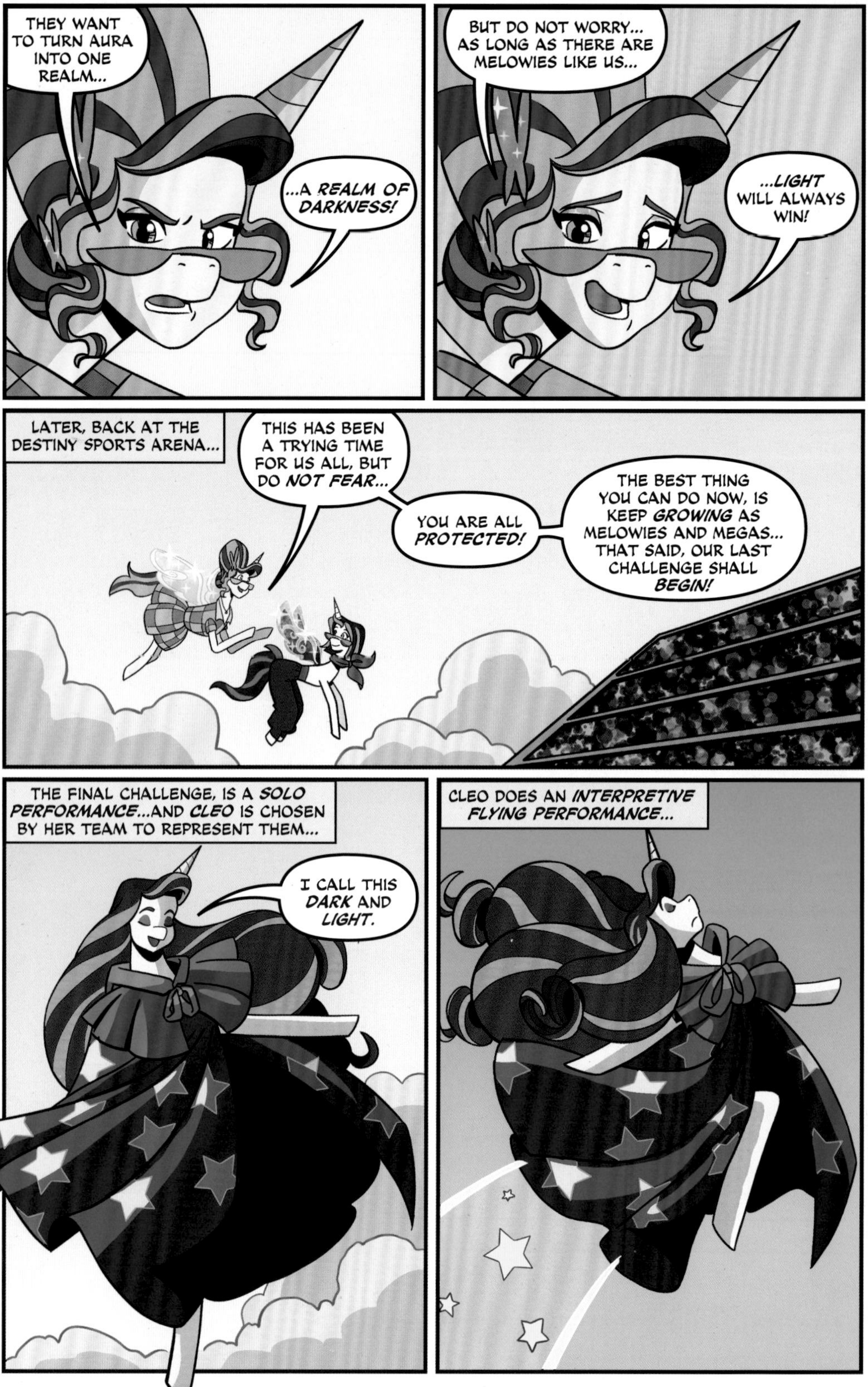
THEY WANT TO TURN AURA INTO ONE REALM...
...A REALM OF DARKNESS!
BUT DO NOT WORRY... AS LONG AS THERE ARE MELOWIES LIKE US...
...LIGHT WILL ALWAYS WIN!
LATER, BACK AT THE DESTINY SPORTS ARENA...
THIS HAS BEEN A TRYING TIME FOR US ALL, BUT DO NOT FEAR...
YOU ARE ALL PROTECTED!
THE BEST THING YOU CAN DO NOW, IS KEEP GROWING AS MELOWIES AND MEGAS... THAT SAID, OUR LAST CHALLENGE SHALL BEGIN!
THE FINAL CHALLENGE, IS A SOLO PERFORMANCE...AND CLEO IS CHOSEN BY HER TEAM TO REPRESENT THEM...
I CALL THIS DARK AND LIGHT.
CLEO DOES AN INTERPRETIVE FLYING PERFORMANCE...

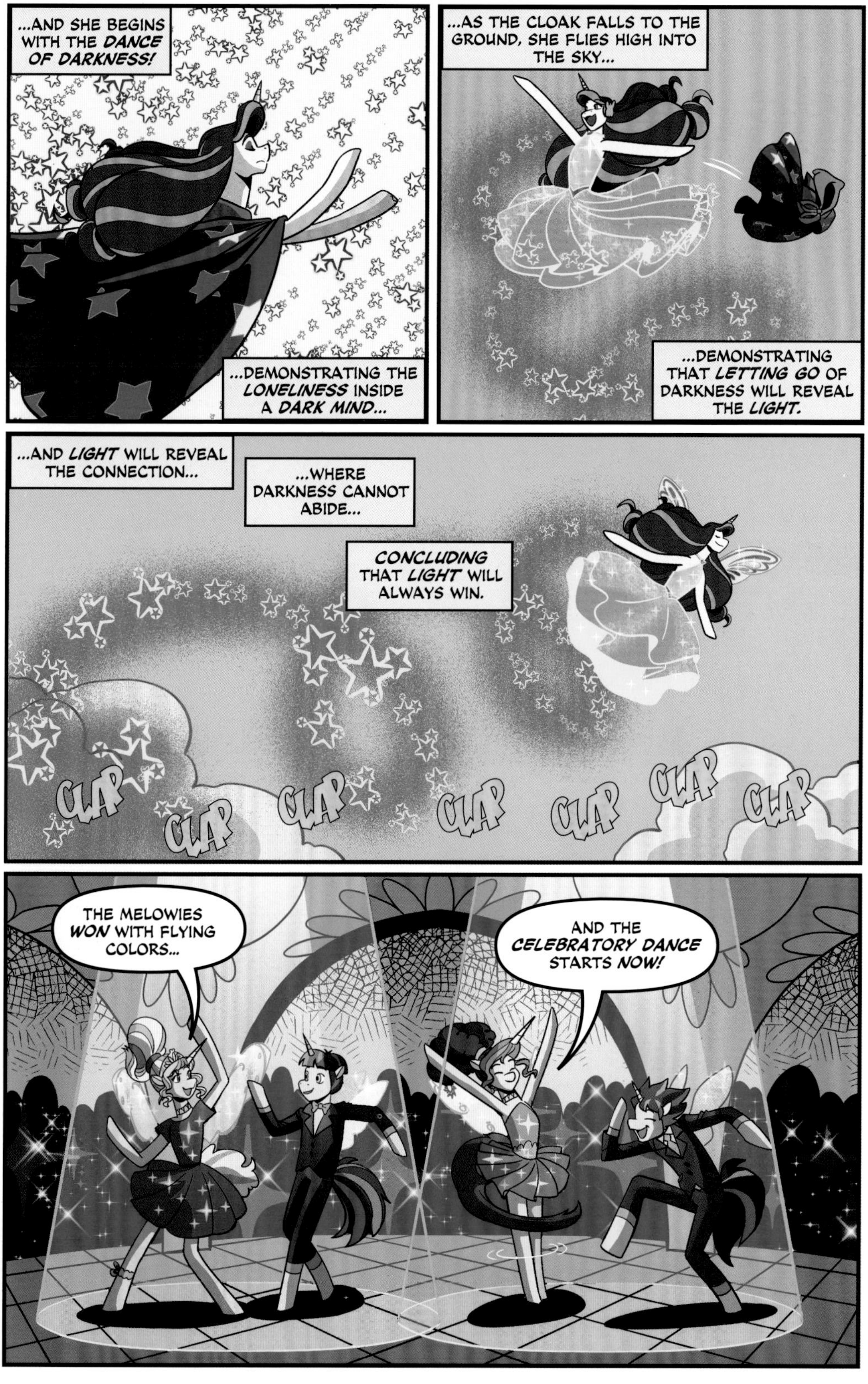

...AND SHE BEGINS WITH THE *DANCE OF DARKNESS!*
...DEMONSTRATING THE *LONELINESS* INSIDE A *DARK MIND*...
...AS THE CLOAK FALLS TO THE GROUND, SHE FLIES HIGH INTO THE SKY...
...DEMONSTRATING THAT *LETTING GO* OF DARKNESS WILL REVEAL THE *LIGHT.*
...AND *LIGHT* WILL REVEAL THE CONNECTION...
...WHERE DARKNESS CANNOT ABIDE...
CONCLUDING THAT *LIGHT* WILL ALWAYS WIN.
CLAP CLAP CLAP CLAP CLAP CLAP CLAP
THE MELOWIES *WON* WITH FLYING COLORS...
AND THE *CELEBRATORY DANCE* STARTS *NOW!*

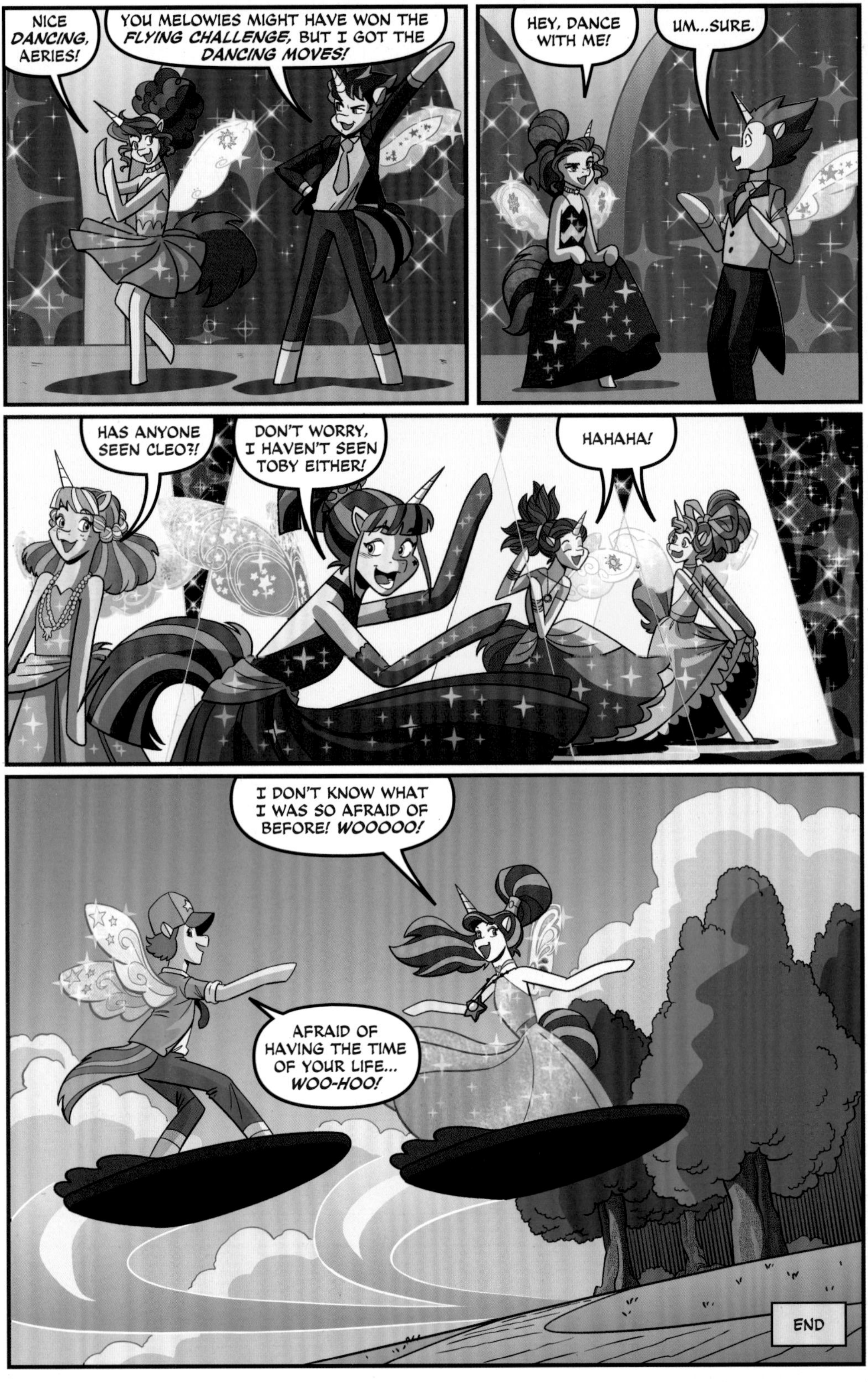
NICE DANCING, AERIES!
YOU MELOWIES MIGHT HAVE WON THE FLYING CHALLENGE, BUT I GOT THE DANCING MOVES!
HEY, DANCE WITH ME!
UM...SURE.
HAS ANYONE SEEN CLEO?!
DON'T WORRY, I HAVEN'T SEEN TOBY EITHER!
HAHAHA!
I DON'T KNOW WHAT I WAS SO AFRAID OF BEFORE! WOOOOO!
AFRAID OF HAVING THE TIME OF YOUR LIFE... WOO-HOO!
END

WATCH OUT FOR PAPERCUTZ™

Welcome to the triply magical premiere volume of MELOWY 3 IN 1 #1, by Cortney Powell and Ryan Jampole from Papercutz—those True Believers dedicated to publishing great graphic novels for all ages. I'm Jim Salicrup, Editor-in-Chief and Fluffy's Official Walker, here to offer up a few behind-the-scenes bios regarding the creators who bring you MELOWY. But first, just to clarify what MELOWY 3 IN 1 is exactly, allow me to explain that the three MELOWY stories collected in this volume were originally published as three separate MELOWY graphic novels, volumes 1-3 to be precise. Thus, MELOWY 3-IN-1! There, that wasn't too complicated. Now on to our creative crew…

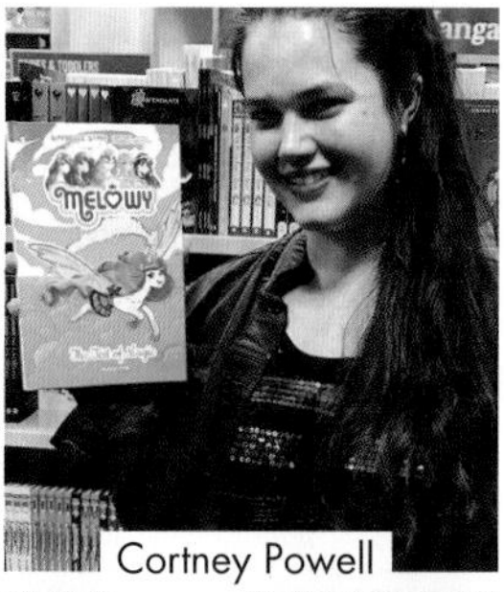
Cortney Powell

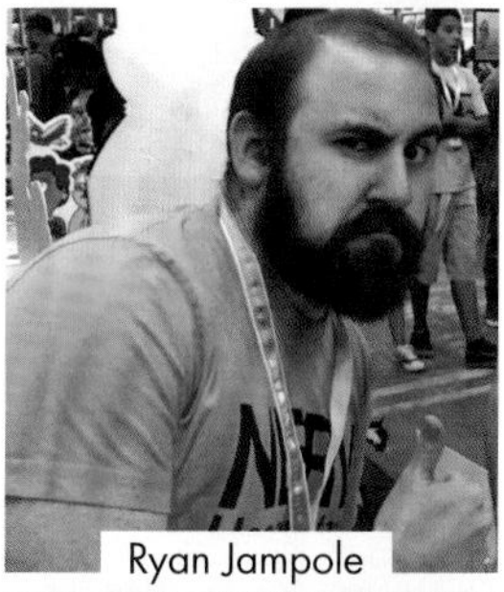
Ryan Jampole

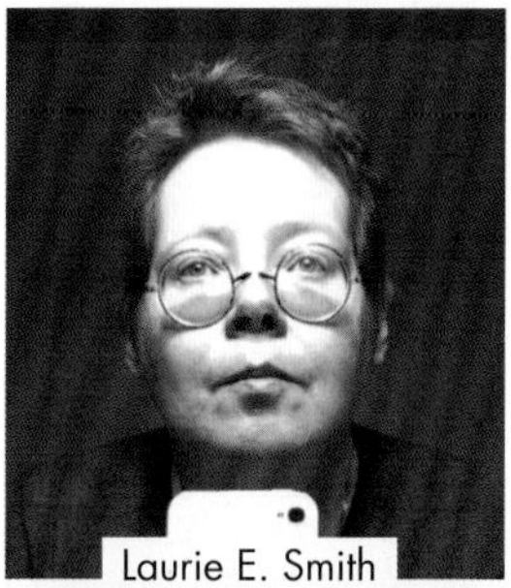
Laurie E. Smith

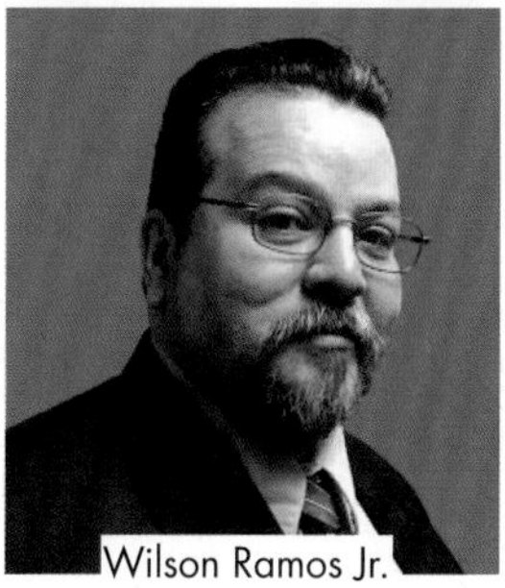
Wilson Ramos Jr.

Cortney Powell, the writer of the MELOWY graphic novels, was born in Alabama, but lived most of her life in the magical realm of New York City. Cortney is a writer, poet, actress, filmmaker, animal-lover, and yogini. At an early age Cortney met Batman co-creator Bob Kane and filmmakers Francis Ford Coppola and Lloyd Kaufman at the San Diego Comic-Con. At the prestigious Professional Performing Arts School, she was proud to star as Enid in cartoonist/playwright Lynda Barry's play "The Good Times Are Killing Me." A fan of such comics as BARBIE, LENORE, and LITTLE LULU, Cortney worked on revising the DISNEY FAIRIES scripts for an American audience for the Papercutz graphic novels. Her magical comics journey continues as the writer on the MELOWY graphic novel series, where she believe the most powerful magic of all is: Love.

Ryan Jampole is quite an accomplished comicbook artist, and has even been nominated for the prestigious Harvey Award, one of the highest honors in the field. Ryan hails from Queens, New York, and attended the High School of Art & Design and the Fashion Institute of Technology—which explains why the fashions showcased by the Fashion Club were so impressive! Among Ryan's many comics credits, he has drawn MEGAMAN and SONIC for Archie Comics, DEXTER'S LABORATORY and CODENAME KND for IDW, and both GERONIMO STILTON and THEA STILTON graphic novels for Papercutz.

Laurie E. Smith has been a professional comicbook colorist for the last 25 years. She lives in Winnipeg with her husband, fellow artist George Freeman. Laurie earned a B.A. (Honors) in English from the University of Winnipeg and has taught courses on comic art at various technical colleges in her home province. In 1996 she was nominated for an Eisner Award for her work on "The X-Files" series of comics. Although art is her profession, writing has been a lifelong love and she recently published her first science fiction novel, "The Codex of Desire," under the pen name Lauren Alder.

Wilson Ramos Jr. is a freelance comic artist who has worked in the comics industry for over 25 years. He has worked as a colorist, letterer, inker, penciller, and art director in digital and print comics, posters, brochures, trading cards, magazines and scores of projects for Marvel Comics, DC Comics, Dark Horse, Random House, Papercutz, and many others. His recent projects include the Independent Publisher Book Award-winning God Woke written by the legendary Stan Lee. Wilson is also a popular sketch card artist who has work for Topps, Upper Deck, Cryptozoic Entertainment, and Dynamite Entertainment. In his spare time, Wilson works on his creator-owned comicbooks Team Kaiju and Ninja Mouse published by Section 8 Comics. Ramos lives in New York City, where he attended The High School of Art & Design. He received his Bachelor's of Fine Arts Degree in Graphic Design from Mercy College. Wilson has been working full-time as a freelance artist, after working on staff for several years at Marvel Comics.

All four of these MELOWY creators are incredibly talented and we're thrilled to have them contributing not only to MELOWY but to other Papercutz graphic novels as well. Speaking of which, don't miss MELOWY #5 "Melloween," coming soon to your favorite booksellers and libraries—it won't be any fun without you!

Thanks, Jim

STAY IN TOUCH!

EMAIL:	salicrup@papercutz.com
WEB:	papercutz.com
TWITTER:	@papercutzgn
INSTAGRAM:	@papercutzgn
FACEBOOK:	PAPERCUTZGRAPHICNOVELS
FANMAIL:	Papercutz, 160 Broadway, Suite 700, East Wing, New York, NY 10038

Go to papercutz.com and sign up for the free Papercutz e-newsletter!

MORE GREAT GRAPHIC NOVEL SERIES AVAILABLE FROM

PAPERCUTZ™

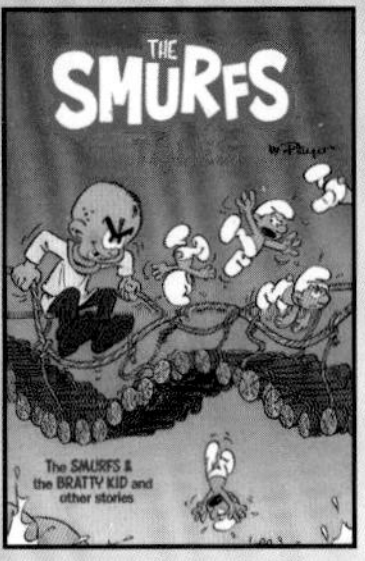
THE SMURFS
The SMURFS & the BRATTY KID and other stories
THE SMURFS TALES

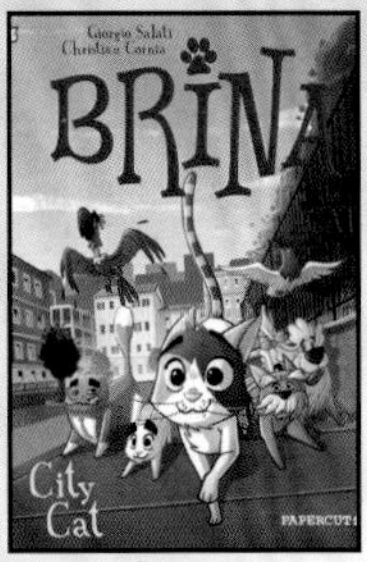
Giorgio Salati
Christian Cornia
BRINA
City Cat
BRINA THE CAT

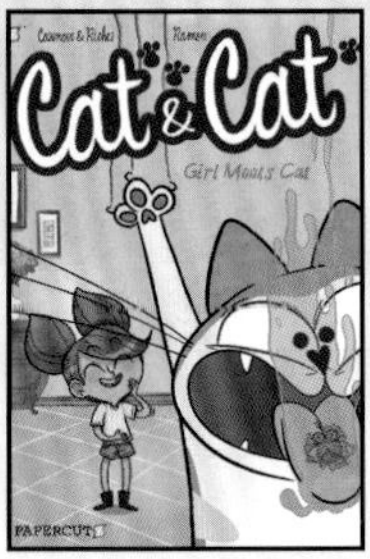
Cat & Cat
Girl Meets Cat
PAPERCUTZ
CAT & CAT

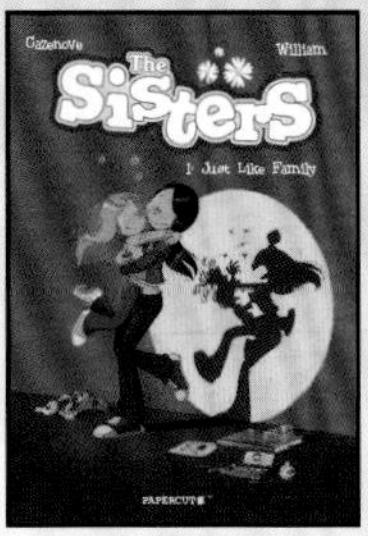
Cazenove
William
The Sisters
Just Like Family
PAPERCUTZ
THE SISTERS

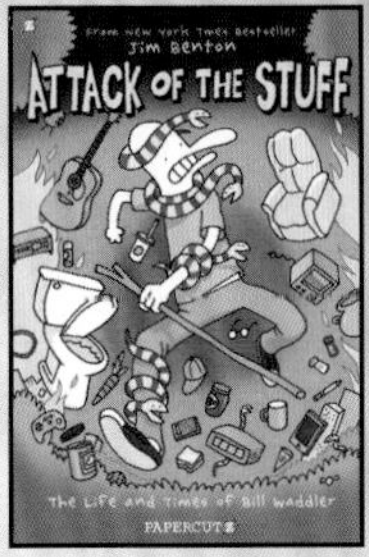
Jim Benton
ATTACK OF THE STUFF
The Life and Times of Bill Waddler
PAPERCUTZ
ATTACK OF THE STUFF

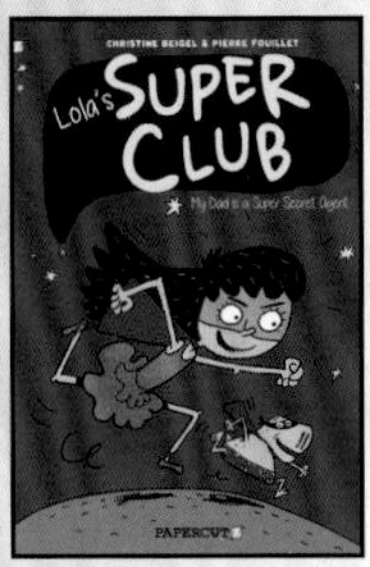
CHRISTINE BEIGEL & PIERRE FOUILLET
Lola's SUPER CLUB
My Dad is a Super Secret Agent
PAPERCUTZ
LOLA'S SUPER CLUB

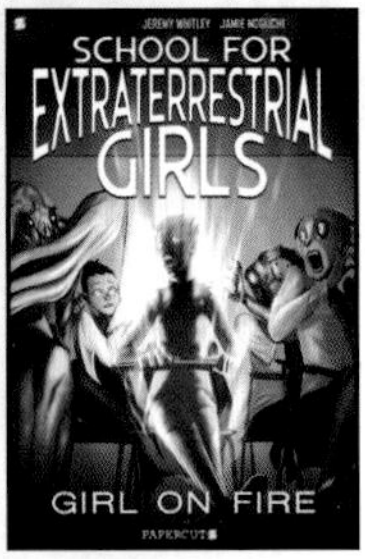
JEREMY WHITLEY
JAMIE NOGUCHI
SCHOOL FOR EXTRATERRESTRIAL GIRLS
GIRL ON FIRE
PAPERCUTZ
SCHOOL FOR EXTRATERRESTRIAL GIRLS

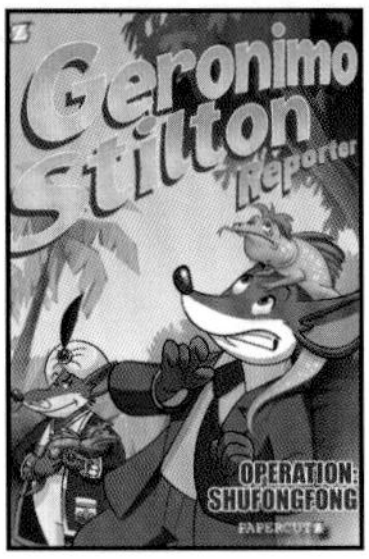
Geronimo Stilton
Reporter
OPERATION: SHUFONGFONG
PAPERCUTZ
GERONIMO STILTON REPORTER

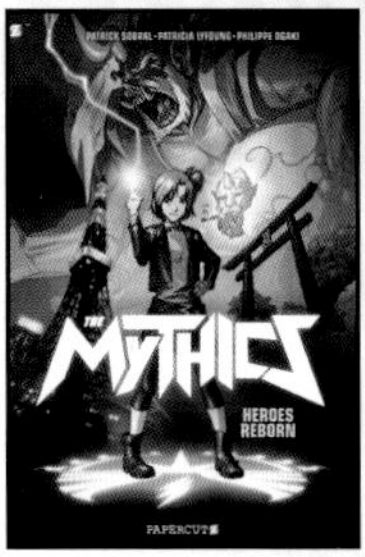
THE MYTHICS
HEROES REBORN
PAPERCUTZ
THE MYTHICS

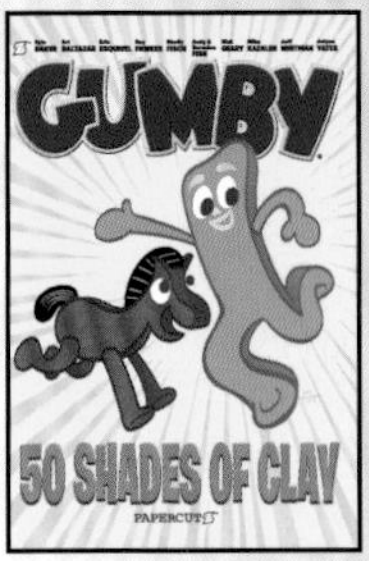
GUMBY
50 SHADES OF CLAY
PAPERCUTZ
GUMBY

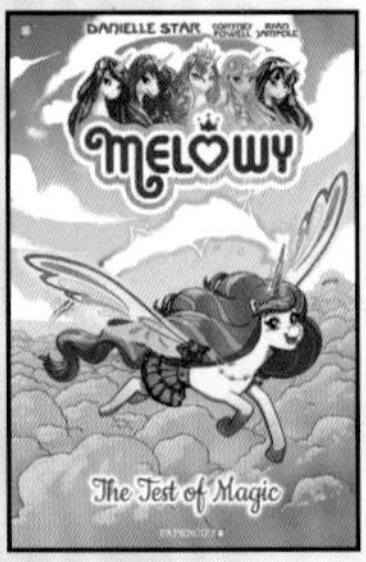
DANIELLE STAR
Melowy
The Test of Magic
PAPERCUTZ
MELOWY

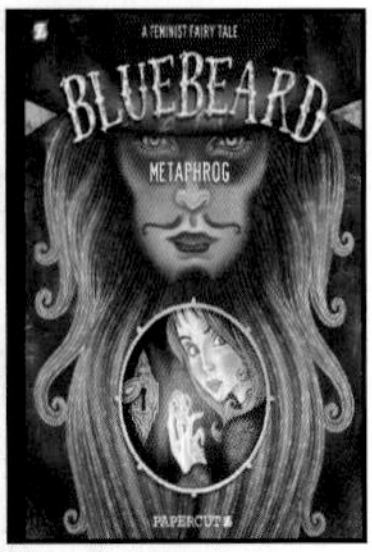
A FEMINIST FAIRY TALE
BLUEBEARD
METAPHROG
PAPERCUTZ
BLUEBEARD

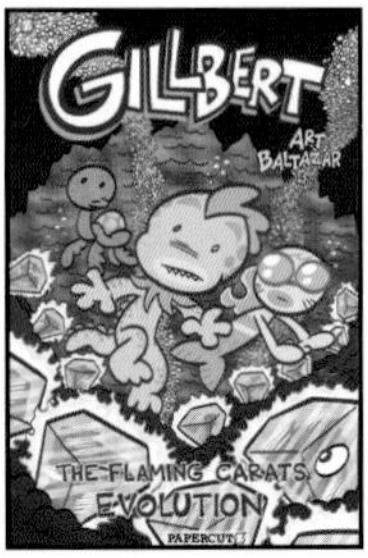
GILLBERT
ART BALTAZAR
THE FLAMING CARATS EVOLUTION
GILBERT

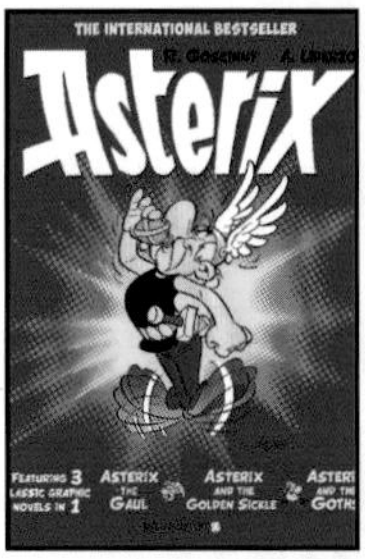
THE INTERNATIONAL BESTSELLER
R. GOSCINNY
A. UDERZO
Asterix
FEATURING 3 CLASSIC GRAPHIC NOVELS IN 1
ASTERIX THE GAUL
ASTERIX AND THE GOLDEN SICKLE
ASTERIX

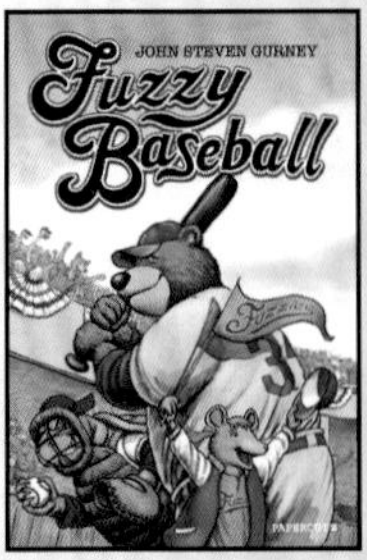
JOHN STEVEN GURNEY
Fuzzy Baseball
PAPERCUTZ
FUZZY BASEBALL

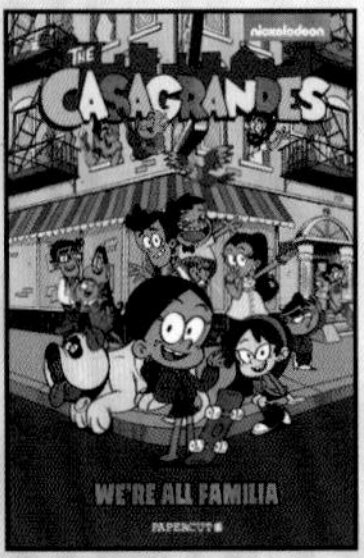
nickelodeon
THE CASAGRANDES
WE'RE ALL FAMILIA
PAPERCUTZ
THE CASAGRANDES

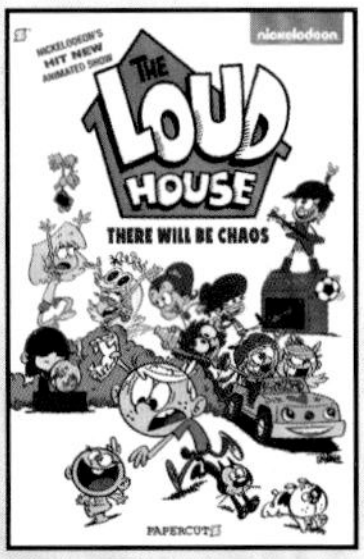
NICKELODEON'S HIT NEW ANIMATED SHOW
nickelodeon
THE LOUD HOUSE
THERE WILL BE CHAOS
PAPERCUTZ
THE LOUD HOUSE

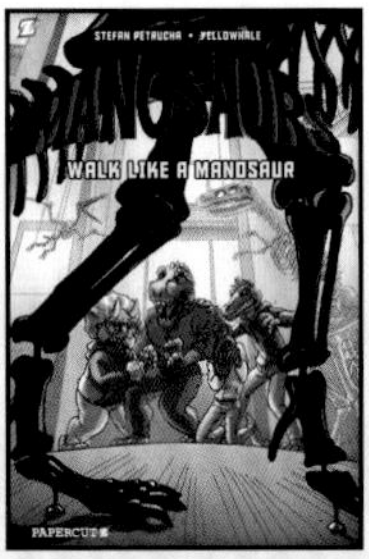
STEFAN PETRUCHA • YELLOWHALE
MANOSAURS
WALK LIKE A MANOSAUR
PAPERCUTZ
MANOSAURS

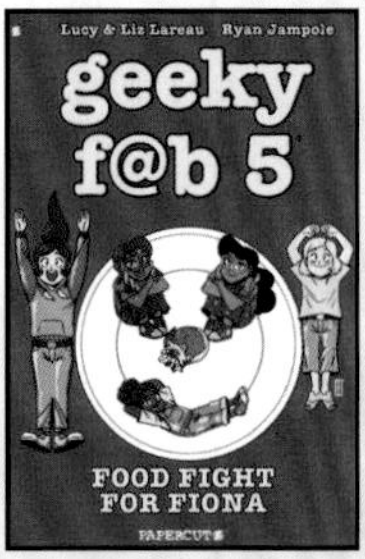
Lucy & Liz Lareau
Ryan Jampole
geeky f@b 5
FOOD FIGHT FOR FIONA
PAPERCUTZ
GEEKY F@B 5

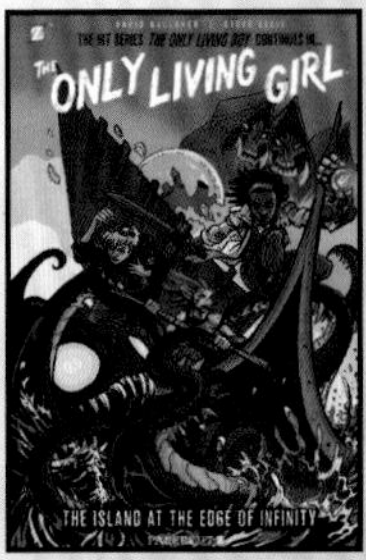
THE ONLY LIVING GIRL
THE ISLAND AT THE EDGE OF INFINITY
PAPERCUTZ
THE ONLY LIVING GIRL

papercutz.com

Also available where ebooks are sold.